A MAN *of* BREEDING

JAMES S. KELLY

A MAN OF
BREEDING

James S. Kelly

ISBN: 978-1-961677-74-6

Library of Congress Control Number: 2023913399

Printed in the United States of America

Published by

info@thequippyquill.com
(302) 295-2278

Other Books

By JAMES S. KELLY

Westerns
A Man of Breeding
A Breed Apart
The Downtrodden Breed

Mysteries
I Didn't Forget
Not In My Backyard Interned

Civil War
Magnolia

Viet Nam War
The Long Walk Home

ACKNOWLEDGEMENTS

Spouse
Patricia

Children
James Jr.
Mark
Nancy
Michelle

Friends
John and Nancy
Orchard Robert and
Marilyn Lang Don and
Noreen Pate Lyndon Beauchene

Relatives
Jim and Ethel
Lancaster Thomas Kelly
Maryann Kelly

CONTENTS

PROLOGUE

The Oregon Trails Land Company had negotiated with Spotted Tail, a chief of the Ogallala Sioux, for an experienced Indian guide to lead a wagon train from Independence, Missouri, to Oregon in April 1864. Spotted Tail told the company he knew an individual who'd taken two trains across the Indian Territory over the past few years without encountering any problems. After they negotiated a fee, Spotted Tail sent Tommy Sanchez to Independence to meet company officials and the wagon master. Although he was in his early twenties, he was experienced beyond his years and came from a family of leaders in the Sioux Nation.

It took him nearly ten days to travel the distance. He arrived after dinnertime and went directly to a livery stable, where he brushed down his horse and gave it some hay and water. After making sure his horse was comfortable, he went into town in search of a room. None were available. He couldn't determine whether the town was full or they wouldn't rent rooms to Indians. After he ate at one of the saloons in town he went back to the livery stable, put his bedroll over a couple of hay bales in one of the empty stalls, and decided to sleep there overnight. He took off his jacket, placed his handgun within reach, and covered himself with the blanket he carried in his bedroll. This wasn't the first time he had slept with the horses.

He was awakened an hour later by loud noises. An argument between three or four people seemed to be escalating, and soon a girl was crying and screaming. He heard a young male voice yell, "Stay away from her!"

Sanchez's father had advised him early in his life not to interfere in the affairs of others, especially whites, so he turned on his side and ignored what was going on in the other stall within the livery barn. But the pleading of the girl was such that he couldn't drown it out. He put the gun in his waistband and quietly moved toward the voices. They must have been oblivious to him as he turned the comer of the stall, for no one looked up. Two men had a young boy and girl cornered in the rear of the stall. One of the men was pounding on the boy while the other had the girl on the floor and was tearing at her clothing.

Sanchez said, "Let them go."

The man holding the girl pulled up her dress, baring her legs, and was tearing at her under- garment. The one pounding on the boy turned around to look at Sanchez but didn't release the boy. "If you know what's good for you, breed, you'll get the hell out of here."

Before either of the men could move, Sanchez took two quick steps and hit the one molesting the girl on the head with his gun; the man rolled off the girl, who quickly got to her feet. Sanchez pressed his gun to the head of the other man and told the girl to take the boy and run. "I'll take care of these two."

The boy was holding his head and leaning against the back wall. His face was swollen and blood covered the right side of his face. The young girl grabbed his arm and pulled him away from his assailant, and together they ran from the livery. There was a moment after she grabbed the boy's arm when she looked directly into Sanchez's eyes and something unspoken passed between them.

The man Sanchez hit was getting to his feet while the other glared at him and said, "You made a big mistake, and when we see you again, we're going to kill you."

Sanchez didn't know what to do with the two. He wondered if he should take them to the sheriff, but being an Indian, he didn't have much faith in white sheriffs, and since the girl and boy were gone, it was his word against theirs. "You two can be on your way. I'll keep your guns." They glared at him as they took their time leaving the livery stable.

He decided to pick up his gear and camp out of town, in case the two came back with friends. He found a good spot shielded by a couple of cottonwoods about two miles out of town and a hundred yards off the road with an unobstructed view. Within an hour, he saw four riders coming from town. He wasn't sure they were trailing him, but when all four stopped where he had exited the road and started toward the cottonwoods, he assumed they were looking for him. Rather than leave, he decided to make a stand. The two trees gave him as much cover as he needed, and besides, he didn't know if he could outrun them. He took out his rifle and waited.

He still couldn't make out who they were as they took their time tying their horses to some scrub and then spread out as they approached the cottonwoods. When they were about thirty paces from him, one of them pointed toward the cottonwoods and shouted, "We're going to kill you, breed, and there's not a thing you can do about it."

He assumed it was one of the men from the livery stable. As soon as the threat was uttered, Sanchez raised his rifle, aimed, and shot one of the men in the shoulder. The man yelled and fell forward. Sanchez called out, "If the rest of you don't want the same thing, then drop your guns and take your friend with you."

There was a period of uncertainty, so Sanchez shot another of the riders in the shoulder, and their decision was made. The other two dropped their guns and raised their hands. Sanchez called out, "Take the other two with you and get out of here. I'd advise you not to follow me; I won't be as generous the next time."

All four were on their feet with two helping the wounded onto their horses. Sanchez watched until they were out of sight. He assessed his options and decided he couldn't go back into town, so he packed up and made his way west. The wagon train company would have to find another guide. He knew that he had had to intercede or they would have molested the girl and beat up her friend. He could hear his father's words warning him not to interfere. Every time he failed to heed his father's advice; it was he who had to move on.

CHAPTER ONE

Those who saw Tommy Sanchez ride into town noted that he sat high in the saddle and seemed to take in his surrounding with little movement of his head. He was dressed as any cowboy in that area with jeans, a flannel shirt, checkered scarf around his neck, and a black Stetson hat. His dark skin could easily indicate Indian or Spanish blood lines or that of a cowboy who spent much of his time outdoors. The only other thing that set him apart was the long black hair neatly falling from the back of his Stetson.

The noonday sun reflected off a Remington rifle in a scabbard on the right side of his horse while a single gun was in a holster strapped to his right hip. Dust was caked to the horse's hoofs indicating he had come via the dry riverbed. His mount continued down to the Saddleback Saloon with little direction from his rider. He dismounted slowly, keeping a keen eye on his surroundings, and loosely tied the animal to the hitching post in front, so that the horse could use the watering trough. There was only one other horse tied up in front of the saloon on this mid-day of the week.

Assessing someone's height and weight while they're in the saddle is difficult. Once dismounted, it was obvious Sanchez stood about five feet ten inches and weighed around one hundred sixty-five pounds. He took time to orient himself to his surroundings, carefully eyeing the row of shops lined up on either side of Second Street in Laramie, Wyoming, before leaving the security of his mount. Most of the businesses were still working out of tents; others were housed in wooden structures that hadn't been finished. All were being built three feet above the street to protect the structures from the frequent flash floods that occurred in the fall and spring.

He walked up the stairs and looked over the cafe doors poised as a sentry to the entrance of the Saddleback Saloon. He saw a large single room, measuring about forty by fifty feet. His gaze moved to the left where a rectangular bar stood and then to the right where stairs led up to second-floor rooms. The remainder of the room was littered with tables and chairs. There were seven people in the saloon that he could see from the cafe doors. Three were playing cards at a table in the far end, another man was standing at the bar, two working girls were seated at a table across from the bar, and the bartender was busy polishing a glass.

All looked up as he pushed through the cafe doors and strode to the bar. One of the girls took her time checking him out before walking up and asking if he wanted company. He ignored the question and asked the bartender for a beer as he slapped at the dust he had accumulated from his long ride. He nodded at the question posed by the bartender that he was a stranger to the area and acknowledged a greeting from the cowboy standing at the other end of the bar by nodding his head. He continued to ignore the girl beside him, who finally walked back to her chair and sat down in a huff. While sipping his beer, he appeared to be deep in thought, taking in everything in the room. Finally, he looked up and addressed the bartender. "Is anyone hiring?"

The bartender said he didn't know of anyone, but the cowboy at the bar spoke up. "I think the Bar 6 is still hiring. It's about three miles south of here. You just follow the road out front and you'll run into it. Ask for Herb Teller, the foreman."

Sanchez finished his beer, thanked the cowboy, and walked toward the exit. As he reached the cafe door, he hesitated while looking out into the street and then exited, walked down the saloon steps, mounted, and rode in the direction of the Bar 6. The girl who had previously approached him at the bar got up, walked to the cafe door entrance, and watched as he rode out of town. "Looks to me like a half-breed," she said to no one in particular.

The road was well traveled and it took him about thirty minutes to cover the three miles to the Bar 6; he didn't meet anyone on the trail.

The ranch house, an adobe-colored structure with a dark brown roof, was set back about two thousand feet from the entrance to the ranch.

As he rode up to the house, he asked a cowboy to point out Herb Teller and was directed to the bunkhouse, which lay one hundred yards to the right and behind the ranch house. The bunkhouse was similar to others Sanchez had seen at other ranches with bunks on either side of a large room and a fireplace near the entrance. Herb Teller, a broad-shouldered man of average height and a diagonal scar on his right cheek, was talking to another cowhand as Sanchez entered. To the question of if he was hiring, he asked Sanchez his name, where he came from, and whether he had experience in breaking green horses.

"My name is Tommy Sanchez, and the best way to explain my experience is to show you."

"Toss your bedroll on that bunk in the far corner and meet me at the corral you saw as you rode in. We have two green horses that none of the hands can ride. If you can break these two, you have a job. If not, we'll give you a meal, a place to sleep tonight, and then you're on your way," Teller responded.

Teller and several of the cowhands were lined up on the rails circling the corral as Tommy entered the enclosure and approached the first green horse with a halter. The cowboys started laughing and talking among themselves as Tommy seemed to be talking to the horse, caressing its head and rubbing his withers and hindquarters.

"Ask him his name and see what he says!" one of cowhands yelled out.

Tommy ignored the taunts and continued to walk around the animal while rubbing his hands all over the horse and talking to it in a soft mono- tone. The ritual lasted about thirty minutes before he placed a halter on the horse and then a blanket. As Tommy continued this ritual, the taunts ceased. It was obvious the cowhands were skeptical, yet they wanted to see what would happen next. The horse seemed to be mesmerized by this approach and allowed Tommy to put on a saddle. While Tommy walked the horse around the closed corral, he continued to talk softly to the horse.

After a couple of laps around the enclosure, he moved the horse up against the wooden rails and mounted. As he walked the horse inside the corral, the talking among the cowboys erupted again. The gist of the dialog was that Tommy was lucky and wouldn't be successful with Thunder, which was the worst horse anyone had ever tried to ride. One cowboy, called Slim by the others, was the most vocal. "I'll bet you five dollars that you won't even get a blanket on Thunder."

Tommy continued riding the green horse around the corral for another fifteen minutes and then dismounted. The second horse was led into the corral by a cowboy who took the first mount from Tommy. Sensing that Thunder would be more difficult, Tommy followed the same procedure but took more time between each stage before attempting to mount Thunder. He was thrown just as he sat in the saddle.

Slim yelled out, "I told you so!"

Tommy got up as the cowhands jeered. Instead of forcing the issue with the horse, Tommy repeated the procedure twice more, taking sufficient time to calm the animal by talking to it and rubbing it all over. The second time he tried to mount the horse, Thunder bucked and threw him just as he was putting his leg over the saddle.

Slim couldn't resist. "Maybe if you kissed him on the lips, he'd be nicer to you."

On the third attempt Tommy mounted Thunder and rode the horse around the corral to stunned silence and then applause, except from Slim, who yelled out, "You must've given him something!"

Teller was impressed. "Where did you learn how to do that?"

Tommy was reluctant to be specific. "I learned the technique from an old friend, but the procedure needs to be repeated a few more times before the horses will respond to any rider."

Teller smiled and shook his hand. "Clean up and join us for supper. I think the boss wants to meet you and you have a job."

Most of the cowhands approached Tommy as he was heading to the bunkhouse and introduced themselves and complimented him on breaking the two horses. Slim didn't come by, nor did he offer to pay the five dollars. Michael Jacobs, the owner of the Bar 6, joined the fore- man and cowhands at the evening meal, complimented Tommy on the demonstration he put on that afternoon, and welcomed him to the Bar 6. "I didn't believe anyone could ride Thunder, but you sure did." Jacobs was looking at Sanchez as he spoke.

Michael Jacobs came from Ireland in 1850 and opened up a freight office in Wyoming for a company located in Chicago. He was a frugal man, and after a decade of hard work, he was able to buy the Bar 6. He had a Midas touch and soon had the largest herd of cattle in the state of Wyoming. When gold was discovered in the Dakotas, the rush was on. Cattle prices were at a premium, and Jacobs became a rich man almost overnight. He was an easy-going man but understood that the wealth he possessed gave him a perceived sense of power, and when necessary, he exercised that power. Those who felt that power were enraged but couldn't do anything other than seethe and wait for their opportunity when and if it ever came. Consequently, Jacobs had a few detractors. His most vocal critic was another rancher who had been engaged to a pretty school teacher. Jacobs had met the couple at an annual dance, and it was love at first sight for the teacher and Jacobs. She broke her engagement and married Jacobs three months later. Their love was short-lived, however; she died giving birth to their son four years into the marriage.

For six months after the tragedy, Jacobs was a recluse and relied on Herb Teller to run the ranch and Maria, his housekeeper, to nurture the child. The six months seemed to be an elixir. After that he worked at increasing his holdings and becoming richer than before. He never remarried; his son and the Bar 6 were his life.

Work on the ranch was at a steady pace, and though the hours were long, Teller allowed a certain amount of freedom in performing tasks assigned if they were completed on time. The routine was probably the same at every cattle ranch in the country. Cowhands worked six days, Monday through Saturday noon, and went into town on Saturday night, had a few drinks, played cards, visited the girls at the Saddleback Saloon, and then staggered back home and slept it off on Sunday. This cycle had been repeated for generations. Tommy usually went with the cowboys but didn't gamble and left the girls alone. Other than a couple of beers, he saved his money. He liked the area and wanted a place of his own. Tommy's goal was to buy a small spread and raise cattle. He felt his wandering days were finally over.

One afternoon while he was working a horse in the corral, Mike Jacobs approached him. "If I bought some green horses, do you think you could train them as you did Thunder and the other horse?"

"Yes sir. I can train most horses, though there are some that might not be worth it. If you know what I mean." With that Jacobs walked off. Tommy didn't know what to make of the short conversation but went about his business and didn't give it another thought.

Tommy knew that Slim harbored resentment and ultimately there would be a confrontation.

It came three months after he was hired and while they were on a roundup near the town of Laramie. As was the case on roundups, the cook rang the bell for dinner and the cowhands hurried to get in line and have first choice, which on this night was beef from a freshly slaughtered steer. Tommy and Slim arrived at the same time and each felt they were ahead of the other. Tommy was willing to let Slim go ahead, but when Slim elbowed Tommy out of the way, the die was cast.

Slim was in front of Tommy when he turned and said, "You think you're something special, but you're nothing but a half-breed. Just because you got lucky with a couple of horses doesn't make you top dog. The rest of us have been here a lot longer than you, so you keep your place."

Tommy just smiled, and that's when Slim lost it. "I'm going to knock that smile off your face, breed, right in front of everyone."

One of the other cowhands yelled, "Teach him a lesson, Slim."

Slim swung a right hand, but Tommy was prepared. He ducked and drove a hard right into Slim's solar plexus and then a left to his jaw. Slim dropped to the ground holding his jaw and several of the cowboys grabbed Tommy and tossed him to the ground. That's when the foreman ran up and yelled at everyone to break it up. By this time, Slim was vomiting on the ground. The foreman was the doctor out on the range and he examined Slim. It appeared that Slim's jaw was broken, and it was obvious he wouldn't be working for a few days. Teller wrapped his jaw with a bandage and had two cowhands put Slim under one of the wagons and cover him with blankets. Teller would have the cook take him back to the ranch the next morning in one of the wagons. The local doctor would be able to treat him there.

After he treated Slim, Teller walked over to Tommy. "Slim can't work for at least a week, so I'm going to dock you a week's worth of pay and give it to Slim. I don't care who started the fight, I've got a job to do and I can't afford to be undermanned. You keep your temper in check or you're out of here."

The rest of cowboys were back in the chow line, but Tommy didn't feel hungry, so he grabbed his bedroll and lay down underneath one of the wagons. He now knew that there were other cowhands besides Slim who harbored some animosity toward him. He'd have to be careful.

Subsequently Tommy was docked a week's wages, which were paid to Slim. Teller was a fair man and deducted what Slim owed Tommy on the unpaid bet. Tommy didn't complain to Ja- cobs; he accepted his fate.

Teller placed Tommy temporarily in charge of training and breaking horses while Slim was recuperating from the beating Tommy had administered. When Slim was able to take back his position, the foreman assigned him to fence mending on the northern part of the property. Slim had been working at the Bar 6 for over two years and felt that he'd been doing an acceptable job, so he approached Teller. "Why am I being given a lousy job and the breed gets mine? I'm a top hand and besides I have seniority."

"The order came from Mr. Jacobs. I work here just like you; your new job is to mend fences," Teller responded very abruptly.

"But he's a breed."

"I don't want to hear about it, just do your job," Teller responded.

Fence mending was a tedious job. Sometimes the rider would stay out two or three nights at a time, but in all cases he was back by noon on Saturday and ready to go with the rest of the crew when they went into town. Over the years, Slim had become friendly with a local tough in Laramie named Bull Larkin. They played cards or had a beer and sometimes took a girl upstairs for the night. Slim hadn't been in town for a few Saturdays and Larkin was concerned. After Slim recuperated, he told Larkin about the fight with Tommy but left out the part where he swung first and added that Sanchez hit him from behind. "You want me to take care of him?" Larkin asked.

"No, I've got my own plans for the breed," Slim responded.

Slim wasn't the only one at the Bar 6 who was envious of what Tommy had accomplished in his short tenure at the ranch. Two others cowboys shared Slim's jealousy but weren't as vocal about it. They sensed that Mike Jacobs favored Tommy because of his ability with the horses, even though Slim had seniority. They sided with Slim but they needed their jobs and therefore stayed quiet.

Tommy had created a legend among the cowboys at the Bar 6 and soon word reached the other ranches in the area of the strange and successful method he used to break horses. Soon after their conversation at the corral, Jacobs decided to buy some horses that other ranchers were willing to get off their hands at a cheap price. With Tommy turning them into useable mounts, Jacobs made a substantial profit.

Over the next six months Tommy and Jacobs became closer, and Tommy started to confide in Jacobs. He shared with him that his goal was to own a spread where he would raise cattle and horses. By this time, Tommy was earning a bonus for every green horse that was brought to the Bar 6 for training and a small percentage of the profits from reselling the horses that

Jacobs bought and Tommy trained. So close was their relationship that Jacobs was investing Tommy's wages and bonuses.

Although the average cowhand's salary was thirty dollars a month plus keep, Tommy was averaging fifty dollars a month, and his investments grew to five hundred dollars by the end of his first year at the Bar 6. He confided in Jacobs that he was looking at a hundred-acre parcel. "I wonder if you'd look at it, Mr. Jacobs, and give me your opinion?"

One day the two rode over to look at the parcel and meet with the owner. Jacobs handled the negotiations, and they settled on a price of $240 with an option to add an additional two hundred acres at three dollars an acre if Tommy exercised the option within three years. The parcel bordered the northern part of the Bar 6 and shared a common creek.

Although Tommy shook hands on the deal, Jacobs made the deal conditioned on his personal agreement with Tommy and a review of the purchase agreement by his attorney. Subsequently, Jacobs had his attorney draw up the purchase agreement as well as a personal ser- vices agreement with Tommy. For the first year, Tommy would continue to work at Jacobs's Bar 6 for four days and the other three he could work his own spread. He'd be paid seventy percent of his present salary but wouldn't share in profits from the horse breaking and resale business. In return, Jacobs would lend him enough stock to get started at the end of the first year.

Saul Freedman had come to Wyoming four years earlier and set up practice in Laramie in one of the tents used by tradesmen and businessmen until their businesses prospered and they could afford stick-built buildings. When the documents were drawn, Freedman rode out to the Bar 6 and showed them to Jacobs, who signed off on the deed and his personal services agreement with Tommy and gave Freedman a draft on the Laramie Bank for the purchase amount. Jacobs was acting as agent for Tommy who was on a roundup and wouldn't be back until the end of the week. When he returned, Jacobs would send him into Laramie to sign the documents and have the deed recorded. In the interim, Freedman would have the seller sign the agreement and deed, and once Tommy signed, Freedman would transfer the funds to the seller.

Jacobs was like an expectant father waiting for Tommy to return from the roundup. Giving him the news that the deal was completed was equally exhilarating. It was too late in the day so he suggested that Tommy go into Laramie the next morning and sign the agreement. They had dinner and a bottle of wine to celebrate the new venture and then talked of the future. Jacobs had a young son to carry on his heritage and now he also had a young man who he considered a friend to mentor. This was the happiest he'd been since his wife died. The two men shook hands before Tommy left for Laramie the next morning.

"Tommy, I'd go with you, but I promised my son that I'd take him fishing and I can't go back on that promise. I hope you understand?"

"No problem, Mr. Jacobs I'll just ride in, sign the documents, and come right back here. See you this afternoon."

It was Saturday morning and the cowboys were getting cleaned up to go town. Before Tommy left for the attorney's office in Laramie, he polished his boots, took a bath, put on his best jeans and a clean shirt. There were no women on the ranch, so the laundry was handled by a Chinese father and son who lived in a tent behind the bunkhouse. The only English they knew had been taught to them by Tommy. He was especially fond of the young boy, who he was teaching to ride and rope. In addition, he taught the father to ride and promised both a job on his spread if it didn't work out for them at the Bar 6. This was to be a red letter day in his life. He would be a property owner; no longer would he be a second-class citizen. They may call him a breed behind his back, but not to his face if they wanted a job on his spread.

Saul Freedman was not in his office when Tommy arrived to sign the documents. A note on his office door indicated he'd be back at two o'clock. Tommy had an hour to waste so he rode down to the Saddleback Saloon and ordered a beer. It was early on Saturday afternoon, and only a small group of cowhands from the Bar 6, some transients, and a couple of working girls were in the saloon. Tommy could see out of the corner of his eye that two of the Chinamen who worked in Wong's Laundry were delivering clean sheets and bar towels to the bartender.

Before they could leave, their exit was blocked by Bull Larkin. Sheriff Harker and his main deputy were trailing a couple of cattle rustlers near Cheyenne and had left Larkin, a part-time deputy, in charge during their absence. Tommy had seen Larkin on two previous occasions in the company of Slim. They appeared to be similar personalities. On one occasion, Slim had pointed to Tommy while talking to Larkin and they both started to laugh.

Larkin was a big kid who liked to harass the Chinese who worked at the laundry. He thought it was funny that they walked in a single file wherever they went, whether it was for laundry delivery or going home after work. He especially like to trip one of them while they were in single file and see if the others would fall down as they tried to get out of the way of their fallen comrades. Today he was holding the long hair of the two laundrymen in one hand and threatening to cut it off. Those in the bar thought it was great sport. That is, all except Tommy. He knew what it was like to be singled out if you were different, and in the next moment his whole world turned upside down.

"Bull, let them alone, they're not bothering you." He said it without much emotion.

Larkin didn't respond. Later, several of the saloon patrons thought he didn't hear Tommy; others thought he just ignored him. Larkin asked the bartender for scissors, and when the bartender didn't respond quickly enough, Larkin yelled at him again. Before he could get the scissors, Tommy spoke. "Bull, I asked you to let them go. They're not bothering you. Haven't you got something else to do besides bother these two?"

This time Larkin heard him, and though he didn't release the laundry workers, he turned with a sneer. "Hey, breed, shut the hell up or you'll be the one whose hair will be cut off. I'm not someone you can hit from behind."

Tommy put down his beer and turned slowly to face the deputy. He spoke in a very quiet tone. Later, several in the saloon, when questioned, said they didn't hear what he said. "I don't think so, Bull. You've had your fun for the day, now let them go and we can get back to our beer."

Larkin's face turned red. He didn't have enough intelligence to assess a situation and then decide what to do. He was the type who reacted first and then if necessary thought about it later. While holding onto the hair of the two Chinamen, he slung them to the side and both fell against the bar. The silence was deafening. It seemed that everyone in the saloon was holding their breath; no one knew what would happen next except Larkin. He was about ten feet from Tommy when he drew his weapon and aimed it at Tommy. "Breed, you're under arrest for interfering with the duties of a law enforcement officer. Give me your gun."

Tommy didn't move. "I didn't come here to interfere with anything, but you've no call to treat them like that. I don't know how the others feel, but I don't like it. They weren't bothering you. They've a right to go about their business without being bothered, same as anyone else. You're supposed to be acting sheriff and up- holding the law, not harassing the people in this town. How would you like it if someone did that to you? I'm not going to jail with you. If the sheriff wants to talk to me about this, I'll be at the Bar 6. He knows where it is."

"I don't need the sheriff 's help. I can take you myself. Now drop your gun belt on the floor or I'll shoot you right here." Larkin was smiling as he looked around the room to make sure the others saw him as he moved even closer to Tommy.

As Larkin moved toward Tommy, he waved his gun sideways while taunting him. Suddenly two shots rang out in rapid succession, and a large spot of blood starting pouring from Larkin's head. He was dead before he crashed to the floor and landed on his face. Tommy had killed before and felt no remorse, but today was different. In an instant he knew that his plans for the future were finished and he wouldn't be buying the property. He would become a fugitive and be on the run for the remainder of his life. He could hear his father's words ringing out in the silence of the bar room.

CHAPTER TWO

Everyone, including the bartender, exited as soon as they could, leaving Tommy alone with the late Bull Larkin as though it was a vigil. Tommy knew that when the initial shock of the shooting was over, someone would try to arrest him. He walked to the front entrance and looked over the cafe doors. He could see a few men across the street pointing at the saloon, so he found the rear door and walked out; no one was in the back. Tommy walked around the side of the saloon and approached his horse tethered to the hitching post. One of the men across the street pointed toward him but didn't make any move in his direction. He mounted Jupiter and rode out of town before the locals could regroup and try to arrest him.

The ride back to the ranch was the loneliest ride of his life. He wondered what Jacobs would say and do. Would he turn him over to the sheriff or would he tell him to leave the ranch immediately? Several of the Bar 6 ranch hands had been in the saloon and rode back ahead of Tommy to report the shooting. Jacobs was waiting for Tommy on the front porch. Several of the cowboys including Slim were watching as he rode up. Jacobs came down the steps as Tommy dismounted and asked him to follow him into the ranch house. The one-story adobe included a large living area with a: fireplace on the rear wall, an office area at other end of the room, and two bedrooms, one on each side of the living area. Jacobs asked him to be seated and tell him what happened. Tommy told him his side of the story.

"Why didn't you stay out of it?" Jacobs asked.

"I've seen people like Larkin act like he did and no one would do anything. Those
Chinese were just doing their job. I asked him to stop and he ignored me. In fact, he told me he was going to arrest me and then he pulled a gun. You know what would have happened. He'd have thrown me in jail and for fun would cut my hair and probably beat me up. He'd get away with it because he was appointed a lawman. What choice did I have? When I got out, I'd have killed him anyway. I just saved myself the humility of being beaten and my hair cut because he felt like it. I'd like my money now. I think it's time for me to leave before a vigilante committee comes calling and you turn me over to them."

Jacobs face turned red. "Is that what you think of me? I want you to stay. Let me talk to the sheriff when he comes out here. He won't try to take you. I have too many men loyal to me and have some influence in this county."

"You don't owe me anything, Mr. Jacobs. It was my doing and I know they'll want to hang me. You don't need to get involved."

But Tommy agreed to wait a few days, stay on the ranch, and see what developed. Jacobs and Tommy walked out the front door and down the steps. Slim and a couple of cowhands were waiting. "You're going to turn him over to the sheriff, aren't you, Mr. Jacobs?" Slim asked.

"That's my business, Slim. I'm still the owner of the Bar 6 and I decide who goes and who stays, remember that."

"But he shot Larkin when he was trying to arrest him."

Teller walked up at that moment. "Mr. Jacobs told you, Slim. If you know what's good for you, you'll shut up and get about your business."

The next day Jacobs sent for Saul Freeman to solicit his advice. Freedman suggested they wait and see what the sheriff had to say. It was two days before the sheriff came out to the Bar 6 with an arrest warrant for Tommy, charging him with murder.

Judd Harker had been sheriff in Albany County for ten years, primarily because no one else wanted the job. Prior to being sheriff, he'd been a mule skinner, drover, and even worked at the Bar 6. He had difficulty holding a job and never forgave Jacobs for firing him. The two men just didn't like each other. Judd was of average height but thick in the shoulders. His most distinguishing characteristic was that he wore cologne most of the time, possibly thinking him- self to be a ladies man. Few men crossed him for fear of his hair-trigger temper. At least one of his prisoners who antagonized him was shot in the back while trying to escape.

He rode up to the ranch house with Fred Higgins, his main deputy and the one who was with him in Cheyenne when Larkin was shot. Jacobs and Tommy saw them approach and remained sitting on the porch drinking tea until the two dismounted. Both Jacobs and Tommy rose. Jacobs was holding his Remington; Tommy had a pistol in his holster strapped to his right hip.

There were no introductions; that wasn't Harker's way. He was a direct man. "I've got a warrant for your man charging him with the murder of Bull Larkin. Me and Fred are taking him back to town." He handed the warrant to Jacobs.

Neither he nor his deputy had touched their weapons, but they noticed that Tommy had a gun holstered on his right hip, and Harker had heard from eyewitnesses how Larkin had a gun on Tommy but was shot twice anyway. He'd be cautious with this one. Tommy didn't read the warrant that was given to Jacobs. The sheriff probably figured that Tommy couldn't read and that's why he handed it to the owner of the Bar 6.

Jacobs read the warrant carefully." It says here that this was premeditated. How can that be when Tommy didn't know he was going into town until that day and only went into the Saddleback to wait for Saul Freeman? Now I've heard from several of the people who witnessed the shooting. All Tommy did was ask Bull to leave the Chinese alone. You know how Bull was. He thought he was king almighty. Tommy didn't draw down on him either. It was self defense from my view."

Harker became impatient. "I don't care what you think and how many witnesses you spoke to. He's going with me and he's going to stand trial for murdering my deputy. Now if you know what's good for you, you'll get out of the way or I'll take you in as well. Are you going to let us have him?"

The tension was high when Jacobs answered while Tommy shifted his position, swung his jacket open, and let his right hand hang free near his weapon. "He's not going with you. This isn't about Tommy, it's about you and me, and I'm not letting you get away with it. You were a lousy ranch hand and a worse sheriff. How could you leave an animal like Bull Larkin in charge of anything?"

Harker was angry and didn't like being put down in front of his deputy. Both he and his deputy were poised to take action, but the look in Tommy's eyes told them what the witnesses to the shooting reported. Larkin had his weapon on Tommy when Tommy drew and shot him twice between the eyes. That was enough for Harker to realize that he and his deputy were no match for Tommy, let alone Jacobs and some of his cowhands.

The immediate tension dissipated, but not Harker's anger. "You have twenty-four hours to deliver him to me in Laramie or I'll go to the fort and get some help. No one's going to shoot one of my deputies and get away with it. Twenty-four hours, that's all. And if you still won't deliver him, I'll get a warrant for you as well. And so the breed won't try to escape, Fred's going to sit out- side the Bar 6 and shoot him on sight if he tries to leave." Harker and his deputy mounted and exited the ranch.

Several of the cowboys, including Slim, had witnessed the confrontation and wondered if the sheriff had the balls to arrest one of the richest and most influential men in the county. They weren't sure. Jacobs and Tommy sat down in chairs on the front porch.

"This isn't good, Tommy. We can hold off the sheriff and his deputies, but not the army. We've got to figure a way to get you out of here tonight. The deputy will be a problem: he's probably hiding out there watching the ranch. I know you didn't ask for this, but it's something you'll have to live with and not here, but somewhere else. You'll be a wanted man. Going to trial here wouldn't work. I think you'd be shot trying to escape. That's Harker's way. I have enough cash on hand to give you what you've invested plus a month's wages, but I think it's best if you leave tonight. Come by in an hour and we'll settle up."

After Jacobs gave him his money, Tommy went back to the bunkhouse to get his gear. He knew that Slim had been trying to stir things up and wasn't sure if any of the other hands would side with Slim if there was a showdown. Chances were they were happy here and would back up Jacobs if there was a confrontation with the sheriff, but not the army. The problem was that he needed to get away fast, slip past that deputy, and put as much distance between himself and Fort Laramie as he could. This was Tommy's country; he knew every water hole and hideout spot between here and the Colorado Territory and he knew how to live off the land. He'd been trained by the best. Once he slipped past the deputy, he knew it'd be difficult to find him.

He pretended to be asleep and waited until the other cowhands dozed off before he slipped out with his personal possessions and made his way to the corral. As he neared the corral someone slipped out of the shadows and put a rifle to his back. Instinctively he pivoted and with his right arm pushed the rifle aside and hit the stalker on the side of his face with his left fist. The adversary dropped the weapon and slumped to the ground. Tommy could see it was Slim, so he hit him twice more. He dragged the unconscious Slim to the corral, gagged him, and tied him to the rail. He unloaded Slim's weapon, broke the stock over a boulder near the water well, and threw it down the shaft.

For a half-mile outside the ranch the terrain was flat and then turned rolling for another mile before becoming flat all the way into Laramie. Tommy sensed that the deputy would be positioned behind a small knoll about a half- mile from the front entrance and be able to see anyone coming down the trail from the ranch. Tommy exited at the rear of the ranch and walked his horse for a half-mile before turning south toward Colorado so he come up behind the deputy. He covered the ground in about two hours and rested. His instincts for survival and his ability to hear any threatening sounds had been honed in his ancestors and passed down to all of the braves.

He heard the deputy's horse and the deputy move around trying to stay awake and keep warm. He tied his horse to a piece of tumbleweed and crawled up to within ten feet and directly behind the deputy who was sitting down, leaning against his saddle and having a cigarette. He could see that the deputy wasn't carrying a sidearm, only a rifle, which was resting on his lap. He spoke to the deputy softly. "Do you want to live through this night?"

There was a moment of silence before the deputy responded, "Yes."

"I want you to move very slowly. Let the rifle drop from your lap, then get up and start walking toward Laramie. I'll leave your horse about two miles from here. I know it's three miles to Laramie, but you can make it in an hour and that's all the head start I need. If you follow me or wait around to see which way I'm headed, I'll kill you. Do you understand?"

"Yes." With that the deputy headed toward Laramie and didn't look back. When Tommy could see that the deputy was a quarter of a mile away, he mounted, grabbed the reins of the deputy's horse, and rode away, leaving the deputy's rifle and saddle on the knoll. The son of Tasunka Lyotake, the buffalo bull, was free.

CHAPTER THREE

With the telegraph spreading throughout the West, law enforcement officials could be waiting for him anywhere he went. The odds were that Harker would think Tommy would flee either west to Utah or south to the Colorado border. He knew Sheriff Harker wouldn't rest until he had him in jail and probably would arrange for an escape that would have dire consequences and therefore save the county a trial. The Colorado border was thirty miles to the south and Denver another hundred and twenty miles farther south. He decided to skirt Denver to the east and go south to Pueblo.

It took him a month on horseback to make the trip while staying clear of any settlement and activity. He had nearly six hundred dollars on his person and wanted to deposit it in a bank as soon as possible. But his first concern was his appearance. The long black hair from his youth had to go. Other changes had to be made and in such a way that he wouldn't be recognized from a wanted poster. He found a pair of old scissors in his saddlebag and cut his hair close to the skin.

At a trading post over the border and east of Fort Morgan he switched from a Stetson to a sombrero. The white man at the trading post asked him, "What do you want me to do with the Stetson?"

"Give it to someone. I don't need it anymore," Tommy responded. Before he reached Pueblo, he grew a mustache, which he allowed to grow into a bushy stump; he looked more Mexican than Indian.

The town of Pueblo, Colorado, on the Arkansas River was the dividing line between Mexico and the United States in the mid-1800s. The original settlement was at Fort Pueblo near present-day Pueblo. It was the focal point for trading between the Indian tribes, the fur trap- pers, and buffalo hunters. This came to an end in 1854, when a band of Utes massacred the small settlement at the fort on Christmas Eve. Subsequently the Utes were captured and transported to a reservation in Oklahoma. Consequently, Indians were not welcome in the town. His change to a Mexican look was fortuitous.

Tommy camped out of town and went to one of the local bars to see what was going on in town and who was hiring. He was told there were only a few ranches but that he probably could find work with some of the buffalo hunters who'd set up south of town. He rode south and came upon some hunters butchering an animal. He dismounted and walked over to two hunters who were on their knees butchering an animal. "My name is Sanchez and I'm looking for work."

"You skinned any buffalo before?" one of the men responded, looking up.

"Some."

"Well, let's see what you can do. There're some old clothes on my mule that you can use. We'll pay two dollars an animal. There's enough work for three months, then you're on your own." s

With that, Tommy Sanchez became a buffalo skinner. The job was messy, but the hunters paid as soon as the skin was removed. Saloons were numerous, and along with a couple of whore- houses, there was plenty of nightlife for a young man. The first month in Pueblo, Tommy was too tired to think about women, and if he ordered a beer, he was able to make it last for a few hours at a time.

Other than the two hunters, the only acquaintances he made were transients like him. He didn't want to get too close to anyone for fear they might remember something about him that would help Harker track him. On occasion he'd have a beer with Jethroe Simmons, a buffalo skinner himself. On Saturday evenings, they'd sit in the back of one of the saloons and talk about work or watch what else was going on in the saloon. It was a way to pass the time for the next few months. Tommy knew that it was only a matter of time before he'd be moving on.

Tommy usually ate with the two buffalo hunters, but on this Saturday evening, he and Jethroe decided to splurge and have a steak at the Branding Iron Saloon. They finished dinner and were enjoying coffee and especially the young blond waitress who was taking an interest in Jethroe. When they finished, they walked out the back of the saloon where they had tethered their horses. As they were nearing the horses Tommy saw a flash of movement to his left, but before he could react, he and Jethroe were hit from behind and were on the ground fighting for their lives. Tommy didn't have time to get out his gun, but he kicked one man's legs out from under him, quickly got to his feet, and hit his assailant over the head with his gun.

He turned to see about Jethroe, who was on the ground moaning while his assailant was running away. Several of the male customers of the saloon came up and took charge of the assailant Tommy fought and who was still unconscious on the ground. Jethroe had been stabbed in the stomach and blood was pouring out of his wound. Tommy was on his knees beside Jethroe trying to stop the bleeding when Jethroe looked up and said, "It was Brock Masters who stabbed me."

He died before a doctor could attend to him. The town marshal and two other men went after the assailant who stabbed Jethroe. Soon they were joined by about twenty men, and within a few hours they caught Masters hiding behind the garbage at the rear of the saloon. Justice was swift in Pueblo. The two were tried the next day and hung the day after. The town marshal complimented Tommy for handling one of the assailants, and over the next few weeks he couldn't buy a beer in any of the half-dozen saloons in Pueblo because he was treated as a hero.

What he didn't want was notoriety. The local newspaper ran a feature on the assailants, the town marshal, and Tommy. There wasn't much coverage on Tommy because he refused to be interviewed by the editor of the paper. He was suspicious of everything, and when a couple of strangers came into town, he stayed out with the buffalo hunters for a few days until they left. Perhaps he was suffering from paranoia, but he sensed his time was limited, so at the end of the week he collected his wages, thanked the two hunters, and moved on.

"We've got enough work for a least a month if you want to stay," the older of the two hunters told him.

He didn't want to tell the two hunters why he was leaving so he made up a story. "It's time I move on. The killing kind of turned me off on the town."

He really wanted to put more distance between himself and Sheriff Harker and didn't want to tell the two hunters that. He wasn't that close to Jethroe, but he stopped by his grave on his way out of town and wondered out loud if trouble would be following him to the next town.

As with his journey to Pueblo, he avoided settlements and any activity, and it took three weeks to cover the distance to Durango. On his first day in Durango, he met with the local banker, deposited his funds, and asked him, "Is there any work available?"

John Cole had been the president of Durango National Bank for the past three years. He was a tall and broad-shouldered man standing about six feet and weighing one hundred eighty pounds. His parents were deceased and he'd been raised by his paternal uncle, who sent him to the best schools in the East. But John was immature, and before he reached the age of thirty, he'd run through his inheritance and some money set aside by his uncle. As a last resort his uncle arranged for this opportunity at the Durango Bank, a subsidiary of the Chicago National Bank in which his uncle was a major stockholder. He told Cole that he'd either succeed in Durango or he'd disinherit him. Cole was an ambitious man and had an incentive to increase the bank 's holdings with the objective that if he was successful, he could go back to what he called civilization, namely the East Coast.

"The only one I know that may need some help is Frank Waidner, who has a ranch ten miles southwest of town. It's little run down, but it has some potential. Durango is a young town, perhaps a little rough at the edges, but I think it'll be a fine city someday. We have an ex-lawman turned preacher by the name of Hogue who's formed a citizens' council to handle any law-and-order problems. A circuit judge and marshal come every two months to handle any serious is- sues that come up. I think you'll like it here. This is a place for ambitious young men."

After Tommy left the bank, Cole looked at the deposit slip and wondered how a Mexican could accumulate such an amount. He had access to some of the wanted posters that came to Parson Hogue, but hadn't seen one for a Mexican. He'd have to keep an eye on this one.

The Waidner ranch was more like a spread with a few head of cattle, some sheep, and about six horses. Frank Waidner was an affable man about fifty years old, short in stature but outwardly friendly. Tommy introduced himself as Tommy Sanchez from Mexico City and said that John Cole suggested he see Waidner for a job. "If John Cole recommends you, then I can use some help. The pay isn't much, but my wife's cooking is the best in the county and at least you'll be well fed with a roof over your head. The hands I had in the past didn't seem to know how to care for livestock, so most of them are strung out in the hills to the south. I made a count of the cattle and horses last year when we branded them. I don't know exactly how many sheep we have, but I believe they'll number about a hundred. Our brand is the double W."

Waidner sensed the younger man's reluctance and suggested that they sit down to supper. He could decide after he sampled his wife's cooking. Tommy agreed. Waidner had a lot of questions about Tommy's background and experience, which Tommy answered without divulging very much. It was the apple pie that closed the deal for Tommy. He could honestly say that he'd never been fed so well in his short life.

Waidner and his wife were delighted. Before the apple pie, Waidner gave him a quick tour of the ranch facilities before it got too dark. There were several corrals and holding pens and a small barn with a room in the front. "This is your room. It's not much, but it's warm and the roof doesn't leak."

"First thing in the morning I'll go out and round up the cattle, then the horses, and finally the sheep and see what we have and what shape they're in," Tommy said. "It looks like your corrals and pens will hold them temporarily.

Soon as I see what we have, I'll start working on getting them in better shape. I may be gone for a few days. Perhaps your wife can pack some food for three days. What I don't use, I'll return."

Frank Waidner never had help that looked at situations as an owner would. Here was some- one who seemed to know what he was doing. Although Waidner didn't know Tommy very well, he sensed that this was an opportunity that he should take advantage of. "We'll outfit you for three days if you think that's enough. I have a good horse I'm willing to let you use."

Tommy declined. "I'm comfortable with mine, and besides, he's worked cattle before and I can trust him."

He stowed his bedroll on the small cot in the corner of the room in the barn and checked out what had been left behind by former occupants. There was an old jacket, a worn Stetson, and a couple of blankets. He figured he'd clean the place up after he made the roundups. He left the ranch at five in the morning. There was a supply of food rolled up in a cloth bag by his horse as he saddled the gelding. He checked the food; there was enough for a week. Well, he wouldn't starve out in the hills.

Mrs. Waidner asked her husband if it was wise to send the Mexican out to check their stock when they didn't know him. Frank Waidner said he had a good feeling for the young man and if they were to stay and work the ranch, they needed someone who knew the ranch business. "Do we have enough to pay him wages?" she asked.

"With the money from the sale of some of the sheep last year and the money from our other visitors, it'll be enough to keep us going for some time. We need someone who can help us or we're going to lose this place. I don't trust many men, but this one has a way about him. He may be running from something, but I still trust him."

It was late September. There was snow on the upper elevations, but the streams were running full and the grass was starting to turn. Tommy marveled at the expanse and the solitude. The barbed wired fences he came across were mostly in disarray, so he made a mental note and put that task on his to do list. He'd been out a day when he came over a rise and saw about thirty head of cattle grazing in a small glen near where Waidner said he might find them. He came upon them slowly and checked their brands; these were Waidner's cattle. In the areas to the south and west he found eight more strays with the WW brand. He rounded them up and drove them slowly toward the other thirty.

It was late so he decided to camp near the cattle. Mrs. Waidner had packed thick slices of ham and lamb along with a freshly baked loaf of bread. Tommy could get used to this life. It was cool and the silence so inclusive that he could hear a wolf in the distance calling for his mate. This was pure heaven for a cowboy, but that wasn't Tommy's goal in life. He wanted his own place where no one could tell him what to do or when it was time to move on. He figured that his stay would be temporary with the Waidners. They were a nice couple and he'd work hard to get their place in shape, but he couldn't see himself working for them for the rest of his life.

Waidner said he had forty head of cattle at the last roundup. Well, there were thirty-eight here and he'd come across two carcasses about two miles north. Each had the WW brand on that part of the hide that hadn't decomposed or been eaten.

The next morning he set out for the ranch about ten miles to the north. It took him almost twelve hours to drive the cattle the ten miles.

Once he had them in the corral, he took care of his horse before letting him loose in one of the holding pens. Waidner came out and congratulated him on bringing in the cattle and invited him up to the ranch house for supper.

"I'll be up as soon as I clean up," Tommy said. He was surprised to see two Indians sitting at the table when he entered. Waidner introduced the two Indians as Weasel skin and Little Eagle. Weasel skin was the taller of the two and seemed easier to understand. They were Comanche and were only two of about ten from their village that had survived from a combination of too many wars and not enough food. They told them about their village, their chief, and a way of life that was lost. They didn't know how it was lost, but it was. "One day we were hunting and fishing and the next the buffalo was gone and we were hungry."

Tommy listened and remembered his father telling him that their way of life could not be sustained with the onslaught of the white man. Sitting Bull had told him to assimilate in the white man's world, for there was nothing left for him in their culture.

At the end of the meal, Weasel skin took out several small nuggets of gold and laid them on the table in front of Waidner. "We pay for white man's food," he said.

Waidner argued that it was too much, but Weasel skin was adamant. "Indians don't need gold; we like white man's food."

Tommy was amused at the scene, but soon learned from Waidner that Weasel skin and Little Eagle came to the ranch several times a year and on each occasion traded gold for food. "I asked them where they found the gold, but Weasel- skin is cagey and won't reveal his source or its location. It's always the same story. He and Little Eagle were wandering one day and stumbled across the gold and he can't remember where they found it."

On a subsequent visit, Weasel skin traded gold for Tommy's sombrero. Over the next two years Tommy was able to increase the herd of cattle and break all the horses Waidner had. He increased the herd of horses with some of the wild mustangs he found in the hills to the south and later broke them. While he was breaking the mustangs, Waidner and his wife would sit on the corral rails and cheer him on. It was a far cry from the heckling that he received from Slim and some of the cowhands at the Bar 6, and he enjoyed the difference. Tommy rebuilt all the corrals and added some new holding pens. Waidner and his wife were delighted and soon their relationship became very close.

One day while he was feeding the stock, Waidner asked him if he'd be interested in being his partner in the ranch and that when he and his wife passed on, their interest would be transferred to Tommy. "You think about it. Though the winters are long and cold, I think there's enough potential in the remaining months to make this a successful and profitable operation."

"I appreciate the offer, Mr. Waidner. Do you mind if I think it over for a few days? Any agreement I make has to be conditional on building my own home on a portion of the ranch."

"I don't see that as a problem," Waidner responded.

Tommy thought about it for a few days and couldn't see any reason why he shouldn't accept the offer, so he did. The Waidners usually drove to Durango each Sunday to hear Parson Hogue give his fire and brimstone speech. On each occasion, they invited Tommy to join them, but he was reluctant to go, always citing work that needed to be done. Finally he agreed to go with them one Sunday and hear the part-time parson and constable speak. He was amused at the fire in Hogue's oration and equally surprised at how well the townspeople attended his weekly meeting even if it was held in a saloon. Mrs. Waidner told him that the wives came to see what the saloon looked like and what preoccupied their husbands on some evenings and the husbands came to satisfy the wives. Durango didn't have any official law enforcement department, but Hogue, as head of a citizens' committee, functioned in that capacity when needed. Each Sunday following his sermon, the citizens' committee met to enact or enforce some law they created.

There were very few Indian inhabitants of the town of Durango. One exception was Maria Cortez, a housekeeper for an elderly woman named Katherine Short, who'd lived forty of her sixty-five years in Durango and seemed to be the town's conscience. Tommy was introduced to Katherine Short and Maria

Cortez at one of the socials held after each Sunday service. Maria was a quiet woman about thirty years old and the daughter of a Comanche chief. They'd been on the run when they were captured by the army. After spending time at one of the Indian agencies, Maria came to the attention of Katherine Short and agreed to become her companion in return for being taught to read and write. It was a good bargain for both individuals; they were more like mother and daughter than employee and employer.

Soon Tommy made a habit of coming to supper on Sunday evenings at the Short home and, after six months, would stay over occasionally. Theirs wasn't exactly a romance, just people of similar backgrounds enjoying each other's company. Katherine Short approved of the socializing.

John Cole was a frequent visitor to the ranch; soon he and Tommy became friendly. They would go off for a couple of days each year to hunt for elk. Their backgrounds were different, but both men loved the outdoors and hunting.

As Parson Hogue's flock increased, he agreed to relinquish his duties as the unofficial law and John Cole took over as head of the citizens' committee. They were looking to name a town marshal and Cole asked Tommy if he was interested. Tommy said he wasn't. Subsequently the town's blacksmith, Joe Michaels, was offered the position and he accepted. It was a one-man position, but if the town grew as Cole was sure it would, he promised Michaels he could add deputies in the future.

It was in the fall of 1877 when John Cole and Parson Hogue showed up unexpectedly at the ranch. Tommy had been out rounding up a couple of strays and was putting them in a holding pen when the two rode up and tied their horses in front of the Waidner ranch house. Both were inside talking to Waidner as Tommy entered the ranch house. He could tell that the dialog be- tween Waidner and Cole was serious.

"Come on in, Tommy. Parson Hogue and John Cole have brought us some bad news. You need to hear this."

They sat by the fireplace drinking black coffee while Cole told the story. "A party of seven men was following a trail somewhere south of here when they got lost. The trail was marked by scorched spots on tree branches, something the Spanish initiated when they came to this territory many years ago. Somehow the group got above the tree line and couldn't find any more marks. They decided to split up into three groups and take a day to see if they could find a way out and then join up at a designated place. Two of seven were lifelong friends by the names of Phil Prouty and Jean LeDroit. While out trying to find an escape route they came across nuggets of gold in a hole in the mountain near the Upper Vallecito Creek. They stuffed their saddlebags with some of the gold and returned to camp but didn't tell the others about their find. Prouty marked the trailby carving his initials in a marker placed near the gold cache."

Mrs. Waidner came in and filled up their cups with fresh coffee before Cole continued with his story, "One of the other groups found a way out down Smelter Mountain and across the Florida River. As they reached Smelter Mountain, the others became suspicious of Prouty and LeDroit because their animals appeared to be over- loaded. They forced them to open their saddle-bags. When they discovered the gold stuffed in the saddle bags they tortured Prouty and LeDroit to tell where they found the gold. Subsequently the others killed the two and threw their bodies in the creek near Smelter Mountain. There apparently was a further falling out of those that remained; greed had taken over. Three conspired against two. One of the two was killed while the other escaped with some of the gold and came into Durango.

"The survivor's name is Jenks. He got drunk at the Silver Dollar Saloon and bragged about the gold and how he got it. The bartender told me, and I told Sheriff Michaels, who has Jenks in custody and wants to form a posse to go after the other three. No one knows the area better than you, Tommy. I'd like you to go along as their guide and the representative of the citizens' committee. We'll pay you ten dollars a day plus provisions. I assume you'll be out about a week."

"Do you think there's a gold mine out there with nuggets lying in a pile?" Tommy asked.

Hogue responded, "I know the Indians trade in gold, but I don't think it's from some mine. Years ago, there was a group of prospectors who found gold south of here. They packed their mules with as much gold as they could, but in doing so they dumped most of their provisions and consequently ran out of food. On their way out, they came across a Ute village whose men were out on a hunting party, leaving the women and children alone. The sight of the prospectors with long white beards and dirty clothes apparently scared the woman and children, who'd been sitting around a campfire eating their evening meal when the prospectors came upon them. The women and children ran off leaving the food for the prospectors who devoured the food, got drunk, and inadvertently set fire to one of the tents. The wind was up and the fire spread, burning the entire village.

"When the Ute hunting party returned and learned about the prospectors, they became enraged and took out after them. They caught them on a small plateau overlooking Vallecito Creek and killed all the mules and every prospector except one. He managed to escape and tell the story. I think Weasel skin and his friends eventually found the gold at the bottom of the plateau near Upper Vallecito Creek. Rather than own up to the massacre, they invented the story of a mine. The gold's as real as you and Waidner, but the source isn't."

"I don't think I'll go. There are plenty of people in town who can handle this."

"But none have your experience as a tracker. That's why we're here," Hogue quickly responded.

"Who else is in the posse?"

Cole was quick to respond. "In addition to the sheriff, there's Jess Kellum, the livery stable owner, and two cowhands who are good with a gun."

"Do you know anything about the two cow-boys?" Tommy asked.

"I personally interviewed them and they're good boys," Cole responded.

Finally, Tommy agreed and rode into Durango to meet with the sheriff. There were five in the party. Had Tommy known that most of the townspeople had declined to join the posse, he wouldn't have come. Cole and Hogue hadn't divulged that information to him. The posse started out about ten in the morning after the other four were sworn in by the sheriff. Tommy didn't know exactly where the gold cache was, but he could lead the party to the upper Vallecito and back without getting lost.

They were on the trail only a few hours when Tommy could see the makeup of the posse was going to be trouble. He didn't know who recruited the two cowboys, but it was obvious they weren't on the posse to do their civic duty; they had gold on their mind. They made about seven miles the first day, and Tommy suggested to the sheriff that they camp and get a fresh start in the morning. Jess Kellum, the livery stable owner, came to Durango ten years earlier with his wife and two young girls and opened up the business. Tommy asked him why he came on the posse. He said he'd had a poor year and needed the ten dollars a day that Cole promised. The sheriff was a competent individual, though this was his first time leading a posse. Tommy wondered if he'd be able to handle the two cowboys who said their names were Rufus and Jake.

Rufus was about five foot seven and wiry. Jess was the taller of the two, though not by much, but had a habit of not looking you in the eye when talking to you. Each carried six shooters on their right hips.

Tommy found the tracks of the three horse- men and four pack mules about noon the next day and could see they were headed for Upper Vallecito Creek. Everyone in the posse was confident they'd catch up to the three shortly since the four mules carrying the gold was slowing them down. But capturing them would take discipline, and Tommy wasn't sure he could count on the others. He'd been on several raids in his teens. In each case there was discipline, and none of the party was wounded or lost their lives.

The posse followed the tracks of the horsemen all day and camped the second night. It was obvious the three ahead weren't concerned about being followed or else they didn't have the skills to cover their tracks.

Around noon on the third day Tommy, who was in the lead, held up his hand to signal everyone to stop and rode back to the group." I saw three men about three hundred yards ahead with their horses and pack mules. Apparently, they stopped to rest by the creek. I wasn't able to see what was in the pack mules, but it's probably the men we're looking for. How do you want to handle this?" He addressed his question to the sheriff.

The sheriff turned to the other three and asked if anyone had an idea. Rufus and Jake suggested they go in fast and shoot them all. Kellum didn't say anything so the sheriff turned to Tommy. "What do you think?"

"I don't like the idea of going in shooting. Someone in the posse could get hit. Besides, we're not positive they're who we're after. I wouldn't want to kill innocent people. I think Kellum and I can work our way on the other side of them and signal when we're in place. Then the three of you can close in and we'll have them in a trap."

The sheriff said that was a good plan. After Tommy and Kellum circled behind the three and positioned themselves behind a small rise, Tommy gave a sound like an owl to signal they were in place. The sheriff and the two cowboys walked slowly into the clearing with their guns drawn, and the sheriff told the three to raise their hands because they were under arrest. One went for his gun and Tommy shot him in the shoulder. The wounded man dropped his gun and fell on his side, clutching his shoulder. The other two immediately threw down their weapons and surrendered.

The sheriff and Kellum checked the bags on the mules and saw the gold. "These are the men, the sheriff said.

It was too late in the day to start back, so they bandaged the shoulder of the wounded man and secured him and the other two with handcuffs to a tree. Then they made camp. Now the problem was how to get everyone and the gold back to Durango safely.

Tommy asked the sheriff if he could talk to him privately. They walked about twenty paces from the others. "Those two cowboys are a concern to me. It's going to be tough enough to get the three you arrested back with the gold without any other problems. I don't want to keep worrying about Jake and Rufus."

The sheriff was surprised at what Tommy had to say, but had gained respect for his instincts. He'd come up with a workable plan to capture the three and the sheriff was relying on him to get them all back safely. "What do you suggest?"

Tommy responded, "To be on the safe side, I want to split them up. You ride or walk with Rufus and I'll keep Jake in sight at all times. If they have something planned, we'll have a better chance that way. And if I'm wrong, then I can apologize later."

The sheriff heeded his advice, but nothing happened the first day on their ride back. They camped where they'd camped two nights before; it was a good location along the creek. That evening the discussion turned to the gold, what the reward was for capturing the three, and finally who was the rightful owner of the gold. Tommy wasn't the least surprised that Rufus and Jake led the discussion. Their feeling was that the gold belonged to no one, so why not divide it up among the five on the posse. Jake felt his claim was as good as the citizens of Durango.

Tommy didn't participate in the discussion, but Kellum did. "I think Jake and Rufus have a point.

The sheriff didn't agree. "Everyone on this posse took an oath to bring back the three fugitives and the gold. What Jake and Rufus are suggesting is that we kill the three fugitives, and that's not going to happen. I'm going to recommend a good reward for everyone, but the fugitives and the gold are going back. I don't want to hear any more talk about the gold."

Tommy kept an eye on the three fugitives while the discussion was ongoing and saw that each had a grin on his face. Jake and Rufus weren't finished. Tommy could see them talking to Kellum after the meeting. He couldn't hear what they said, but it seemed like a sales pitch to him. Tommy wasn't sure what would happen next, but he was sure the discussion hadn't ended.

The next morning before they broke camp, Rufus and Jake made their move. They walked their horses down to the creek telling Kellum that they were going to fill their canteens. As the other three were lifting the prisoners on to their horses, the sheriff asked Tommy and Kellum where Jake and Rufus where; neither knew. After a quick look down at the creek, it was apparent they were gone. Kellum checked the provisions and found that two days of food were missing.

The sheriff turned to Tommy. "What do you make of this?"

Tommy looked around at the others before he responded. "I think they mean to have the gold and we're in the way. My guess is they 'll try to ambush us. Their best chance for getting away with it is to kill all of us. I don't think they want to share. If we don't show up in Durango, no one's going to be looking for us for at least a week. Even then, they may not send a search party. Look how hard it was to recruit anyone for this posse. Rufus and Jake probably think this is their one chance in life to have something. They don't look like the type of men who're going to make it in this world. I say we have a fight on our hands if we're to stay alive and make it back to Durango."

The sheriff was more and more acquiescing the decision making to Tommy, who was feeling the responsibility shifting from the sheriff to himself. He knew he was their best chance for survival and decided to act. "Sheriff, I suggest that we cuff the prisoners' hands behind their backs. That way they won't have control of their horses if there's trouble ahead. I think you should be in the lead with a mule on either side of you, then Kellum with the two prisoners shielding him. I'll bring up the rear with the wounded prisoner with the other two mules. The trail isn't that wide and we're traveling at a slow pace. This way we can control our group and probably protect ourselves once the shooting starts. Those two boys don't have rifles, only handguns, so they have to get up close. My guess is that they'll be close to the trail when they try to ambush us. They'll try to take us out at first and then dispose of the three prisoners. My guess is they'll make an attempt early today. They won't want to wait until we get closer to Durango."

The sheriff looked at everyone. "You heard the man; let's get moving."

The prisoners were apprehensive. They knew their fate was sealed. If they returned to Durango, a rope was waiting for them. If Rufus and Jake took the gold, they wouldn't leave anyone alive. Tommy was comfortable with the sheriff, but Kellum puzzled him. He was the type who would try to negotiate first and take action only as a last resort. Tommy felt sure he'd fold once the shooting started. Tommy had gotten to know him the last few days. Kellum talked about his business, his wife, and his children. It was obvious he was a loving father and husband, but Tommy could sense despair. He was a nice man in a hostile country; he'd be more suited to the East and would have a hard time coping in the West if he remained.

When they put the three prisoners on their horses and cuffed their hands behind them Kellum objected that they were being mistreated and nearly had the sheriff convinced when Tommy said no. "We're not going to take a chance with the two out there trying to rob and kill us and these three free to break and put us at risk. Their hands are going stay cuffed behind them."

About ten in the morning they stopped for a fifteen-minute break in a clearing along the trail that paralleled Vallecito Creek. They were putting the prisoners back on their horses when shots rang out and the sheriff fell on his side. He had been hit in the shoulder and right leg. Kellum froze and Tommy grabbed him by the collar and slung him to the ground. Under intense fire, Tommy quickly ran to the sheriff and dragged him to safety. Two of the prisoners jumped off their horses and fell to the ground before crawling behind the three lawmen. The wounded fugitive was down between the mules and wasn't moving. There was a pool of blood around his head, and Tommy assumed he was dead. The horses had scattered but the mules stayed where they were.

It appeared that the shooting came from some trees ahead and to the right of the trail. "All we want is the gold. Send one of the prisoners out with the mules and we'll let all of you go." It was Rufus who called out to them.

The sheriff was conscious and Kellum was applying a tourniquet to his leg and checking the wound in his shoulder. "What do you think?" the sheriff asked Tommy.

"It won't make any difference if we give them the gold or hold on to it. They'll killus anyway. They can't afford to leave us alive. They know once we get to Durango we'll telegraph their description to all the towns in the area. The problem is time is on their side; they can wait us out. Our food, water, and extra ammunition are on one of the mules. If we can get to the food and water, we could wait them out, but you need medical attention. I don't want to sit and wait for them to decide about our lives; we have to do something. I'm going to try to circle around them and see if I can surprise them. If I can get out of here, we have a chance and may get them in a crossfire. Can you and Kellum hold on while I make a play?"

"What if you don't come back?" Kellum seemed dazed.

"I'm thinking positive. I hope you do the same." They both nodded.

Kellum turned to the sheriff. "I say we give them what they want and they'll let us go. We don't need the gold. I want to get back to my wife and children and you need help. I'm going to send one of the convicts out with the mules."

Before the sheriff could respond, Tommy said, "No one is going to do any such thing. I'm a little bit more experienced working with the likes of Rufus and Jake. They won't let us live. Do I need to tie you up with the other prisoners or are you going to listen to me?"

Kellum hung his head, and the sheriff said he'd hold onto Kellum. "Take them down, Tommy. We'll be okay. Go!"

Tommy started crawling on his stomach back down the trail. Since they didn't fire at him, he assumed they couldn't see him from their vantage point. About one hundred yards down the trail he moved into the bushes on the left side of the trail. He assumed that they would be protecting their right flank and wouldn't expect anyone to come from the other side of the trail, which was bordered by Vallecito Creek. He wasn't sure if they had stolen the spare ammunition when they split this morning, but Tommy was confident that he had an even chance now that he was away from the others.

He crossed the creek west of the trail and started up the bank on the other side, staying about forty feet from the creek. He couldn't see Kellum or the sheriff, but he sensed he was abreast of them after about thirty minutes of crawling through the bush. He confirmed that when he heard Rufus yell out again with the same offer. He now had a good idea of their location. They were probably overly confident and might not be as alert as they should be.

After he covered another twenty yards, he decided to recross the creek. He slid along his belly and then stopped when he heard Rufus and Jake talking. They were discussing what they'd do with the gold. Apparently San Francisco was in their future, or so they thought. A chill went down Tommy's spine when he heard Jake say that they would kill all of them. They'd come this far; this was their chance at a big stake. They had the advantage, but this was Tommy's arena.

As a boy he'd been taught by his elders how to sneak up on his prey without alerting them to his presence. When he was fifteen he was in a raiding party on an Indian village. He and another young brave got up close to the enemy without them becoming aware of their presence. Then they killed four of the enemy before the village knew they were there.

He was up trail from Rufus and Jake and was able to get within ten feet of them. They were sit- ting down behind a couple of fallen tree trunks and their guns were holstered. He could hear them clearly. One was suggesting that they go in with guns blazing; the other was saying they could just wait, because the lawmen and prisoners couldn't get to their food or water. They were especially aware of Tommy; he made both of them nervous.

Tommy decided to make his move and stood up. "If you boys want to live, don't make a sudden move. I've got the drop on both of you."

Rufus reached for his gun and Tommy shot him between the eyes. Jake raised his hands and Tommy walked up and disarmed him.
"Sheriff, I'm coming out. I have Jake, but Rufus is dead."

Two of the fugitives were alive, Kellum was a distraught and the sheriff had two gunshot wounds and had lost a lot of blood. Now with the addition of another fugitive, Tommy wanted them to move as fast as they could. At least Kellum was able to put Jake and the two fugitives on their horses and cuff their hands behind them. Tommy decided not to waste time burying the two dead men. He had one of the prisoners drag them over to the side of the trail and cover them with brush.

Kellum objected. "These men deserve a Christian burial."

"You can stay and perform the service, but the rest of us are leaving now." Tommy became impatient with him, but Kellum saddled up and joined the others.

Because of the sheriff's wounds, Tommy decided to cover as much ground as they could before nightfall. He wasn't sure they could make the campsite they had used on their first night on the trail, but he was going to try. Kellum seemed to withdraw even more into himself and Tommy was constantly prodding him to help. He'd seen men like Kellum before. They weren't equipped mentally to handle the brutality of the frontier. With the sheriff hurt and another prisoner added, he knew the odds weren't in his favor to get all of them back without another serious incident.

With nightfall slowly approaching, Tommy found a suitable spot to stop for the night. By his calculations, he guessed they were about two miles short of the first night's camp. Rather than unload any equipment and then have to repack in the morning, he broke out enough water and food for a short meal and told everyone to get some rest. He'd stand guard tonight. Jake wanted his handcuffs removed so he could go to the bathroom. Tommy refused. "You'll have to make do, but the cuffs aren't coming off."

The sheriff's condition deteriorated during the night, and the next morning Kellum seemed even more withdrawn than before. It took Tommy another thirty minutes to get everyone saddled up while the best he could do for the sheriff was change his bandages and tie him to his saddle so he wouldn't fall off. He was oblivious to all the threats, the complaining, and the attempts to delay departure. Tommy was in survival mode and wouldn't listen to anything. His focus was to get the sheriff some medical attention and the others to the safety of Durango.

John Cole was alerted that the group was coming into town. He was shocked when he saw how drawn and haggard they were. They virtu- ally smelled. About ten of the town's men headed by Parson Hogue showed up and took charge of the three prisoners. The town doctor had the sheriff brought to his office, and Kellum's wife and children ran up and threw their arms around him and led him away. He was mum- bling incoherently.

Cole took charge of the gold nuggets and said there'd be an accounting and rewards for all who served on the posse. Before he left for the Waidner ranch, Tommy told Cole the entire story and why he left Rufus and the other dead prisoner out on the trail. Cole congratulated him, but Tommy wasn't sure of John Cole at this time. Tommy was still angry at being conned into going on the posse. He wondered if Cole was his friend or just an opportunist.

Cole was ecstatic about the success of the posse but not as much as he was over the number of gold nuggets they recovered. By Sanchez's own words they hadn't checked how much was in the saddlebags, so it was up to Cole to make an accounting. This was the chance he'd been waiting for ever since he was forced to take this job in the middle of nowhere. He sat back in his chair and poured himself an ample glass of sherry and contemplated his future. His was in a position of trust in Durango and decided to use that position to maximize the situation. He made an inventory of the nuggets and decided to put aside twenty percent for himself. Since he was the only one who'd be making the inventory, he decided that thirty percent was workable. By the end of the day, he'd convinced himself that fifty percent was more appropriate.

The question was how to get the nuggets out of the bank without creating any suspicion and without having to explain to his secretary and full-time teller what he was doing. He decided to tell his two employees that he hadn't inventoried the nuggets because of his work load and would get to them over the next two weeks. Since the gold didn't belong to anyone, it wouldn't raise a fuss of any kind. In the interim, he'd store the nuggets in the vault, and since he was the only one with access to the vault, his two employees wouldn't be able to tell what he was up to. Starting tonight, he'd take home a sample in his briefcase.

Over the following two weeks he took half of the nuggets home and inventoried the remain- der and gave a copy to Pastor Hogue and the citizens' committee. One of the committee members raised a concern about the accounting. He was familiar with gold and had seen the load the mules were carrying. He suggested there should have been more. Cole responded that about one- third of the load was nothing but rock and that's why there appeared to be a disparity. The other committee members refused to comment.

CHAPTER FOUR

After a quick meal washed down with hot coffee, Tommy excused himself from the Waidners and went to his room in the barn. He hadn't slept in nearly sixty hours and didn't bother taking off his clothes. He awoke twenty-four hours later, took off his boots and clothes, washed up, and went back to bed.

John Cole showed up about dinnertime two days later, and when Waidner offered him a room for the night, he accepted. The trial for the two surviving murderers of Prouty and LeDroit plus Jake was taking place two days hence. He wanted Tommy back in town to give testimony to their crimes. The citizens' committee planned to hang them the day after that. Tommy refused.

Cole was surprised. "You have a responsibility to see this through. The sheriff is recuperating but isn't able to testify for at least another week, Kellum is a basket case and just sits on his porch crying. His dear wife doesn't know what to do. She's considering selling the livery and moving back east. So you have to come in for the trial. We need you. Besides, this case has statewide attention and there's three reporters in town to cover the trial and hanging. If you don't testify, they may leave. This is good publicity for our town. You have to come in." "John, you helped me when I came here two years ago. You set me on the right course and introduced me to my partner, Frank Waidner. For that I'm grateful. But you ask a lot from a friend- ship. You talked me into joining that posse. In fact, you kind of shamed me into going. The only reason I went is because I was your friend, but you lied to me. That wasn't a good posse you put together. I could tell within a half-day that those two cowboys had their own agenda and that Kellum wasn't suited to be out there. I don't know whether you're on a power trip or not. All I know is that I'm not going into town to give testimony. You'll just have to wait until the sheriff is well enough to testify. He's a good man and deserved better from you. And don't bother sending those reporters out here. I won't talk to them."

Cole was stunned and tried to get Frank Waidner to intercede with Tommy, but Waidner said no and refused to be drawn into the discussion. Tommy left Cole sitting in Waidner's front room and went to bed. When he came up for breakfast early the next morning, Cole had al- ready gone back to Durango.

Tommy had made so many improvements to the ranch buildings that Waidner said he didn't recognize the place. They weren't getting rich, but they were more than breaking even. Mrs. Waidner realized that Tommy had been an answer to their prayers. She didn't think they'd make it through another winter before Tommy arrived. And Tommy could see enough potential that he was looking at a place on the ranch to build his own home.

Waidner was sort of an amateur architect and drew up a set of plans for a two-bedroom home on a small plateau overlooking the creek that meandered through the ranch. Mrs. Waidner was like an expectant mother. She'd already started on curtains for the windows and sheets and pillowcases for the bedroom. Tommy had met Maria Cortez at the church social a couple of years ago and she'd come out to see the location that Tommy had selected. He was planning on marrying her but hadn't asked her yet. The posse was a distant memory. The sheriff had recovered and the two fugitives and Jake were hung, even if the trial took a month more than John Cole wanted. Tommy, Kellum, and the sheriff received a bonus of two hundred dollars each for returning the men and the gold. Jess Kellum had a heart attack and died a year after returning with the posse. The city appropriated the remaining gold for future city developments.

One afternoon, Tommy and Waidner were laying out the rooms on the ground at his planned home site. They were crosschecking with the plans Waidner had drawn up to make sure it was what Tommy wanted before they started cutting timber. Mrs. Waidner had sent a picnic basket with them and they were taking a break eating sandwiches when they saw John Cole approach. Tommy had only seen him a few times over the past two years. Their blossoming friendship had ebbed and neither had gone out of their way to resurrect their past rapport. They exchanged greetings and Waidner offered some of the food and a drink to Cole, who said he wasn't very hungry, but a cold glass of water would wash away the dust from his ride out there.

Cole took out a wanted circular from his pocket and showed it to Tommy and Waidner. Posters during this period of time didn't carry an actual photograph of a fugitive, just a sketch and a reward posted on the bottom with the name of the agency issuing the warrant for arrest. "A Pinkerton detective was riding through and had a bunch of wanted posters with him. He asked the sheriff to look at the posters to see if any of them fit someone he knew. The sheriff took his time and looked at all of them. One of them triggered something, and the sheriff withdrew it and put it in his pocket when the detective wasn't looking. The man in that poster is wanted for murder of a law enforcement officer in Laramie, Wyoming. The circular depicts someone who has long hair, and the sheriff and I think it could be you. I thought I'd ride out to see what you have to say."

"It seems to me that you've already made up your mind if you rode all the way out here. It's hard for me to believe that sketch looks like me, but I'll put your mind to rest. That's me they're looking for. But that was in Wyoming. That poster doesn't have much validity out here un- less someone takes me back there, and that's not going to happen."

Waidner was stunned. He hadn't expected there'd ever be a problem with Tommy. "There must be more to the story other than it's you in the wanted poster."

"I was in Laramie on business and had to wait for my attorney, so I stopped in the Saddle back Saloon. The sheriff was out of town and left a loud-mouth deputy in charge during his absence. He was harassing a couple of Chinese laundrymen and I asked him to stop. He ignored me, so I asked him again, and he pulled a gun on me and said he was going to take me to jail and cut my hair. The sheriff had a reputation of shooting prisoners in the back who were trying to escape. I didn't want to be the next on the list so I shot the deputy. My employer interceded for me and tried to reason with the sheriff, but all he got for his effort was the threat that he'd be arrested too, so I left town."

Waidner turned to Cole. "You know enough about Tommy to know that what he says is true. He's a hero in this town. He's not the kind of man who shoots for no reason. He saved two men on that posse. I believe his explanation, so what are you going to do?" Waidner was calm, but he was looking intently at Cole.

"I don't know what I'm going to do. We're a law-abiding town and it doesn't look good that we have a wanted man in our midst and not do anything about it. It doesn't look good, that's all I'm saying."

Waidner was livid. Tommy's coming to the ranch was the best thing that ever happened to him and his wife. He was looking forward to growing old and turning the ranch over to Tommy, who he loved like a son. "Let me tell you what you're not going to do. You're not going to tell anyone about this conversation, and you and the sheriff are going to destroy that circular and forget it ever existed. Now I'm not threatening you, but I'm telling you if you turn in Tommy, I'll be your enemy for the rest of my life. It looks to me like this is some sort of payback because Tommy wouldn't go into town and testify, when you wanted."

No dialog occurred between Tommy and Cole. In fact, Cole wouldn't look directly at Tommy. He turned around and went back to Durango.

"Frank, I don't want you to get upset, but I'm going to move on. Cole's made up his mind. He has a sense of what's right, and I don't think you can convince him that what he's going to do isn't fair. He hasn't forgiven me for not testifying and thereby showing him up in front of all those reporters."

"Wait a few days and see what happens. That can't hurt. Can it? We need you here."

It looked like Waidner was going to cry, so Tommy put his arm around him and gave the old man a hug. "Cole is full of himself. He sees himself as the ruler of Durango, and he's going to make a decision that I'm not going to like. He won't get his hands dirty; he'll have the sheriff wire the Pinkerton detective, and the next thing you know is someone will come out here for me and that someone is going to be killed because I'm not going to jail for killing that loud mouth. It's best I move on. I'll be out of here at daybreak. I've kept most of my money here at the ranch, but I have a few hundred in Cole's bank, so I'll give you a check for that amount and maybe you can cover it. If not, I'll let you know where to send the balance. My share of the ranch is really yours anyway, so no need to settle on that score."

Tommy could've been a prophet. As soon as John Cole returned to Durango, he met with the sheriff and directed him to contact the Pinkerton detective. From Cole's viewpoint, Tommy admit- ting that he was the one on the wanted poster couldn't be ignored. The sheriff promised he'd send a telegram the next morning. The sheriff did send the telegram but waited a week before he sent it. If Tommy wanted to run, the sheriff wasn't going to get in his way. He had never for- gotten what Tommy had done for him and the others on that posse.

Their last meal together was a sad one. Mrs. Waidner couldn't stop crying and Frank Waidner used every persuasive argument he could to change Tommy's mind. But in the end, he could see Tommy's concern, and he and his wife accepted their fate. The ranch would never be the same, and Waidner and his wife would pass away within the next three years, but not without seeing John Cole brought down. Cole was caught embezzling bank funds and stealing almost half of the gold Tommy and the posse had recovered.

Cole thought he was so clever sneaking out some of the gold each night, but his teller had become suspicious when Cole kept putting off auditing the gold. It wasn't that the teller was such an honest man; he had asked Cole for a raise in salary and Cole had turned him down. So one evening he followed Cole home and looked in a window at the side of the house and that's when he saw Cole taking some nuggets out of his briefcase. So the teller became a responsible citizen and turned Cole in to the citizens' committee. Some of the members of the committee had felt all along that there had been more gold than Cole's audit showed. The sheriff went to Cole's house and confronted him while his deputy sneaked around back and went into Cole's house. He found some of the gold nuggets under Cole's bed. Justice was swift and John Cole was sentenced to eight years in the Colorado penitentiary.

Tommy was sure they wouldn't be able to contact the Pinkerton detective quick enough to have him return to Durango within a week. By that time he would be south along the Santa Fe Trail and would disappear into the great South- west. He'd miss the woman Maria and maybe he'd send for her, but deep down inside he knew that she wasn't the one he wanted to spend the rest of his life with. She was a good person but too convenient.

The year was 1879; it had been three years since Sitting Bull had defeated George Arm- strong Custer at the Battle of Little Big Horn. Tommy had been so busy at the Waidner ranch that he didn't find out about the battle until a year after it happened. He wondered where his father was and how he was coping with life after his great victory.

His mind wandered back to the time he first became aware that Sitting Bull, Tasunka Lyotake, was his father. It was about the same time he became aware that his mother wasn't Indian but white. She was short and thin with fiery red hair and spent a great deal of time alone. He remembered her most for teaching him to read and write in Ute and later in English. He had complained to his father that he wasn't getting enough time to play with his friends. Sitting Bull told him to pay attention to his mother and learn what she was teaching him. The relationship be- tween his mother and Sitting Bull was strained. Even though she was the wife of Sitting Bull, many in the village never let her forget that she was a captive. Sitting Bull could've solved this easily but he didn't. He couldn't bring himself to give her the support and love a woman needed.

However, when the time came when she could have been liberated, she chose to remain in the culture that had captured and imprisoned her.

She didn't want to take the chance in the white world when it was offered; too much stigma was attached to women who were repatriated. Tommy had resented her many times but couldn't help but feel the love she bestowed on him. When he realized how fortunate he was, it was too late; she was dead. He wished that he'd been a better son. He asked Sitting Bull about her many times, but his father was either too busy or unwilling to share any of his feelings for the woman.

His father took his mother for his wife when he was twenty years old and she was seventeen. She'd been captured on one of his tribe's many raids on wagon trains. At the time, Sitting Bull didn't have a wife, and when she was brought into the village, he asked the chief if he could have her. He purchased her from her captor for two fine ponies. When Tommy could speak English fluently, she told him about her early life, her father and mother, and that her name was Elizabeth Kelly. Her family wasn't poor, but feeling their opportunity was greater out west, they joined a wagon train that was attacked in the southern Dakotas. All the adult men and women were killed; only the children and young adults were spared. They were taken to Tommy's village initially, but eventually some were taken to live at other villages while others, unable to cope with the hard and sometimes cruel life, died soon after their capture. She had died when Tommy was thirteen.

Tommy grew up with the young men of his tribe learning how to hunt and fish and eventually was allowed to go on raiding parties. Because of his lineage, the fact that he was halfwhite and half-Sioux was overlooked. His first major action was with a Lakota war party led by Red Cloud that attacked a wagon train bringing supplies to Fort Phil Kearney on the Powder River in Wyoming. The Lakota viewed the presence of the fort, which protected the Bozeman Trail, as a threat to their territory. Soon after the attack, a patrol led by Captain William Fetterman rode out from the fort to drive off the raiding party. Red Cloud's force lured him far from the fort and massacred the soldiers to the last man. Tommy was fifteen and completed his right of passage.

Because he was fluent in English, Tommy accompanied Red Cloud to the signing of the Laramie Treaty with General William Tecumseh Sherman. Red Cloud relied on Tommy to read and then translate the document to him and the other elders. Tommy voiced his concern to Red Cloud that the Indians weren't getting an effective treaty. But the old men were tired of fighting and were grasping at straws with the hope that this treaty would last, so they signed. It brought an end to the war along the Bozeman Trail and granted the Lakota Nations enormous portions of Wyoming, Montana, and the Dakota Territory. But like most treaties with the Indians, the white settlers found ways around the treaties, and again hostility between the two cultures broke out.

The elders utilized Tommy's understanding of the English language and his fair looks to have him act as a liaison with trappers and subsequently act as a guide to wagon trains who wanted to cross the Lakota Territory. The elders had a threefold purpose. They wanted to control access to their territory, they wanted the wagon trains to move expeditiously through their land and not afford the settlers an opportunity to homestead on their land, and they wanted to charge a fee for Tommy's services. The fees collected were essential to buying food and thereby supplement their rations. Soon Tommy was not only talking as a white man but started dressing similarly. The only thing he didn't change was his long hair.

During the next two years Tommy acted as a guide to three wagon trains. On one of these trips he became friendly with an old cowboy named Jess Felton who was quite handy with a six-shooter. He taught Tommy how to shoot and how to draw quickly. Most of all he taught him how to remain calm and take his time before reacting to uncomfortable situations. After a few months of practicing, Tommy became more proficient than his teacher. Training came naturally to him because his life in the Indian village was

regimented and all the young braves were always in training and therefore trying to prove themselves.
Before Tommy left the wagon train,
Felton took him aside. "You have a skill with a weapon beyond what most men have. It's up to you to use it wisely and not just because you can. Do you understand me?" Tommy nodded that he did.

His skill with a handgun would be a benefit to him for the remainder of his life, but another skill he learned would allow him to succeed in the white culture. On a subsequent wagon train he was guiding he learned an art in breaking horses. Wild horses were abundant on the ranges, and the male members of the wagon train frequently captured some of these mustangs and tried to break them. Most were unsuccessful, but on this particular wagon train was a man named Andrew Cork, who was born in Scotland and had a unique way with horses. His method was not the traditional one Tommy had been exposed to but rather a method that was less traumatic for both rider and animal. The principal was simple but difficult to master for someone who didn't have a great deal of patience.

Cork showed Tommy how to gain the horse's respect and especially its trust. Soon Tommy was breaking green horses brought along on the wagon trains or picked up on the grassy prairies. And he was breaking them faster this way. He was able to supplement his fee for guiding the wagon trains by breaking horses after the wagon train stopped for the evening meal. He then sold the animal to members of the train. It was during this wagon train that he found and broke his current horse, Jupiter.

These two years taught him the skills of handling a six-shooter and breaking horses and gave him an insight into the white man. Here was an industrious group who continued to improve their lot in life. It was in direct opposition to the pastoral way of life he had experienced up to now. His observation was that his way of life was going to be continually impacted by the white man. If he wanted to succeed in life, he had to change his perspective and try to make his way in the white man's world. His father and the elders had no choice. They didn't have the skills to compete with the white man; all they could do was wage war to defend their way of life. It was not what they wanted, but what was forced on them by white expansion. Sitting Bull was no fool; he saw the inevitability of the white culture. Yet he had no choice; too many of his people were depending on him to hold out.

The story was different for his son. He understood how the boy was torn between both cultures and he approved of Tommy trying to make it in the white culture. "You can always come back to us and I would welcome you," his father said.

Tommy's skills in breaking horses allowed him to obtain employment. However, at the first two ranches where he worked as a cowhand, he could immediately feel the discrimination that came with being half-white and half-Sioux. It wasn't until he was hired by the Bar 6 and subsequently by Frank Waidner that he realized not all white men were prejudiced and that there was a chance for him to succeed in their world.

He followed the Santa Fe Trail until he reached the outskirts of Santa Fe. He had always wanted to see a large city and decided to stay for a few days and then be on his way again. He had heard about a place called California.

CHAPTER FIVE

Lars and Helga Hansen left Norway for America soon after they were married. They were sponsored by Lars's oldest brother, Frederick, and his wife Ingrid who had a farm that was too large for them to manage by themselves in western Pennsylvania, in a town called Titusville. All three of their children had died soon after birth and the doctor had told Frederick that his wife's health would be in jeopardy if she had any more children. There was a twenty-year differential between the two brothers, and Frederick acted more like Lars's father than his older brother.

Yet the two couples worked well together and shared the same home for seven years until Lars and Helga's first child, Lars Junior, was born. The farm prospered and both brothers shared equally in the proceeds from their labor. When Lars and Helga's second child was born, a little girl whom they named Sarah, the brothers built a second home on the farm, and Lars and Helga with their first two children moved in. Subsequently a third child, whom they named James, was born to Lars and Helga.

The hard work in managing such a large farm before Lars arrived had taken a toll on Frederick and Ingrid. He died in 185 5 and Ingrid two years later. Frederick and Ingrid left everything to Lars and Helga. The farm continued to prosper as did the neighboring area. A major milestone in this country's history and for their little town of Titusville, Pennsylvania, occurred in 1859 when Colonel Drake struck oil in Titusville. A gold rush-type stampede took place, and the peaceful existence they all enjoyed vanished with the wind. The problem was that there wasn't any planning to this oil boom. Wells were dug too close to others in an attempt to retrieve as much oil in as short a time as possible. The geological formations had not been analyzed properly, and soon the flow of oil along the ground turned the area into a mud flat. Derricks were erected and produced for a short time, then burned down and a new derrick would be built. The debris littered the countryside. Land speculation fever took over and farms proximate to the initial oil finds near the Hansens' farm were leased at enormous annual rents.

It was about this time that their oldest son, Lars, drowned in a lake on their property. Initially it was thought that he suffered a cramp. It was only later that the family realized the ex- tent of his malady. Lars was a handsome young man with blond hair and the most imposing eyes ever seen on an individual. He excelled in school and was always the leader in sports. On the surface, Lars appeared to be a rugged young man with a great deal of energy, whether it was at work on the farm or at play with his friends. But unknown to him and his family was that he suffered from a form of epilepsy. The seizures weren't evident other than that he appeared tired at times. He rationalized that the fatigue came from working too hard or playing sports.

When he was exhausted, he'd rest for a few minutes or lay down, and when he rose, he was as energetic as before. Probably his parents over- looked the signs because he'd become his father's right hand and they were counting the days when they could turn management of the farm over to him.

Wildcatters were in such a rush to find oil that they'd promise anything to secure the rights to land. Soon many of the leases were in default and the land in dire straits. Oil mixed with the soil turned into mud. Lars and Helga held off for as long as they could, but the offers were so good that they finally relented and sold the land in 1864. The loss of their eldest son may have given added impetus for the sale. Everyone in the family was distraught and was looking for a change of scenery.

The government was advertising almost free land in Oregon. Both America and the British had laid claim to Oregon and planned to settle the dispute by counting the number of American settlers versus British settlers by 1880. Whichever country had the most settlers by that date could claim the territory. It seemed like an opportunity and at the same time some sort of salvation for the Hansens. The oil rush was destroying the area surrounding their home, their oldest son had died on the river adjoining their property, and they felt the offers were too good to turn down. So they sold their farm.

The contract for sale called for a large down payment with annual payments tied to the amount of oil produced from the wells on their land. They placed most of their money in the First Union Bank of Harrisburg. Half of the proceeds were divided equally into separate trusts for Sarah and James to be dispersed to them when they reached the age of twenty-one. In the event one of them died before reaching their twenty-first birthday, the trust would then go to the surviving sibling. The other half of their funds was placed in a trust for Lars and Helga with Sarah and James as beneficiaries.

The Hansens switched trains in Chicago and continued to Independence, Missouri, which was the jumping off point for wagon trains heading to the Oregon Territory. It was an ideal location. Participants could arrive by steamboat, cargo ship, or covered wagon, be outfitted for the journey, and then join a wagon train. There were twenty families that signed up for this particular trip leaving April 3, 1864; fifteen would make the trip. Sarah was fourteen at the time and James was twelve.

The journey to Oregon by wagon train would take six months, mainly due to the use of the slower-moving oxen in lieu of horses to pull the covered wagons. Initially wagon trains used horses, but horses couldn't feed off the prairie as oxen or mules and were quickly replaced. It was also a safety feature since hostiles didn't normally attack wagon trains drawn by oxen because they didn't want to be laden with the slow-moving animals. Life on a wagon train was fairly mundane. The men on the train, under the guidance of the wagon master or captain, tended the livestock brought along for food and milk, and maintained the wagons, which had a habit of breaking down on a continuous basis.

Originally the Conestoga wagon was used, but it was too large and cumbersome for the journey and was continually getting stuck in the mud. They were quickly replaced by the prairie schooner, a wagon about four feet wide and ten to twelve feet in length. When the Hansens saw the prairie schooner, they nearly backed out even if it meant the loss of their deposit, but Sarah and James pleaded to continue and the parents relented. The wagon would be their home for the next six months, but they wouldn't live in- side the wagon.

That was reserved for the food they were required to bring plus any clothes or personal items they needed. Each person was required to have at least five hundred pounds of food for the six-month journey. For the Hansens, that meant two thousand pounds. Staples such as flour, beans, coffee, and bacon, however, were stored in barrels strapped to the side of the wagon.

Women cooked and tended the children who were prone to cause mischief. In some cases wagon masters had to halt the train so that some nervous parent could look for a child who had strayed too far away. Members of the wagon trains rose early, left by seven, stopped for lunch at midday and made camp around five or six in the evening. Since the wagons were loaded with food and clothing, all the wagon train members walked alongside their wagons during the trek. Even during inclement weather, they walked alongside their wagons.

It was a communal group when it came to work and cooking; all chores were shared. Sarah cooked alongside her mother while James helped with the livestock. The problem was finding enough wood for the fire. In many cases wood along the trail was sparse due to the number of wagon trains that had the same agenda. In which case, buffalo chips were used in lieu of wood. Evenings were the best time for members of a wagon train. After dinner they sat around the fire and talked of their pasts and their desires for the future. Occasionally communal singing and dancing kept their spirits up during the long daily treks. Everyone slept on the ground, mostly under their prairie schooner and generally were asleep by nine. They'd awake at five the next morning and the cycle would start again.

The company that sold space on the wagon trains was apprehensive about sending less than twenty families on the trip, but the fifteen that made up this trek voted unanimously to make the journey. They were introduced to the wagon master, Charley Crisp, who briefed them on his responsibility, his authority, and their responsibilities. Next the local army garrison commander advised them that there wouldn't be a military escort during their trek. He explained that the troops in his area were spread too thin due to the demands of the ongoing civil war. Throughout their route, forts were spaced approximately forty miles apart on most of the Oregon Trail and manned with about thirty men each. But these men were constantly being harassed by the tribes in the area and spent their time chasing after them or running them off. He further stated that wagon trains were a prime target of marauding Indians along the Oregon Trail because the Indians saw this influx of settlers as having a direct bearing on the loss of buffalo, thereby creating a shortage of food.

In spite of his warnings the members of this particular train felt the risk was worth it and they voted to go on. But Sarah was concerned. "Do you think we should turn back?" she asked her father.

Her father asked Charley Crisp who said he was concerned but felt there were enough able- bodied men on the train to prevent an attack.

Her father then told Sarah, "I think we'll be okay."

Young James Hansen was the image of his father, built square and sturdy, but Sarah, with long blond hair and deep blue eyes, was a head turner. At fourteen, she had blossomed into a sensual young woman. At least one of the young single men on the train asked Lars for her hand; two others just wanted to court her. The rite of passage had come quickly for her and she didn't know what to make of all the attention she received from the males on the train. In addition to the two who wanted to court her, there were two others that doted on her every word, helped with her chores, and sat with her at dinner. Sarah was becoming frustrated. "They're around me every minute and I don't have time to myself," she confided to her mother.

Sarah's mother just smiled and told her to enjoy the attention; soon she'd be able to have first pick from among the eligible young men. Schooling for Sarah had come easy because she'd been a vociferous reader since she was five. Lars and Helga had a minimal education and were proud of Sarah's ability to read and write, so she was given the prestige of keeping their accounts and reading and explaining their contract with the wagon train company.

The Oregon Trail went from Independence, Missouri, through Nebraska, southern Wyoming, and the southern part of the Dakotas before reaching northwest Oregon. The train made steady progress traveling at a rate of eleven miles a day, and after one month they were near the western edge of Nebraska. When they reached the upper Platte River, there was an increase in the number of Indian sightings. None of the sightings were provocative, but the wagon master increased his sentries at night and the number of outriders in the daytime. The women called a meeting and voiced their concern about the number of Indian sightings. Since each wagon had one vote, it was necessary for husbands and wives to agree. Lars and Helga asked Sarah and James for their opinion. They wanted the adventure and urged their parents to continue, if they thought it was safe. The vote by the members of the train was unanimous to continue.

The next afternoon, one of the outriders came back into camp at a gallop and reported to the wagon master that there were about fifteen Indians who appeared to be armed about a mile ahead. It was nearly three o'clock, so the wagon master decided to play it safe. He stopped the wagon train and, as on other nights, had the wagons form a circle and stationed four men spaced equally apart around the interior of the circle. All the men in the wagon train would rotate with the four on a four-hour basis throughout the night. Weapons were checked and rechecked and their defense plans reviewed again to be sure all knew what to do in the event of an attack. There was no singing and dancing that night.

The evening passed without incident. The next morning they assembled and set the course for the next day, ate breakfast, and hitched up their wagons. Everything seemed normal when they broke camp and formed the wagons into a single file. Early in the morning they saw Indians riding parallel to them about a mile to the north.

The number of Indians had increased from fifteen to seventeen.

That night they followed the same ritual as the night before. Their nerves were beginning to fray, and several of the women demanded that they return to Independence. It was the first time Sarah suggested to her parents that perhaps they should turn around. The Hansens voted to turn back but were outvoted nine to six. The next day the number of Indians had increased to twenty and made everyone on the wagon train apprehensive. Nobody slept that night. The wagon master doubled the guards on the interior with shift changes every two hours. They had reached the point of no return.

The next morning, they'd driven only a half-mile when they were attacked by twenty Indians approaching from the north at 90 degrees to the line of wagons. The wagon master immediately ordered the wagons into a circle and to break out their weapons. On their first pass the hostiles killed the wagon master and two of the other men. This put the members of the wagon train in disarray for a short time until Lars Hansen took charge and directed their defenses. He set up barricades throughout the circle of wagons and had the women and older children reload rifles for their male family members. The smaller children hid under their parents' wagons.

This seemed to stabilize their defenses for a few hours as the Indians continued to circle while firing on the wagons. The hostiles rode by on the sides of their horses with one leg visible while firing over the horse's neck. Next the Indians fired flaming arrows into the circle of wagons and soon the canvas on two of the covered wagons ignited, and Lars had to dispatch some of the men to put out the fire, which made the defenses shorthanded.

Lars and the rest of the men were holding their own. They hadn't lost any more men while the Indians lost three of theirs, but the odds favored the hostiles. Time was on their side, and by afternoon, half of the men in the wagon train had been killed or severely wounded. It was then that four Indians broke through their defenses and killed one man and wounded another and forced the defenders to fall back under their wagons with the women and children. Soon all the Indians had penetrated the circle of wagons and hand-to-hand combat ensued. Although the men and women fought bravely, they eventually were overwhelmed.

They couldn't defend against the Indians and fight the fires at the same time. The survivors, both men and women, were systematically slaughtered; only the children were spared. The Indians looted the wagons, and when they were finished, they set everything on fire and killed all the oxen. The children were rounded up; those that couldn't walk were killed. Sarah and James Hansen and two other males about fourteen years of age were the only ones spared. Five of the Indians had been killed in the raid, and the Indians spent time lamenting over them before carrying the children off to their village.

James was crying continuously and Sarah tried to console her brother and make him understand that his survival was the most important thing for him at this time. That seemed to have some effect on him and he calmed down. To keep her mind off their predicament, Sarah thought back to her early life, her mother, her father, and the brother that had died. To see her mother and father slaughtered was a very traumatic experience, and that sight would be with her forever. Her religious training and faith helped her get through the day.

The four captive children were tied around the waist and in turn tied to each other and then by a long rope to one of the Indians' ponies. None of Indians spoke English, but the message was clear: keep up or be killed. They reached an Indian village late at night. None of the four captives had had food or water since morning. When they reached the village, the four captives were tied to wooden stakes and left there until morning. The next morning their captors re- leased them long enough to relieve themselves and then gave them some water and ground meal.

During the first week, they were worked under the direction of the women of the tribe who continually beat them if they didn't complete their chores or were slow to respond. They were fed in the morning with some sort of corn mash and in the evening were given food discarded by the adult Indians. The four captives became scavengers and fought each other for any scrap of food they could find. The other two male captives were bigger than James, but they were no match for James and Sarah working together. She was his big sister and wouldn't be denied her and James's share. None of the captives were aware that the Indians had let it be known that they were available for a ransom. But since their immediate relatives had been killed and any other living relative was back east and unaware of their predicament, the window of opportunity for them to be rescued was slowly closing.

Sarah's first two years as a captive were ones of survival for her and James. Their hours were long and the beatings by the women were common even though she and James made every effort to please their captors. Their task was to skin buffalo and chew the skin to make it tender for the men of the family they belonged to. In addition, she had to supply kindling for the fire used to cook the evening meal for the village. During the first winter, she nearly froze. Her clothes were discarded rags and she slept in an unheated tent with James and the other captives.

Sarah was an intelligent young woman and had an affinity for languages and quickly gained an understanding of her captives' language. Soon she was able to tell if they were talking about her and the other captives. She tried to teach James their language, but either he didn't want to or couldn't comprehend, so Sarah would translate for him. The malnutrition and rags she was forced to wear didn't diminish her beauty. Soon the young braves were spending time around Sarah, which made her more unpopular with the single women of the tribe.

One day, a Sioux hunting party arrived at the village and was treated as family by the Lakota Indians of the village. Sarah was separated from the other three captives and traded to the Oglala Sioux. She tried to say good-bye to her brother, but she was forced onto a pony and quickly whisked away. Her last memory of him was him standing and crying out to her. It nearly broke her heart.

Her new Sioux captors moved continuously around Wyoming and northern Nebraska and came into contact with many whites. In all cases, Sarah was either hidden or restricted to an area where she couldn't be seen. Although she was given work and expected to do her share, the beatings ceased and she was adopted by an older couple and allowed to live with them; she was considered their daughter. She was given freedom within the camp and better clothes to wear and enough food to eat.

One day she observed a white man presumably trading with the chief of the village. She found a clean piece of bark and with a partly burned stick she fashioned a note that gave her name and the word "help" scratched on the bark. When the message was finished, she went about her work furnishing kindling for the evening meal while gradually getting closer to the white man's horse. She knew she couldn't approach him directly, so she planned to put the bark in his saddlebag. When she thought she wasn't being observed, she made her way closer to his horse, but there were no saddlebags, so she stuck the bark under the horse's blanket. It was partially sticking out, but she had to take a chance.

She learned the white man was a French trader who had taken a Sioux woman as his wife and was considered a member of the tribe. Soon after the Frenchman left, she was summoned to the tent of Spotted Tail, the chief of the village, and shown her message. He asked her what the writing meant. She knew it was useless to lie so she told him the truth and was given to the women for discipline. She was beaten by the women, but not severely enough that she couldn't do her work. From that time forward she was under continuous surveillance.

Sarah was beginning to think it was hopeless and only death would free her, but she was seventeen and becoming a mature woman. The elders of the village must have noticed because they told her she was going to marry one of the young braves of the village. She protested to no avail and went through extensive training by her adopted parents in the ritual of courting. Initially three young men started the courtship. They'd bring presents to her new parents and would play a flute outside her teepee. She thought it was amusing but still wouldn't con- sider becoming active in the ritual. The elders weren't impressed with her delaying tactics and decided she was to pick one of the three suitors or the elders would select her new mate. After two weeks, there was an addition to the number of suitors and she was told she was to become his wife. He was a very important chief. His Cheyenne wife had died last year and his child needed a mother.

Like the others, her prospective groom would bring presents and walk by while playing a flute. Sarah declined to go outside to give him any indication she was interested until her Indian parents forced her outside their teepee one night while he was playing the flute. He smiled at her appearance and considered that as a yes.

"I'm not going to marry you." He obviously didn't understand her because he smiled back at her.

One week later she became the bride of Tashunka Wilco, better know as Crazy Horse, nephew of Spotted Tail, the chief of the village. During her first two years in captivity she'd been treated slightly better than the dogs and many times had to fight them for scraps of food to stay alive. But at the same time, she hadn't been sexually molested; she was a virgin. Now her status had changed. Crazy Horse was the war chief of the Sioux and was considered a great warrior. Everyone knew of Crazy Horse and his exploits. The children sang his praises and the women told her about his conquests. She learned about the war for the Bozeman Trail, where he was victorious, as well as the Fetterman Fight and the Wagon Box Fight he won. Sarah was to become an Indian princess. She decided to accept her fate and see what the future would bring.

The wedding ceremony started in the morning with dancing accompanied by four or five drummers and a couple of flute players and lasted until late afternoon. Sarah, along with her adopted Indian parents and Crazy Horse and his friends, separately inspected their new home. Then the two groups joined together and the newly married couple walked through the village to the site of the dancing, sheltered by a blanket held over their heads by four warriors.

When Sarah first saw Crazy Horse, she was frightened of him and at the same time in awe. At the ceremony, he wore his hair long and free with a headdress that had a red hawk feather in it. She'd been bathed by the women of the tribe and given a white beaded dress to wear. Her blond hair was long and free-flowing, similar to Crazy Horse's. Even the women who had beaten her when she tried to communicate with the Frenchman were taken with her beauty. Her intended spoke very little English. She, however, had mastered the Oglala Sioux dialect and was able to converse in his language.

The ceremony was concluded by the medicine man when the new couple returned to their new home. At this point the couple separated and Crazy Horse entered their new home and let the entrance flap remain in the open position, signifying that he would accept his new bride. Sarah was taken by some of the women of the tribe for a final ritual and instructions for her wedding night and then carried in a blanket by six of the women to her new home. Seeing the flap open, the six women carrying Sarah walked in and deposited her at the feet of her husband who then tapped her with his rifle and declared, "You are mine."

Sarah had been given instructions by her new parents on the various wedding rituals. That evening she was to cook a meal for Spotted Tail, her adopted parents, and the close friends of Crazy Horse. Many of the women of the village assisted her by starting a fire and providing food for the entire wedding party.

After the meal the wedding party departed. She didn't know what to do, so she stood there waiting for him to tell her what to do. Her dress was held together in the back by leather cord. He walked toward her, reached behind her, and undid the fasteners. The dress dropped to the ground. He ran his hands over her body and she shivered with anticipation. He took her hand

and led her over to a bed near the fire. He pointed to the bed and she crawled under the main blanket. He lay down beside her and pulled her on top of him and started to explore her body. She'd been instructed by the Indian women on what would happen, but until she experienced it her- self, it didn't mean anything. He started kissing her mouth and cheeks and then her throat while fondling her breasts. She stiffened when his hand reached between her legs and forced them apart. She was expecting him to penetrate her, but his fingers massaged her sweet spot and she experienced her first orgasm.

It seemed like an eternity before he penetrated her. The anticipation was overwhelming but the pain intense at first and then she got lost in desire and felt her body leave and then return with a climax. She lay in his arms for a while and then he started the procedure over again and entered her for the second time. She lay there in ecstasy and screamed her pleasure. For two years she had been made to feel like an outcast; for another two years she had had no one. Now she was the wife of the war chief who didn't beat her but treated her with loving care. She didn't know what tomorrow would bring, but tonight was the most exciting night of her life.

She asked if she pleased him. He smiled and replied in his native tongue, "Very much."

CHAPTER SIX

The treaty of Fort Laramie seemed to bring stability to the entire area. The Indians were promised most of Wyoming, Montana, and Nebraska, and Crazy Horse and his band along with their wives and children moved to northern Wyoming. Sarah gave birth to a boy in 1869 and a second son in 1870. The communal life in their village was peaceful; Crazy Horse spent time hunting and fishing; she spent most of her time with her two babies and his young daughter Naiwa. Then gold was found in the Black Hills of the Dakotas and their peaceful existence was replaced with apprehension. Crazy Horse was angry at the number of settlers being allowed onto the land given to them through the treaty.

Though Sarah wasn't completely in his confidence, their relationship had gone far be- yond captive and master. She was treated with respect, and her position was that of spouse to the war chief. At night he would share his frustration with her. She would listen and occasionally interject her opinion. At first, he was unapproachable, but after a few years and with her loyalty confirmed, he would share some of his plans; she was his sounding board.

Though she wasn't invited to a meeting in late 1870 between Crazy Horse and Sitting Bull, he told her about their plans that evening. He was going to lead a raid on the surveyors of the Northern Pacific Railroad. The raid would be more of a nuisance to the railroad, but to Crazy Horse and Sitting Bull, it would give the U.S. government a message that the Indian nations wouldn't be satisfied until the migration to the Dakotas ceased. Sarah was concerned that what he and Sitting Bull were planning was foolish and she voiced her concerns.

"Why risk losing more braves over some- thing as trivial as the surveyors? These small battles are nothing but nuisances to the whites, but it's something they can rally around. Why give them this ammunition?" Crazy Horse didn't respond.

The nomadic lifestyle of the Indians was one of the most difficult adjustments for Sarah. The constant uprooting of the entire village and moving it to a new area, sometimes over a hundred miles away, was necessary to this lifestyle. Sarah always planted a garden and was unhappy when she had to move before the plants grew and produced anything. She was concerned that their entire existence was dependent on the migration of the buffalo, so she shared her concern with Crazy Horse. "We have so much land, why not put down roots, grow things, and establish something we can count on? I was raised on a farm. I know how to grow things to eat." He was unable or unwilling to give her an answer.

Yet Sarah was amazed at how mobile they were. It took less than three hours to disassemble the teepees, gather up their belongings, and move toward the next site. As soon as the next site was selected, all would work in unison to establish a village similar to the one at their last location. Soon she was as proficient dissembling and reassembling as anyone in the village. No wonder the U.S. soldiers had difficulty in tracking them.

Her two sons and her adopted daughter, Naiwa, made a game of these movements. Naiwa was five years old when Sarah married Crazy Horse, and although the transition for her was strange, she soon became a devoted daughter and was a willing member of the family. Sarah spent time teaching her to read and write.

Most of the Montana Territory was still primitive with very few white settlers. Crazy Horse spent most of the next few years hunting, fishing, and caring for his young family. Sarah had now become fluent in his dialect of Oglala Sioux and was an important member of the tribe.

Crazy Horse could communicate in English, but she was able to make him more confident when he spoke the language after she taught him to read and write. It was a difficult adjustment for him at first, but as the trust developed, he was able to become her pupil. She didn't embarrass him. No one knew of their arrangement, and for that he was grateful. Soon the elders were using her as their interpreter with white traders and new settlers and allowed her freedom to travel to other villages and white settlements to buy supplies.

It was during these leisure years that Sarah found she had a talent for drawing and sketching. Art supplies were non-existent in the village and there was no money to pay for such frivolous things. She learned to sketch on smooth fabric made by the women of the tribe. When her capability reached a point where she was able to sketch a human subject, she found ways to develop colors from adobe, flowers, and bark and then embellish the sketch in colors. Most of her subjects were the women of the tribe who were flattered that she was able to capture their likeness for all to see, but she soon progressed to Indian village scenes in bright colors. She openly wondered if there was any value in the sketches.

In the spring, accompanied by a few braves, she went to a settlement across the border in Colorado to purchase salt and other items that were in short supply in her village. Since they had few dollars and little gold coin, she bartered for staples they needed. Several of the women of the tribe were proficient in making colorful blankets, which were in demand in the white communities. She had made several trading trips in the past and had a good idea what the white settlements wanted.

The proprietor of the local general store bought two of her blankets, which were more than enough to offset the cost of the supplies she needed. Before going, she asked if he'd be interested in some of the sketches she brought along. He looked at the three she showed him and liked them all but wasn't sure they 'd sell, although he did offer to trade for them. She asked if he had any art supplies. He smiled and led her over to the comer of the store and showed her pencils, crayons, brushes, and some canvases. She asked him to trade the value he placed on her sketches in art supplies.

Since it was her first visit to this town, she caused quite a stir. The local minister asked if she needed assistance to escape from her Indian captors. She proudly responded, "I'm the wife of Crazy Horse, chief of the Oglala Sioux, and his emissary."

Her desire to leave had long since been forgotten; she was now a committed member of the tribe. But believing that she was a captive of her Indian escorts, the minister called upon the local sheriff to rescue her. The Indian escorts were told to leave while Sarah was detained. Sarah was in tears as she was escorted to the minister's home where she was greeted by his wife. "I know you must be relieved to be with your own people. You can stay as long as it takes for you to become acclimated. My husband and I will help you in every way we can to put this terrible ordeal behind you." The minister's wife embraced Sarah as she spoke.

"Why can't you believe me? I'm not a captive; I'm the wife of Crazy Horse. I shudder to think what he'll do when my two escorts return and tell him you've detained me. Did you ever think about my children? You've deprived them of their mother."

"We're only doing this because we love you. We have experience in these matters. We've been successful in repatriating two other women who found themselves in a situation such as yours. It's really for your own good," the minister's wife responded. She was shown to a room she'd be using. Sarah sat down on the bed and tried to see how she could persuade these people to let her go home before a war began.

The two escorts returned to their village the next day and reported what happened to Crazy Horse and Spotted Tail, who counseled restraint. The council was called to discuss the situation and a plan of action was formulated.

Sarah spent the first night at the minister's home, but she didn't sleep. She thought about her plight and what she could do to prevent the confrontation she knew would come. Crazy Horse was not one to give up any of his possessions without a fight. Though she never saw him in battle, she knew from the few confrontations she had witnessed that he would think clearly and then would be relentless in his attack.

The minister and his wife were eating breakfast as she came down the stairs. They offered her breakfast, but they really wanted to convince her that she was better off with her own people.

"My husband is not one to be disrespected. By taking me, you have shown disrespect and he will retaliate, and very soon, I imagine. I believe he loves me very much, but besides that he has to save face in order to remain the leader of his tribe. I don't think either of you understand the peril you've placed this town in."

"Sarah, we've talked to the commandant at the fort and alerted him to the possibility that Crazy Horse might attempt to take you back by force. He has a detachment of thirty men and is prepared to defend us if need be." The minister seemed very sincere to Sarah, if not a little naive.

"Sir, my husband can call upon eight hundred warriors at a moment's notice. None of you, including the soldiers at the fort, would survive. You must let me return to my husband and family."

The word spread quickly that there was a beautiful blond woman who'd been rescued from Indians by the minister. It didn't take long for the commandant of the fort and several of his young officers to drop by the minister's home and offer their help to Sarah. "Sir, I'm not a captive of the Sioux, but the wife of Crazy Horse and a valuable member of the tribe."

The two young officers stayed for tea while the commandant met with the sheriff to plan their response in the event of an attack by Crazy Horse. Sarah was flattered by the attention of the two young officers, but made sure they knew that she was a married woman and that it would be inappropriate for her to attend a dance with them at the fort tonight, even if chaperoned by the minister's wife.

Two days went by and still no sign of Crazy Horse. She was surprised he hadn't come by now. Finally, three days after she was detained, Crazy Horse and two companions made their way to the town where Sarah was being held. The first to see him coming was the sheriff, who sounded the alarm, and twenty of the townsmen responded in the street with weapons. Two others were sent to the fort to alert the commandant. Much to their surprise, only three Indians came into town, one of which they assumed was Crazy Horse. None of the Indians was armed.

Sarah saw the activity in the street but wasn't sure what caused the commotion until the minister came home and told his wife and Sarah that Crazy Horse and two other Indians had arrived. "Sarah, you're to stay here until the sheriff determines what his intentions are." The minister seemed very agitated and kept looking out the window.

The Indians dismounted, and Crazy Horse, who could carry on a conversation in English with a degree of confidence, asked the sheriff if he could see his wife. By this time the commandant had arrived, and the sheriff asked him what should be done. The commandant said that it seemed natural to him that Crazy Horse should see his wife provided that she wasn't alone with him. One of his officers would accompany Crazy Horse to the minister's home and would remain until Crazy Horse left. The other two Indians would remain with the sheriff.

Crazy Horse and a young officer walked to the minister's house and were greeted by the minister's wife and Sarah. They sat down together and had tea. Crazy Horse's English wasn't perfect, but under Sarah's tutelage, he was able to converse well enough to be understood, though he greeted her in his native tongue. "I've come to take you home if you want," he said.

Here was a man she'd been intimate with for the past few years, and only once had he told her he loved her, yet he seemed sincere, and she wrapped her arms around his waist and told him that she was ready. The young officer who'd accompanied Crazy Horse to the minister's house blocked the door, but Sarah gently pushed him aside. "This is my husband, and I'm going home with him. I understand your concern, but this is my life and this is the man I wish to share it with. Now please let us leave." The young officer moved aside.

They walked down the main street with an entourage of the minister, his wife, the young officer, and many of the townspeople behind them. When they reached their horses, the commandant asked Sarah if she was going of her own free will. "Sir, I appreciate your concern, but this is my husband and I'm returning to my village and my people."

The minister wasn't convinced. "She's a white woman who was captured years ago.
Surely you can see that she's intimidated by him. We need to intercede on her behalf, even if she's unwilling. It should be done in God's name."

The commandant was looking at the big picture. He didn't want an Indian uprising. He knew of Crazy Horse's reputation and was impressed that he had come without weapons and a war party to get his wife back. "She's an adult, and her desire is to return with him. I'm not going to interfere."

All four mounted their horses. "I want to thank all of you for your hospitality, but this is my life and my husband. Please visit us at our village. We are quite like you in many ways, so come see for yourself." Sarah turned her mount and led her companions out of the town.

Crazy Horse couldn't help but smile at the stunned expressions on the faces of the towns people. When they reached their own village, the elders met them and told Sarah how happy they were that she had returned and how much they had missed her. Even the women who'd been so cruel to her when she first arrived wept for joy upon her return, and at last Sarah felt loved by her husband and her people.

She experienced a tragedy the next year with the loss of her first son. He contacted tuberculosis and died at the age of four and they buried him in an unmarked grave along the Powder River. She remained in mourning for nearly three months. During that period she reflected on her life and the fact that her parents were dead and her brother perhaps still a captive. She had been accepted by the Sioux, but it wasn't the same as having one's blood relatives at hand during periods such as this. When she emerged from her period of mourning, she asked Crazy Horse to find her brother. He said he'd send someone to the Lakota village where he was last seen by Sarah and make inquiries, but he counseled Sarah not to have hope.

Crazy Horse was unsuccessful. There was no record of James, and those who were contacted didn't even remember the boy. Sarah was sad but didn't give up hope.

Her peaceful life came apart in 1876 when General Crook ordered the Indians in her village to report to the reservation. Crazy Horse and the other bands ignored his request, and Crook sent troops to arrest them. Sarah begged the elders to let her go and talk to General Crook. "What do we have to lose by my talking to him and sparing us the upheaval and perhaps something greater?" she asked.

As much as they trusted her due to all the effort, she had made to protect their interests when dealing with white settlers and the fact that she had returned of her own free will when the inhabitants of a small town sought to restrain her, Crazy Horse and the elders resisted her entreaty. She and the rest of the village retreated to the surrounding hills just minutes be- fore Crook's troops arrived, forcing them to leave all their possessions behind, including Sarah's art supplies. Since no Indians were found, Crook ordered the village burned and the capture of any horses left behind.

She and Crazy Horse watched in shock as their village was burned to the ground. During a snow storm that night, Crazy Horse regrouped his band, recaptured their horses, and retreated farther north. Their food supply was low, but they traveled as quickly as they could in the snow and reassembled in southern Montana. They were given food on the way by other tribes who heard of their plight. Sarah felt empowered by now and shared her concerns with Crazy Horse. "This can't go on any longer. You've got to make peace. They outnumber us and eventually we'll be arrested, killed, or placed on a reservation. What about our son and daughter? Are they going to be at war all their lives? We owe them a life."

Crazy Horse listened but disagreed. "Every time we agree to a treaty, they use it to force us into a smaller territory and then force us to defend the land they forced us onto. I may be the war chief, but that doesn't mean I enjoy being at war all the time. They are going to give us no peace until we're all dead. They want our land and they mean to take it. I could give in now and sue for peace, but that would make no difference.

They'd find some reason to move us from one area to another until there is no other area."

She knew he was correct, but she had to do something. "Then negotiate something we can live with, not something that we can't hope to obtain." She at least had his attention.

Later the same year, General Crook made another initiative to force the Indians onto the reservation. He sent a detachment from Fort Laramie under Colonel Reynolds to locate the Indian camp along the Powder River in Montana. Reynolds was supported by the Crows and Shoshone Indians while Crazy Horse was supported by the Cheyenne. Initially Reynolds's troops pushed the Indians back, but Crazy Horse rallied his band and forced Reynolds to retreat and regroup a great distance away in a place outside Sheridan, Wyoming. This unforeseen retreat had a subsequent impact on Lt. Colonel George Armstrong Custer. Reynolds's mission was twofold. The first was to force Crazy Horse and his band onto the reservation and the second was to back up Custer as he rode against the Sioux in southern Montana.

Again, Sarah pleaded with Crazy Horse to make peace. "The time when you have the greatest negotiating power is after a victory. General Crook will be shorthanded and will welcome peace."

Flushed with victory over Reynolds, Crazy Horse and his Cheyenne friends, numbering about one thousand, made their way to the Little Big Horn where they joined up with Sitting Bull. Sarah and her son and daughter traveled with the other members of the tribe about a day later. The night before the battle, Crazy

Horse was agitated. He told Sarah that their time had come and they would be victorious tomorrow.

She counseled patience. "Winning could really be a defeat, especially if it incenses the nation and they send more and more troops to capture us."

"They have their own problems. Their civil war has drained them and they can't sustain an active campaign," he countered.

"Once that's over, they'll come looking for us. We'll be at the top of their list. Do you want that to happen to us? Our two children will always be on the run." He walked away without answering.

She along with the other women and children were positioned behind one of the small hills about a mile from the main Indian force. Sitting Bull, with an assist from Crazy Horse, ambushed Custer and killed the entire Seventh Cavalry. It really wasn't much of an ambush because Custer seemed to walk right into the middle of the large Indian contingent with his eyes wide open and his arrogance flowing over. Sitting Bull had seen the victory in a dream the night before.

Sarah could hear the battle, but she didn't witness the slaughter. The other women of the tribe told Sarah about the heroic exploits of Crazy Horse, who seemed to be everywhere during the battle. At one point he rode back and forth within range of Custer's troops, who fired at will but without any result other than to inflame Sitting Bull's forces.

Sarah did not share in the thrill of victory; she sensed how this would be viewed back east and counseled for negotiation with General Crook. She knew their days were numbered and that the U.S. government would spare no expense to either arrest all of them or force them onto the reservation or maybe even kill them all. This defeat was a stab in the heart of the nation. The eastern media would declare the massacre of Custer and his men as shocking and unprovoked and would demand that Sitting Bull and Crazy Horse be captured, tried, and convicted. It didn't matter that Custer had perpetrated many atrocities, destroyed entire villages, and killed anyone he caught there.

"This massacre will be looked upon as an insult to the U.S. government's sovereignty," Sarah told him. Even if Crazy Horse heard her plea, the battle was like a narcotic that prevented him from hearing her.

After the battle of Little Big Horn, Crazy Horse led his followers back to the area of the Rosebud in Southern Montana; Sitting Bull and the others disbanded. This was their way; they were more defensive than offensive in nature. They wanted to hunt and be left alone. No longer would they band together for a concerted offensive. This was their last hurrah. They would fight small battles, lose many of their braves, and scatter. Sarah begged Crazy Horse to move south and out of General Crook's areas. Confident in their own invincibility with their victory over Custer, Crazy Horse and his band were not being realistic. They didn't realize that this sense of invincibility was tied directly to the number of other tribes they could enlist. Soon the other tribes were captured or dispersed and the strength in numbers they had attained at the Battle of the Little Big Horn would never again be realized.

In early 1877, Colonel Miles led his fifth infantry in a relentless pursuit of the Sioux and their Cheyenne followers, making it difficult for Crazy Horse and his band to stop long enough to obtain food; they were being worn down by Miles's endless pursuit.

Crazy Horse counterattacked and led about eight hundred warriors against Miles, but the general was a cagey veteran of the Indian wars. He disguised his cannons as wagons, and as Crazy Horse at- tacked, Miles uncovered the cannons and fired on the Indians. The Indians not caught in the cannon fire escaped with Crazy Horse to the mountains and, under the cover of a snowstorm, left in the middle of the night. This was indeed a momentum changer, because more and more of the Indian bands were scattering or surrendering. They were out of food, the buffalo had been decimated, and the tribes lost their superiority through numbers.

In the spring of 1877, General Crook sent a message to Crazy Horse through Red Cloud. If Crazy Horse and his followers would surrender, he and his people could have their own reservation in the Powder River area of Montana. Sarah begged him to accept. After counsel with other members of the tribe, he, Sarah, and the two children along with Short Bull, Little Big Man, and about eight hundred of his followers went to Fort Robinson, Nebraska, adjacent to the Red Cloud Agency, and surrendered.

Sarah met with General Crook when they arrived at the fort. "What will happen to us?" she asked him.

"My orders are to allow you to enter the Red Cloud Agency pending a decision by
Washing- ton on what to do."

The Red Cloud Agency had been started in 1871 after Red Cloud met with President Grant, the Interior Ministry, and the commissioner of Indian Affairs. Red Cloud had taken a neutral position in 1876 during the battles at Rosebud and Little Big Hom and acted as a peacemaker between Crazy Horse and

General Crook. This made him a valuable intermediary, and President Grant had rewarded him with the agency. Grant felt that having the Indians in a reservation where they could be monitored would ease some of the tension between the Indians and the white settlers. The Red Cloud Agency had a staff of thirty to forty employees assisting the agent in charge to deliver rations to the thirteen thousand Indians living there. Though the majority of the Indians living in the reservation led peaceful lives, there were small bands that were constantly causing trouble such as rustling and raiding wagon trains. In 1874, after one of the agency men was killed by a band of hostile Indians, Fort Robinson was built to protect the agency and its employees.

The promise of a separate reservation for Crazy Horse, Sarah, and their followers fell through. The commissioner of Indian Affairs denied the reservation primarily because Crazy Horse had been involved in the massacre of General Custer. Sarah asked General Crook to intercede, but he told her the main obstacle was the commissioner of Indian Affairs' demand to have the Indians disarms.

Sarah was passionate. "We need to hunt, and in order to hunt we must have weapons. Most of the violations are initiated by white settlers. You know I'm correct. The peace commission that toured the prairies in 1875 concluded that most Indian violence was provoked by whites." Crook told her that his hands were tied.

The two had become friends. Sarah found in General Crook someone who was sympathetic and whom she could trust. He on the other hand was flattered that a beautiful young woman would seek him out for his wisdom and counseling. At one of their meetings, she shared her concern for her brother who was left with the Lakotas when she was traded to the Sioux. Crazy Horse had sent an emissary to the last known village where James had been held, but the tribe had moved and no one knew where they were at this time. She asked the general to use his net- work to determine where the boy was.

It took nearly six months before he gave her the good news. Her brother had been rescued several years ago and was in Harrisburg, Pennsylvania. Sarah was thrilled and kissed the general on the cheek; he immediately blushed. She started writing to James Hansen detailing her life over the past eight years.

CHAPTER SEVEN

To help resolve the impasse of giving up their weapons in order to have their own reservation, General Crook suggested that Crazy Horse and Sarah travel to Washington and meet with President Hayes and the commissioner of Indian Affairs to plead their case. Crazy Horse was uncomfortable. He didn't like meeting with the white dignitaries, and besides, they didn't have the money to make the trip. General Crook said he could find funds to pay for the trip, but Crazy Horse was still uncertain. "Every time we meet, we come away with less of our land and are forced to fight to keep what little they give us, and they leave us without our dignity."

Sarah understood, yet was pragmatic at the same time. "We don't have much left. Why not see if we can convince them to give us peace and a reservation. Our children deserve that from us." For once he agreed.

The two along with Red Cloud, Spotted Tail, and a military escort provided by General Crook traveled to Washington, D.C., by train to meet with President Hayes and the commissioner of Indian Affairs. The train seemed to stop at every town along the route. At each stop they were greeted by crowds who wanted to see the blond, blue-eyed beauty with the Indian war chief who was the killer of General Custer. Much of the crowd was curious and controlled, but at a couple of stops along the way, some shouted out obscenities and demanded that Crazy Horse be arrested for his role in Custer's massacre. Their military escorts quickly ushered them inside the train and they continued on their journey.

They were given the presidential suite at the International Hotel off Pennsylvania Avenue and informed that their room and meals were paid for in advance. Sarah and Crazy Horse became the toast of Washington during their ten days in the nation's capital and easily overshadowed the eloquent Red Cloud and persistent Spotted Tail. With her long blond hair flowing down her back over her Indian dress, and Crazy Horse with his high cheekbones and regal posture, they were in constant demand by the power elite in Washing- ton. The requests for interviews were numerous.

Each interview of Sarah focused on her capture by the Lakota who killed her parents and everyone on the wagon train and the reason why she didn't escape when she had the opportunity. She responded that she loved her husband, her children and their life in their village. Crazy Horse was asked about the battle of Little Big Horn. He responded that Custer could've re- treated because of the large number of Indians that had assembled against him, but he was too arrogant. He was asked if he killed Custer; he replied that it wasn't him. He was asked about the other battles, and he answered as truthfully as he could. Though he was fluent enough in English, Sarah's presence gave him confidence and he was able to answer most questions without her interceding. There was a charm about the couple that the capital hadn't seen in years, and the press and the public couldn't get enough. The strong relationship that actually existed between the two was evident through- out their stay.

Some groups protested their acceptance in the nation's capital. Several papers criticized the president for meeting with a known murderer. His advisors were recommending that he not meet with the Indian delegation, but when the president saw Sarah and Crazy Horse together at a luncheon, he decided to keep the meeting scheduled later in the week.

Prior to the scheduled meeting with the president, the couple was free to travel around the nation's capital at their leisure. Reporters followed them everywhere. Sarah was in awe of all the attention they generated; Crazy Horse was aloof and would rather have stayed at the hotel and forego all the trips around town that she planned. One day they were treated to a carriage ride down Pennsylvania Avenue; the next day they were hosted at the Smithsonian Institute and Library of Congress.

One of the highlights of their visit was a ride from the capital to Baltimore and back on the side-wheel steamer called Sue. This was the first time Crazy Horse was impressed with anything in Washington and he, through Sarah, even though his English was passable, asked many questions about the boat's speed, number of passengers it could carry, and the steam apparatus that provided the propulsion. On the way back to their hotel, the large throngs gathering along the route cheered as the two droves by. One over anxious admirer jump into their carriage and offered flowers to Sarah; Crazy Horse grabbed him by the arm and pushed him out of the carriage. Sarah squeezed his arm in appreciation.

There were photos of the two posted everywhere in town, and wherever they went, they were asked to take a photo with complete strangers. As usual Crazy Horse was reserved while Sarah was realizing a dream corning true. She was someone. Those years of being a captive had all been forgotten and this trip was making up for all of that misery. They were hosted at lunch every day by a different group trying to get their story. A couple of magazines wanted to buy their exclusive stories. "We'll make a decision after we return to our village, and if we're interested, I'll notify you in writing," Sarah told them.

Just before their departure from Washington, Sarah received a letter from her brother James Hansen. The bond between them hadn't been broken. If anything, their ordeal had made them closer. He was shocked that she had married Crazy Horse. Everyone back east thought he was responsible for the massacre at the Battle of Little Big Horn and that he personally killed General Custer. James's local U.S. representative, Mark Solart, was working out the details of his trip to Washington so he could see Sarah. James felt that Solart was somewhat self-serving, but if he could help, it was okay with James. He suspected that Solart wanted to meet Sarah.

The day his parents were slaughtered and he and Sarah were taken prisoner had always been a weight upon James' shoulders. He saw his father fall and rushed to him. Even at his young age he knew his father didn't have long. He looked for his mother but couldn't see her. His father was saying something and James put his ear to his father's lips and heard his father say there was money for him in the First Union Bank of Harrisburg and then he died. At that moment he was hit over the head and when he woke his sister was trying to comfort him.

He remained a prisoner of the Lakota Indians for six years before he was rescued by a group from the

Seventh Cavalry, led by George Arm- strong Custer. He felt forever grateful to Custer for his release. Over the next three years he worked his way back home, doing odd jobs at Fort Laramie, working in the slaughter houses of Chicago, and finally arriving in Harrisburg just after his twenty-first birthday. He had a few dollars saved and was able to hire an attorney to see if in fact he had an inheritance in the First Union Bank of Harrisburg.

The first thing James had to do was establish his identity. His mother and father were dead, probably his sister as well, and he couldn't re- member anyone he knew in the Titusville area. But his attorney was relentless and after six months was able to establish James's identity sufficiently enough for the bank to release funds, which had swelled to a small fortune. The problem was that there was three trusts, one for Lars and Helga Hansen and the other two for James and Sarah. Though the parents were dead, proof hadn't been provided to the bank. James's attorney said he would work on that.

James's share was made available to him while Sarah's was retained by the bank. He was twenty-two years old, single, and with sufficient funds to start a new life. The problem was he didn't know what to do. That's where the bank stepped in to help. Franklin George, the bank president, suggested that he buy a small general store in Titusville. The widow who owned the store wanted to move to Philadelphia and live with her children. He could learn about business without too large an investment.

James was a hard worker and with some advice from his banker and his attorney made the store very profitable, such that he was able to hire a store manager and have more time for leisure. But he was restless and looking for some new venture. He approached Franklin George again and asked his advice. Harrisburg was growing and now was the capital of the state. George suggested he buy up commercial property around the city and hold it for a few years. It appeared that he had sufficient income from the general store for his monthly expenses; he was single and therefore could speculate a little. The problem was that James was astute enough not to want to risk that much capital or take on too much debt.

The banker suggested an alternative. "James, your father's instruction was that in the event either you or Sarah died, the trust would go to the other. This is 1876; Sarah hasn't been heard from for over ten years. I believe you've waited long enough; the money is rightfully yours. I'd check with your attorney to have your sister and parents declared dead, and our bank will make the rest of the funds available to you."

James was stunned. It never dawned on him that Sarah wouldn't return, and he didn't feel comfortable taking his parents' money even though they were dead. He sought counsel from his attorney who agreed with the banker. After a week of ambivalence, he had Sarah and his parents declared dead and several months later all their funds were transferred to his account. He immediately bought the land the banker had identified and after a year buyers appeared and his fortune grew. By the time James was twenty- four, he was on his way to becoming a millionaire. He was asked to run for city council, which he declined. He was a little concerned that he may be moving too quickly and things could get out of hand if he wasn't ready. There would be plenty of time for that.

When he was told that Sarah was alive and wanted to communicate with him, he was happy and eagerly responded to her first letter. After he responded, he realized the delicate situation that her being alive had created. He was torn between telling her about the trust funds and not telling her for obvious reasons. He decided to adopt a wait and see attitude until he sorted everything out. This marriage of hers had startled everyone. He wondered how she could endure being the wife of a blood-thirsty savage. These were the people who had killed their parents. He wasn't going to give his hard-earned money to any savage, so he decided he wouldn't tell her about her inheritance.

At the agreed to date and time, James Hansen arrived at her hotel and was escorted to her room along with Representative Solart. Sarah couldn't believe how tall James was. He towered over her and Crazy Horse. Sarah could see in his eyes and in the manner, he carried himself the image of her beloved father. She wept for joy and James held her in his arms. The introductions were uncomfortable for James and Crazy Horse, who excused himself so that the two siblings could talk in private. Representative Solart wanted to stay, but Crazy Horse was quite persuasive and the congressman reluctantly left the two alone.

"Some of our parents' friends wanted to come, but the notoriety surrounding Crazy Horse was too much for them to bear and they declined. Everyone I know thinks he's the cold-blooded killer of General Custer. However, they want you to know that they admire you greatly and hope someday that they'll be able to visit with you. I feel like they do, but I know you've always had a level head and wouldn't take up with someone if he didn't have some redeemable traits."

"My husband is Crazy Horse who is a legend among his people and admired and feared by many. He's been a heroic warrior, yet he has an integrity about him that makes him a great leader that others seek to follow. It's true that he was at the Battle of Little Big Horn, but so was I. The newspapers are incorrect; he did not kill Custer. He's won many battles, but he's never scalped anyone. During the eight years we've been together, he's honored, loved, and respected me. I could ask for no more from any man. You need not like him, but I do; I am his wife. In some eyes, I'm a second-class citizen because I'm a squaw, but in my village, I'm held in great regard and I interface with many of the white dignitaries as an emissary for my people. You are my brother and I love you, but you'll have to accept me as I am with an Indian husband and you'll have to give him the respect that he deserves."

James didn't agree with his sister, but he decided that he wasn't going to raise the issue again. She was articulate and an ardent advocate for her husband, her way of life, and her adopted Indian family. They spent the remainder of the day sightseeing and reminiscing about their parents. As a favor to James, Sarah reluctantly agreed to allow Representative Solart to join them for dinner at the hotel that evening. Solart had been instrumental in arranging the meeting between her and James and she felt an obligation to him. She asked Crazy Horse if he wanted to join them; he declined. She knew Solart to be self-serving but also knew that without him she wouldn't have been able to have this reunion with her brother.

As it turned out he was quite charming and a member of the House Subcommittee on Indian Affairs. They discussed ways he could be helpful and the type of legislation that was needed to secure their reservation for perpetuity if the president gave his approval. She agreed to personally mention to the president how helpful Solart had been to her. In return he would be her voice and advocate in Congress. He escorted her and James to their rooms in the hotel. She wasn't surprised that Solart asked her to come back to his room, which she declined with tact and grace. It was amazing to her that at least three men had made a pass at her while she was in D.C., yet no one had ever made such a move on her in the Indian culture.

James was amazed at how well his sister advocated the position of the Indians and how well she interfaced with males and females alike. His sister was a superstar. She brought him a picture of Crazy Horse that she painted. He didn't like Crazy Horse, but it was obvious that the picture was painted by someone with a great deal of talent. His conscience was bothering him. He wanted to tell her about the money, but his dislike for Crazy Horse clouded his vision and he didn't divulge the information. Solart didn't know about the money, but he was aware that Sarah had been declared legally dead and wondered what James as going to do about it. James told him, he'd take care of it when he returned to Harrisburg.

Before the couple went home, they were invited to a party at the vice-presidential mansion. At dinner, Sarah sat to the left of the president while Crazy Horse sat to his immediate right. James was at a table with Congressman Solart. Most of the conversation was between Sarah and the president; Crazy Horse had little to say. After dinner a military band played and the dignitaries got up to dance. While Sarah was dancing with President Hayes, he complimented her on her beauty and for the work she was doing to bring peace to the West. Crazy Horse was amused at the attention she was receiving but played the patient husband.

Before dessert was served, President Hayes issued a proclamation and presented it to Crazy Horse. He proclaimed Sarah and Crazy Horse as honorary residents of Washington, D.C. Then the mayor rose and gave them the keys to the city. She danced with Congressman Solart, her brother James, and two senators from a southern state. One let his hand slip down below her waist and he squeezed her buttocks.

"Senator, are you aware that my husband is Crazy Horse and he's scalped twenty six men? Now if I told him you were getting fresh with me, I shudder to think what he would do." The senator apologized and soon Sarah saw him depart the vice-presidential mansion. He didn't return.

The meeting with President Hayes and the commissioner of Indian Affairs went well. Red Cloud, Spotted Tail, and Sarah tried to make the president understand the plight of the Indian. He promised to look into their need for a reservation with sufficient land to feed the tribe. Sarah as advocate pointed out the difficulty for a group that lived off the land and killed animals for food to be deprived of weapons to hunt as well as to defend themselves. "The white settlers are the aggressive ones. Without weapons, the Indians are at their mercy. President Hayes, it would be a shame to destroy a group who founded this country." Crazy Horse understood what was being discussed, but Sarah was presenting such a strong case that he declined to comment. He had been blessed with a beautiful and intelligent wife. The president promised a quick study and answer.

She and Crazy Horse escorted James and Congressman Solart to their train. James and Sarah promised to write. She saved her special gift to the end. "I painted this from memory. Each time you look at this picture of our mother and father you'll realize how lucky you and I were to have them as parents and that I will always love you." James was so overcome with emotion that he could hardly communicate. She smiled as he got on the train and waved good-bye.

James Hansen was distraught. He had taken Sarah's money with the best of intentions but lost his perspective when faced with a situation he couldn't understand. He felt betrayed by Sarah. Crazy Horse and his people were the ones who had murdered their father and mother and here she was married to one of the bloodiest savages in history. He could not bring himself to confess to her what he'd done and, worse, why he hadn't corrected the situation, but he didn't. Try as hard as he could to hate her, he admired her. She was beautiful, smart, committed to a cause, and from the picture she painted of their parents, a very talented artist.

On the trip home to the Red Cloud Agency, Sarah and Crazy Horse stopped in Chicago and were invited to dinner by the mayor. Again the spectacle of a major Indian figure with his blond, blue eyed wife caused enough disruption that the chief of police had to cordon off the entire block around the restaurant. There were no protests in Chicago, just an admiring public who couldn't get enough of the famous couple. The mayor took them for a steamboat ride out on the lake; Crazy Horse became seasick. Sarah, the dutiful wife, tended to her husband and broke off the planned festivities. The couple adjourned to their hotel in town and left early the next day. While they were making love that night, he pronounced his love for her for only the second time; it was also the last time.

Sarah's role became more pronounced when they returned from their Washington trip. Crazy Horse became even more withdrawn than he had previously. He didn't expect anything from the dignitaries in Washington and saw his way of life disappearing and nothing could be done to salvage it. It was Sarah that Crook and the other white settlers at the agency communicated with and it was she they shared their concerns with, hoping she would convey their message to Crazy Horse. Most of the whites at the agency distrusted the aloof Crazy Horse and resented his white wife. Indians at the Red Cloud Agency were jealous of the prestige that Crazy Horse and Sarah enjoyed. Included in that group were Red Cloud and Spotted Tail, who'd traveled with them to Washington but were completely overlooked the entire time and in essence were supporting players; consequently, their feelings were hurt. Sarah desperately tried to hold everything together while attempting to find a place for herself and her husband in the growing white society.

In May 1877, General Crook, acting on a rumor that Crazy Horse was planning a rebel- lion, ordered his arrest. Crook hadn't received any communique from the president or commissioner of Indian Affairs about an agency or reservation for Crazy Horse. But he was receiving constant pressure from his superiors to force the Indians onto a reservation. Since Crazy Horse was the best known Indian in his area, he became the target. But the arrest was delivered in the form of a summons, and because Crazy Horse and Sarah were unaware that he was under arrest, they ignored it. They, along with their two children, headed northwest and entered the Spotted Tail Agency.

Hoping it would all blow over, Crook opted to do nothing, but in September, acting upon direct orders, General Crook sent troops to arrest Crazy Horse. Much jealousy had developed as a result of the Washington trip. Red Cloud, Spotted Tail, and other Indian leaders felt slighted because Crazy Horse and his blond wife were getting all the attention. They planted a seed in General Crook's mind that Crazy Horse was planning a rebellion. When the troops arrived at the Spotted Tail Agency, Sarah negotiated an additional day so she could prepare Crazy Horse for the trip. They talked through the night and Sarah finally convinced him that the best solution was to tell General Crook that he had no intention of inciting a rebellion. Before he left with the soldiers, He squeezed Sarah's hand and told her, "You've been a good wife."

The next day Crazy Horse was led back to Fort Robinson near the Red Cloud Agency. Sarah remained behind, expecting that as soon as Crazy Horse met with General Crook and assured him that he wasn't planning any disturbances in the area, he'd be released. However, once Crazy Horse reached Fort Robinson, security personnel at the agency sought to imprison him. When he resisted, he was stabbed in the abdomen by one of the soldiers. He died that evening. Sarah wasn't notified until three days later. She and her two children along with six of Crazy Horse's band left for the fort immediately and claimed the body. General Crook met her when she arrived.

"He came to tell you he had no intention of starting a rebellion. He was tired and wanted the reservation. Why couldn't you wait until Washington decided one way or the other?" she demanded.

"I tried to delay but was given a direct order. He wasn't supposed to die. A couple of our soldiers overreacted and then he overreacted and before we could stop it, he'd been stabbed. I'm so sorry. I didn't want this to happen. Please accept my apologies," Crook responded.

Sarah, her two children, and six of his best friends left Fort Robinson with the body of Crazy Horse. By the time she reached Wounded Knee the procession had grown to a few hundred. At the burial, at least one thousand Indians were present to pay homage to a great warrior. Red Cloud and Spotted Tail made the trip and wept as dirt was placed over Crazy Horse's final resting place. Sarah's daughter cried with her, but her son vowed vengeance on the soldiers who killed his father. Crazy Horse was thirty-five years old.

Her people over the last eleven years were the Sioux, and now her husband was dead. Any friends she made within the Indian culture had been scattered, killed, or imprisoned. She had to make a life for herself and her children. It was obvious there was no life for her within the Indian culture; most were starving and couldn't help her even if they wanted to. She went back to Fort Robinson with the children to seek employment. General Crook was most supportive and offered her a position as interpreter. Although she was only fourteen when she was captured by the Lakota, her early education had been extensive. Subsequently she read many books covering history, geography, and mathematics that General Crook was able to obtain for her. Although many of the officers' wives resented her, General Crook strongly suggested that she be allowed to tutor some of the children. For the first time she was the bread winner for her family. Within a year, funding had been provided to build a school at Fort Robinson and Sarah was appointed by General Crook as its first teacher.

Her son, whom she called Lars after her father, was becoming difficult to control. He preferred his Sioux name of Tashunka Wilco, which was also his father's. It was a family tradition to take the father's name when it was vacated. Crazy Horse had taken the name from his father who vacated it for him, and like his father, young Crazy Horse wore his hair long and free flowing. His personality was similar to his father, very aloof and quick to respond. But he was sensitive to the fact that he was a half-breed and didn't like the taunting of the white boys as he grew up in the fort.

When he was eleven, he savagely beat the son of an army major, and but for the fact that General Crook interceded on Sarah's behalf, he would have been shot by the major. The next year he ran away. Try as hard as she could with limited resources and the stigma of being a squaw, she was unable to trace him. She heard rumors that he was riding with a band of hostiles, pillaging and destroying wagon trains and attacking isolated settlers. He was his father's son without the conscience of Crazy Horse, who had waged war against the army but was well respected as a great leader.

Her stepdaughter Naiwa was seventeen years old and of marrying age. She had been courted at the Spotted Tail Agency, and Sarah and Crazy Horse had given permission for her to marry one of the braves who came courting. Soon after Sarah went to Fort Robinson with her son Lars, Naiwa married and went to live at the Spotted Tail Reservation. After the school was built on Fort Robinson, Sarah enrolled Lars, but he was always finding an excuse to skip school. He was bright, could read and write, but wanted to be a rebel. He still carried the psychological scar that his father had been killed here by soldiers.

"Schooling is something you need to make your way in this life," Sarah told him. "The buffalo are gone and all you'll find out there is a way of life that is no more. Your father under- stood this. That's why we went to meet with the president. We wanted a reservation for ourselves and our people. I beg you to try." He walked away from her and left the fort.

General Crook was her most ardent sup- porter. Sarah was twenty nine years old and still a beautiful woman. Life without her husband and son made her life empty. She was employed at the agency, but none of the white women would socialize with her and when she approached them within the fort confines, they would turn and walk the other way. The only clothes she wore were what she'd been wearing the past twelve years. Crook suggested that she end her mourning and shed the Indian garb and start dressing as a white woman.

Although she was considered a piranha by the women at the fort, the same didn't apply to the young officers who found her fascinating. There were constant invitations for picnics, walks, and an occasional dance at the fort. On one occasion, she attended one of the dances at the fort escorted by two young officers. The response by those at the dance was mixed; the men were fascinated by her beauty while the woman saw her as a scarlet woman. Romance was out of the question even if she was so moved, because General Crook was like a protective father and made the young officers very uncomfortable.

Sarah had written to James on four occasions, but hadn't received a reply; she wondered if James was ill. Even if Sarah hadn't told James about the death of Crazy Horse, the newspapers back east carried the story for a week and everyone was talking about his death. James went back to Harrisburg and shared his concerns with his financial advisor/attorney Charles Howard about Sarah, her Indian husband, and the fact that he'd declared her legally dead and she hadn't received any of the money from her trust. His attorney assured James that he hadn't done anything wrong, but James was depressed and sought the counsel of his minister. The minister told James that his actions under the law were probably legal, but his actions were morally wrong and he at least owed his sister something. The minister couldn't tell him what to do; it would have to be his conscience that would guide him. James's problem was that his assets had increased twofold but he wasn't liquid. If he was to pay Sarah back, he had to sell something. He decided on a different course of action.

General Crook suggested that Sarah leave the area and all memories that it contained. After the first Indian agent was fired for embezzlement, the new agent, John Mcintyre, a Presbyterian minister, agreed to take over the agency for a year while they searched for a replacement. It was his intent to pursue his ministry in California. During his time as agent for the Red Cloud Agency, he became Sarah's sponsor and friend. By the end of his first year, true to his word, he, his wife Patricia and daughter Nancy, along with Sarah as their nanny, planned a journey to California. Mcintyre had enough funds for the trip and was assured that his position as minister of the First Presbyterian Church of Los Angeles would be waiting. So he was comfortable with risking the journey.

Although his wife was slightly nervous about the attention he was giving Sarah, she believed him to be a man of God and was doing what she would do if given the chance. She welcomed Sarah and entrusted Nancy to her care. By this time Sarah was without any of her children and was delighted to spend as much time as she could with their young daughter.

CHAPTER EIGHT

As before, Tommy skirted the main populated areas as he made his way down the Santa Fe Trail to the old town of Santa Fe. In 1880, Santa Fe was in the midst of an economic boom. The addition of the Atchison, Topeka and Santa Fe Railroad and the invention of the telegraph helped fuel the economy. But corruption was rampant and President Hayes appointed Lew Wallace as territorial governor to clean up the area. Wallace was so successful that the famous outlaw Billy the Kid swore that he'd come to Santa Fe to kill him.

Tommy had nearly one thousand dollars accumulated from his labor at the Bar 6, working for Frank Waidner, and his share of the reward for his work on the posse. He deposited the funds in the Santa Fe Bank and then started to look for work. He tried to hire on at several ranches, but for whatever reason there wasn't any work available. Joseph Beers, the manager of the Santa Fe Bank, suggested that Tommy had enough capital to go into business. He pointed out that the local livery stable was for sale. The former owner had died and the widow was anxious to sell and move back east. She wanted two hundred dollars but probably would take one fifty. With the population expected to increase, Beers assured Tommy that he could make a comfortable living from the business. Beers handled the negotiations, and soon Tommy was a business owner and a valuable client of the bank.

He made an inventory of his business and found that it was a viable enterprise. The widow provided ledgers for the past three years and it was obvious that her husband kept a good set of books, but for some reason they were only making expenses. Tommy could attribute some of the previous owners' problems to poor management, but it seemed to him there was something else. On his first day as the new owner, he tallied up the sales for the day and came up short. He knew the rig had been rented out twice that day and that the employee he inherited, by the name of Frank Culler, had handled those transactions.

He called Culler into the makeshift office at the end of the day and asked about the proceeds. Culler initially said the renters didn't pay.

"Frank, I saw you accept money from both people who rented the rigs. So where is it?"

"That's mine for doing the work."

"Frank, you get paid a daily wage, nothing more. If there's a bonus for good work, I decide that, not you. I want the money and then I want you off my property."

"You can't fire me. I've been here longer than you. If you know what's good for you, breed, you'll forget the whole thing."

"Frank, I want the money now. If you don't pay me, you're going to be carried out of here on your back."

Culler made a mistake when he swung at Tommy and missed and was hit twice by Tommy. He landed on the ground hard and didn't move. Tommy checked his pockets and retrieved the rental fees and then dragged Culler by his feet out of the livery stable and left him at the edge of the main street. Tommy was sure that Culler was the reason why the widow had wanted to sell the business.

Later Culler let it be known that he was sucker punched and when he next came face to face with the new owner he'd better be armed. But he backed down when he came face to face with Tommy at the local saloon; Tommy was wearing his six-gun. He looked Culler in the eye and suggested he look for work in another town. A couple of days later Culler left town.

Tommy let it be known that he was looking for help. At least ten men applied, but a young Navajo Indian by the name of Henry Garcia was the one who got the job. It wasn't because Garcia was Indian that he was hired, it was just the manner in which he presented himself and his desire for the work. Tommy assessed his livery business and tried to put himself in the position of his customers to see what would satisfy them. He took a chance and instituted a delivery system for those who needed to rent a mount or a carriage. As long as he got a day's notice he had Garcia deliver the mount or rig to the individual and then pick it up at the end of the day.

Word spread about this service and Tommy couldn't keep up with the increase in business so he hired another Navajo, a young man by the name of Fernando recommended by Henry. Soon his bank account was increasing and Beers suggested that he look into acquiring another business enterprise. Tommy wasn't sure; success was coming too fast and he feared the notoriety that went with it.

With the coming of Governor Lew Wallace, the area soon took on a law and order flavor, and people were willing to get involved and new businesses were being started. The town council hired a law and order sheriff who was slow to anger but quick with a gun.

Soon the lawless element moved out of Santa Fe or ended up in the cemetery. Tommy met the sheriff, and although he wasn't someone he could cultivate as a friend, he respected the job the man did in cleaning up the town. With the success of his business he was invited to join the Santa Fe Businessmen's Association. It was an eye opener for Tommy who could see first hand how the town's movers and shakers thought and how they planned for the continued increase in the economy. Al- though he was successful in everything he tried, the insight would be beneficial if he were to expand.

He now had four employees, Henri, his brother Tomas, his cousin Enrique, and Henri's best friend Fernando. Business was good, but he needed to expand. There were plenty of wild horses roaming the range. Tommy had an idea and sent Tomas and Enrique to round up some of the mustangs. Most were too wild to be worth too much, but many, with a little work, could be domesticated. Tommy set about training the four Navajos to use his method of training horses. After two months of training they were able to break enough horses to make the venture profitable. Similar to the Bar 6 operation, Tommy and his crew took on horses owned by other ranches or individuals and broke them for a fee. The operation was becoming larger than the area around the livery stables could contain; they had to have another place to set up the horse training operation.

Henri and his family lived on the Navajo reservation south of Santa Fe. Tommy talked to the elders and they agreed to let him run his horse training operation on the reservation in return for two steers a year. Soon the horse training operation had doubled what they were doing at the livery stables and Tommy was spending more time at the reservation. That's where he met Marie Garcia, who was Henri's sister. They started keeping company; she was a pleasant woman, though self-conscious about her English, so Tommy learned Navajo. She was reluctant to be seen in public with him and preferred that he meet her at her parents' place.

Because his past tenure in other locales was short, he wasn't interested in settling down. She seemed to accept the attention she was getting without a commitment, and her mother accepted him as a special visitor and allowed him to stay in the guest bedroom. Marie would visit him at night and leave before daybreak before her parents and siblings rose. He knew everyone in the family knew of the affair, but as long as Marie was in her bed by morning, no one said anything.

Tommy liked the family and spent many days fishing and hunting with her brothers and sometimes her father. They swapped stories of life in Indian villages, raids they had gone on, and occasionally talked about women they knew. He liked the family atmosphere. It brought back pleasant memories of his child- hood, and yet it introduced sadness within him when he saw the interaction of Marie with her parents and siblings and realized he didn't have any family. He'd always been a loner and wondered if the rest of his life would be as a loner. He couldn't have a permanent home until the issue of Laramie was settled.

Spanish colonial architecture still permeated the town buildings, and Tommy started to look at developing a small retail section for future growth. Businesses requiring retail space generally put up tents as their offices when they came to town and built only after they were sure their particular endeavor would succeed.

Tommy saw an opportunity to provide rental space for those individuals. With the help of Joseph Beers, he hired an architect and started negotiations to buy land to build a retail strip. This was the most ambitious project he and the town had attempted, so Tommy went to the city council to propose his development and seek their guidance.

The city fathers were receptive and apprehensive at the same time. They weren't sure that the town could support such an undertaking, and they didn't like the aspect of condemning several of the old buildings for the planned site. They didn't turn him down but asked that he reconsider the demolition of two of the buildings. They wondered if he couldn't rehab the buildings and fit them within his development plan.

He brought their concerns back to his architect and asked him to look at the impact of leaving two of the buildings standing and integrate them within his plan. "If you can make the changes they ask for, I think we'll be approved," he told the architect. He didn't have a home of his own yet. He'd been living in a rooming house run by the widow Leachman. It was a pleasant arrangement. She served two meals a day and changed his linen twice a week. He was a busy man and the lifestyle at the rooming house was relaxing and at times rewarding. He'd met several other businessmen in his situation and developed friendships he hadn't experienced before. After his business started providing him a respectable living, he moved into the new Santa Fe Hotel because it gave him more flexibility to meet clients and other businessmen. The restaurant was good and the management provided him a conference room with a telegraph whenever he needed it.

The four Navajos working for him rounded up about two hundred horses over a six month period and were able to break half of them. Tommy's business had taken on another dimension. He was working with horse buyers and brokers beyond the confines of Santa Fe and sometimes New Mexico. The telegraph was an ideal instrument to tap into this source of buyers. It was through the telegraph that he found out the U.S. Army's buyers required a continued supply of fresh mounts for the cavalry. They were willing to sign an exclusive contract if he could deliver three hundred mounts a year. The offer was tempting, but he wasn't sure that Henri and the others could continue rounding up horses and breaking them without additional help. Things were moving so fast for him that he was nervous and decided to take his time, so he declined the army contract.

Two couples and a child entered the hotel together. The older couple, who seemed to be with their daughter, indicated they'd register for all of them while the younger couple entered the temporary banking office located in the lobby of the hotel. The young man was square built and of medium height while the woman with him was petite but very beautiful. She was barely five feet tall with long, flowing blonde hair that was adorned with blue flowers and an Indian headband. Her escort talked to the banking clerk who upon inspection of a bank draft issued him about three hundred dollars in new bills.

While the gentleman was counting the bills, two masked men walked into the hotel lobby. One of the gunmen trained his gun on the hotel clerk and the three visitors who were registering. He ordered the clerk and the visitors to sit on the floor with their backs to the registration desk and be quiet. The other gunman walked into the bank office and pushed the attractive couple aside and demanded that the teller place all the bank's cash into a sack he shoved into his chest. At that instant, a well dressed man of medium height walked down the stairs and stopped at the landing and looked over the situation that was unfolding.

The gunman in the lobby saw the man come down the stairs and trained his gun on him. "You, on the stairs, join the others on the floor and keep quiet, if you know what's good for you."

The man on the stairs didn't move. He appeared to be taking in everything while trying to assess what he should do. This enraged the gunman, who took a couple of steps toward him and shouted, "I told you to get over there on the floor. If you don't move now, I'm going to put a bullet in you. Now move."

It was early afternoon and there were only a few people in the bar. The silence was deafening as the gunman in the banking office went about his business while the gunman in the lobby was staring down the man on the stairs. The four on the floor in front of the registration desk turned to look at the man on the stairs.

The silence was finally broken by a quiet voice. "There's not going to be a robbery today. Leave all the money on the floor and get on your horses and leave now."

The gunman in the bank office heard the threat and turned to see what was going on. The four sitting on the floor were staring at the man on the stairs, afraid the gunman would shoot him. It took Ed Orchard, the gunman near the stairs, a few seconds to get over the shock. The hairs on the back of his neck rose and his cheeks flushed. He'd heard that voice before, but where? Then the events of that afternoon almost ten years ago came back in a flash. It couldn't be, but the voice was the same, and though he was dressed as a gentleman and his hair was neatly combed, he spoke in the same quiet manner and he looked like the same person.

Orchard remembered Bull Larkin laughing while holding onto the long hair of the Chinese laundrymen and a half-breed standing at the bar telling him to let them go so that everyone could go back to their beer. Larkin didn't think it was funny and told the half-breed he was under arrest. He had a gun trained on him from sixfeet away when the breed drew and shot the deputy in the forehead.

The robber in the bank office yelled,

"Shoot him, Ed!"

Ed Orchard had been an outlaw for over ten years and involved in a few shootouts with the law. He raised his hand to silence the other gunman and then seemed to be trying to decide what to do. When he spoke his voice seemed higher and more agitated. "Wait, Jimmy! I've heard that voice before."

Jimmy wasn't following what his brother said. "He's only a dude, you can take him easy, shoot him."

Ed Orchard again signaled his brother to be quiet and spoke directly to the man standing at the bottom of the stairs. "Are you the one from the Saddleback Saloon?"

The man looked around the room as though carefully choosing his words before answering. "I am, and this is the last chance you have. Drop the money on the floor and leave. I won't trail you. Chances are you can make it over the pass before the sheriff can form a posse and follow you."

Ed Orchard assessed his options and knew what he had to do. "Jimmy, leave the money on the floor and move to the doors and grab our horses. I'll cover you."

Jimmy couldn't believe what he was hearing. "Ed, there's two of us and this guy doesn't have a gun that I can see. This is too good a score. I'm for taking him now."

"Jimmy, do as I say and we'll all live through this. I've seen this guy draw and fire. He's the fastest I ever saw. I saw him take that guy in Laramie who had a gun pointed at him and was just six feet away. He was able to draw and fire two shots before the deputy could twitch. This is death looking us in the eye. Move to the door. I'll cover you until you get to the horses. We have to take his word that he won't come after us. Move, I told you."

"Ed, no one's that fast. You've never backed down from anyone in your life," Jimmy said.

"Believe me he's that fast and I saw it. He's as cool as one gets." Ed motioned for his brother to move.

Jimmy reluctantly dropped the canvas bag on the floor and made his way to the door as Ed backed out, and then both ran to their horses. Not a shot was fired. Ed couldn't tell if the man at the landing was carrying a gun, but he knew it was too much of a chance to take. He'd rather live to see another town.

Those in the bar weren't privy to the situation unfolding in the lobby. The two couples were stunned and no one talked as the well dressed man walked down the stairs toward the exit and out into the street. He strode down to the livery stable as one of the couples watched him exit through the door. Only the hotel clerk was conscious enough to shout after him, "Thank you, Mr. Sanchez."

Tommy knew that he'd have to move on. The gunman had identified him, and the two couples would tell the sheriff what happened as well as the reference to Laramie. It wouldn't take long for the sheriff to wire Laramie and get the full details. He knew that Judd Harker wouldn't sleep until he had Tommy in his custody long enough for a fake jail break and a bullet in the back. He didn't think it would be difficult to sell his livery business. He'd already had a good offer and was sure it was still available. He also had the option of selling to the Navajos. They knew the business, were honest, and could make a living while paying Tommy on an installment basis. If they were interested, he'd set it up with the bank manager and try to leave by the end of the week.

Every time he tried to do something good it backfired on him and he had to run again. He made a vow that he wouldn't intercede again un- less his own life depended on it. That woman in the banking office was beautiful and there was a certain familiarity to her, but he couldn't place her. The man she was with was a very lucky man. Normally the only time Tommy carried a gun was when he went to the Indian reservation. Today was no different. He had planned to go out to the reservation in the afternoon, and although the area was generally law abiding, the ride out to the reservation was long and anything could happen.

The next morning Tommy approached the bank manager, who had heard about the at- tempted robbery and asked Tommy many questions that he was unwilling to answer. Tommy told him his plans to leave the area and sell the business to Henri and his brother. He asked the bank manager to set up the agreement and handle the quarterly installment payments they would make if they accepted the offer.

Joseph Beers was deeply distressed. He really liked Tommy and didn't want to lose him as a customer. "There's nothing that bad that could make you leave. Let me work on it for you. I know a lot of people. The shooting in Laramie had to be self defense. I know you. I've never seen you look for trouble; I've never seen you lose your temper. Can't you take a few days to think this through?" Tommy wouldn't respond to the plea.

Henri couldn't believe what he was being told nor could he believe his good luck. He admired Tommy and didn't want to take advantage of any problem Tommy was having. "Tomas and I can run it for you until you return. We're honest and we'll run it as though you were here."

Tommy smiled and put his arm around Henri. "I want you to have it. Your time has come. You deserve this opportunity. Make sure you share it with the others. I'll be okay. Don't worry about me."

"What about Marie?" Henri asked.

"I'll tell her, and maybe when I'm settled I can send for her. You, Tomas, and Enrique have a great opportunity here and I'm grateful for your friendship. The bank manager will set up the paperwork, and it should be ready for signature tomorrow. I have to leave quickly."

"This is about what happened at the hotel.

You backed those two down without even a gun. How did you do that? I heard one of them say you were the fastest gun he ever saw. I've never even seen you use a gun. Did he have the wrong person?" Tommy didn't answer.

Sheriff Jed Stone of Santa Fe was out in the desert trailing a horse thief and didn't get back in town until two days after the incident at the hotel. He was summoned by the mayor and the town council and told of the incident and asked what he was going to do. He went back to his office and check the wanted posters but didn't pick up on anything, so he went down to the livery stable to talk to Tommy, who was at the Navajo reservation and wouldn't be back until later. Stone asked Henri to have Tommy come see him when he got back.

Tommy visited Marie and told her he had to leave and didn't know when he'd be back and that perhaps he would send for her after he was resettled. He didn't believe what he was telling her nor did she believe what she was being told.

CHAPTER NINE

James Hansen arrived at Fort Robinson the day before Sarah, the minister, and his family planned to leave for California. He had been in contact with General Crook over the past six months and shared with him his plans to visit with Sarah. He asked the general to keep his visit a secret and treat it as a surprise. The night before Sarah and the minister were scheduled to depart General Crook invited them to his quarters for a farewell dinner. Most of the officers and their wives turned out. Over the past year there had been a softening in the position of the women at the fort and they at least tolerated Sarah. The minister had a lot to do with the change of attitude, and he took every opportunity to ease some of the strained relationships. Here was a young woman who got up early, taught school, tutored some of the fort's children in the evening, and on weekends worked in the fort's medical clinic. The diehards wouldn't change, but some of the others seemed to understand what a nice person she was.

The minister, his wife, and Sarah arrived at the fort about six in the evening and, after a short cocktail period, were served venison and assorted vegetables. After dinner, General Crook gave a farewell speech and said he had a surprise for Sarah. At the appropriate moment, James Hansen opened the main door and strode up to his sister. Sarah was stunned and began to cry.

The minister and his wife had never met James and weren't aware that James was Sarah's brother.

After introductions were made, James and Sarah took a stroll outside. He'd rehearsed what he was going to say for nearly a year, but as the time approached, he wasn't sure he could confess what he'd done. Sarah could see that he was having a difficult time in expressing himself so she suggested they sit down and he tell her what was on his mind. "James, don't worry. I've been through a lot and I can help; please tell me what the problem is."

Slowly he told her about the last words their father said to him about the three trust accounts he'd set up. He shared with her his investments and gradually confessed that he took her trust and their parents' trust after he thought she was dead. She didn't interrupt though she wondered why he didn't tell her about the trust when they met in Washington. He told her of his prejudice toward the Indians who captured him and killed their parents and which became manifested in Crazy Horse. He told her of his conversation with his minister and how he realized he'd been selfish and insensitive to her plight.

"I've moved all my assets into a partnership with you as my partner. Everything I have and everything I've earned has been accounted for and placed into this partnership. I hope you'll forgive me and let me share the next year with you making up for lost time and all that you've been deprived of. Our partnership is worth nearly a million dollars. Most of our assets are in property, but I've liquidated some property so that we have about thirty thousand dollars to spend if you want. I understand you're planning to go to California. I'd like to make it a vacation and go with you to see some of the West and especially California."

"This is coming so fast; I don't know what to ask. You're my brother and I love you. I can't con- done what you've done, but I can understand.

Why don't we put that behind us? But what about the minister and his family? They need my help with their daughter. I can't just leave them. They've been wonderful to me" "Why don't I go with you to California?" Over the next hour James explained the partnership agreement and gave it to Sarah to sign. He indicated he could give her some cash now if she needed it. She asked that he hold on to it temporarily. They finally walked back into the auditorium where the minister and his family were talking to General Crook. James explained what had transpired over the last hour and a half and asked the minister if he and his family would mind if he accompanied them on their trip to California. They talked for another hour and finally said they'd be delighted. Sarah thought General Crook would cry at the news. Sarah was like a daughter to him and he was de- lighted about her good fortune.

After the shock over her good fortune had passed, she thought about her children. She asked the McIntyres and James if they could postpone their trip for a few days while she visited her daughter Naiwa and give her the good news. Pastor Mcintyre indicated that he didn't have a specific date to arrive. He'd told the foundation that he and his family would arrive before the end of the month. So if Sarah could finish her business so that they could reach Los Angeles by the end of the month, he saw no problem in delaying their departure.

They made the trip to the Spotted Tail Reservation in a day and spent a day with Naiwa and her family. General Crook provided a detail of two men to accompany them on their trip. James was amazed at how freely Sarah moved in the Indian culture and how much feeling there was between Sarah and her adopted daughter. James was still uncomfortable around Indians, still remembering his years of captivity. Sarah left her adopted daughter some money and said she'd send some money quarterly to help her. She asked Naiwa about Lars, but Naiwa didn't know where he was, nor had he visited her since she was married. After a tearful parting, James and Sarah made their way back to Fort Robinson.

James arranged for their passage on the Atchison, Topeka and Santa Fe Railroad. Sarah paid the fare for the minister's family to show her appreciation for the support they'd given her over the past year. She was leaving the only life she'd know as an adult and moving into the white world as a wealthy young woman. She had some concerns, but she'd been able to cope in the past, so why not in the future? Instead of leaving the next day, they would leave at the end of the week. Mcintyre assured them that a couple of days wouldn't impact his position and that he was delighted for the company and help on the Journey.

The train was comfortable, but forty hours in a confined place was hard on all the passengers. Finally they reached the town of Lemy about fifteen miles from Santa Fe and rented a carriage. They planned to spend two nights in Santa Fe and tour the oldest town in North America before traveling back to Lemy and then on to Los Angeles. James had planned ahead and made reservations for them at the Santa Fe Hotel. The trip from Lemy took a couple of hours, and soon they were in the bustling old town. James had brought a series of bank drafts with him so he wouldn't be carrying a lot of cash. While the minister and his family were registering, James and Sarah walked into the Wells Fargo office located in a room in the lobby of the hotel.

James introduced his sister to the teller and provided identification along with the bank draft for three hundred dollars. Just then, they were pushed aside by a burly masked gunman who ordered them to the side and leveled his gun at the teller and demanded all the cash in the till.

Sarah could see there was another man in the lobby who was armed ordering Pastor Mcintyre, his wife, and daughter to sit on the floor in front of the registration desk. Sarah had never experienced anything like this before and clung to James. She could see the terror in Mrs. Mcintyre's face as she clung to her daughter and husband.

Just then a well dressed man walked down the stairs in the lobby and stopped on the landing. He was a slim, dark skinned man about five feet ten inches tall and appeared to be of Mexican descent. The masked gunman in the lobby ordered him to join the others on the floor in front of the registration desk, but the man just stood there as though trying to determine what he should do next. The gunman in the lobby shouted at him and told him to move now.

Yet the man stood there ignoring the gun- man's threats. When he spoke it was in a very calm manner, but Sarah could hear it very clearly and wondered where she had heard that voice before. "There's not going to be a robbery here today. Place the money on the floor and get out of here. It'll take the sheriff some time to raise a posse and go after you. I'll not come after you."

The gunman in the bank yelled for his partner to shoot the man, but the other one said to be quiet. Then he said the strangest thing. "Are you the one from the Saddleback Saloon?"

The man on the stairs took his time to respond. "Yes I am. I'm not going to tell you again. Leave the money on the floor and go."

"Shoot him, Ed!" the man in the bank office yelled.

"Jimmy, leave the money on the floor and go for the exit. I'll cover you until you get to the horses."

"Are you crazy, Ed? There's two of us, and he doesn't even show a gun," the gunman in the bank office protested.

"Jimmy, believe me, we're looking at death here. This guy is no one to fool with. He's the fastest gun I ever saw. I'm not taking any chances. I saw him draw and put two shots into a guy's forehead in Laramie and that guy was six feet away and had a gun trained on him. I'd rather live to rob another bank."

Reluctantly the gunman near Sarah and James dropped the sack of money on the floor and went for the horses. The other gunman backed up and went through the door after his friend.

The teller moved quickly and picked up the sack full of money; Sarah and James went over and helped up the McIntyres. They were staring at the man from the stairs, who calmly walked out the front door without saying a word to any of them. They were stunned. Bank robbers gave up the money; no one was shot; and the one who had backed them down never produced a gun.

McIntyre asked, "Who was that?"

The desk clerk said he was Mr. Sanchez who had a room at the hotel. "Is he a gunman?" Sarah asked.

"He's a businessman. He owns the livery stable and rents out horses and carriages. I think he's going to build some commercial buildings across the street. I've never seen him with a gun," the clerk responded.

"The gunman in the lobby said he was the fastest gun he ever saw, and then he referenced Laramie and I think the Saddleback Saloon," James said.

Sarah had only seen the man for those few moments when he told the gunmen to leave, but she couldn't help but think he was familiar. He looked like a Mexican, but he could be an Indian. She strained to think where she saw him before, but she was grateful that he was there. Whoever he was, that gunman was respectful and didn't want to go up against him. He reminded her of Crazy Horse who had that aura about him; men respected and feared him.

The sheriff was out of town, and they were leaving the day after tomorrow, but Sarah was mesmerized about the man and wondered if she'd see him again, perhaps at dinner that evening. The topic of conversation during their evening meal at the restaurant was the attempted bank robbery and especially the man who stopped it. The whole dining room was buzzing about the event. They finished dinner and were going up the stairs when he entered the lobby and asked for his room key.

It was awkward for them to come back down to the lobby so they resolved to thank him to- morrow. Sarah again wondered if she knew him. But they were disappointed the next morning because the man had risen early and left the hotel before they went to breakfast.

"James, how could anyone be so fast that he made someone who had a gun pointed at him run away?" Sarah asked.

"I don't know. It seems farfetched when you think about it. But that man was scared enough that he was willing to leave the money rather than face that man. I wonder what happened in Laramie."

"The room clerk said he owns the livery stable. Maybe we could pick up our rig at the livery stables and see some more of the
surrounding area as well as the town."

James was smiling. "That guy has you hooked. You think you know him?"

Sarah gave James a playful slap on the arm as the minister and his family joined them in the lobby. "You two seem happy this morning. It seems you're over the episode that happened right here,"Mrs. Mcintyre said.

"We thought we'd go down to the livery stables and drive around some in our rented carriage. It's a nice day and I'd like to see some more of the surrounding area. We can be back by lunch. Perhaps we may run into our hero and personally thank him," James replied.

James grabbed Sarah's arm and the five of them walked down to the stables. A couple of young Indians were servicing one of the rigs as they entered the stables. Sanchez wasn't visible so they asked for him. One of the young men said that Mr. Sanchez was at the bank and would be back in an hour. "Your horse and carriage are ready if you want to use them."

It seemed unanimous, and the five climbed into the carriage and drove out of town with James driving. They were just leaving the stables as Sanchez came out of the bank, but they didn't see him. When they returned around noon, he wasn't at the livery stables or the hotel.

Sarah had made her mind up that she was going to see him before she left Santa Fe.

In order to be fresh for the long trip starting tomorrow, the McIntyres decided to go to bed early while Sarah and James went to dinner at the hotel by themselves. After they were served a second course, Sanchez entered the dining room and was seated at a table along the far wall. Sarah wanted to thank him and asked James what she should do. He suggested she send a note with the waiter and see what his response would be. She asked the waiter for writing paper and a pencil and wrote Tommy a note. She watched as the waiter gave him the note and as the waiter pointed out Sarah, Tommy smiled his acknowledgement and responded in writing. She asked if he would join them for an after- dinner drink in the lobby; he responded that he would be delighted.

Sarah and James were sitting in the lobby when Sanchez appeared. He shook James's hand and then Sarah's before he sat down across from them. "You have a very lovely wife, Mr.Hansen."

Sarah and James laughed at the same time, but it was James who responded. "Sarah is my sister; in fact, she's my beloved sister."

They passed the time with small talk for a few moments. Sarah couldn't keep her eyes off him and hung on his every word. She was positive that she'd seen him before. But where? Just when Sarah had the nerve to ask Tommy where he came from and especially about the situation the day before, Henri Garcia came into the lobby and told Tommy that a horse was down with colic. Tommy excused himself, shook James's hand, kissed Sarah's, and left with Henri.

CHAPTER TEN

The town of Tombstone, Arizona, was founded by Ed Schieffelin in 1879 when he came upon a silver strike about twenty miles from the city. The town was aptly named after Schieffelin's Tombstone Mine. Schieffelin told anyone who'd listen that he got the name from a soldier who came upon him while he was prospecting south of Tombstone. The soldier told him that the only thing he'd find out in this god forsaken land was a tombstone. The news of the silver strike spread across the country, and by 1880 the population of Tombstone had increased to one thousand people. Tommy Sanchez heard of the strike while he was in Santa Fe. In trying to decide where to move on at a moment's notice, he decided to see what the isolated town of Tombstone would have in store for him. He could spend a few months there and then decide what to do.

Whereas Santa Fe was becoming a cosmopolitan city, Tombstone was at the other end of the spectrum. Most of the shops were housed in makeshift tents; there were very few stick built structures, yet there was a feeling of excitement that Santa Fe couldn't match. Tommy took about a week to make the journey and carried about two thousand dollars in cash with him, which he deposited into the Wells Fargo Bank established soon after Schieffelin struck the mother lode. He left an equal amount in the Santa Fe Bank.

By now his assets totaled around ten thou- sand dollars and he had a small income each month from the installment sale to Henri and the Navajos. He thought it was good business to leave some of his cash in the Santa Fe Bank and give Joseph Beers an incentive to see that Henri and his partners lived up to their bargain. Again, as in Santa Fe, Tommy made friends with the bank manager, John Wolcomb, who gave him an overview of the town's business opportunities. Most of the men in town were trying to strike it rich by finding gold or silver, so Tommy had no problem in purchasing the only livery stable in town. The owner couldn't wait to get cash and be outfitted for prospecting. Included in the sale were two carriages, two old horses, a two story structure that housed the livery stables, and two shacks on an acre of land.

As in Santa Fe, Tommy interviewed for help and selected a young Apache Indian named Joaquin as his assistant. Joaquin was somewhat reserved. Tommy understood that an Indian trying to make a living in a white world would be reserved and self conscious. Yet the boy, aged nineteen, not only seemed grateful for the opportunity but had an energy about him that seemed contagious. He was living with his parents and siblings in a shack about a mile south of town and was the sole supporter of his parents and the younger siblings. When Tommy visited Joaquin, he was shocked at the living conditions they were forced to share and asked if they'd like to live in the loft at the livery stable. The father was a proud man and refused.

Tommy persisted and said that he needed someone on the premises at night and that it would be a bargain for both himself and Joaquin's family. They could sleep temporarily in the loft while one of the other buildings was rehabbed into suitable living quarters. The father accepted the offer.

Tommy immediately started to improve the livery business similar to his operation in Santa Fe and enlisted Joaquin and his family to round up horses to expand the operation. His parents didn't know much about horses, but his Apache cousins did and were adept at rounding up strays on the range. Tommy had a lot of patience and started showing them how to break the horses without all the bits used by cowboys. Fifteen horses had been broken and a holding pen set up on some of the acreage behind the livery stable. It took a little more patience to break horses to the carriages, but in six months' time his operation was up and running. Joaquin's mother and father took care of boarding while Joaquin and his younger brother spent time training the horses.

Soon another business venture became available. The owner of a freight hauling business was stricken with silver fever and was anxious to sell his business and start prospecting. Tommy took over a business that just needed a little care and hard work. Soon he was hauling supplies out to the mining camps and bringing silver bullion back for the assayer. He hired two more Apache's recommended by Joaquin and before long his business was as good as, if not better than, the one in Santa Fe. He wondered how long he'd be able to stay here before some- thing else came up and he'd have to move on.

The town was still rough, and Tommy wore his six-gun strapped to his right side but wasn't forced to use it for nearly a year. As the silver strikes increased, a new element entered the town in the form of gambling, saloons, and whores. It was 1881, and Wyatt

Earp and his two brothers were the law in the town. This group brought in some of the most famous gunmen of the day including Bat Masterson and Luke Short. But there was another noticeable group in Tombstone calling themselves the Cowboys, seemed to be antagonists. They always seemed to have money to spend but didn't appear to work. One evening some of this group was celebrating at the new Bird Cage Saloon. Included in that group was the famous gunfighter Luke Short. As the party broke up, Short came back to the livery stable to get his horse. He was startled by Joaquin's father and pulled his gun and ordered the old man to come forward.

The father was a proud Apache and wouldn't move for God almighty. Short decided to teach him a lesson and shoot him in the leg. As he aimed his pistol, someone behind him told him to drop the gun or he'd meet his maker. Short was drunk and belligerent and started to turn around. Tommy hit him over the head with the barrel of his gun and Short fell to the ground. Tommy took Short's weapon and dragged him over to one of stalls and laid him on the hay. Tommy was in the livery office when Short woke up and wanted to know who hit him. Tommy told him he did because he was going to shoot one of workmen. Short was angry and told Tommy that the next time he saw him, he'd kill him.

"That's provided you can," Tommy said.

"What do you mean? Do you know who I am?"

"As far as I'm concerned you're a lousy drunk, and the only reason I didn't shoot you last night is because you're a friend of Wyatt Earp. But you couldn't take me on your best day."

"Give me my gun and we'll go at it right now."

Tommy got up from his desk and handed Short his six-gun. "I've got a suggestion for you that's painless and will probably not hurt you as much as trying me."

Tommy led Short out to the back of the livery stable where there were two bottles sitting on a table about forty inches off the ground. "You and I will fire at the same time. You take the right bottle and I'll take the left and you can find out if you'd stand a chance against me."

"You're pretty confident, aren't you? Well, I'll play your game but then I'm going to kill you.

Who's going to count to three?" Short asked.

Joaquin had joined them outside. He'd seen Tommy draw before and wondered what Short would do after they played the game. "Joaquin will count. We can do it as much as you want if you think you got conned."

They stood side by side facing the table and Joaquin counted to three. When he got to three the left bottle shattered and Short's gun was still in his holster. "You jumped the count. Let's do it again," Short demanded.

Joaquin replaced the bottle on the left and started the count again. The left bottle shattered and Short's gun was still in his holster when the count went to three. Short knew there was no reason to play the game again. He had lucked out. The livery stable owner was the fastest gun he ever saw and he didn't want to go up against him.

"The only thing I ask is that no one in town knows how fast I am," Tommy said.

"Do you think I'm going to tell anyone?" With that, Luke Short walked off and went to the Bird Cage

Saloon to celebrate his near brush with death. He was a renowned gunfighter and no one had ever bested him. He knew it was different when you actually went up against someone as opposed to the game he had just played, but that livery stable owner was too fast to even try.

As time went on, he and Tommy enjoyed a beer now and then, not for anything in particular, just to pass the time of day. They seemed especially comfortable with each other.

One evening the two were having a beer when another gunfighter by the name of Charlie Storms came into the Bird Cage and started yelling at the bartender. Tommy knew Storms by reputation. When he was drinking, Storms could be a mean one and someone to avoid if possible. Luke Short, on the other hand, thought he was the best gun hand around and wasn't likely to take much guff from anyone. Soon words were exchanged between Storms and Short. Storms intimated that Short got his reputation by shooting his victims in the back or when they weren't armed. That was the last straw, and the two went outside.

Tommy followed them outside trying to act as a peacemaker, but the rift had gotten too wide and no one was listening to him. Storms was standing in the street facing both Short and Tommy, who were on the boardwalk. Just then Storms reached up and grabbed Short's arm and tried to throw him into the street, but Short wasn't as drunk as Storms and held his ground. The idea was to make Short stumble while Storms went for his gun, but Short was too fast and he shot Storms, once in the torso and once in the head. Storms was dead before he hit the ground.

Luke Short was arrested, but with Tommy giving evidence that he was acting in selfdefense, the matter was dropped. Soon Short moved to Dodge City and bought into the famous Long Branch Saloon where he remained for the next two years. Tommy heard that Short later died of consumption, but not before being involved in another famous gunfight. After moving to Fort Worth in 1883 and becoming a partner in the White Elephant Saloon, Short came into conflict with another famous gun- fighter by the name of Jim Courtright who was the former marshal of Fort Worth. It seems that Courtright had a new profession, that of selling protection to the saloon owners in town. When he approached Short, he was rebuffed. Short told him he didn't need any stinking protection.

Courtright was incensed and demanded satisfaction. The two men walked outside and strolled down the street while continuing their verbal argument. Eventually the two faced off against each other and went for their weapons. Courtright's gun got hung up in his holster and Short shot his right thumb off. Since Courtright couldn't hold a gun in his shooting hand, Short took his time and fired four more shots, killing Courtright.

Tommy would go into the Bird Cage from time to time to have a beer when he was thirsty, but he left the whores alone. He'd been keeping company with a married woman whose husband had abandoned her and two young children. She'd come into his office one day at the livery stables and asked for a job. "I've watched you, Mr. Sanchez, and can see that you've got an eye for business. Now I have a skill that I think can be beneficial to you and give me employment. Joaquin and his relatives are honest people, but they don't seem to know anything about bookkeeping, and I'll bet you're losing money tracking your income and expenses. I can set up your accounts and make it easier to see what your cash flow is and what your problems are in accounts receivable."

"Have you kept books for other businesses?" Tommy asked.

"I kept the books for a general store in Tucson before we came here. I'll do a good job for you, and it will help keep my kids fed. Why don't you give me a try?"

"I'll see how it goes for a couple of months if that's okay with you, Mrs.-?"
"I'm Janice Hutchison, Mr. Sanchez. Jan will be just fine."

It was one of the smartest moves Tommy ever made. She set up journals for each of his profit centers and soon Tommy could see where the problems were and made corrections accordingly. Tommy still hadn't purchased a home in Tombstone even though he was moderately wealthy. His insecurity due to having to leave the last three places quickly made him apprehensive. But he did rent a home at the end of Main Street and furnished it with items he purchased at the local emporium.

With the office in the good hands of Janice Hutchison, he decided to take a couple of days off and go hunting with Joaquin. When he got back in town the afternoon of the third day, he immediately went to the livery stables. Jan Hutchinson was in the office.

She looked up as he walked in. "Did you have a good time hunting?" Jan asked Tommy. "Not bad. Is there anything going on that I should know about?"

"Well, there was something I wanted to talk to you about." Tommy sat down and turned to- ward her.

"I see you don't have any lady friends, and I was wondering if you'd like to keep company with me? I was married for a few years and I enjoyed some of the benefits of married life, if you follow me. I'm not beautiful, but I know some men find me attractive, so would you like to come to dinner at my house this evening?"

Tommy sat for a few minutes trying to comprehend what he'd just been asked before he blurted out, "What time?"

They kept separate houses but their relationship was intimate. Tommy enjoyed her two children and taught her son to ride. The four of them could be seen almost every Sunday in a carriage going into the hills for a picnic.

The saloons were bringing in a great deal of money primarily from the mines, and Tomb- stone was flourishing. Tommy 's bank account was increasing, and he was thinking about buying another business. He had a livery stable, was breaking and selling horses, had a flourishing freight business, and owned several commercial buildings. One of these building housed the famous Tombstone Epitaph, the successor to the original newspaper, the Nugget. Tommy's only association with the newspaper was as an advertiser.

His banker friend was continuously bringing him opportunities, but Tommy was careful.

The latest investment proposal was intriguing to Tommy but different from anything he ever tried. There was enormous wealth in Tombstone and no cultural outlet except for the entertainment the saloons provided. Several of the businessmen had formed a group to develop a plan to open an opera house for the town. Tommy was asked to invest in the project. The plan called for an opera house to be established in the largest of Tommy's commercial office buildings. It seemed to make sense since Tommy 's building was large enough to support the enterprise.

There was always excitement in   Tombstone, whether it was nightlife, an occasional fight in the street, or a gunfight. One day Franklin Buckskin Leslie and Billy "the Kid" Claiborne decided to settle their differences in the middle of Main Street. Tommy was sitting on the porch in front of the Bird Cage Saloon when the two went at it. It seemed that the law was live and let live. Tommy never found out why there was a confrontation, but Wyatt Earp didn't seem concerned and wasn't too interested in questioning Tommy, who saw the entire confrontation. Later Earp explained that sometimes a small situation gets out of hand and someone gets killed. That's the way it was. What started as an explanation of how things worked in the sheriff 's office soon blossomed into a friendship between the two.

Doc Holliday arrived in Tombstone one day along with his constant companion, Big Nose Kate, and they became full time inhabitants of the Bird Cage Saloon, drinking and gambling. No one knew how it began, but the relationship between Holliday and Wyatt Earp flourished. They were frequently seen together in the Bird Cage. Earp ran the faro game and Doc ran the poker game. The friction between the so called Cowboy element and the Earp Brothers started slowly but soon erupted into petty little squabbles and confrontations. The Cowboy element was headed by Ike Clanton, and their primary source of income was rustling cattle and robbing an occasional supply wagon.

Tommy felt the sting when one of his freight wagons carrying silver from one of the mines was robbed. When money or silver was carried after that, Tommy had two men riding shotgun on the freight wagons and one man tracking the wagons as it returned. There were two other attempts to rob his freight wagons, but the robbers were thwarted when the outrider came up behind the robbers as they were trying to stop the freight wagon. Clanton had a ranch outside of Tombstone, but it didn't appear to Tommy that there was enough livestock on the ranch to support the number of cowboys in his entourage. Tommy suspected that the robbers were some of Clanton's associates.

When Clanton came to town one day, Tommy let him know that he didn't appreciate anyone trying to rob his freight wagons. "What make you think it was me?" Clanton asked.

"I didn't say it was you. Just pass it around that I don't like it." Clanton and his Cowboy group gave him a wide berth.

One of his freight drivers was out sick one day so Tommy took his place and delivered sup- plies to one of the mines near the Tombstone Mine of Ed Schieffelin, who'd become a good friend of his. Schieffelin had become wealthy and after a few years had sold most of his holdings, some of which he sold to Tommy, and was enjoying the good life. It was this day that the conflict between the Clantons and the Earps erupted and the famous gunfight at the Ok Corral took place, in an alley nearby. Billy Clanton and a couple of the Cowboys were wounded or killed during the gunfight.

Significantly, the OK Corral was the livery stables owned by Tommy Sanchez, and the notoriety that followed was unprecedented. Reporters flocked to the town and soon every- one appeared to have witnessed the gunfight. Joaquin and his family were present at the livery stable office during the gunfight and were interviewed sixtimes. Their pictures were taken and money was pressed in their pockets to help gain an interview with the elusive Tommy Sanchez, who was making himself scarce. While the re- porters were in town, Tommy spent time away from Tombstone fishing and hunting with a couple of Joaquin's relatives. He didn't want any part of the hysteria generated by the gunfight.

Immediately after the gunfight, County Sheriff Johnny Behan arrested the Earps and subpoenaed Joaquin and his parents to give their version of the gunfight, but Joaquin and his parents continually said they didn't see anything.

During the trial, one of the Cowboys said that Ike Clanton knew Tommy would be out of town that day and used that as an excuse to take over the livery stables, and for all practical purposes Joaquin and his family were imprisoned during the gunfight. Tommy convinced Joaquin and his parents to testify. The Earps were exonerated and soon another feud began between the Earps and the Behan followers. Eventually this resulted in the wounding of Virgil Earp and the killing of Morgan Earp. But that was only the beginning. Subsequently, Wyatt went on a rampage and eventually killed all four men who were responsible for the wounding of Virgil and the murder of Morgan.

Tommy was successful in escaping the number of visiting reporters, but the Tombstone Epitaph was another issue. A featured article identified him as the owner of the OK Corral and that he had previously owned a livery business in Santa Fe. His options were dwindling, but he was tired of running. He liked the seclusion of the town and the fact that he was successful here; he didn't want to leave. Intuitively he knew that other papers would pick up on the article and that someone would come with some form of warrant or more than likely a wanted poster and he'd have to defend himself. He decided to talk to Wyatt Earp and see what he'd suggest. Virgil was really the town marshal, but Wyatt was the titular head of the family, and Virgil ac- quiesced to Wyatt on most matters.

Since Earp ran the faro game at the Bird Cage Saloon, he was able to use one of its private rooms on the second floor whenever he wished, and this is where they met. Tommy took his time and told Earp what happened in the Saddleback Saloon in Laramie on that fateful afternoon. He also told him about the posse he led to get back the gold for the town in Colorado and how he had stopped an attempted bank robbery in Santa Fe. He told him about Judd Harker and how any- one he didn't like seemed to get shot while trying to escape from his jail.

"Have you tried to get a pardon?" Earp asked. "No. All I've done in the past is just move on hoping that no one could find me. It seems I have a touch for business and when you become successful, you draw attention to yourself. I guess I could become a bum, but you'd probably throw me in jail and then you'd find some wanted poster on me and I'm back in the same situation."

Earp couldn't help but laugh. "You're a funny man. Are you really that fast with a gun?" "I seem to be," Tommy responded.

"After a couple of beers one evening Luke Short told me about the run-in he had with you. Now after hearing about Laramie and that hotel episode, I think you're as fast as he said you were. Well, no one's going to arrest you here. Besides, I don't think a Wyoming warrant can be served in this state. I personally know the governor, and he couldn't give a shit about what some other state wants. Why don't you hire an attorney and see if you can get a pardon? You're probably rich enough to buy one. Check out who wants to be governor of Wyoming and see what he wants to get you a pardon. What's the price of being left alone?"

"I'm going to take your advice. If I have to leave, just let me know and I'll move on."

"It's not going to happen while me and Virgil are here."

The committee to develop a plan to refurbish Tommy's commercial building into an opera house was meeting at noon in the Bird Cage Saloon. Chairing the meeting was John Wolcomb, the president of the Tombstone National Bank and a personal friend and advisor to Tommy. Others present were Tommy; George Sinclair, a local rancher; Geoffrey Combs, the owner of the Bird Cage; and Saul Schwartz, the owner of the Tombstone Epitaph. A preliminary architectural plan had been submitted by a firm out of Santa Fe and had been approved. Today's meeting was to address fund raising and a time schedule for the ambitious plan. Tommy's view was to raise at least fifty percent of the funds needed before they started the retrofit of his building. He didn't want to start tearing his building apart and then find out they couldn't reach their financial goal and he'd be left with a gutted building and sub- sequent loss of income.

His bookkeeper, Jan, had worked up a pro forma for five years. He had passed out copies to the committee members at a previous meeting and was seeking some feedback. Most agreed with the approach, and when put to a vote, it carried on a four-to-one vote. Geoffrey Combs had voted no, but didn't give a reason. The group finished lunch and were developing an investor's list when they were interrupted by two men who walked up to their table.

Tommy looked up and didn't recognize either of them at first. Almost eight years had passed since he last saw Judd Harker the day he came to arrest Tommy for killing his deputy. Harker was heavier and had grown a beard, and when he smiled, his yellow teeth showed. The other man was unfamiliar to Tommy, who assumed he was one of Harker's deputies.

Harker's voice was more of a snarl when he faced the group. "I don't mean to interrupt you fine gentlemen, but I wonder if you're aware that there's a killer in your midst." Harker sneered as he pointed to Tommy.

Tommy didn't move. Harker wasn't pointing a gun at him, nor was the other man with Harker." You're a long way from home, Judd. Why don't you turn around and go back where you came from?" Tommy said.

Harker drew his gun and aimed it at Tommy. "I'm taking you back to Laramie so you can hang for killing my deputy. Now get up or I'll shoot you where you're sitting."

He motioned for his deputy to get behind Tommy, but before he could move, Wyatt Earp walked into the Bird Cage. Tommy had noticed that the bartender sent one of his waiters out as soon as Harker started the confrontation. "No one's going to shoot anyone here unless it's me doing the shooting. Now put your gun down and don't make any sudden moves."

"Who the hell are you?" Harker asked.

"I'm Wyatt Earp, and I don't give a shit who you are and what you want in my town unless you want to tell me who your undertaker will be."

The color drained from Harker's face as he stared at Tommy, trying to assess his chances of shooting him and surviving Wyatt Earp. "I'm Sheriff Harker, and this man is wanted for killing my deputy in Laramie, Wyoming."

"You have until I count to three to drop your weapon on the floor or I'll kill you and the guy you brought with you, "said Earp. "One, two

"He didn't get to three because Judd Harker dropped his weapon and the other man raised his hands.

Earp pointed at Harker and his deputy. "I want you two to come with me to the jail. If you don't, I'll kill you right here. Tommy, you come with us. Let's see if we can sort this out. Virgil's out of town and I'm acting sheriff." Earp's gun was still in his holster.

Tommy, Harker, and his deputy sat in front of Earp's desk as Earp spoke to Harker. "Show me your warrant."

Harker produced a folded worn paper and handed it to Earp, who took his time reading it. "It seems to be legal, but it's pretty old. How do I know it's still valid?" "You have my word as a law enforcement officer. Now can I take my prisoner back with me to Wyoming?"

"I don't know. I want to check a few things out first before I say one way or another. It'll take at least three or four days. In the interim, you and your deputy keep a low profile. Where are you staying?"

"At the Tombstone Hotel. You know, Marshal Earp, there's some in this town would be glad to get rid of Sanchez."

"Now who would that be?" Earp asked.

When Harker didn't respond, Earp said he'd see him in a couple of days. Until then Harker and his deputy wouldn't be able to carry a firearm in the town of Tombstone.

"How are we going to protect ourselves?"

"Well, against Tommy, you wouldn't have a chance even if you carried five guns each. I think I'll let your friends in town look out for you until I can get to the bottom of this." With that he dis- missed Harker and his deputy and asked Tommy to stay.

"Someone wants you out of town. I'll bet they wired Harker to come here. I'm going to check this whole thing out. You've got no worry; they're not going to take you while I'm around. But I'd stay clear of them until then. You might want to find out who sent for them."

Tommy spent the next two days watching Harker and his deputy and who they contacted while in town. Either they were forewarned or smarter than Tommy thought, because neither were approached or approached anyone in town. The few friends he had in town were at a loss to understand why anyone here would go out of their way to cause him any trouble.

Earp was suspicious. The first thing he did was wire Laramie and ask who the sheriff was and the status of the warrant for Tommy Sanchez. It took three days to get his response. Then he met with Tommy, Harker, and his deputy in his office.

"Well, the warrant is legal and it's enforceable in Wyoming, but not in Arizona. The problem is that Sheriff Harker isn't a sheriff; he's probably a bounty hunter impersonating a sheriff. It seems that Harker was voted out of office six years ago. He got on the wrong side of a man named Mike Jacobs, a rich rancher outside Laramie. So this means that Harker can't enforce anything here. But our governor is upset with Mr. Harker for coming here and upsetting one of our leading citizens and causing him undue stress, and he wants Harker and his so-called deputy arrested and sent to jail. Now what do you think about that?"

It was the deputy that spoke up first. "Harker told me he was a sheriff and wanted to enforce a warrant. He agreed to pay me fifty dollars. I thought he was legit. I don't want to go to jail. I'm sorry I ever met this son-of-a-bitch."

"Well, that just about says it all, doesn't it," Earp added.

"He's still a killer, and no matter what you say, that warrants legal. He has to pay for killing my deputy."

"Well, he not going to pay while he's in Arizona, but you got two choices, spend three years in Yuma or get the hell out of here as fast as you can because I'm drawing up a warrant for your arrest, and any bounty hunter can collect one hundred dollars for bringing you in dead or alive. You have one hour head start and then I'm posting the warrant. Now get the hell out of my town."

"What about our weapons?" Harker asked.

"I'll bet if I give you your weapons, Tommy will come looking for you. My advice is to leave now and count your blessings that I don't let him go after you."

Tommy didn't take any chances that Judd Harker wouldn't change his mind, so he followed at a discreet distance for a day before he turned back, reasonably assured that they wouldn't return. To be sure, he had the Indians keep a lookout in the direction the two left and as an added measure he wore his sidearm for the next few days. He and his girlfriend,

Jennifer, talked at length trying to determine who wanted him out of town. They couldn't think of anyone.

CHAPTER ELEVEN

Two weeks after Harker and his associate left town, Tommy was informed that the commit- tee to bring an opera house to Tombstone was meeting for a working lunch. Tommy retrieved the plans to rehab his commercial building, looked over the plans again, and was prepared to brief the committee that he was in favor of the changes.

George Sinclair called the meeting to order as soon as the Bird Cage had delivered sandwiches and beer for the committee. The chairman, John Wolcomb, was on vacation; yet, the remaining four members could vote on the changes to Tommy's building. He quickly ran through the minutes and raised the issue of the changes the committee requested. Tommy grabbed the plans and was ready to cover the changes requested at the last meeting, but before he could speak, Geoffrey Combs raised the issue that the committee hadn't approved the selection of Tommy's building for the opera house.

"I thought the issue was resolved last meeting when we voted four-to-one to approve the building. This meeting is to discuss changes. That's why Tommy went to the expense of having the plans changed. Am I missing something here?" George Sinclair asked.

After several minutes of discussion between Sinclair and Combs with Tommy and Schwartz, the owner of the Tombstone Epitaph remaining silent, Combs said. "I changed my mind and I think Sol did also, so I want another vote to determine if we're to move forward with Mr. Sanchez' building."

Sinclair called for a short recess and asked to speak with Tommy in private. They stepped out of the room for a few minutes and Sinclair said, "I think the deck is stacked. Combs waited until Wolcomb went on vacation before he called for this meeting."

Tommy was listening intently. "What do you suggest?"

"They can't have a quorum if you and I leave and refuse to vote."

"You mean just leave?"

"Yes and we wait until Wolcomb returns and then we can have a meeting. I smell a polecat and I think its Combs. He's got an agenda."

Sinclair didn't return to the meeting, so Tommy went back in the room and picked up his plans. "George and I are ready to meet again but after John Wolcomb returns."

He smiled at both Combs and Schwartz as he picked up his plans and left the room. He'd sensed some friction between himself and Combs and wondered if there was more to it than just dislike. He'd have to keep an eye on Combs and Schwartz as well.

Soon the uproar over the warrant subsided and thing were back to normal, but Tommy was no longer on the committee to get an opera house for Tombstone and wasn't interested in helping in any way. As soon as Wolcomb returned, he resigned from the committee and withdrew his building from any consideration. His interests were expanding, and he started looking in other lucrative areas in the Southwest. His banker, sensing his depositor had an acute business mind, was constantly recommending other business ventures. If

Tommy succeeded, the bank would also benefit. He started traveling to some of the surrounding towns to see what financial prospects might be available; he'd be gone for up to a week at a time. Joaquin and his family could easily handle the day-to-day operation, and with Jennifer watching the receivables, he was able to use his time more profitably by seeing what else was available.

From the time Fort Huachuca opened in 1877, the detachment there was in constant need of cavalry mounts since the Chiricahua Indians led by Geronimo were constantly raiding the new settlers in Arizona. On one of his trips out of town, Tommy signed a contract with the fort commander and had Joaquin and his brothers deliver the mounts. Since Joaquin and his brothers were Apache, Geronimo and his band left them alone and allowed them to move freely between the fort and Tombstone.

Tommy's next trip was to Bisbee, where copper had been found in 1877. He wanted to see if there was an opportunity to expand his freighting business. He'd been sending his wagons to the rail spur outside Santa Fe, picking up supplies, and then transporting the goods to the miners and citizens in Tombstone. He felt it was a stretch but doable to expand his operation all the way to Bisbee. He met with two of the largest mining operators and signed a six month contract. The mining operators were willing to take a chance but wanted an out clause if Tommy couldn't produce.

He was riding back at dusk and estimated that he was about two miles from Tombstone when he heard a shot and felt Jupiter falter then drop to one knee. He quickly dismounted and saw that Jupiter was shot in his right rump. Tommy was afraid the horse would go into shock, so he forced the animal on his side and examined the wound. It was a little too deep for him to try to remove the bullet, so he gave Jupiter some water and then grabbed his Remington.

The shots had come from his right side. He waited another five minutes and then started to crawl in a circular direction toward the origin of the shots to see if he could get around the shooter. It took him thirty minutes to reach the spot where he thought the shooter would be, but the shooter had disappeared. Tommy found a spent casing and tracks heading toward Tombstone and noted an anomaly in the right front hoof of the shooter's horse. Tommy pocketed the spent cartridge and walked back to Jupiter. The horse was on his feet and appeared to be noticeably hurt, so Tommy gave him some more water and slowly walked the animal the two miles to Tombstone.

When he reached his stables, he had Joaquin and his father work on the animal. The father was especially adept at treating sick animals. After carefully examining Jupiter, the father heated a knife, and with Tommy and Joaquin holding onto the animal, he extracted the bullet in the horse's rump. They cauterized the wound and moved the animal to one of the holding stalls. The father said he thought Jupiter would be okay in a couple of days, but no riding for two weeks because he thought the wound would need that much time to heal.

Tommy took the slug from the father, examined it carefully, and went to his home. It was too late to do anything tonight, but the first thing in the morning he'd walk down the street and see if he could pick out any markings in the dirt that would indicate that the shooter had come to Tombstone.

After breakfast he strolled down the street toward the Bird Cage Saloon, carefully looking for any tracks that could belong to the shooter's horse. He found the tracks and followed them to a horse tied up to the rail in front of the Bird Cage Saloon. Just to be sure, he lifted the horse's right front foot and saw the anomaly in the shoe. Tommy walked up to the front of the Bird Cage and looked over the cafe doors at the entrance. He could see several regulars, a couple of girls, and one or two businessmen sitting at one table. At another table was Geoffrey Combs, two of his associates, and a stranger. Tommy decided to sit on one of the benches on the walkway outside the Bird Cage and see who would claim the horse. Thirty minutes later, the stranger who was at Combs's table came outside and looked around. Tommy had the latest Tombstone Epitaph in front of his face and was able to watch the stranger without being seen. The stranger didn't seem to be in a hurry as he walked up to his horse and started to mount.

He turned quickly as he heard Tommy ask, "Why'd you take a shot at me out on the Bisbee Trail?"

The stranger turned and flipped open his coat, exposing a six-gun in a holster strapped to his left hip. Several people walking by the Bird Cage stopped to watch. "I don't know what you're talking about. I just came into town to get a drink and now I'm leaving, so you'd be wise to get out of my way, if you know what I mean."

Tommy didn't move. "I have no problem with you leaving town as soon as you tell me who sent you to ambush me."

"You're starting to get me riled, Mister, now let it go and be on your way," the stranger responded.

Tommy, who was on the walkway in front of the saloon, shifted his position so that he was looking down and straight at the stranger. "I want you to drop your gun and come with me to the sheriff's office and settle this matter." Tommy's voice was very calm.

The stranger almost laughed out loud. He shifted his weight to his left foot and drew his revolver. Halfway through his draw he cried out in pain and dropped his gun. He reached over and grabbed his left shoulder where Tommy had shot him. After putting the gun back in his holster, he walked down the stairs and pushed the stranger toward the sheriff's office. Someone had told Virgil Earp about the confrontation in front of the Bird Cage, and he was halfway across the street when the shot was fired. He continued walking slowly up to the two who were now in the street.

"This guy tried to bushwhack me on the Bisbee Trail, but instead he shot Jupiter. I tried to get him to go to your office and settle this, but he pulled a gun on me and I shot him." Tommy said.

Virgil questioned several of the townspeople who'd watched the shooting. At least two told him that Tommy asked the stranger to go to the sheriff's office and settle it and that the stranger pulled a gun but Sanchez drew faster." Someone call the doctor," Virgil said. "Tommy, you and this guy come to my office. I want to find out what's going on."

When they arrived at Virgil Earp's office, Tommy handed him the casing that was left along the trail where someone had tried to ambush him. He also gave him the slug taken from Jupiter. He told Earp about the mark on the horse's right front shoe and how he trailed it to the Bird Cage and waited to see who would claim the animal. "So you didn't actually see him take a shot at you?" Virgil asked Tommy.

"No, but this is pretty conclusive, don't you think?" Virgil nodded.

"I never saw this guy before, so I'd like to know who paid him to ambush me. While I was in the saloon, I saw him talking to Geoffrey Combs and two of his associates," Tommy said.

Virgil turned to the stranger, who now was being treated by Dr. Harold. "Why did you try to ambush Sanchez?"

"I didn't do any such thing. He's a liar. I never saw him until he braced me outside the Bird Cage."

Virgil turned to his deputy. "Bring this guy's horse over here, see if he's carrying a rifle, and then get Geoffrey Combs. I want to hear what he has to say."

While they were waiting for the deputy to return with the gun and Combs, Virgil interrogated the stranger and found out that his name was Frank Jessup from Santa Fe and he was looking for work. He didn't know Geoffrey Combs and he didn't ambush Sanchez.

The deputy returned with the stranger's horse and said that Combs would be over shortly. The stranger was carrying a Winchester, and the shell Tommy picked up on the Bisbee Trail and the slug from Jupiter matched the bullets in the Winchester. Virgil checked it out and found that it had been fired recently. The deputy had checked the horse's hoof and confirmed what Tommy said about the shoe. In addition, the clay on the hoof matched the soil on the trail.

"I'm pretty much convinced that you tried to bushwhack Sanchez and that may get you twenty years in Yuma Prison," Virgil said. Virgil had Jessup take everything out of his pockets and the deputy took everything out of Jessup's saddlebags. Most things were what a cowboy would carry with him from town to town. What set Jessup's personals apart was the two hundred dollars in cash that he had in his shirt. "For a cowboy who's looking for work, you seem pretty well heeled. Where did you get the two hundred dollars?"

"It's mine and I earned it," Jessup fired back.

"Okay. I'll want to check on the place you earned it. So let me know and I'll check it out." Virgil got out a pad and pencil and asked for the information. Jessup didn't provide it.

About this time Combs arrived at the jail and wouldn't make eye contact with either Tommy or Jessup. When Virgil questioned him about the shooting on the trail, Combs denied any knowledge of the shooting and said he didn't know Frank Jessup.

"Then why were you talking to him this morning at the Bird Cage?' Earp asked.

"He came to our table and asked if we knew if anyone was hiring. I thought I was being courteous to buy him a drink, but that's all there was to it." Combs was indignant that he'd been called out of a meeting to run over to the jail and was too busy to give the sheriff any more of his time. He just got up and left.

Virgil placed Jessup in a cell. "You've got a problem. The evidence says you tried to bush- whack Sanchez, and I'll bet someone hired you to get him. If I were you, I'd tell who put you up to this and save yourself a lot of time in jail. After they convict you, it'll be too late. Of course that's my opinion, and it's really up to a judge and jury, but you're going to stay in jail until the circuit judge comes next week. You ought to get your- self a lawyer. You're going to need one."

"That guy that shot me was lucky. My hand got caught in my coat," Jessup said.

Virgil laughed. "That's the luckiest thing that ever happened to you because if not, you'd be dead. Tommy Sanchez is the fastest gun there ever was and probably ever will be. You sleep on that."

CHAPTER TWELVE

The Arizona Territory was young, and there was a shortage of judges. In order to handle all the judicial work for a new and emerging state, judges were each assigned to a specific district. It was their responsibility to visit each locale within that district on a periodic basis, hence the name circuit judge. Judge Samuel L. Carson was assigned to the southeastern part of Arizona, which included Fort Huachuca to the west and Bisbee to the south. Normally Carson would be in Tombstone every two months but could vary his itinerary if he was contacted by telegraph and could then assess his trial load and reprioritize his schedule if necessary.

The circuit was made possible because every judge could be contacted by telegraph, and in an emergency another judge could leave his district and fill in if it was important. Homicides were the highest priorities, followed by robberies and other felonies. Attempted murder, as in the case of Frank Jessup, was prioritized right behind murder. The trial was to be held in the Bird Cage Saloon because it could hold the most people.

There were only three attorneys practicing law in Tombstone; one was Tommy Sanchez's attorney and was applying for a pardon to the state of Wyoming for him. Another drew up wills and real estate contracts and had no experience in the court room. The other was retained by Frank Jessup; his name was Martin Merry weather. He had limited experience but was aggressive and tried to present a favorable case for Jessup, but the majority of the evidence, even though circumstantial, was against him. The state of Arizona was represented by State Attorney General McKinney Johnson, who, similar to Judge Carson, was a traveling prosecutor. When the jury retired to deliberate, Jessup's attorney approached the judge to see if a deal could be made if Jessup told them who paid him to kill Tommy Sanchez.

Carson set up a meeting to discuss this latest development. He invited Virgil and Wyatt Earp, Jessup, his attorney, Tommy Sanchez, and the attorney general. While they were discussing a potential plea by Jessup if he revealed who hired him, the jury foreman passed word to the judge that they had reached a verdict.

"I'm inclined to let this go to a verdict, but if you want to talk, I'll listen, but I won't make any promises in advance," Judge Carson told every- one present.

Jessup and his attorney moved to a corner of the room and were in a heated discussion. Tommy couldn't make out everything that was said between the two, but he distinctly heard Merry weather state that a fast jury usually meant a guilty verdict. The two seemed to reach accord and walked back to the table.

"Here's what I propose, Judge Carson, if Mr. Johnson is amenable. Jessup changes his plea to guilty and he receives a sentence of two years at a penitentiary other than Yuma, which might mean a death sentence to Mr. Jessup if he was incarcerated there. In return he identifies the person or persons who hired him."

Judge Carson turned to the attorney general. "What do you think, Mr. Johnson?"

"I certainly would like to know who set this up, but I don't want to agree to anything until I hear who it is. For all we know, he can give us a name of somebody we don't know and have no way of arresting unless we extradite the individual. He has to tell us first, and if it's someone who's accessible then I might agree to some re- duction in his sentence, but that's after I hear the verdict."

"Well, you heard it. Mr. Johnson wants to hear what the jury has to say. I tend to agree with him. What say you, Mr. Merry weather?"

"What will Mr. Johnson accept as a sentence if we give him the name?"

"I want to hear the jury speak. If the verdict is not guilty, Mr. Jessup is free. If he's found guilty, then we can meet again and you can plead your case."

Judge Carson called the jury back into the court room and asked the foreman to read the verdict. The verdict was guilty of attempted murder. Tommy was looking at Geoffrey Combs, who was sitting to his left on the other side of the aisle. It was as though the color had drained from Combs's face. He and his two associates immediately left the Bird Cage.

Merryweather asked the judge for a meeting prior to sentencing. The judge agreed and asked everyone who participated in the first meeting to come back into the office the Bird Cage provided for him.

When they were seated, Judge Carson spoke directly to Jessup. "This is an informal meeting, so if you've got something to tell us, now's the time before I pass sentence."

Before Jessup could speak, his attorney interrupted. "What's on the table for my client if he tells what he knows?"

Judge Carson looked at McKinney Johnson for an answer. "You've got a problem, Mr. Jessup. You've been convicted as the one who attempted to murder Tommy Sanchez. I'd like to get who- ever hired you, but if you produce a name, how do we know we can prove what you say is true? It would be your word versus theirs, unless you have some proof. No matter what happens, you're not going to be set free. The name means nothing; it's the proof that you have to trade. The judge and I are honorable men, but we're not fools. I think the first thing you have to do is give us a name or several names."

Merry weather nodded to Jessup, who took a drink of water and told his story. "I was approached by Judd Harker in Laramie last month and shown a wanted poster on Tommy Sanchez. Harker told me that Sanchez shot and killed his deputy and that when he went to Tombstone to arrest Sanchez, Wyatt Earp wouldn't let him. He said that Sanchez was wanted dead or alive. Since he couldn't go back to Tombstone, he wanted to know if I'd be interested in either bringing Sanchez back to Laramie or killing him. He told me that it was worth four hundred dollars one way or the other. I'd be given two hundred dollars once I reached Tombstone and two hundred more after the job was done. Harker had a contact in Tombstone who was keeping him informed about Sanchez and who would come up with the money. He said the man's name was Jeff Strait who worked for Geoffrey Combs at the Bird Cage.

"If I wanted the job, I had to contact Strait and collect the two hundred dollars from him. I was broke and needed work; Harker advanced me twenty dollars so I could get to Tombstone. I thought I was doing law enforcement business and that it would be okay. I got into town two weeks ago and met with Strait at the Bird Cage. He told me about Sanchez and his trip to Bisbee and said it would probably be best if I did the job out of town. He gave me two hundred dollars and said I could have the balance after I did the job.

"Sanchez was pointed out to me by Strait and I staked out his livery stable. When he went off to Bisbee, I asked the Indian at the stables when he'd be back and he said in a week, so I waited six days and then went out about two miles down the Bisbee Trail and found a good spot. I'm a good shot with a rifle and assumed that it'd be a piece of cake. I went out three consecutive days and waited until dark. On the third day, Sanchez showed. I didn't know I missed. When I went to the Bird Cage, Strait introduced me to the owner who asked if I had a successful day. I said I did. When I asked Strait for the balance, he said that they wanted to wait until Sanchez's body was brought in. He said to hang around a day and then they'd pay me."

"Was Combs in on it?"

"I don't know. I just assumed that Strait was fronting for him, especially when he said they'd pay me. That's all I know."

Judge Carson turned to Johnson. "What do you think, McKinney?"

"It's thin. Just because you say it doesn't mean it's true. What proof do you have that Harker and Strait conspired to have you kill Tommy Sanchez?"

"I have the wanted poster on Sanchez and a note in Harker's handwriting to introduce me to Strait."

Judge Carson turned to Johnson, who took it as a cue to continue the interrogation of Jessup. "Do you have these with you?"

Merryweather reached into his briefcase and handed the two items to Johnson, who took a few minutes and looked at the judge. "These couldn't get anyone convicted of anything. It's his word against theirs. I couldn't recommend any reduction in sentencing off these two items. Perhaps if we can confront Strait, he'll give up Combs."

Judge Carson turned to Virgil Earp. "Maybe Wyatt can bring Strait in here and we can question him while Jessup and his attorney are present."

When Wyatt Earp went to the Bird Cage saloon, he was told by the bartender that Combs and Strait had gone to Santa Fe on business and didn't say when they'd be back. "Kind of sudden, wasn't it?" Earp asked. The bartender just shrugged his shoulders.

Carson and Johnson concluded there was nothing they could do other than passing sentence on Jessup. They called the court back in session, and over Merryweather's strenuous objections, Judge Carson sentenced Jessup to ten years at Yuma for attempted murder. In private, Judge Carson, McKinney Johnson, Virgil and Wyatt Earp agreed to keep Jessup in the Tombstone jail for ten days while Wyatt went to Santa Fe to find Strait and bring him back.

CHAPTER THIRTEEN

The first leg of their trip to Los Angeles was through Tucson, Arizona, aboard the Southern Pacific Railroad. Sarah was disappointed that her time with Tommy Sanchez was short lived; she was unable to see him that morning before they departed by carriage to Lemy for their trip to Tucson, twentyfour hours away. The McIntyres were excited and their daughter in awe of the experience of the West. Travel by rail was in its infancy, and many of the facilities were non-existent or makeshift at best. There was no dining on the train, but box lunches were available for a price. Restroom facilities were a portable pot in a room at the rear of the coach. There was some flexibility in that the seats in the coach section could be moved so that passengers could either face forward or to the rear of the train, making it ideal for families traveling together.

They had just settled down to enjoy their box lunches when Sarah, who was facing to the rear of the train, saw two riders paralleling the train and grab onto a metal handle attached to the rear of each car and apparently board the train. She remarked to James that it was a funny way to get on board the train. James had heard of train robbers and, without anyone except Sarah seeing him, immediately put his cash into his sock. The rear door of the railway coach burst open and two masked men with guns drawn shouted to the passengers to give them all their valuables as they walked down the aisle.

When one of the masked men approached James and Sarah, he made mention that she was a comely bitch and reached for a brooch she had fastened to her jacket over her right breast. In so doing, he grabbed her breast, and she retaliated by sticking him in the hand with a hair pin. He let out a loud shout and reached to strike her, but she was too quick and jabbed him in his other hand with her pin; he dropped his weapon on the floor. James grabbed the man's arm, pulled the robber toward him, and wrapped his arm around the man's throat while Sarah picked up the weapon and placed the barrel against the robber's temple. The second robber ran down the aisle threatening everyone unless Sarah and James released his accomplice.

They were at a standstill until the second man pointed his weapon at the Mcintyres' young daughter and demanded Sarah hand over the weapon. Sarah didn't want to jeopardize the girl, but she didn't want to give in to the threat. "We'll release your accomplice as soon as you holster your weapon and leave the train, but I'll not return your weapon. I can assure you that I'm an excellent shot and have fired a weapon many times. If you shoot the girl I'll shoot you and then your accomplice."

Sarah turned the weapon and pointed it directly at the head of the second robber. "This can end two ways. Both of you alive and off this train or both of you dead and an innocent child destroyed," she said as she stared at the robber.

Jane Mcintyre was hysterical and her minister husband was counseling Sarah to give up her gun and let the gunmen have everyone's valuables. The rest of the passengers remained quiet as the drama unfolded. But Sarah had been under pressure in other situations and knew that it wasn't likely that the gunman would shoot a little girl. He was using her as leverage and probably couldn't believe that a woman could stand up to him. The other robber being restrained by James tried to grab Sarah's weapon, but James was too strong for him and squeezed tighter on his neck and told him not to move or he'd break his neck.

Sarah didn't know whether the gunman believed that she was a good shot so she gave him a demonstration. She aimed carefully and shot the overhead lamp at the rear of the coach. Everyone turned in unison and saw what she hit and turned back in awe to look at the little blond woman as she threatened a masked gunman.

Before anyone could respond, Sarah continued, "Now I suggest that you move backward toward the rear of the coach. We'll follow with your friend. Believe me; I will shoot both of you if necessary."

The silence was deafening. The armed robber didn't know what to do, but he chose the lesser of two evils, holstered his weapon, let go of Nancy Mcintyre, and started moving backwards. James took this as his cue and forced the other robber to his feet and began pushing him toward the rear of the coach. Sarah was to the right of James and had her weapon aimed directly at the retreating armed robber. When the four of them reached the door, the armed robber opened it, and all moved to the ramp at the end of car. With both robbers facing the stairs, Sarah ordered both men to jump or she'd shoot them. They jumped and began rolling over and over but eventually came up on their feet.

James was stunned. "Sarah, where did you learn to shoot like that?" She smiled and said she'd tell him later.

The passengers thanked Sarah and James, and all of them asked her if she really would've shot the robbers if they didn't leave. Sarah responded that they had given her no choice. One of the passengers stated that she was sure one of the robbers was the notorious Black Bart who'd been robbing trains and stagecoaches in this area for the past three years.

But the McIntyres were not as forgiving. Pastor Mcintyre spoke to her. "I know you thought you were doing what you thought was best, but the risk was too great, and the risk wasn't yours but someone other than you. The result was good, but not the trauma it caused my wife and me. Nancy wasn't your daughter."

Before they reached Tucson, a middle aged man approached Sarah and James and identified himself as the editor of the Tucson Daily and complimented both for the heroic action they took. He wanted to do a feature for the Daily and asked if he could ask them some questions. Sarah was reluctant, but James was so exhilarated and so proud of his sister that he tentatively agreed, but with a caveat that she may refuse to answer some of his questions. Sarah had not been totally forthcoming with her brother on her life with the Oglala Sioux and probably never would. Some things such as the raids she experienced, been on, and observed were better left unsaid. James would probably never understand.

The second leg of their trip would be by stagecoach since the railroad didn't extend to San Diego or Los Angeles. Rather than book pas- sage on the existing line, James had contracted for a private coach with a driver and another man to ride as a guard.

It would take six days of continuous riding in the coach to reach Los Angeles. They'd be able to use the existing stage line's stops for resting, food, and, if necessary, a change of horses.

The six days became eight days because of the constant stops required for the young girl who wasn't used to a trip as strenuous as this and the women who needed frequent rest stops. Bill, the driver, and his partner, Shorty, were the owners of the private stage line and made the round trip to Los Angeles or San Diego once a month. Whereas the usual fare was two hundred dollars each, the chartered coach was double that price. James had been very generous and paid the entire fare for the McIntyres, but the once strong relationship was barely intact since the incident on the train. Jane Mcintyre wouldn't speak to Sarah, who in turn was hurt and didn't understand. Her husband said to give Jane a few days and she'd come around. "Jane was watching everything unfold and she didn't have any say in the action taking place," he told Sarah.

At one of the stops along the route, they had about a thirty minute wait to change horses, so James and Sarah took a walk around the way station and James asked her about her ability to fire a weapon.

"When I was married to Crazy Horse, I went on several raids before I gave birth to my first child. My husband took pleasure in teaching me to how to fire a rifle and a handgun that he captured as trophies on some of his raids. I was grateful that he did, because our village was raided by another tribe once while he was away on business. There were no men left in camp and only myself and several of the other wives. The only weapons available were bows and arrows except for my handgun. It was only a small raiding party, and

I think I caught them off guard as I fired first at one of the raiders and then another. I didn't hit anyone, but the sight of a little blond pregnant Indian squaw was probably more than their masculine egos could take and they broke and ran."

He laughed. "Weren't you afraid?"

"No. Crazy Horse taught me very well and to only fire when I had no other choice. One of the myths about Crazy Horse was that he was a cold blooded savage. I can assure you he was not. He took no pleasure in killing. His goal was always to provide food for the village and protect our way of life. It was only when he thought there was no other choice did he fight."

"Do you miss him?"

"In some ways I miss him; in others no. I want to assimilate into white culture and see if I can be productive. He wouldn't have survived in this society. He was very uncomfortable when we were in Washington; he needed to be free."

They arrived in Los Angeles at ten a.m. on the eighth day of their trip and were in dire need of bath and clean clothes. Sarah and James were met by an Overland Transfer employee and driven to the prestigious Pico House, built in 1869 in the middle of the town. They said good-bye to the McIntyres who were met by the deacon of their church. Sarah and James agreed to visit with them within a couple of days, but both couples knew that probably wouldn't hap- pen. The trauma of the attempted train robbery and Sarah's action couldn't be assimilated by the McIntyres.

James had arranged for adjoining suites at the Pico House for himself and Sarah. His intent was to lavish her with the best that money could buy for the next few months. His conscience was still bothering him for his initial greed and his insensitivity for all that Sarah had been through. The Pico House had gas lights in all the rooms while the rooms and suites on the second and third floors had baths. This was one treat that Sarah thoroughly enjoyed, and James was kept waiting an extra thirty minutes before Sarah was ready for dinner in the lavish restaurant of the Pico House.

Los Angeles in the 1880s was being transformed from an unruly city to a small industrial juggernaut. Law and order had come to the town; the stigma of being the first murder capital of the United States was forgotten, and progress was manifested by the number of commercial enterprises developing in the city. The city had been embarrassed when it was featured in the Los Angeles Times and New York Times for the blood spilled in its streets and was making every effort to distance itself from that part of their history.

Still the Los Angeles that Sarah and James came to visit was bustling with activity. Every- thing seemed new, big, and expensive. Their first stop the next day was to the First National Bank where James presented a letter of credit and was able to draw funds to use on their vacation.

Preston Miles, the bank president, was taken with Sarah and James and invited both to dinner that evening as his guest at the famous Delmonico Steak Restaurant in the Prescott House on Main Street. Sarah was like a little child in a candy store. After years of deprivation and poor living conditions, she was thrown into the world of fine food, exquisite fashions, and superb accommodations. James was content to spoil her. Miles was an entertaining individual who spent most of the evening staring at the beautiful Sarah. The remainder of the time he spent informing them about the growth in Southern California and recommended that they tour the state and judge for themselves.

Over the next week they visited every monument within the area and once, on a lark, went with Prescott Miles to Chinatown for lunch. Chinatown in the 1880swas a small enclave yet an active commercial area along Calle De Los Negros with laundries, restaurants, and vegetable stands. The Chinese who came en masse to help plan and build the railroads had fallen into disfavor once the major portion of the railroads were completed. They had difficulty in finding employment and soon found that the only employment available was in menial jobs such as dishwashers in restaurants, laundry workers, and vegetable stand sellers. But their plight paled in comparison to the Native Americans in California, where racism was prevalent. Indians were forced to the outskirts of society and were gradually moved to areas that could hardly sup- port anything let alone human beings.

Preston Miles was becoming quite attentive. Sarah had been widowed three years, and al- though she had had a short affair with one of the lieutenants at Fort Robinson before she left, she hadn't been courted by anyone except Crazy Horse. Preston was in his fifties and slightly overweight, and though Sarah found him an interesting dinner companion, she didn't want to encourage his constant attention. She shared her concerns with James who suggested they use this time to travel and see the rest of the state. Preston was disappointed that Sarah wouldn't be available for the next two months, but realized it was he who had suggested they see California.

Sarah was emphatic that she would never ride in another stagecoach. Though the rail- road connecting Los Angeles and San Francisco hadn't been completed, their proximity to the sea made that a viable alternative. James booked passage for them on the steamboat Marigold and set sail for Santa Barbara, a day away by steamship. Before they left Los Angeles, James made reservations at the internationally famous Arlington Hotel for a week. Prescott Miles drove them to the steamer in his personal carriage and exacted a promise from Sarah that they would have dinner as soon as she returned. Before she could react, he grabbed her in his arms and kissed her passionately with an open mouth. It was James who pulled him off, and Sarah hurried up the gangplank.

The steamer was lavishly appointed with a large restaurant, parlor, and sitting area and an observation deck on top. Sarah was simply dressed and felt self conscious when confronted by other women with the latest fashions. James promised a shopping spree once they reach San Francisco. Since neither James nor Sarah had ever been on a steamer, they had fun running up the stairs and skipping on top of the second deck. The steamer docked at Stearns Wharf, and a carriage drove them up State Street to the Arlington Hotel, which for that time was one of finest hotels in California. Santa Barbara in the 1880s was a bustling community.

After a couple of days of sightseeing in Santa Barbara, Sarah relented, and they took the stagecoach over the San Marcus Pass and stopped at Kinevan Tavern for lunch before continuing onto Santa Ynez. However, this was the era of stagecoach robberies, and Sarah and James were not to be denied the pleasure of a hold up. Just as the stage came over the pass, they were stopped by two masked men who demanded that the driver and shotgun rider throw down their weapons and then the strongbox. The passengers were allowed to remain in the coach and weren't searched; the bandits were only interested in the strongbox, which was sitting at the feet of the driver and shotgun rider. After the bandits left, the stage continued on to Kinevan Tavern and the passengers were given liquid refreshments and a box lunch; the stop took twenty minutes.

It had been a long day, and Sarah and James were exhausted when the stage drew up in front of the Central Hotel on Sagunto Street in Santa Ynez. The hotel had been open for a year and featured running water in the rooms, which were spacious but not ornate.

Over the next three days they visited the Santa Inez Mission and were hosted by Don Ortega at his annual roundup. Sarah was delighted with the hospitality shown her and James but was appalled at the plight of the Chumash Indians who were barely surviving at the poverty level. She questioned her host about the Indians and was basically patronized and told that the Chumash were living the life they desired. She and James visited other ranchos, and Sarah fell in love with the beautiful rolling hills and magnificent climate.

James had promised her a shopping spree in San Francisco, and that's what she received. Her wardrobe during the trip from Fort Robinson had been simple. Her first taste of the many upscale women's stores was intoxicating, and she spent the next three days being fitted in the manner of a wellto-do woman. At night they dined at the most luxurious restaurants and by day traveled by carriage and occasionally by the horse drawn street cars that seemed to be every- where they went.

But after ten days of excitement that only San Francisco could provide, James said it was time for him to go back east and tend to their financial operations. He wondered if Sarah wanted to go with him or stay on the West Coast. The excitement of the city was nice, but Sarah still had her feet planted on the ground and soon saw that this wasn't her way of living. In addition, she wanted to see her home town and see if she could establish a life there.

CHAPTER FOURTEEN

The final leg of the transcontinental railroad from Sacramento to San Francisco had been completed, and they decided to leave immediately from the bay area and go east. The McIntyres were settled in their Los Angeles mission, and Sarah telegraphed them with a promise that she would spend time with them when she returned to the West Coast, but they didn't respond to her suggestion. Sarah understood James's need to return and review his investments, but she wanted to make an attempt to contact her son while they were traveling cross country. So Sarah asked James if they could make an attempt to find Lars on their way east. James agreed, so before they departed, he and Sarah met with the Pinkerton Detective Agency in San Francisco and gave them a description and the last known location of her son, Lars Hansen or Tasunka Wilco, as he liked to be called. The Pinkerton Agency, with offices throughout the states, contacted the head of their Omaha, Nebraska, office and scheduled a meeting for Sarah and her brother.

The trip by train from coast to coast was normally seven days if the trains were on schedule. Omaha was approximately the mid point. They boarded the East Coast Express and met with Pinkerton Agent James Jefferson four days later.

The accommodations aboard the East Coast Express were excellent for that era. Sarah especially like the suite she and James shared. There were two bedrooms, a sitting area, and a room with a sink, tub, and running water. Restroom facilities were located at each end of the individual cars. They arrived a day early in Omaha and immediately went to the Pinkerton office. Agent James Jefferson was out in the field and wasn't expected until late that night. The receptionist said she'd let him know they were in town as soon as he checked in. James had booked two rooms at the Excelsior Hotel in downtown Omaha for two nights, expecting that Jefferson would have some information on Sarah's son by the time he returned.

James T. Jefferson was a tall, thin man about fifty years old with an engaging smile and a firm handshake. He'd been a former lawman, serving as town marshal in several small towns before joining the Pinkerton Agency ten years earlier. The receptionist had sent a messenger to the Excelsior telling James and Sarah that Jefferson could meet them at the agency at nine the next morning. When they arrived, Jefferson came out to meet them and escorted them into his office. He offered them some refreshments, which they declined.

The file on Sarah's son was on his desk. As he opened it, he said, "There's some good news and some bad. I've located your son, but he and some of his friends from the reservation set fire to a rancher's barn and are being held in a small town about ten miles from here awaiting trial. I don't know why they burned the barn. The sheriff said your son and his friends went to the ranch to seek employment and obtain some food but were turned away, so they retaliated by burning his barn. The damages run to about a thousand dollars, and the rancher is pressing charges."

"If we paid the damages, could Lars be released?" James asked.

"I know the rancher is mad, but getting paid for the damage to his barn might persuade him, but I don't know about the sheriff. He seems like a hard case."

"What if we went over there and talked to the rancher and the sheriff together?"

"It's okay by me, but if this is your son, you may not want to go over there. He may not want to acknowledge you as his mother or your brother as his uncle in front of his friends."

For the first time Sarah spoke. "We won't know the answer to that unless we try. I'm a realist, Mr. Jefferson. My son takes after his father and may be long past the time when I can influence him, but if I don't try, I'll regret it the rest of my life. So when can we go?"

Jefferson nodded. "I'll telegraph the sheriff and tell him that we'd like to meet with him and the rancher this afternoon and see if they 're interested in some sort of financial settlement. That will at least encourage the rancher to meet, but as I said before, the sheriff is a hard case. I should have an answer in about two hours. The only place to wait in this small town is the saloon or here in my office. I would suggest my office."

It was eleven o'clock when the telegraph message was relayed that the parties would meet at two o'clock in the sheriff 's office. Jefferson had a four passenger rig at his disposal, and he along with Sarah and James drove to the small town of Lost Gap.

In less than an hour Sarah and James had reached an agreement with the sheriff and the rancher to drop the charges against Sarah's son and his friends if James would pay the rancher one thousand dollars and the sheriff one hundred dollars. James gave each a draft for the amount, and the release was signed by the sheriff. It was only a matter of the sheriff opening the cell doors and telling the three that they were free.

The problem was that Sarah still hadn't talked to her son, nor had she disclosed her relationship to the sheriff, so she asked the sheriff if she could have a few moments with Lars some place private before he was officially released. The sheriff told her there was a storage room ad- jacent to the jail; it was small but private. James asked her if she wanted him present.

"I think this is between Lars and me. Just wait, and if everything goes well, then I'll intro- duce him to you."

As Sarah waited for Lars in the small storage room, she wondered ifhe'd mellowed or was still bent on becoming a version of his late father. The cuffs were still on Lars as the sheriff led him into the storage room where Sarah was waiting. Sarah asked that the cuffs be removed, which the sheriff did reluctantly but said he'd be waiting outside if she needed him. As soon as the sheriff left, Sarah walked over to Lars and put her arms around him and kissed him on the cheek. Lars made no outward movement to acknowledge her existence.

There were two chairs in the room. Sarah sat in one and asked Lars to sit in the other facing her,but he refused and remained standing. "I've missed you, Lars."

"My name is Tasunka Wilco. I don't know any Lars."

"Okay, if that's what you want. I'm sorry to hear that you're in trouble."

"They wouldn't give us a job and they wouldn't feed us because we're Indians, so he got what he deserved."

"Is it worth going to jail? This way of life will only bring you into conflict with the law."

"What do you care, you're white."

"I'm your mother and I love you. I loved your father whether or not he was an Indian. I searched for you for a long time. It's only been recently, since I've been united with my brother and your uncle, that I've had the resources to find you. I'd like you to come live with me."

"What do the sheriff and the white man have to say about this?"

"My father and your grandfather left me an inheritance. I'd like to help you get a new start and a chance to succeed in this world, even if it's in what you call the white man's world. I'm here to take you home if you'll let me."

"Would I have to go to the white man's school?"

"I'd want you to get a good education. Their schools are the best. Why not give it a chance and see how it goes? Your options are not very good the way you're going now, so why not try another direction?"

"What about my friends?"

"I can get the charges dropped, but that's as far as I go with them."

"I suppose that I'd have to cut my hair?"

"Lars, I love you and I'd like to see you get a chance in this world, but I'm not going to sit here and negotiate with you on every little issue. You either want to make an effort or you don't. The life you're living now doesn't even provide you any form of a livelihood. If you continue, you'll end up dead or in jail. That doesn't seem like much of a life to me. I would think you'd at least make an effort to break out of this life."

"What about the charges against us?"

"My brother paid the rancher for his dam- ages, and the charges against all of you have been dropped. My brother James is outside. I'd like you to meet your uncle. He was captured by the Lakotas at the same time

I was and was released after six years; he a very nice person and he'd like to meet you. We're on our way to Pennsylvania where I was born to see if I'd like to live there. I'd like you to come with us. In either case you are free."

"I don't want any woman telling me what to do. I'm a man and the son of Crazy Horse. My people look to me as a leader. I will lead my people and recapture what is rightfully ours." Lars got up, walked outside past James Hansen, and asked the sheriff if he was free to leave with his friends. The sheriff said they were free, and Lars and his two friends walked down the street to the livery stable and picked up their horses. Sarah saw Lars ride out of town with his friends and she started to cry. James put an arm around Sarah and held her for a moment.

Jefferson walked up to Sarah. "He's young. If you want, I can follow up periodically and keep you informed."

Sarah smiled. "I don't think he realizes how difficult his life can be when he's on the run all the time. I hope with a little time he'll come around." James gave Jefferson their address before they left the next morning on the train to Pennsylvania.

They passed the next three days aboard the train taking them east. Initially Sarah was distraught and spent most of the first two days in her cabin. But by the third day she was her old radiant self and joined James in the sitting parlor. They arrived in Philadelphia the morning of the fourth day and hired a livery to take them to the Putnam Hotel where they stayed overnight. The next morning they boarded the train to Harrisburg. James had telegraphed the Harris- burg Bank telling the bank president that he and Sarah would arrive by train the next afternoon.

As they stepped off the train, James bought a newspaper from a street vendor. The headlines read, "Crazy Horse's wife coming home." The article was not flattering to Crazy Horse and painted him as a ruthless savage and the plotter of the massacre that took the life of George Armstrong Custer. Sarah was guilty of these atrocities by association or, in her case, by marriage. She was referred to as the white squaw of Crazy Horse. Both she and James were initially stunned, but James's shock grew into outrage. The only person he had told of their itinerary and the fact that his sister was alive and had been the wife of Crazy Horse was Franklin George, the president of the Harrisburg Bank.

James was still fuming when he rented a carriage. He and Sarah made their way to the bank and a confrontation with George. They entered the bank and saw George talking to one of his tellers. James, with Sarah close behind, stormed up to George and shoved the paper in his face.

"I was as surprised as you," George offered. "Let's go into my office and we can discuss this in private." George took Sarah by the arm and pointed to his office. James followed.

George offered them a chair and some refreshments, but James was still angry and stood facing Franklin George. "You're the only one who knew we were coming here and that Sarah was Crazy Horse's wife. How could you use that personal information as though it was fodder for idle gossip? I trusted you and you've betrayed us."

"James, I didn't. Someone in the bank went into my desk and read your file. I think we've pinned it down to two people, and both have been suspended. I'm terribly sorry. I wouldn't cause you any pain and certainly not your beautiful sister. What can I do to show my good faith? I hope this doesn't impact our business relationship?"

James wasn't pacified but didn't know what could be done to alleviate the situation. "The damage has already been done, and I'm sure other papers will pick up on it. My sister had a life thrust upon her that she didn't choose, but she made the best of it, and now someone wants to make her life difficult again. It's not fair. While we're here we can sign the papers transferring my sister's share to her, giving her the right over her property. I want you to explain all her rights to her and how she can enforce them if need be."

Two hours later they finished their business and James took Sarah to his home on the south side of Harrisburg. The family farm in Titusville had been sold before the Hansen family made the trek west. The royalties they received from the oil wells drilled on their former farm had helped James purchase several tenements, commercial buildings, and this home on an acre of land. Sarah was surprised at the size of James's home and how sparsely furnished the four bedroom home was. She knew her days would be filled with decorating and she relished the thought.

Sarah spent the next month redecorating their home and getting acclimated in the com- munity, which seemed easy on the surface but more difficult than she imagined. The newspaper headlines that greeted them were only the start of a campaign to treat her as though she was an enemy. Subsequent articles summarized her captivity and the fact that she gave birth to two boys, that she probably was with her husband at the Battle of Little Big Horn, and subtly indicated that she was as guilty as Crazy Horse for the death of General Custer. James was furious and tried to find out who was behind this, but to no avail. The articles were no longer on the front page, but enough damage had been done to Sarah's reputation that she was reluctant to be seen in public. James contacted the Pinkerton Office in Harrisburg and asked them to investigate.

Sarah wanted to see her old home in Titusville even though James explained that she would be disappointed because of all the derricks on their former farm. But she persisted and so they took the train to Titusville. James had been home a few times, but this was the first for Sarah since her capture. The small town had changed dramatically since the discovery of oil. Sarah remembered only a general store in the town whereas now there were about twenty retail shops to service the increase in population and the wealth the town had experienced since Colonel Drake drilled the first well here.

Sarah and James visited their old farm, but as James had warned, Sarah couldn't even identify the place now. They spent the remainder of the day intown trying to find any former residents. If they existed, none appeared to come into town so they left on the four o'clock train back to Harrisburg.

It took nearly a week before the local Pinkerton agent contacted James and delivered his report. It seems that Franklin George, a pillar of the community and a married man with four children, had a mistress who he confided in. It was she who had contacted a reporter at the Harrisburg News named William Climb who apparently paid her for the information, though the Pinkerton agent didn't know how much she was paid. James took the report and told the agent that he would get back to him after talking to his attorney.

Charles Howard was the attorney James contacted after he was released from captivity. Howard was able to help him reestablish his identity and subsequently realize his in- heritance. It was he who introduced James to Franklin George. When he read the Pinkerton report, he apologized to James and asked what he wanted him to do.

"I want to change banks, prosecute George's mistress, and let the public know what a scoundrel Franklin George is."

Howard took a few seconds before he responded. "Well, I think that can be accomplished if you really want to. I know this has been hard on your sister."

James was surprised at Howard 's cavalier attitude. "You don't realize what she's been put through. She's a beautiful woman who was captured by savages who killed our mother and father and forced into marrying one of them. Subsequently she was rescued and put up for public ridicule by someone who wouldn't know what to do if faced with the trauma she's experienced. So yes, I really want to, and if you're not in our corner, I'll seek legal representation elsewhere. Perhaps you have a problem since you introduced me to your good friend Franklin George who's responsible for this notoriety."

Howard hadn't expected this outburst from James, but he soon recovered. "James, I'm in your court and will do as you ask. I'm ashamed about Franklin's conduct as well and will help you in making the changes you desire. What about First National of Pennsylvania? Their financial statement is sound, and the chief operating officer is a personal friend. Why don't I set up an appointment for you and Sarah and see what you think?"

Sarah's feeling were hurt, but she wasn't going to give anyone satisfaction or hide out anymore, so she made it a point to go shopping every day and let anyone know who wished her ill that she wouldn't be intimidated. Many of the storekeepers were sympathetic and went out of their way to be helpful; others were condescending and would wait on her but would gossip be- hind her back.

On her way back home one day she came upon a middle-aged woman sitting in the gutter. The woman appeared to be sick. Sarah stopped and asked if she was ill but received no response. She reached down and touched the woman's shoulder to see if she heard her. When the woman looked up Sarah thought her to be Indian, so she spoke to her in the Oglala dialect and noted some degree of recognition from her. She helped the woman up and took her home and called for Dr. Fordham to come to the house.

Fordham was a young doctor who was just starting a practice in Harrisburg and certainly wanted to please such a beautiful woman as Sarah Hansen. He'd been introduced to Sarah at a church box social and immediately was smitten. He'd called upon her with her brother's permission, and the couple went to dinner a few times. Nevertheless, the stigma of being Indian in that day and age wasn't lost on the medical profession, and John Fordham was reluctant to examine the older woman and wouldn't have unless Sarah insisted. But he didn't want the fact that he was treating an Indian to become public knowledge.

His preliminary diagnosis was that the woman was suffering from malnutrition. He wanted to end the examination there, but Sarah made him continue and had to smile as she spoke to the woman and assured her that she wasn't going to be molested by the young white man. After Dr. Fordham was finished he gave Sarah a prescription in her name for some vitamins and suggested that the Indian woman be given some soft food and a lot of liquid. Sarah thanked him and said she would get back to him if she was available for an ice cream social in the town next weekend.

The woman was bewildered at the attention being given to her by the small, blond, blue eyed woman and especially bewildered by her ability to communicate in a language she herself had heard many times. The woman told Sarah in bro- ken English that she went by the name of Naomi and was Iroquois but had lived in an Oglala village for two years and had picked up the language. She'd done housework and laundry for a family in Harrisburg until one day the woman of the house said the family was moving to Philadelphia and wouldn't be taking her with them. The couple's name was George. Obviously James had exacted retribution on Franklin George, but it had also caused Naomi to be without a place to live and work. That was two weeks ago and she hadn't been able to find a position since then. After her meager savings had run out she was forced to live and beg in the streets and hadn't eaten much during that time.

When James came home he questioned the reasoning of bringing the woman to their home and not to one of the soup kitchens in the city. Sarah said that the woman needed a place to live, someplace where she was wanted and could contribute, and someplace where she felt welcome. James objected, but knew that it was a losing battle. He also admired Sarah for wanting to help someone who probably could easily have been her if he hadn't come to her aid. So Naomi moved into one of the bedrooms and became their housekeeper and companion to Sarah.

With Naomi's help, Sarah plunged into the redecoration of their home and started painting again. She found a well known artist by the name of Phyllis Gaines who gave instructions to a few selected students who had promise. Sarah asked Phyllis to look at her paintings and offer an opinion. The teacher was astonished and told Sarah she had an innate talent that was superior to her own. All she could do was help Sarah realize her potential. She suggested Sarah could expand her talent if she'd use better equipment and canvases. She agreed to work with Sarah on what art supplies to buy and suggestions on how to expand her horizons. She acted more as consultant than teacher.

With Phyllis Gaines help and encouragement, Sarah gave a small exhibition of her work, which was primarily oil paintings of Indians, their villages, and family gatherings. The Harris- burg News sent one of their reporters to the exhibition and wrote a complimentary article about Sarah's work. This would have been acceptable had not the reporter continued with a review of Sarah's history, especially that she was the late wife of the notorious, savage Crazy Horse. Sarah refused to become angry and just accepted it as the way some people would always view her and that nothing she could do would change that viewpoint.

Sarah had begun to notice a change in James's behavior. As Naomi took on a larger role in their home, James spent less time with them and took his evening meals elsewhere. Initially Sarah thought it was business that occupied his time, but soon realized that it was something else. She tried not to pry and instead casually asked him about the change, but got nothing other than he was working hard on their investments.

Sarah and Naomi were in town shopping and decided to stop at a small restaurant run by an older couple that Sarah had met when she first arrived in Harrisburg. The couple wasn't concerned about serving Naomi as were other establishments in the town. When they were seated, Sarah looked over the menu while asking Naomi what she wanted to eat. It was then that she spotted James and a young woman sitting at a corner table. Sarah told Naomi to wait while she walked over to where James and the young woman were sitting. He was so engrossed with his companion that he didn't notice Sarah until she was at their table. She smiled at the woman, who looked up. "Hi, I'm Sarah
Hansen and I'm James's sister."

James almost fell off his chair as he got to his feet and self consciously introduced his companion to Sarah. "This is Jennifer Craylor. Her father owns the bank that's working with us on our investments."

Sarah hadn't seen her brother so flustered before and assumed it was the young woman he was with that was the basis for his embarrassment. The woman looked up at Sarah. "Please, won't you join us?"

"You look as though you were deep in conversation and I don't want to intrude. Naomi is with me, and it's probably best if we eat separately. How about coming to dinner this week and we can get better acquainted?"

"That would be nice. I'll look forward to the invitation," the young woman responded.

Sarah went back to her table. Naomi smiled and suggested that James had a girlfriend. Sarah assumed that was the reason that James had been so scarce the last few months. She wondered what James's intentions were. It would be interesting to see how it played out.

Dr. Fordham continued to call and seemed to be an earnest suitor, but from Sarah's viewpoint there was no romance, just companionship. He proposed to her at one of the church socials. She tried to delicately turn him down but didn't succeed. He couldn't take no for an answer and demanded to know who she preferred to him, especially since she wasn't so choosy the first time. He knew he made a mistake when he said this, but it was too late. Any chance he had for Sarah Hansen being the future Mrs. Fordham went up in smoke that day.

The invitation to dinner was sent to Jennifer Craylor but wasn't accepted. Subsequent invitations were sent with the same result. There was always a family function or a trip or someone was ill in the Craylor family. Sarah read in the society section of the Harrisburg News about the many parties Jennifer's family had at their estate. Occasionally she read that her brother was one of the attendees, but an invitation was never extended to her. When she finally confronted James, he was embarrassed and said the time wasn't right for both families to get together. Sarah was heartbroken, but her time in the Indian culture had conditioned her not to show any outward feelings. Still, the insensitivity of her brother would remain with her forever. She'd been home a year and realized it wasn't her home anymore. Her history with Crazy Horse was like a lamppost out in front of her house. If her brother had problems with that, then how could she assimilate into this society? The answer was clear. She couldn't.

But there were some bright spots in her life. Naomi had become a loyal servant and companion, and

Sarah's paintings had gained notoriety in Philadelphia and New York. She had a profitable showing at the famous Latrelle Gallery, and from all indications she could make a reasonable living from her art work. Two of her landscape paintings sold for prices above her expectations. Surprisingly, James didn't seem interested in her talent, nor did he or Jennifer Craylor attend any of her showings. The portrait business was lucrative, but Sarah felt that niche wasn't something she wanted to cultivate. Be- sides, Cecelia Beaux seemed to have a monopoly on the portrait business on the eastern seaboard and was considered at that time to be the greatest female portrait painter of her day. Sarah was privileged to meet the famous artist once and receive a critical appraisal of her landscapes. Sarah was also introduced to Emily Sartain, the head of the Philadelphia School of Design and a well known impressionist painter in her own right.

She enrolled in Sartain's school and met many of the rising women artists of the day. While at the school of design, she met a lovely young fellow artist by the name of Susanne Petrolla from a wealthy family in southern Pennsylvania. Petrolla took an interest in Sarah's work and made numerous suggestions, some of which Sarah thought were very good, which she incorporated into her work. The two became friendly and at times would paint together at Sarah's home. Susanne would take the train to Harrisburg, stay for a week while they painted, talked of life, and then would take the train back to the school of design where she was staying.

Sarah introduced the young woman to James, hoping there would be an attraction and that James would get out from under the influence of the Craylor family. Though Susanne was a lovely young woman, James didn't pay any attention to her other than being cordial. He declined several attempts by Sarah to bring the two people together, either at dinner or via a picnic. In fact, he seemed to stay away from home more than usual while Susanne was there.

Sarah and James's home had four bedrooms, one for each of the inhabitants. The fourth originally was an office for James but was gradually taken over by Sarah for her art work. When Susanne visited, she'd sleep on a studio couch in that room. On evening while James was out and Naomi had retired earlier, Sarah and Susanne shared dinner alone and consumed some wine, which made Sarah a little tipsy. After they cleared the dishes, Sarah said she was going to bed and kissed Susanne on the cheek. In turn, Susanne embraced Sarah somewhat passionately and kissed her on the neck. Sarah freed her- self and said goodnight to her friend and went to her room. She was surprised at the embrace but assumed she had imagined it to be more than what it was because of the amount of wine she had consumed.

Sarah was awakened about two hours after retiring; someone else was in bed with her. Susanne had pulled up Sarah's nightgown and was fondling her breasts and kissing her on the neck. Then the young woman, who was nude, pushed herself between Sarah's legs and flicked her tongue in and out of her vagina. Sarah was starting to feel pleasure but had no intention of allowing this to continue. She placed her hand under the young woman's chin and lifted her head as she slid off the bed and adjusted her nightgown.

"You misunderstand my attention, Susanne. I'm not the woman you'd hoped for. Please return to your room and in the morning I think it would be best if you returned to Philadelphia." Sarah didn't show anger, but was firm. Susanne, completely nude, stood facing Sarah, smiling as though taunting her. Then she turned and walked out of the bedroom door while swaying her hips for Sarah's benefit.

It was two weeks later before Sarah returned to the school of design. Susanne wasn't there. One of the girls said that Susanne had told Miss Sartain that she was taking a vacation with her family. One of the other female artists asked Sarah how she had enjoyed her week with Susanne. Sarah knew there was some sort of implication there, so she confronted the young woman who told her that Susanne was a known lesbian and had told several of the girls that she was going to have Sarah. Not wanting to be the butt of any more jokes or jeers and realizing that she had learned everything she could at the school, she told Emily Sartain that she was going to end her time at the school.

Harrisburg could not be her home in the future. She'd been unable to establish any worthwhile relationships other than with Naomi. Her relationship with James was strained and they hardly saw each other. Sarah set up a meeting with their joint attorney, Charles Howard. She'd previously asked him for a complete analysis of all her holdings to determine how much was in real estate, what percentage was in securities, and how much was liquid. The real estate was bringing in a monthly income that would allow her and Naomi to live comfortably. The securities would function as long term investments and would act as a safety valve in the event her real estate investments deteriorated.

Over the years she and James gradually divided all the real estate investments so that they no longer were in a partnership. She arranged to have most of her cash put in the form of drafts that she could place with a bank when she resettled. The paintings were another asset, but with her growing notoriety, she could leave her paintings at various galleries or have them transferred to others of her choice.

When she had all her plans finalized, she asked James to have dinner with her, just the two of them. She wanted to discuss an important matter with him. James was so smitten with Jennifer Craylor that he was oblivious to any- thing Sarah had done over the past few months. He was shattered when she divulged her plans to return to California, and a nagging feeling of guilt arose within him that made him feel even worse. He knew that he had forced this issue and immediately wanted to do anything he could to make it up to Sarah. He'd force the issue with the Craylors, but Sarah knew that forcing someone to be accepted wouldn't work in the long run.

"You'll always be my brother and I'll always love you for the way you came and rescued me, but we've got to live our own lives and this thing with Crazy Horse and now Naomi seems to have created a chasm between us. I've never felt com-fortable here, and I think you can get on with your life once I'm out of the way. Naomi and I are going back to Omaha and see if we can find Lars and then
continue on to California."

CHAPTER FIFTEEN

When Wyatt Earp caught up with Geoffrey Combs in Santa Fe, he was sitting at a table at the far wall in the Hotel Santa Fe restaurant; he was alone. Earp approached Combs and sat down across from him, and leaned against the wall. Combs didn't seem surprised to see Earp and offered him a glass of wine as he sat down.

Earp took the glass of wine offered and took off his hat. There was a buzz in the restaurant; several of the patrons recognized Earp and were constantly looking his way. "I came to talk to you and Jeff Strait," Earp said as he sipped some wine.

"Well, as you can see, I'm right here, but Jeff didn't get off the train at Lemy. I suspect he's on his way to Wyoming. Did you know he was from there?" Combs seemed to be enjoying the cat and mouse game; Earp wasn't.

"Kind of sudden, wasn't it?"

"He'd been talking about going back to Wyoming for some time, and now seemed to be a good time."

"Why did you come along?"

"I had some business in Santa Fe that needed my attention."

"Jessup claims Strait paid him to kill Tommy Sanchez and seemed to think that you were in on it. As soon as the verdict was read, the two of you leave town. Quite a coincidence, don't you think?"

"That's silly, Sheriff. I didn't have anything to do with the ambush of Tommy Sanchez. As far as Jeff is concerned, well, he's his own man. I don't speak for him. If you were coming to arrest us, I think you made the trip for nothing."

"I don't think so. I may not have gotten to Strait before he high tailed it out of here, but I believe I've flushed out a polecat, if you know what I mean."

Combs was furious but smart enough not to cause a confrontation even if Earp was out of his jurisdiction. "I don't have anything more to say to you, Sheriff. If you don't mind, I'd like you to leave my table unless you've got a warrant."

Earp had been dismissed but didn't move. "Tell me about Tommy Sanchez being taken off the Opera House Development Committee. I didn't say anything at the time, but it looks like you don't like Tommy and probably were behind Jessup's attempt. You've got my attention even if you don't want it. When I get back, I'm going to put out a warrant on Strait. It'll be interesting when we catch him, to see if he gives you up. If that happens, I wouldn't want to be you with Sanchez in the same town."

Combs didn't say anything nor did he look up as Earp left the table and went over to the bar to have a drink.

Before Earp left the next day he checked with the hotel manager to see who Combs arrived with. The manager confirmed that Combs was alone. When Earp went back to Lemy he checked with the railroad dispatcher who confirmed that Jeff Strait didn't get off the train at Lemy. Earp wondered why Combs was after Sanchez.

Combs knew he'd made a mistake in under-estimating Tommy Sanchez and now was concerned about what Earp had alluded to. At first he had just wanted to slow down the Sanchez real estate expansion, and then when those ploys didn't work, he wanted him out of the way. But it was a mistake to listen to Judd Harker who had his own agenda. Strait was now a problem and Combs would have to take care of him sometime in the near future. He had to make sure that Strait wasn't arrested. He knew too much. Maybe Harker had a use after all. But Sanchez was still a problem. He wondered how long he could wait before he took care of him permanently.

Tommy continued to expand his business empire. It wasn't that he became rich overnight, it was the steady way he was accumulating valuable properties and businesses with a steady stream of income. Tommy had almost a monopoly on the freight business from the railroad station in Lemy to the towns in northeast and northwest Arizona. The telegraph was a boon to his imaginative mind. He was constantly asking people in town what was needed in the way of retail items. Then he would search the country for these items and bring them to Tombstone. Soon he realized that it would be profitable to open his own general store. There were times when he purchased items that sat in the back room of his store for lack of interest, but in most cases he was right on the mark in anticipating the consumer's needs.

Santa Fe was ruined for Tommy. He didn't want to go back and explain to the sheriff his tie to Laramie, Wyoming, and therefore the Santa Fe market wasn't open to him. In fact, he never went to Lemy. All freight pickups were handled by Joaquin and his crew. The expansion of his business fulfilled a need he had to prove that he belonged in the white world and he wasn't just some dumb half breed. There were times when he was referred to as that half breed, and he was sensitive to the discrimination, yet he didn't retaliate even though he could have very easily. The experience of working with the group to bring an opera house to Tombstone made him more secretive and less willing to participate in community affairs. Tommy became a loner. Even his relationship with his sometime live-in girlfriend and permanent bookkeeper was not overly intimate. They had sexual relations and he spent time with her and the two children, but he didn't allow her to get too close; he held her at arm's length. It seemed to Tommy that he was looking for something elusive that was out there somewhere but he just hadn't found it.

The Combs situation puzzled him until one evening when, during a more intimate moment, Jan shared with him the fact that she and Geoffrey Combs had had a relationship for a year before Tommy came to town. It was probably the reason her husband went off and left her. As her relationship with Combs became more intense, the physical and mental abuse began. She was afraid and started to withdraw from her other friends. Combs became obsessive and accused her of being unfaithful with other men, even though she wasn't. She finally broke it off, but Combs threatened her if she ever became friendly with another man. It wasn't that Combs wanted her; he just didn't want anyone else to have her. Tommy was the first man she had known in an intimate capacity since she broke it off with Combs. He apparently was afraid of Tommy and hadn't threatened her since she started seeing him.

"Why didn't you tell me this before, certainly before the Jessup's trial?" Tommy asked.

"I was afraid," she responded.

Tommy had been trying to find out who was behind the attempt to force him out of Tombstone and the reason for this campaign. Jan's rev- elation seemed to answer that question and now he had to decide how to handle it from this point forward. Jan also shared with him the secret retreat that Combs had in the mountains where he went to get away from the constant noise and commotion at the Bird Cage. She'd been there once and therefore was able to give him directions. Tommy didn't plan on visiting Combs at the retreat unless it was necessary. He decided to seek a meeting with Combs to see if the issue could be resolved. In the back of his mind he was hoping to resolve the issue so that he could get back to what he did best, but he sensed that the meeting would be futile. Having to leave Santa Fe and previous to that leave the Laramie and Durango areas was always on his mind. He was constantly planning for the day when he'd have to leave Tombstone.

His attorney was working on a pardon for the Laramie killing, but the process was bogged down with current politics in the state and the fact they couldn't get either candidate who was running for governor to commit to helping them. Without the governor, there wouldn't be a pardon. Tommy asked his attorney to contact Mike Jacobs, the owner of the Bar 6, and ask for his advice. He hadn't communicated with Mike since he left Laramie but assumed that Mike would help if he could.

He found Geoffrey Combs sitting at a table by himself enjoying breakfast one morning. Tommy walked up and asked if he could have a moment of his time. Combs said it'd have to be quick because he had a very important meeting immediately after breakfast.

Tommy got right to the point and told Combs that he knew it was him that was behind the Jessup affair, the opera house fiasco, and a campaign to have him leave Tombstone.

"Says who?" Combs responded.

"I do. But I'd like to put all of that aside and see if we can come to a mutual resolution and put the past behind us," Tommy responded.

Combs put his fork down and glared at Tommy. "Since I don't know what you're talking about, there can hardly be a resolution. Now if you'll excuse me, I have that meeting to attend that I told you about." With that he pushed away from the table and walked upstairs to one of the conference rooms. Tommy wondered if he should be carrying his gun for a while.

Over the next couple of months the two adversaries avoided each other. Tommy didn't go into the Bird Cage and Combs didn't visit the livery stables. One day, Jan asked if she could speak to him before he left for the day. "It seems our relationship has started to fall apart. I'd like to see if we can put a little fire back in it. Why don't you come for dinner tonight? The children are staying with the Williamses so we have the house to ourselves. I'd like to see if we rekindle our relationship." Tommy said he'd be over at seven.

Jan was a pleasant woman and a good book-keeper and Tommy welcomed her friendship. He'd been intimate with her over the past two years but didn't promise her anything beyond friendship. He cleaned up and got out a bottle of fine wine and walked over to her house. She greeted him with a kiss and thanked him for the bottle of wine and asked him to open it while she grabbed two glasses. They toasted each other, and she indicated dinner would be ready in a few minutes. The fare was venison and mashed potatoes with rice pudding for dessert. They chatted about business, Joaquin and his family, and his new business ventures. About nine o'clock they moved to her bedroom and he undressed her and caressed her body as she got into bed and waited anxiously for him to undress and join her.

They made love; she was especially active, and Tommy met her with equal fervor and they fell asleep in each other's arms. About one in the morning, Tommy was awakened by the sound of a floor creaking, and then the bedroom door burst open and shots were fired at him and Jan as they lay in bed.

Tommy's reflexes were honed through years of cavalry raids on his village and he was a light sleeper. As the door burst open he rolled off the bed and reached for his gun in the holster on the floor. As he continued to roll, he landed on his back and started firing at the shadows inside the room. There were two of them, and Tommy 's first shots hit one of the intruders, who fell at the foot of the bed. Tommy continued shooting and saw the second intruder stumble back toward the door and run out into the living area.

Tommy got up and chased the man outside and fired as the individual was fleeing. He'd emptied his gun and went back into the house to get more shells. He turned on the kerosene lamp and saw the blood on the bed sheets and the limp body of Jan Hutchinson. He checked for a pulse; she was dead. The gunman, lying on the floor at the foot of the bed, was dead; he'd been shot in the head.

As he was putting on his pants, Virgil Earp, closely followed by Wyatt Earp, ran into the house with guns drawn. "Two men rushed in and just starting firing. I returned fire, hitting the guy lying at the foot of the bed and chased the other outside. I ran out of ammunition, but I think I winged him. When I came back, I found Jan. She was dead."

Virgil checked Jan and confirmed that she was dead as well as the gunman on the floor. "I don't recognize him." He said.

Joaquin and his father showed up next and offered their help. The old man had been a tracker when he was younger and offered to track the assailant. The two Earps and Tommy told him to lead the way. Although it was dark, there was enough of a moon for the old man to follow the footprints and the occasional drops of blood as he led them behind the retail section and then to the back door of the Bird Cage Saloon.

Virgil and Tommy went around to the front of the saloon and told the old man to go home while Wyatt slowly opened the back door and made his way through the kitchen into the bar area. In the meantime Virgil and Tommy entered the front and asked the bartender where the wounded man was. The bartender pointed to an upstairs room.

"Is there a window in the room? Virgil asked. The bartender nodded.

Wyatt and Tommy walked slowly up the stairs while Virgil went out the back to preclude the gunman escaping that way. Wyatt tapped on the door and asked the gunman to come out with his hands in the air. The response was two bullets through the door. With Wyatt on one the side of the door, Tommy kicked in the door, but there was no response. The gunman lay on the floor. He appeared to be in bad shape but was alive. His empty revolver lay next to him. Wyatt checked him for wounds. He'd been shot in the stomach; it didn't look good. Generally gut shots were fatal in the Old West. Virgil had arrived by then and yelled down to the bartender to send someone to get the doctor.

Virgil got down on his knees and put his mouth up to the fallen man's ear. "Why did you kill the woman and try to kill Sanchez? Virgil asked.

The gunman didn't say anything. He just grabbed his stomach and groaned.

"Who put you up to this?" Virgil continued to press for an answer because he could see that the gunman didn't have much time left.

By this time the town doctor arrived and after carefully examining the wounded gunman, he looked up at Virgil and said the man was dead.

Wyatt went downstairs and grabbed the bartender and brought him upstairs to the room where the body lay. "Frank, I want to know who this guy is."

Frank Phillips had been the head bartender at the Bird Cage for the past five years and, like all bartenders in small towns, knew almost everyone in town and what they did for leisure. "I don't know his name, but I've seen him with Geoffrey and Mike. I assumed he worked for Geoffrey."

"Where's Geoffrey?" Wyatt asked the bartender.

"He's out of town is all I know."

"When did he leave?" Virgil asked.

"Yesterday, about noon."

"Where's Mike?" Wyatt asked.

"He went home early."

"What a coincidence," Wyatt responded.

"Virgil, I'm going over and get Mike Sturgess and see if he knows anything about the shootings. I think we have to see if anyone else in the saloon knows this guy. Maybe you can ask some questions while I talk to Sturgess."

Wyatt scared the hell out of Mike Sturgess when he banged on his door at two in the morning. He told Earp that he went home early be- cause his wife wasn't feeling well and he didn't want to go back to the Bird Cage at this hour. "Why can't it wait until tomorrow?"

Earp told him to put on his pants; he was going back to the saloon to identify the dead gunman. Sturgess complained all the way to the saloon and up the stairs. When he saw the dead man, Wyatt could see immediate recognition. "Who is it? And don't tell me you don't know who he is. I'm not going to buy that."

"He's Harvey Wilson; he does odd jobs for us here or gofer jobs when we need them. Why's he dead?"

"He killed Jan Hutchinson and tried to kill Tommy Sanchez tonight at Jan's house. You're coming with me to look at the other one Tommy killed."

Leaving the doctor to handle the dead man in the Bird Cage, Virgil, Wyatt, Tommy, and Sturgess went to Hutchinson's house and went into the bedroom. Tommy had a kerosene lantern and shone it on the dead man's face. Again, Sturgess's face gave away the fact that he recognized the dead man.

"He's Wally Furgon and he hangs around with Harvey Wilson, or at least he used to. We use both of them at times for various odd jobs. I hadn't seen him in weeks, and just so we under- stand each other, I don't know anything about the shootings." "Where's Combs?" Wyatt asked.

"I don't know. He said he was going to be out of town for a week. He's the boss. I don't question him when he says he's taking off."

"Come on, Mike, you know everything that's going on at the Bird Cage. You're Combs's right hand man. I'll bet you sent Wilson and Furgon to shoot Tommy and got Jan instead. This is cold blooded murder and you can hang for this, so I suggest you start talking now while we're in a good mood and not in a hanging mood." Wyatt was really pushing Sturgess for some answers.

"I don't know anything about the shootings and I haven't seen either Wilson or Furgon for a couple of weeks and you've no right to talk to me like this. I never even fired a gun."

"No, but you could pay someone to do it for you. What have you got against Sanchez and Hutchinson? Was she you ex girl-friend and Sanchez was stealing your action?"

"I don't know what you're talking about. I'm a happily married man and I didn't have anything to do with this. Now can I go home?"

The funeral for Jan Hutchinson was two days later. The entire town turned out; that is, everyone but Geoffrey Combs. Jan's children attended, and the older of the two asked Tommy what was going to happen to them now that their mother was dead. "Are we going to live with you?"

Tommy knew that the children were staying with the Williams family the night of the shooting. The next morning he went over the Williamses' house and talked to Frank and Ethel Williams. He asked them if they could care for the children for a few days while he tried to find a permanent home for them. At the time of the funeral he'd been unsuccessful in finding a permanent home for the children, but he'd made a number of inquiries about the Williams family and all indications were that they were people with their feet on the ground and would be ideal foster parents. He approached Mr. Williams after the funeral and asked him if he and his wife could keep the children permanently. Mr. Williams said they'd like to, but he didn't know if they could afford it.

"Jan was a trusted employee who I knew very well, and I spent a lot of time with the children. I feel obligated to see that they have a good home. I talked to my banker and I can provide financial assistance to you until the children reach eighteen." Tommy told Frank Williams how much money per month they'd receive, and Frank said he'd be happy to take the children home.

The murder of Jan Hutchinson was on everyone's tongue in this town of two thousand and especially since the two killers worked for the Bird Cage. The Tombstone Epitaph in their editorial asked that Geoffrey Combs return as soon as possible and explain why two men in his employ would commit murder.

A week went by with no progress in identifying who paid the two gunmen to kill Jan and Tommy. It wasn't something personal between the two gunmen and Tommy because he had never seen them before. Tommy met with Joaquin and his father and told them he'd be out of town for a few days and asked them to handle business.

"I want to go with you," the father said. "She was our friend as well and I want the man who paid the two, and we all know who it is. I can help. I can track anything."

"I don't know what you're talking about," Tommy said. "I'm going to Bisbee on business. Joaquin, you take over the books. Jan told me you'd been helping her and you were ready to take over if necessary. If anything happens to me, I've made provisions for you and your family, but I don't expect anything will happen to me before I return."

"You're a good man, but you don't have to do this by yourself. You've been like a brother to Joaquin and a son to me. Please let us handle this as a family." Tommy smiled at the old man but didn't respond.

He packed for four days and took his Remington and two six-guns with extra ammunition for the task. He started out toward Bisbee, just in case he was being followed, but reversed his course after a couple of hours and made his way to the Dragoon Mountains, northeast of Tomb- stone. He hadn't been on a raid in over fifteen years, but he had been trained by the best and those instincts were still within him. Jan had told him about the hideaway that Combs had in the mountains and its location.

It took him a half day to locate the small fortress sitting on a hill accessed by a circular path leading up to the main house. That evening he decided to see what was in the compound. After finding a place for his horse, he crawled up the rear face of the hill and came out on a small rise about fifteen feet above and to the side of the main structure. He was fifty feet away, but he could see two outbuildings. One probably served as a barn for the horses and the other as storage. He could make out two armed men, one stationed in the front and the other at the rear of the main house. Every thirty minutes the two guards patrolled around the main house and then returned to their stations. He couldn't be sure, but he sensed there was another man inside the main house besides Combs. He waited another hour and then crawled back down the hill, gathered up his horse and rode to a camp he'd made earlier that evening.

He formulated a plan that he believed would work. He slept until noon the next day and awoke to the intense heat of the Arizona desert. For the remainder of the day he cleaned his equipment, had another meal, and rested until nightfall.

At midnight he tied his horse to a large mesquite bush and retraced his steps of the previous evening. He crawled up the hill, stopping periodically when he heard the two voices of the outside sentries as they patrolled around the main building. He stopped near the same place as the previous evening and waited until the guards made their thirty minute patrol and returned to their station. Then he carefully crawled up behind the man sitting on a chair at the rear of the house. He placed his left hand over the man's mouth while holding him in the chair and hit him with the butt of his revolver with his right hand. The rifle on the man's lap fell to the ground and landed on some rocks, making a slight noise.

Tommy was dragging the man to the bushes when the second man came around the house with his gun drawn. Tommy had no choice but to shoot him in the head. Instantly lights came on in the house and someone moved quickly toward the back door. Tommy held his ground as he crouched behind the unconscious sentry.

The back door opened slightly and someone whispered, "Is that you, Joe?"

When there was no response, the door closed, and Tommy could hear the lock click and then another light appeared in the front of the house. Surprise was still on Tommy's side, so he ran to the back door, kicked it in, and dove to the floor. He believed he was on the kitchen floor. Someone started firing down the hall into the kitchen and Tommy was pinned down.

He heard the front door slam open and someone running toward the barn. A few moments later he heard a horse running down the circular path leading from the main house. He assumed it was Combs making a break for it and leaving whoever it was to hold him off until he escaped or Tommy was dead. He was getting nowhere lying on the floor so he fired about five shots down the hall in the direction of where the shots had come from and dived out the back door.

He was making his way around to the barn when someone came out the front door and around the house toward him and started shooting at him. Tommy dove to the ground, coming up alongside the house. and as the figure came within eyesight, Tommy shot him twice and the figure fell over.

The other gunman was coming to and Tommy asked him if there was anyone else in the compound other than the four Tommy had counted. The gunman said that was all there were. Tommy then asked the gunman if he wanted to live. The gunman nodded that he did. "I want you to run down the hill as fast as you can. I'll give you a ten minute start, but if I see you when I come down, I'll kill you. Do you hear me?"

The gunman nodded and ran toward the front of the house and down the hill. Tommy decided to take a look around to see if there was anyone else here regardless of what the gunman said. The main house consisted of a kitchen, living area, and two bedrooms. Tommy assumed the larger bedroom was for Combs. He checked the storage building and noted it was full of hay and grain. There was one horse remaining in the barn and Tommy put a halter on the horse and climbed on. He rode down the hill to the place where he left Jupiter tethered. He saddled Jupiter, mounted, and trailed the other horse behind.

He'd been trained from the age of eight to track animals such as horses, deer, and buffalo, as well as humans. He'd have no problem tracking Combs even if it was still dark. He thought Combs would head to Tombstone, but to Tommy's surprise he headed in the direction of the desolate Chiricahua Desert.

When daylight came, Tommy could see that Combs was running his horse pretty fast. Tommy knew from experience that a rider couldn't keep up this pace without killing the horse. Every two hours Tommy stopped, giving the horses some water and changing mounts. It was nightfall when he saw a rider on the horizon. Tommy decided to stop for the night and conserve his energy; Combs would be easy to pick up at daylight.

He rose just before dawn and mounted Jupiter and trailed the other horse behind. By noon he came across the rider's mount. The horse was lying on its side and in the last throes of dying. Tommy put a bullet in the horse's head to eliminate the pain and trauma the horse must have experienced over the last few hours.

It was an hour later when he was fired on from a dry wash off to his left. He dismounted and tied both horses to a cactus bush and made his way toward the dry wash. He was within thirty yards of the old creek when he was fired on once and then in succession four more times. He crouched down with his left elbow on his knee and his rifle in his hand watching the wash; he remained in that position for an hour when he was fired on again. He knew that whoever was in the wash was running out of ammunition, so he decided to move slowly toward the spot where the shots were coming from. He crossed the wash about thirty yards south and crawled on his stomach until he came up behind the gunman; it was Combs.

Tommy rose to his feet. "Drop your gun, you don't have a chance."

Combs turned quickly and fired at Tommy but missed. He tried to fire again but was out of ammunition.

"You can drop it now."

"You better kill me because I won't miss the next time," Combs responded as he dropped his gun.

Tommy walked up to Combs, who shrank back against the far bank of the wash, picked up Combs's gun, and walked back to his horses. No other words were exchanged between the two men and Tommy never saw Geoffrey Combs again.

He returned to Tombstone two days later and had Jupiter and the other horse rubbed down and given an extra ration of oats. Joaquin's father asked Tommy how it went, and Tommy just nodded. He rested the next two days while he went over his plans, and when he had them set in his mind, he called in Joaquin and his father and told them he was leaving. He wanted them to have the livery stables, his freight business, and the horse breaking operation. The father said they didn't have the money to buy the businesses but they could run the business until Tommy came back.

Tommy told them he wasn't corning back. "I want you to have the business. You've worked hard, know how to run it, and besides, you de- serve the opportunity. You've been like family to me. I'll have my banker work up a contract, but it will be no money down and monthly payments to my bank. There's plenty of cash flow, so you should have no problem in making the payments."

Joaquin continued to protest, but eventually he and his father were resigned to the decision. Deep down they knew that this was a chance to improve their lot in life. Tommy had his attorney draw up the bill of sale for the businesses he was selling to the Apache Joaquin and his family. Tommy met with his banker and told him his plans and how much he wanted for the commercial buildings. The banker could handle the transactions for a fee, the collection of rents on them until sold, and the monthly payments from Joaquin, and he'd keep his account at the bank open.

It was similar to his departure in Santa Fe, and Tommy was quite proficient in handling this type of dissolution. Deep down he knew it was time to leave. He knew he'd been successful in Santa Fe and now in Tombstone, but there was so much more he wanted to accomplish. The problem was he didn't know what that was, only that it couldn't be done here.

Before he left, he met with Wyatt and Virgil Earp and thanked them for their help and understanding.

"Is Combs corning back to town?" Virgil asked.

"I don't think so," Tommy responded.

It was two years later when a prospector in the Chiricahua Desert came across a skeleton. Some clothes were still on the body. The prospector found identification on the body indicating it was Geoffrey Combs. When the prospector got to Tombstone he turned the identification into the sheriff 's office, but there was no reward and the new sheriff didn't even know who Geoffrey Combs was.

CHAPTER SIXTEEN

Sarah asked Charles Howard to contact James T. Jefferson, the Pinkerton detective who had helped find her son Lars and see if he knew where Lars was. It was two days before Jefferson responded. Lars was last seen near Lincoln, Nebraska. He was wanted for some petty theft, nothing serious, but Jefferson felt that if Lars didn't change, he was headed for prison or worse.

It'd been a year since she last saw her daughter Naiwa, so Sarah and Naomi left Harrisburg, taking the train to Sacramento with a stop in Omaha to meet with Jefferson. James Hansen didn't come to the station to see her off. Sarah was sad and wondered if James would ever get over his prejudice.

It was a day's trip from Omaha to the Spotted Tail Agency to see Naiwa, who had a new baby boy and had named him James, which delighted Sarah. The three women talked about the old days, the future, and when they would see each other again. Sarah gave Naiwa some money and told her she'd send some each year. The time to leave came too soon, but Sarah and Naomi were off to Omaha to meet with Jefferson, who didn't have any further word on Lars.

This was the trip of a lifetime for Naomi, who never in her wildest dreams believed that she would be treated so well in this world. Last year she was on the street; this year she was a companion to a lovely young woman who treated her with respect and dignity. She knew deep down that she'd give her life for Sarah Hansen if necessary. She looked back on her life before she came to Harrisburg and wondered if her sister was still alive. She hadn't seen any of her family since she left their village. There was so little to eat that many in the tribe were eating any stray dog that ventured near. It wasn't like that when she was young. Her life was so much different and so free.

They arrived in San Francisco two days later and spent the next two weeks becoming acquainted with the ebb and flow of this exciting city. Sarah wasn't sure where she wanted to locate, so she decided to hire an agent who specialized in finding homes for people. She leased a small home in a respectable neighborhood about six blocks from the wharf. They were close to shopping, some nice neighborhood restaurants, and the horse drawn trolleys. Naomi and Sarah were like two small children in a candy store as they set about finding pieces of furniture to furnish the small, two bedroom home, which included a large kitchen and a sunny parlor. There was a wraparound porch in the rear of the home. Sarah hired a contractor to enclose two sides with glass and screen in the rear. This would be her studio.

James Hansen may have been preoccupied during the year and a half that Sarah was in Harrisburg, but what he had done for her was invaluable. He had shown her how to take control of her everyday life. Consequently she set about establishing a rapport with a banker, an attorney, and a physician. She'd interviewed three different banks before she selected Market Street Bank, mainly due to the courtesy that James Durham, the manager, showed her and Naomi. He was attentive to her needs and recommended certain procedures to provide a better analysis of her existing assets and made small suggestions on how she might increase the monthly revenue from her commercial and apartment buildings. He analyzed her income and expenses and gave her a sample profile of a budget so that she could manage her day-to-day cash flow.

She started painting again. She'd hire a carriage, Naomi would make a lunch, and they'd go up to Russian Hill for four or five hours or until the fog moved in and it became too cold. She'd become acquainted with a few artists and asked their advice about supplies and where her work would receive the most attention. She took a few lessons from one of the artists teaching at the San Francisco School of Art to improve her ability to mix colors.

Some days she and Naomi would go to Fisherman's Wharf and paint alongside the other fledgling artists, and it was here that she learned which galleries would be receptive to her work. Soon she made contact with the manager of a gallery and asked if she could place some of her work there on consignment. There were numerous landscape painters in the bay area, but none with the perspective of the Wild West and more specifically the Indian culture. The lavish colors of her canvases immediately caught the eye of the gallery's clientele.

The owner of the gallery, John Stevenson, approached her about a one woman showing of her work. Sarah had always painted at her leisure and with scenes that she could remember. Painting with a time table of nine months was perhaps more pressure than she wanted, but the challenge of being able to accomplish the task was what won out in the end. She decided to do landscapes similar to the impressionist style. She used her experience and memory of the Indian villages, the landscape of the prairies, and the endless images of the Indian spirit manifested in their everyday life.

It took her eight months to produce six landscapes paintings that she felt were worthy and asked the gallery owner for an honest appraisal. She could see the answer in his eyes as he reviewed each painting, setting them against her studio wall as he carefully scrutinized every aspect of each painting. When he was finished he warmly grabbed her hands and told her he was delighted that she had chosen his gallery and looked forward to a successful showing next month.

Fueled by praise from the owner of the gallery, she decided to treat herself to some new clothes. She and Naomi went into town and shopped until they were tired. The only argument they had was when Sarah tried to buy Naomi some clothes. Her companion rebelled and absolutely would not look at any dresses. "I have clothes; I don't need any more. You've done enough for me."

The night of the showing was drawing near and Sarah felt pressure unlike anything she had ever experienced before. It was Naomi who was her rock and who told her not to worry. If the gallery owner was convinced, he'd make sure his clientele would feel the same way. "This is a business," she said, "and the gallery owner has an investment in the outcome; it's his responsibility to sell your work."

The clients who came were the elite of San Francisco and the surrounding area. Women wore their finest; Sarah couldn't keep her eyes off the finery, but her beauty trumped any fine clothes that the other women had, and every man that came with his wife made a special effort to meet the tiny blond artist. Some held onto her hand a little too long for their partners.

One particular man paid attention to her all evening, making sure her wine glass was filled. His name was Franz Heller, an importer of fine China with a retail operation on Market Street in the city.

By the end of the evening, the gallery owner had commitments on five of her paintings. The only one that didn't sell was a scene of Indian women cleaning buffalo skin by a stream. This was one of Sarah's favorites and brought back memories of the time when she was sitting with these women doing the same thing, but the clients felt that it was much too stark to put in their drawing rooms. Franz Heller remained to the end and invited Sarah to dinner the following evening. Sarah declined but said she'd be receptive to lunch the next day if Heller could fit that into his schedule. He said he'd call for her at noon, but she said she'd rather meet him at a restaurant of his choosing. He smiled and told her Antoine's was a superb eatery, specializing in fish. She agreed to meet him there at noon.

Heller was waiting for her when she arrived ten minutes late. She apologized for her tardiness, but he was charming and kissed her hand. He was such an entertaining companion that she hardly touched the superb lunch of Dover sole. He told her of his early life in Prussia on a horse breeding farm owned by his family. He was an accomplished equestrian and for a couple of years had served as a captain in the Prussian cavalry. His father had been a merchant in the town of Trakehnen and wanted Franz to go to American as an extension of the family's importing and exporting business.

Sarah wasn't sure she wanted any form of relationship at this time, while she was fur- the ring her career as an artist, but Heller was so charming that she found herself accepting engagements when she really didn't want to. They had dinner at least once a week and once a month went to the opera or a play. Their relationship had been casual up to this point, but he was pressing for a more intimate one and she wondered if he was the man she wanted to be intimate with. His whole persona seemed to overwhelm her, and all she could do was to put obstacles in his way or he'd totally control her.

One evening they went to dinner and then to a performance of Aida at the San Francisco Opera House. Afterward they dined at the Wellington House before Heller drove Sarah home in his carriage. He'd been the perfect escort all evening, and Sarah allowed him to walk her to the door. As she reached in her purse for the keys to the front door, he reached down and kissed her passionately; it caught her by surprise. She wrestled herself away and opened the door and was turning toward him to say goodnight when he pushed through the door and attempted to embrace her. She stumbled backward and he was upon her again, groping and attempting to kiss her. She slipped and stumbled backward against the hall wall and he pinned her up against the wall and fondled her breasts. He was too big and strong and she was being forced to her bedroom and there wasn't anything she seemed to be able to do to stop him.

He grabbed her by the shirt and forced her onto the bed. She was hitting him, but he didn't seem to feel the impact. He forced her skirts up and pulled down her drawers and when she tried to kick him, he slapped her hard across the face. She was stunned, terrified, and didn't know what to do. His pants were down around his ankles and he pushed her legs apart and had his knees between her legs as he was preparing to enter her when he let out a blood curdling scream. He fell off the bed on his back and screamed again. Naomi was on top of him trying to cut him in his genitals. He was trying to fend her off while screaming at the same time When Sarah realized what was happening and she screamed at Naomi, "Get off him and don't cut him anymore!"

Naomi reluctantly moved off Heller but stood poised with the knife if he made a threatening move. Heller turned over on his hand and knees and started to cry. Sarah could see blood pouring from his buttocks where Naomi had slashed him. Sarah got a wet cloth and applied pressure to his buttocks, but the bleeding didn't stop, and she was concerned.

She reached into her nightstand drawer and took out a small revolver, then told Naomi, "go outside and have Heller 's man take you to our doctor. Tell the doctor there's a man at our house with a serious knife wound and we're worried about the amount of blood he's losing. Ask him to come immediately."

Naomi was reluctant to leave and wanted to stay, but Sarah assured her she was an excellent shot and would shoot Heller if he moved off the floor.

When Naomi told Heller's driver that it was Heller who was wounded, the driver wanted to go inside the house but was persuaded by the knife Naomi was wielding to do as she bid.

No sooner had Naomi left for the doctor than Heller started to get up. Sarah leaned over Heller, placed the gun with pressure on the back of his head, and said that she would shoot him be- tween his legs if he didn't lie quietly on his stomach until the doctor arrived. He slowly relaxed and lay down, but not without complaining of the intense pain he was feeling.

At times he cried and pleaded with her not to call the police.

The doctor, Naomi, and the driver returned in forty five minutes. Naomi ordered the driver to remain with the carriage; one look at her knife was all it took. The doctor examined Heller and gave him a small dose of morphine for the pain. He cleaned the wound and stitched it up and suggested that Heller stay off his rear for the next few days. Dr. Feldman said that with a knife wound, he was required to notify the sheriff. Heller begged him not to notify the sheriff and stated that he cut himself. The doctor asked how, and Heller said that was none of his business.

CHAPTER SEVENTEEN

It wasn't as though Jan Hutchinson was the love of his life, but she was a warm, caring individual who had been caught between Tommy and Geoffrey Combs. Tommy still wasn't sure why Combs had hired two men to kill him but killed Jan instead, leaving two orphans. The Williamses were a good family and would look after Jan's children until they were of age. Tommy would track their progress through his banker in Tombstone and would supplement the family's income until the children were of age.

The question for him was where to relocate. He didn't have a financial problem. Henri and his family were paying him for his business in Santa Fe, and he was sure Joaquin would pay each month for the Tombstone operation. The banker in Tombstone had already sold two of his commercial buildings and had offers for the other two. Tommy was worth over one hundred thousand dollars and had a four figure monthly income. He seemed to have a knack for business and was able to make them successful, mainly because he saw what was needed and also hired people who he could trust.

Phoenix and Tucson were young and energetic, but he wanted to go someplace farther away from the Judd Harkers of the world, so he decided on El Paso, Texas, to see what opportunities were available. The Acheson Topeka, Southern Pacific, Texas Pacific, and Santa Fe railroads had been extended to El Paso by 1881. It took him three days to wind up his business and make his way by train to El Paso with Jupiter riding in a car outfitted with horse stalls. The town had grown to nearly twelve thousand by 1883, had added horse drawn cars, and was in a constant state of building. Tommy interviewed two bankers and chose Timothy J. Stearns of the El Paso National Bank not only because he was eager but was astute in seeing investment potential in several areas.

The horse hadn't lost its appeal as one of the main methods of transportation, and since this was a tried and true method of success, Tommy immediately set about to buy a livery stable. There were three on the outskirts of the city, but only one was for sale. Tommy visited with the owner of the livery stable and asked why he was selling. The owner finally admitted that he had difficulty with the business and couldn't find reliable help. Tommy allowed his new banker to handle the transaction even though the banker indicated he thought Tommy was setting his sights too low. Tommy just smiled.

With the livery stable now his, he advertised for help. Surprisingly he had twelve applicants, ranging from middle aged men who were down on their luck to drifters to some Mexicans. He listened patiently to all of them, but Francisco Ortega seemed to have the most knowledge of horses, and Tommy was comfortable with him. Francisco had a wife and two small children who lived on the Mexican side of the Rio Grande River separating the two nations. For each of the applicants, he tested their knowledge of the local area, the number of ranches that were successful, and those that were not. In the end he decided on the Mexican and said he'd give him a three month trial.

Francisco Ortega, like Henri and Joaquin, had a natural affinity for horses and was willing to work to earn the trust of his employer. Tommy asked Francisco about the number of wild horses in the area and was surprised to learn there were still a few herds of mustangs across the border and that they were available to anyone who'd capture them. Tommy asked his banker to verify what Francisco had told him and was assured that this was the case. He and Francisco set out to capture a few of these mustangs and see if they could be broken. He showed Francisco how to gain the animal's respect and then how, through a careful and systematic approach, the horse could be ridden and subsequently carriage broke.

Slowly Tommy replaced his present stock of horses with new ones and instituted his method of leasing carriages and horses. Within six months his was the most successful of the three livery stables. It seemed that Francisco had several cousins who shared his knowledge of horses and were in need of work. As he had done in Santa Fe and Tombstone, Tommy increased the number of his horses and was able to bring in horses from other ranches that were seen as unfit, break them, and subsequently sell them for a profit. He hired a bookkeeper and some of Francisco's friends; after the first year the business turned a sizeable profit.

But Tommy had visions of something bigger than a livery stable. With the four railroads merging in El Paso, he envisioned a freight and import business that would bring products from all over the country to this growing area. Others had similar visions, but they lacked the larger picture and the finances to make it work. With his banker's help and a line of credit, Tommy started importing furniture from the more famous furniture manufacturers in the East and opened up a large furniture store. His retail furniture store was the largest in the Southwest, and with his introduction of installments sales, he captured a large portion of the market. Soon Tommy was more than half way toward his goal of being a millionaire.

Frequently Tommy visited Mexico to find horses, do some hunting, and sometimes camp out. While in Mexico, Tommy made the acquaintance of Don Hernando Lopez, a landowner with a large herd of cattle. Lopez had heard of Tommy's method of training and breaking wild horses and asked for a personal demonstration at Rancho Lopez, located just outside the small town of Nuevo Casas Grande. Previously, Lopez had purchased some of the mustangs that Tommy and Francisco had trained and was cross breeding them with some of his thoroughbred stock.

This was the perfect entree for Tommy, who willingly demonstrated his method before Don Lopez, his family, and many of the other rancho owners in the Mexican state of Chihuahua, which was the cattle center of Mexico. Tommy learned that Lopez and other rancho owners had tried shipping cattle to the States. They had an advantage because of the rail head at Nuevo Casas Grande which had a direct connection to El Paso. But their experience was anything but satisfactory. They'd ship their cattle, but were paid after delivery and sale in the northern markets, and payment was always delayed for some reason or another. They felt that they were being taken advantage of by speculators and con men.

Tommy stayed with Don Hernando for three days, and during that time he proposed a partnership with him. Tommy would give a deposit to Don Hernando amounting to about thirty percent of the market value of his cattle and ship them to the northern markets at his expense and they'd share the proceeds on a 25:75 basis. "So in essence I'd get seventy five percent of the market value of my cattle and you would get twenty-five percent less expenses," Don Hernando said.

"That's true, but you will get nearly one third of your money up front and not have to worry about any shipping costs or losses during transit. Think about it. Why not try it once, and if it works out for you, perhaps you'd like to be my partner and help with contracts with the other ranchos. If I'm as successful as I believe I'll be, why not share in the rewards?"

"Mr. Sanchez, I'm not someone to be trifled with. I can be a good friend or a rotten enemy."

"I wouldn't have it any other way. Let me know your decision. I must leave for El Paso in the morning."

When Tommy came down to breakfast the next morning, Don Hernando had an agreement ready that outlined the proposal that Tommy made to him the evening before. They shook hands, finished breakfast, and Don Hernando drove with him to the train station in Nuevo Casas Grandes. "I will be ready by the fifteenth of next month to ship. Will you be ready?" Don Hernando asked. Tommy said he would be ready.

It was thirty days after the first shipment of cattle from Don Hernando's herd that he received payment in full from Tommy Sanchez. He was impressed and asked that Tommy visit his rancho and talk about the future. He wanted to make one more shipment before he'd agree to a partnership. Tommy acquiesced to his demand, and the next shipment went off without a hitch with the same deposit and the same return of the proceeds.

Don Hernando was hooked. He talked to other rancho owners in the state of Chihuahua and together they rounded up a sizeable herd for the next shipment. They shipped six more times over the next six months with equal success.

Tommy had made adequate use of the telegraph and set up buyers in advance at four different locations in the Midwest. Tommy was becoming richer, and so was Don Hernando.

On one of his visits to the rancho, Tommy was introduced to Don Hernando's daughter, Maria Conchita, who'd been going to school in Mexico City. Maria Conchita was a magnificently beautiful young woman with a smile that would soften any male she came in contact with.

Tommy became one of her admirers and always found an excuse to visit the rancho even if there wasn't any ongoing business between himself and Don Hernando. Soon he was courting the young woman with the blessing of her father. In spite of their age differential, Tommy found her to be a mature and willing companion. She was a skilled pianist, and Tommy loved to sit and listen to her play for hours on end. As the courtship progressed, it became serious, and Tommy asked Don Hernando for Maria Conchita's hand. An engagement party was planned, bringing together family and all of Don Hernando's friends and acquaintances. Many who attended had shipped cattle through Tommy's company. Don Hernando cried as he stood before his family and friends and announced the engagement. The engagement party lasted two days, at the end of which Tommy and Maria were exhausted and decided to get away from all their family, friends, and acquaintances for a few hours. Don Hernando smiled when the two love birds said they were going on a picnic at Sierra Springs, a lush oasis about five miles from the rancho.

Tommy had gotten into the habit of not carrying firearms while he was at the rancho and saw no reason on this beautiful sunny day to break that custom. Today they were lucky; no one else was enjoying the lush greens around a small, running brook. Maria laid out a blanket and the lunch their housekeeper had prepared. Tommy lay back on the blanket and Maria cuddled up in his arms. They were so exhausted that they closed their eyes and soon fell asleep in the noonday sun.

Tommy was the first to wake and immediately sensed something was wrong. He sat up and that's when he saw four men leering down at the couple. Tommy came awake and assessed his options. He stirred Maria and told her to get up, walk to the carriage, and leave the lunch where it was. As he was helping Maria to her feet, he was shot in the back twice and fell over onto the blanket. The last thing he remembered before passing out was one of the men grabbing Maria and pulling at her clothes.

When nightfall came and the couple hadn't returned, Don Hernando and seven of his men rode out to Sierra Springs. They found a bloody Tommy unconscious on a blanket on top of the food the housekeeper had prepared for them. Their horse and carriage was tied to a tree, but there was no sign of Maria. Tommy's wounds were serious and he appeared near death. Four men lifted him carefully into the carriage. Just then one of Don Hernando's riders found the naked body of his beloved daughter Maria; she'd been beaten to death. The father ordered his men not to look at her naked body. He grabbed the blanket and placed it around his daughter's body and openly wept.

He personally carried her to the carriage and lovingly laid her next to Tommy.

One of his men said that tracks indicated there had been four riders recently at the springs and those tracks were heading to the south. Don Hernando ordered three of his most experienced men to see if he could track them and then report back to him at the rancho. He would drive the carriage with the lifeless body of his daughter and Tommy Sanchez back to the rancho.

Men and women cried when Don Hernando returned with the lifeless body of his daughter. Maria's mother had been dead for over ten years, and Don Hernando asked his longtime housekeeper to prepare his daughter for burial. His was the largest rancho in the state and, like many ranchos, had a doctor in residence. He sent for the doctor and asked him to try to save Tommy's life. They carried his body into the guest room that Tommy had been using. The doctor cut off his shirt and saw the two wounds. Tommy was unconscious, had lost a lot of blood, and obviously was very weak because of the amount of time he'd been lying on the blanket before he was found. The doctor told Don Hernando that the only chance to save him was to remove the two bullets. With the help of one of the young women at the rancho, the doctor took out both bullets, cleaned the wounds, and said that Tommy's life was in God's hands.

Don Hernando asked the doctor to examine his dead daughter to see if she had been violated. The doctor was embarrassed when he informed Don Hernando that Maria had been repeatedly violated. The old man broke down and cried.

The three riders sent by Don Hernando returned the next morning and said they'd tracked the four to a small town called Tapa, about ten miles south. They talked to the owner of the cantina who told them that four riders had come to the cantina, stayed only a short time, and then left. No one knew the four or where they went. Don Hernando's men were unable to pick up their tracks. In the interim, the Federales had been contacted and they assured Don Hernando they'd apprehend the four.

Most of her family and friends attended Maria Conchita's funeral, but Tommy was still unconscious. She was buried on a knoll facing the stream that bordered the eastern portion of their rancho. This was her favorite place on the rancho. She'd told her father that she felt at peace here.

A captain of the Federales attended the funeral and reported that they hadn't been able to identify the men responsible for Maria's death and wounding Tommy.   "Has   the American said   anything?" he asked.

Don Hernando responded that he was still unconscious. "It will take time. I want to post a reward of ten thousand pesos for information and capture of the four men responsible. Will you take care of the details?" The captain said he would.

Tommy hovered at the edge of death for the next week and was cared for around the clock by several of the women workers at the rancho. Don Hernando checked on him every hour and prayed for him every day. The doctor told Don Hernando that they 'd know one way or the other at the end of the week. That's when Tommy's fever broke and he seemed to regain consciousness but then lapsed back again. The women tried to feed him when he was awake, but he wouldn't cooperate. Don Hernando was worried that he would die without food or water.

The next morning Tommy was conscious and tried to get out of bed but nearly fell. When he learned that Tommy was awake, Don Hernando came to visit and asked him if he remembered what happened at Sierra Springs. Tommy asked about Maria, but Don Hernando evaded the question and posed his own again. Tommy told him that the last thing he remembered was getting shot and one of the four men grabbing her. "Where's Maria? I want to see her. Is she hurt?" he asked.

"She was raped and murdered. We buried her last week." It was stark and blunt, but Don Hernando wanted to see Tommy's reaction.

Tommy turned white and his breathing became forced. Don Hernando was afraid the shock of the tragic news might make Tommy's heart stop, and he yelled for the doctor. The doc- tor gave Tommy an injection to calm him down. Soon his breathing stabilized and color returned to his face and he asked Don Hernando, "Who were they?"

Don Hernando was embarrassed. "We don't know. We followed them for ten miles but then lost them. The Federales have taken over and are ardently searching for them, but I don't know. I posted a reward of ten thousand pesos."

"I'll get them. What does the doctor say about me?"

"He says you are very weak and it'll take a couple of months for you to recover." Tears were rolling down Don Hernando's cheeks.

"I will walk tomorrow even if you have to hold me up, and in a week I'll be ready to go after them."

"But no one knows who they are or where they went." Don Hernando was trying to empathize with Tommy but he was becoming frustrated; he was a powerful man and he didn't know what to do.

"I will find them." He then turned over and went back to sleep.

The next morning after breakfast, Tommy, with the help of one of the women working at the rancho, walked outside. Don Hernando offered a shoulder and the two walked twice around the riding corrals. Tommy lay down on a hammock on the front porch for an hour and then was up walking again using a cane. The next day he tried a mild form of sit-ups and continued to walk. Soon he was walking by himself without assistance from anyone or the use of a cane. After a few days his appetite came back and he started to regain the twelve pounds he had lost. It was a week before the stitches would hold well enough while he attempted to ride Jupiter. Both the doctor and Don Hernando tried to slow Tommy down and told him to use some restraint, but he was determined to be on his feet as soon as possible and track down the killers of Maria Conchita.

He hated to admit it, but he knew he needed another week of eating and exercise to regain enough strength to be a worthy adversary. In between walking, exercising, and climbing small hills, he practiced shooting with his rifle, hand- gun, and something special. The children would sit for hours and watch him practice his artistry.

At the end of the second week, he was ready and told Don Hernando that he would find them. Don Hernando begged Tommy to take him along. "I know you want to go, but this is a job for someone with my skills. I've done this before. I won't fail you," Tommy said.

He took another mount in addition to Jupiter and loaded his weapons, extra ammunition and rations for a week on the second horse. He found the cantina in Tapa that afternoon. He cautiously entered the small, one story adobe structure and looked around. In addition to the bartender, who he assumed was the owner, there were two peasants sitting at a table against the wall. He hadn't been conscious very long the day he was shot, but he carried in his mind a vivid picture of each of the four men who shot him and killed Maria.

He could see that the two peasants sitting at the table weren't any of the men he sought, so he turned his attention to the bartender and spoke to him in Spanish. "Four men came through here one Sunday afternoon about three weeks ago. I want their names and I want to know where they are."

The bartender continued wiping down the small bar and didn't pay much attention to Tommy as he responded. "They came through, had a drink, and then left. I don't know them nor do I know where they are. I told that to the three men from the rancho and to the captain of the Federales when he was here."

In a flash, Tommy drew and fired. The bartender screamed and grabbed his left ear. The two peasants got up and started to the door, but with his gun, Tommy waved them back to the table. He turned to the bartender." I can do this all day. I have plenty of ammunition and I can hit an ant at thirty paces. I want to know who the men were."

The bartender started to deny his knowledge again, but something in the way the thin Mexican was looking at him told him that this adversary was more of a threat than the four men. Though his voice was shaking, he told Tommy the four were Gustavo Flores, Juan Dominquez, and the Lopez brothers, Javier and Fernando.

"Where are they?" Tommy asked.

The bartender no sooner uttered the words "I don't know" than Tommy shot off part of his right ear. The bartender fell to his knees and grabbed both sides of his face; his hands were full of blood. He screamed the answer." They have a hideout in a box canyon in the Chihuahua Valley. Back in the canyon is a waterfall and a small stream. Their cabin is by the waterfall, but you can't get to them. They have a guard posted at the entrance of the canyon, and both sides of the entrance are steep."

Tommy threw a couple of gold coins on the bar and turned to the two peasants. "Which of you can lead me there? I will pay you or I'll shoot you right here."

The older of the two said he knew the location of the canyon that the bartender identified. "If you promise not to kill either of us, I will lead you near there. These men are bad and you don't stand a chance, so I won't get too close in case they see us."

"That's fine, but if I suspect that you're leading me into a trap, I'll bury you in the sand and let the ants take you and then I'll track your friend and slit his throat. Do you understand?" The peasant nodded that he did.

While the younger peasant helped bandage the bartender's ears, Tommy took out a map he'd been carrying. The older peasant showed Tommy on the map where the box canyon with the waterfall was located. The bartender con- firmed the location. It looked to be about a three- day trip.

Tommy turned to the bartender. "I'll be back with those men. God help you if you have any of his friends waiting for me when I come back. I'll kill you and burn this place down. Do you understand?" He pointed the gun at the man and waited until he nodded that he understood.

He set out immediately with the peasant who said his name was Felipe; he let him ride the spare mount. Tommy knew where he was going and had an idea how to get into the canyon, so he decided to take his time and conserve his energy. At the end of the third day, the peasant pointed to the area where the box canyon was located. Tommy paid him and watched him disappear back the way they came with money in his pocket and the use of a horse. The man seemed honest. Tommy was positive the peasant would leave the horse at the cantina and make sure it was fed and watered until Tommy returned.

'On their way to the canyon, he had looked through binoculars at the mountains enveloping the canyon and could see that the only practical way in was through the front. If the bartender was correct, there was a sentry at the entrance. He spent the remainder of daylight trying to find a place to camp that couldn't be seen by anyone at the entrance to the box canyon, as well as a place that was close enough to the canyon so he could go back and forth in a minimal amount of time.

After he selected his camp he decided to use the nighttime to reconnoiter the area. He spent the entire night getting a feel for the length of the canyon, the steep heights on either side of the entrance, and where a sentry might be stationed. He made his way back to camp and slept until afternoon. His camp was secluded, and he was able to practice with his special weapon for two hours without being seen; then he took a nap.

As soon as it was dark, Tommy made his way back to the entrance and crawled around to the right and then back to the entrance and then around to the left searching for a way up. It was when he was about one hundred yards from the entrance on the left hand side that he saw some movement above, and as he waited, he distinctly saw a flash of fire, similar to someone lighting a cigar, though it could even be a small camp fire.

Going inside the canyon and then up the sheer wall to attack the sentry would be fruit- less. The only practical solution was to go up the other side of the entrance and kill the sentry from that location. The floor of the canyon was only about thirty feet wide, and the walls sur- rounding the canyon were about one hundred feet high at the entrance. He crawled back and found a spot about fifty feet from the entrance on the right side that looked climbable and started up the wall. The going was tough, and he decided to take his time so as not to sap all his strength. It took him about an hour to reach the top. He came up at a point directly across from the flash of light he had seen below. He thought to himself that the sentry didn't sense any threat, because he didn't disguise the small camp fire he used to keep warm.

Tommy waited until his eyes adjusted to the darkness and then could make out one man sitting in front of a small fire. Tommy had carried a six gun with extra ammunition and a rifle up the hill. But it was the other weapon, a bow and quiver of arrows, that could put him at an advantage. He had been an excellent shot with bow and arrow as a child, and the amount of practice he did at the rancho while convalescing made him particularly confident he could hit the man and not alert those in the cabin near the water- fall. A sitting man at about 100 to 125 feet would be difficult, but a man standing at that distance was doable.

When he was ready, he unleashed an arrow that clattered against the rocks near the sitting sentry. The sentry turned his head to see where the noise was coming from and then slowly stood up and turned to face Tommy, who shot him in the heart. As the sentry was falling, Tommy placed another arrow on the bow and was ready in case he missed. The question was what to do now. It was obvious the sentry had a means of going up and down the wall. So where was the access? It was also possible that the sentry would be relieved by someone else, and Tommy couldn't afford to have that happen. Any surprise he might have would be lost, and the odds of him being successful against possibly five other men would be too great.

He had no choice but to descend to the canyon floor and enter the canyon and find the place the sentries used to go up and down the canyon wall. He tied a rope around a solid boulder and lowered himself to the canyon floor and slowly walked toward the waterfall looking for the access. He found it about one hundred yards inside the canyon and slowly made his way up. The sentry was dead and lying on his stomach with an arrow sticking out of his back. Tommy grabbed him by the collar, dragged him into some shrub, and put some branches over his body. Next he put out the fire and waited. It was only eleven o'clock, and if there was a sentry change, it probably would be either at midnight or four a.m. Whether there was a relief or not, he planned to descend to the canyon floor about four o'clock and make his way to the cabin.

Tommy had the ability to sleep while still being alert. There was no sentry change at mid- night, but shortly before four in the morning he heard movement below and then a voice says in Spanish that he was coming up. Tommy hid behind a boulder to the left of the access trail, and as soon as the relief sentry reached the top, Tommy came up behind him, placed one hand over his mouth, and pulled the man back to- ward him. With the other hand he slit the man's throat. Neither of the sentries was one of the four who raped Maria.

He was in full attack mode. The only thing missing was war paint as he made his way along the canyon floor toward the cabin by the waterfall. Soon he heard a dog bark. He'd been pre- pared for this eventuality and waited for the dog to approach him. He shot the dog with an arrow and the dog whined and fell over. Tommy waited about fifteen minutes before he moved forward. He grabbed the animal and pulled it back down the canyon and laid it up against the wall. He hated to kill the animal, but he didn't have much choice.

The canyon slowly widened, and he could hear the waterfall and then make out an outline of a cabin with smoke coming out of the chimney. In addition to the cabin there was a corral, a lean to, which was probably used for storage, and an outhouse. It was four thirty and still dark as Tommy made his way around the cabin, positioning himself near the corrals with a clear view of the doors leading from the cabin, the lean-to, and the outhouse. To make this work, he knew he'd need more than luck.

At six in the morning there was stirring in the cabin, and two of its inhabitants came out and made their way to the outhouse. Tommy raised his rifle and shot one of the men in the shoulder and the other in his leg. Both fell and started to crawl toward the cabin, but Tommy placed two shots in the dirt in front of them and they stopped. The door to the cabin was slammed shut from inside and the glass in a window on the side toward the outhouse was shattered by a rifle pointed out the window. Tommy's position was still obscured from the shooter in the window, and he carefully lit an oily rag, attached it to the tip of an arrow, and fired it into the broken window. Then in succession, he fired two flaming rags on the roof and three more into the broken window.

Soon smoke was billowing out the window and the front door was thrown open, a rifle was pointed out the door, and several shots were fired. One of the men inside dove out the door and came up rolling and firing at the same time. Tommy took his time and shot him in the shoulder, and the gunman dropped the rifle. He made an attempt to grab it, but Tommy was too quick and shot him in the middle of his hand. The gun- man lay back awaiting the outcome.

The fourth man inside finally came out the door firing his handgun randomly while turning in circles hoping to hit his adversary. The smoke had probably blinded the man. Tommy took his time and dropped him with a shot in the shoulder. All four gunmen lay on the ground, crying out in pain and swearing in Spanish. He spoke to the four in Spanish, "Sit there until I'm finished. Anyone trying to escape will be shot."

Tommy waited until the cabin burned to the ground. Then he set fire to the outhouse and the lean-to and waited until everything was ashes. Now that he was sure there was no one else around, he threw a rope to the gunman who had been shot in the leg and told him to tie each of the other's hands behind their backs.

When the gunman was done, Tommy tied that man's hands behind his back and then told them all to sit on the ground with their backs to each other and not move. He wound a rope around all four and walked over to the corral where five horses were standing. Then he came back and bandaged all their wounds and stopped the flow of blood before he saddled all five mounts. One by one he helped the wounded men onto their horses. One of the men, referred to as Gustavo, tried to escape. Tommy shot him in the foot and then bandaged the foot. Each man was tied to his horse so there was no chance for escape. Tommy told them he'd shoot anyone who tried to run

The ride back was grueling. After he retrieved Jupiter and loaded his supplies on the extra horse, he was on his way. He refused to take time for the men to relieve themselves and didn't give them any food, just water. They cried, complained, and hurled insults at him throughout the ride. He'd stop every three hours and pour water into their mouths but would not loosen any of the ropes that bound their hands or let them get off their horses.

Tommy did not sleep; he was tired, but he knew he could maintain this pace until they reached the rancho. Then there'd be time to sleep. When he reached the cantina, he saw that his other horse was tethered to a bush outside the building. He grabbed the horse, tied the halter to the horn on his saddle, and trailed it and the other horse behind him. He was getting tired, and he didn't want to take any more chances with the four men so he tied each of their horses to a lead line that he wound around his saddle horn. They reached the rancho about six in the evening of the third day after leaving the canyon.

Don Hernando and six of his men took charge of the four. "These are the four who shot me and raped and killed Maria Conchita, "Tommy said. "I've done my job and I'm finished with them. It's up to you to deliver whatever justice is reasonable." He fell asleep in the guest room with his clothes on but awakened periodically when he heard screaming and then would fall asleep again. He awoke thirty six hours later and never asked about the four men, nor did Don Hernando furnish any information. No one at the rancho spoke of the incident ever again.

Tommy spent the next two months recuperating and making daily vigils to Maria Conchita's grave site. The stitches in his back had ruptured during the ride back with the four, and he was forced back to bed for a few days and then spent two more weeks recuperating.

When the captain of the Federales came by the rancho and asked about the four men Tommy had caught, Don Hernando said he didn't know anything about it. It couldn't have been Tommy because he was too ill to have left the rancho. When questioned by the captain, Tommy said he didn't know what they were talking about.

"The owner of the cantina said you captured four men. What happened to them?" the captain persisted.

"I'm sorry, Captain, the owner must have me confused with someone else," Tommy responded.

"I don't think so. I'm pretty sure he remembers you because you shot both of his ears before he told you their names and where they could be found. One of the peasants went with you to their hideout, and he and the owner saw you with four men when you picked up the horse that he left at the cantina. So where are they?"

"There must be a mistake because I was here at the rancho recovering from my wounds. Ask anyone."

The captain of the Federales and Don Hernando took long walks to the site where Maria was buried and each unashamedly cried at her grave. The captain, who had also courted Maria Conchita, was persistent and continued to ask everyone about the four men, but he was to be denied and finally left the rancho frustrated. When Tommy told Don Hernando that he was leaving the rancho and the area as well, the old man cried and begged him to stay. "You're like a son to me. What will I do when you leave? Who will I leave the rancho to? You are like me. I still can't bear the pain that her murder has caused. Please stay."

In the end, the old man knew that Tommy would go. He'd lost his true love, and the effort he had expended to track, capture, and deliver the four men to Don Hernando was a tremendous emotional strain on him. He had to deter- mine the purpose of his life and how he wanted to spend the rest of it. He was a wealthy man and capable of creating income. In some ways, he was a man for the ages. Tommy left the rancho, and he and Don Hernando never saw each other again.

CHAPTER EIGHTEEN

The episode with Heller was the tipping point. She'd been uncomfortable in this large city from the beginning, and now she was sure the bay area wasn't for her; she needed a quiet community to live in. Her paintings seemed to sell and she could always send them to any gallery, so being in San Francisco wasn't a necessity. She wondered why Heller seemed so empowered and that she was his for the taking. She definitely hadn't led him on; she was no flirt. Her lease was up in two months, and she had no intention of renewing it. The excitement of the city and the proximity of the retail markets were a plus, but the structure of village simplicity was some- thing she'd grown to love. Naomi had confided in her that she didn't like the fast pace of the bay area and especially didn't like the people who seemed to go out of their way to make her feel inferior.

They were having breakfast in the kitchen when Sarah confided in Naomi. "I'm much more comfortable in a small community. San Fran- cisco is nice, but it's a place I'd like to visit, not live in. What do you think?"

"Whatever you want to do is fine by me, but I don't like the way people look at me. It's like I have a disease."

The question for Sarah was where to relocate. She'd traveled through many locales in California but hadn't spent enough time to get a feeling for what it would be like to live there permanently. She needed a plan. She went to the San Francisco Library to get some background on some of the towns, what type of industries they had, and especially what the weather was like. Since she'd lived in the Midwest for most of her adult life, she decided to concentrate on the coastal areas of California.

"Why don't we retrace our steps by starting in Los Angeles and then go up the coast to Santa Barbara to see what the communities are really like. We haven't spent much time any place, so we can start from the beginning."

With two months to go before they departed, they decided to utilize their remaining time in the bay area by visiting every monument and point of interest. On one of these excursions, they visited the San Francisco Pier and saw the variety of ships docked in the harbor. Sarah was fascinated with a clipper ship by the name of Emerald Gay docked in the harbor. The ship was long and sleek with a narrow bow that had a sculpture of a maiden on the front. She made inquiries to see if there was a way she could have a tour of the vessel. The captain was in the harbor master's office when she made the inquiry. He was taken with her beauty and invited her and Naomi to return to his ship for a tour; she and Naomi accepted the invitation. Jonathan Bird personally escorted them out to the ship in his launch and gave them a tour of the lush clipper ship.

Sarah learned quickly that this charming man from New England was not only the captain but the owner of the vessel as well, and a very proud owner at that. The Emerald Gay was a three masted clipper ship, 270 feet in length and thirty seven feet across the beam, a draft of seventeen feet with a maximum speed of seventeen knots. The vessel was primarily used to transport cargo up and down the coast of California, but it did have four cabins and occasion- ally carried passengers.

"Captain Bird, why are there so many men scurrying all around the ship?" Sarah asked.

Bird pointed out that the ship required at least forty sailors per trip but that they would carry forty five on their next voyage. They'd just returned from Los Angeles and he was contracting for cargo for the return trip to Los Angeles in six weeks. Their tour included the cargo hatch, galley, crew quarters, and four bedrooms below deck. On deck he showed them the sails, masts, rigging, and the helm. He showed Sarah and Naomi how to turn the wheel and how the helmsman navigated. He graciously allowed Sarah to stand behind the wheel and turn it; she was ecstatic. After the tour he invited them to have lunch with him on deck. They gladly accepted even though Naomi was a little suspicious of any man paying too much attention to Sarah. Her knife was always ready if necessary.

During lunch, Jonathan Bird told Sarah and Naomi about his early life in Gloucester, Massachusetts, where he was born. He grew up in a family that owned a fleet of fishing vessels and that's where his love of the sea began. He served as a crewmember on his family ships until he was twenty one, working his way up from cabin boy to first mate. On his twenty first birthday party, his father gave him command of one of their ships. He'd been married once and had two boys who were following in the family tradition. His wife had died when he was forty, and he plunged himself into the family business. His two boys were in their early twenties and each was commanding a family ship. He missed the boys, but they had their own lives to lead and he wouldn't interfere.

He had purchased the Emerald Gay two years ago and decided he wanted to be on his own. His parting with his family was amiable but nevertheless still traumatic .After his wife's death, he decided to sail around the world, and when he landed in San Francisco, it was love at first sight. He was mildly surprised that Sarah was planning to leave and visit Los Angeles. In an offhanded comment, he said she could sail with him to Los Angeles if she wanted.

He asked if he could call on her for lunch the next day; she graciously accepted. "Why don't you come to my home first? I'd like to reciprocate with a tour of my studio."

When he showed up the next day, she displayed several of her paintings that were being prepared for a gallery in Philadelphia. He spent an hour looking at her work and commented, "You are an accomplished artist." She smiled and curtseyed at the compliment.

They had lunch at Fisherman's Wharf and after lunch walked along the wharf. He explained the purpose of each of the ships as they walked past them. She told him about her abduction, subsequent marriage to Crazy Horse, her sudden wealth, and the talent she developed. But what intrigued Jonathan the most was not her artistry. It was true, he was fascinated with the colorful landscapes she painted, but it was the humility she expressed when speaking of her work. He saw in front of him a successful woman, but one with the grace not to flaunt it.

They had lunch daily for the next week and then graduated to dinner and the opera. Sarah was smitten with the tall New Englander, and they quickly moved into an affair. Naomi was constantly trying to preach prudence, but the affair was becoming serious and Sarah knew that she was in love. To preclude any confrontation with Naomi, she would spend the evening with Bird at his home and come back to her place the next morning. She knew Jonathan cared, but didn't know how much until he proposed after a month and a half of a whirlwind courtship. She accepted and they set a date three months hence, which coincided with his return from Los Angeles.

Sarah had planned to leave the area, so she had let their lease lapse. Now she had to look for some other lodgings in the interim. So she and Naomi set out to find a place to live until she was married. She found one place that was almost perfect for her and Naomi, but they wanted a two year lease. Another landlord said he'd promised the two bedroom flat to someone else, but Sarah suspected that they didn't want to let the space to an Indian.

She shared her frustration with Jonathan, who suggested that she and Naomi accompany him on his trip to Los Angeles and back aboard the Emerald Gay. She thought about it for two days and agreed that the trip might be a way for Jonathan and Naomi to become better acquainted and remove some of Naomi's apprehension. She still didn't like living in the bay area. The problem was that Jonathan was well- established in the area and it would be difficult for him to relocate. In addition, he had a beautiful home on Nob Hill, which she'd seen on the many occasions she slept over, and she loved the home.

On the day they were to sail, Sarah and Naomi took a carriage to the wharf and had one of the sailors load their baggage on board. She and Naomi were shown to Jonathan's suite, but Sarah said that was inappropriate and that she and Naomi would share two of the other bedrooms. Jonathan laughed when he heard of the arrangements but wouldn't interfere with his future wife's decisions, at least not at this time. The ship was carrying timber, furniture, and other household goods to Los Angeles but didn't have a cargo for the return trip. Jonathan planned to talk to several middlemen when he landed in Los Angeles. In times past he had to wait between two to four weeks before he had a full load to take back. During that period, they'd live on the ship.

The trip to Los Angeles would take approximately twenty-four hours depending on the winds, so they decided to leave at three in the afternoon so they could dock in the afternoon on the following day. Jonathan had checked the weather, and although there appeared to be a potential storm, it was believed that it wouldn't arrive until the following evening and would probably pass way to the west of their route. They would parallel the California coast sailing about six to ten miles offshore, except near the perilous area of Point Conception, located in the southwestern part of Santa Barbara County. The area around the point had a counter current, and it was at this point where the coastline went directly north to San Francisco and south- east to Los Angeles. Experienced sailors such as Jonathan Bird avoided the area. Along that stretch, they'd move to about thirty-five to forty miles off the coast.

They were on deck as the Emerald Gay left the dock and set sail for Los Angeles that afternoon. Sarah and Naomi retired to their quarters and Jonathan worked with the navigator as they left the bay area and set sail for the city of Los Angeles. The sun was just setting when Jonathan invited Naomi and Sarah to dine in his quarters. The chef had been with Jonathan for the two years he owned the clipper ship and prepared an excellent dinner of fresh fish and seasonal vegetables with rice pilaf. Dessert was an apricot tart. They toasted the chef with a glass of burgundy and then retired to their respective quarters. Naomi had finally confided to Sarah that she was afraid of sailing and it had taken all of Sarah's charm and pleading to get her on board. Consequently she hadn't eaten any of her dinner, nor did she participate in the conversation.

That evening when she was sure Naomi was asleep Sarah quickly walked across to Jonathan's suite and knocked lightly. He instantly opened the door and smiled. "What took you so long?"

"Oh shut up, Jonathan, and take me to bed." They embraced as he shut the door, lifted her in his arms, and gently placed her on his bed. Sarah knew she had loved Crazy Horse, but not in the way she loved Jonathan; this was the love of her life.

Around one in the morning, the boat began to roll. The storm hit, and Sarah excused herself by suggesting that Naomi would be frightened if she awoke and found Sarah wasn't there. Jonathan said he understood and kissed her passionately and said he'd be on the bridge until the storm abated.

Two hours later the ship was rolling heavily in the storm and the timbers started to creak each time the boat tossed and turned. Jonathan had the helmsman steer into the westerly wind, but he was being pushed slowly onto shore. He estimated that the winds had increased to ninety knots while waves were coming across the deck; all hands on deck were tied to each other to preclude anyone from falling over- board. Next some of sails ripped, and Jonathan knew they were in trouble when the main mast cracked in half and fell to the deck.

He rushed below and told everyone to get on deck then banged on Sarah's door and told her they were going down. She and Naomi put on their life preservers and followed Jonathan up on deck. Daylight had broken and they could see the rocks off the coast. One of the lifeboats was in the water and several of the crew were trying unsuccessfully to get in the boat. The rain had lessened, but the winds were still stirring up the sea. A last gust of wind brought a bigger wave that snapped the boat in half, throwing Sarah and Naomi in the water. Neither could see Jonathan.

One minute the three were holding on to each other, the next minute it was just Sarah and Naomi; Jonathan wasn't there. Both women could swim, but not in a stormy sea. It was Naomi who kept Sarah's head above water and it was she who grabbed a rope attached to some floating wreckage and pulled it toward her. Naomi tied Sarah and then herself to the wreckage.

Earlier they had both sensed danger and changed out of their night clothes. They had put on dresses that were now so water logged that they were pulling each of them down. With one hand Sarah unfastened her skirt and slipped out of it and then her petticoats. She yelled at Naomi to do the same; modesty wasn't going to get them drowned.

They were in the water about an hour when they spotted a fishing boat. "Help, help!" Sarah cried.

The SS Maritime had been the first to see the Emerald Gay break up, and though the sea was violent, they attempted to send a gig to see if they could rescue any survivors. Their first attempt was unsuccessful;

their second attempt also failed, and the crew manning the gig had re- turned to the Maritime.

They waited another hour before sending out nine men in a half ton gig. Six men did the oaring and three were bailing as fast as they could. They picked up three survivors who were holding onto a mast and took them back to the Maritime. Other sailors replaced the nine and were now manning the gig, and it was this group that rescued Sarah and Naomi. By alternating crewmen, they were able to rescue fifteen crewmen and the two women from the Emerald Gay. The Maritime captain set up a makeshift survivor's area in one of the cargo rooms below deck. Several of the sailors furnished some of their clothing to Sarah and Naomi, who'd been given a blanket to wrap around them.

All of the seventeen rescued were suffering from hypothermia, but the medical corpsman on the ship could only give them blankets and serve them hot coffee. A few had head and arm injuries and were being treated as best as the corpsmen could. Sarah asked several of the Emerald Gay's crew if they saw Jonathan Bird, but none had.

Several other ships had joined the Maritime by now and were attempting to rescue anyone in the water. After two hours and with other ships joining the search, the Maritime captain decided to continue north and dock at Port Harford, west of the city of San Luis Obispo. He planned to turn over the survivors to the port authority and continue on his way to San Francisco. The captain gave all seventeen survivors the option of get- ting off at Port San Luis Obispo or continuing on to San Francisco. All of the seamen rescued asked to be returned to the bay area.

"We'd like to get off at San Luis Obispo. I must return as soon as possible to Santa Barbara and search for my : fiancé," Sarah told the captain.

Ministers, townspeople, and some city officials were waiting as Sarah and Naomi were taken ashore by some of the crew of the Maritime on the same gig used to rescue the two women. Everyone was polite and accommodating. Word had reached everyone present about the disaster at sea and that two women passengers were being put ashore at their port. Many onlookers also were there to see who the two women were. The first thing Sarah asked the head of the greeting committee was, "Have they found Jonathan Bird?"

Frederick Peters, the mayor of San Luis Obispo, said no other survivors had been found at this time, but from what he was told, the search was continuing.

"Can we get transportation from San Luis Obispo to the Point Conception area?" Sarah asked.

She was informed that the railroad had been connected as far as Los Alamos but that she'd have to take a stagecoach the rest of the way. A minister by the name of Joshua Smith said that Sarah and her companion were welcome at his home until she was able to decide what to do next.

Sarah graciously accepted. One of the others in the welcoming group was John Lewis, the president of San Luis Obispo Bank. Sarah asked to speak to the gentleman in private. "Mr. Lewis, I have considerable assets in the Bank of San

Francisco. Although I've lost all identification, I've established a password with the bank in the event of something unforeseen, such as a robbery."

Sarah gave Lewis her password and asked him to expedite transfer of five thousand dollars into an account in his bank. She was sure that if he wired her description, there would be no problem. Mr. Lewis smiled and said he would take care of it as soon as he reached the city. One of the women provided clothing for Sarah and Naomi, and they changed in the port office. James had prepared her well for taking care of herself.

The minister and his wife were most gracious, and although their home was modest, it was clean and had a homey feeling that Sarah appreciated. She and Naomi stayed with Pastor Smith and his wife for three days, during which time Mr. Lewis was able to open an account for Sarah in his bank and release sufficient funds for her to continue her quest for Jonathan. She thanked the minister and his wife and gave them a generous donation to help them with their work.

They boarded the train to Los Alamos in the morning and arrived before noon and then took the stage in the afternoon to Santa Ynez, arriving at seven in the evening at the Central Hotel on Sagunto Street in the center of the small town. They checked in, and Sarah asked the desk clerk if there was any more news about the survivors of the Emerald Gay. He said they still hadn't found anymore survivors. After checking with the clerk about transportation to Santa Barbara, the two women were shown to their rooms. They cleaned the dust off and went downstairs to dinner in the hotel restaurant.

At the registration desk was the latest Santa Barbara Bulletin brought to the hotel by the stagecoach from Santa Barbara. The headlines and most of the front page covered the ship- wreck, and in a paragraph at the bottom of the front page was a list of survivors.

Sarah was identified as the squaw of Crazy Horse and Naomi as her Indian maid. She was furious but didn't say anything to the clerk. As they were seated at a table in the corner of the restaurant, many of the patrons turned and stared at them. She ignored the other patrons and stared at the menu. Neither she nor Naomi could help but overhear some of the words that were said. One was "squaw" and the other was "white trash." She ignored the contemptuous comments and finished her dinner in silence. Most of the room had cleared by the time they were served.

The stagecoach driver was ill and their trip was postponed by one day, so they were required to stay another day at the hotel. Sarah was furious but was determined to fight through her anger and keep calm. Sarah had been to Santa Ynez before, and in spite of the rudeness of those in the restaurant, she rented a carriage, and she and Naomi drove to the mission in Solvang. Sarah wasn't Catholic, but she wanted to talk to the priest and share some of her concerns. Father Lynch was the resident priest with Fathers Farrelly and Lack as his assists. The mission and all its lands had been deeded back to the Catholic Church during Abraham Lincoln's term as president, and since that time the buildings were in a constant state of flux and repair. The mission was currently under repair by a family named Donahue who had moved into the mission and were helping with the financing. Mr. Donahue was a carpenter, stone mason, and blacksmith and, together with his four sons, had recently completed a living room or sala area for the priests to conduct the business of the mission.

Father Lynch welcomed Sarah and Naomi and showed them around the mission. He stopped during their tour to introduce them to the Donahues who were busy at work. Father Lynch sensed that something was troubling Sarah, and at the end of the tour he suggested that he and she sit on a bench under a tree over- looking the Santa Ynez River.

Naomi decided to go for a walk while the two talked.

The view of the mission lands and the river with its various tributaries was magnificent. Sarah wasn't shy and told Father Lynch of the sinking of the Emerald Gay and the potential loss of her fiance, Jonathan Bird. The priest listened patiently as Sarah told him of her early life, the abduction by the Oglala, her marriage to Crazy Horse, and her sudden wealth. He only interrupted a few times to ask for clarification. When she finished, she confided in the priest, "I feel deep down in my heart that Jonathan is dead and I must pick up the pieces and go on with my life. I just want to find a quiet place for Naomi and me, where I can paint and be free of the prejudice that has followed me for so many years."

After she finished, Father Lynch pointed out to her, "Those people in the restaurant were transient and didn't in any way project the feelings of the people in the Santa Ynez Valley. Things such as this have a tendency to not survive very long. From everything I've heard you can't blame yourself for what you couldn't control. You made the best of a difficult situation, and it took a great deal of courage to persevere in spite of that situation."

Sarah had never met the priest before, but what he said made a significant impact on her and she decided to try to put the prejudice be- hind her. Her first and foremost challenge at this time was to find out whether Jonathan had survived. "Father, you've been very helpful. I hope I'll be able to visit with you again."

Sarah and Naomi took the stagecoach to Santa Barbara the next morning, rented a carriage and driver in Santa Barbara for the remain- der of the day. They contacted the chief of police to see if he had any new information on the sinking of the Emerald Gay. He told them that no other survivors had been found and they were calling off the search. "Would it be possible for Naomi and me to get to Point Conception?" Sarah asked him.

The chief informed her that there were no roads to the point, which was sixty-five miles south of Santa Barbara. "Besides, there isn't any- thing to see even if you were able to get there."

"What about a boat?" Sarah asked.

"Vince Savoy has a small steamboat that he charters, but it's expensive." The chief gave her Savoy's address and wished her luck.

They drove to Sterns Wharf where Savoy had a small office. Vince Savoy was just a few inches taller than Sarah, but his burly build made him seem so much bigger. He told her the trip was dangerous, expensive, and not for women "I was aboard the Emerald Gay with my fiance, Jonathan Bird. I've got to try one last time to see for myself if Jonathan drowned." They agreed on a price and Savoy told her to be at the wharf at seven the next morning and he'd take her to the point.

Naomi was ambivalent; she wanted to go with Sarah but didn't want to be on a boat again. Fear for her mistress won out in the end, and she accompanied Sarah to the wharf the next morning. The steamboat trip took five hours, and they arrived shortly after noon. The winds had died down and the sea was only mildly rolling, so they were able to approach the point close enough to see the jagged rocks and feel the pull of the cross- current that was so ominous to most seamen. None of the wreckage was visible, and Sarah couldn't really tell where the Emerald Gay went down or where she was picked up. It seemed hopeless, and after two hours, she accepted reality and told Savoy to take them back to Santa Barbara. They had stayed at the Arlington Hotel the previous evening, and before they left that morning to go to Point Conception, Sarah had reserved the next three evenings at the hotel. She decided to take a hard look at the Santa Barbara area as a place to relocate.

When they returned to the wharf, there was a message for Sarah from the chief of Police saying Mr. Timothy Bird was staying at the Whitmore in Santa Barbara and asked her to call upon him. She and Naomi drove to the Whitmore House on upper State Street about seven blocks north of the Arlington. Sarah asked the driver to wait with Naomi and went into the hotel and up to the registration desk and asked if Mr. Bird was in his room. A message was delivered by a valet to his room and a response received indicating that Mr. Bird would meet Sarah in the lobby in ten minutes.

Sarah sat down in one of the velvet-covered chairs and waited. Soon she was approached by the registration clerk and a tall, thin man about forty to fifty years old. "Miss Hansen, this is Timothy Bird."

Sarah asked the man to be seated and inquired whether he would join her with some coffee; he declined and sat down across from her. They were the only persons in the sprawling lounge. Sarah introduced herself and told Timothy Bird she was Jonathan's fiancee and was on the Emerald Gay when it was shipwrecked near Point Conception.

"I'm well aware who you are, Miss Hansen, and I know you were out this morning searching for my brother. I wanted to meet you before I re- turned to the East Coast."

"I don't know much about Jonathan's family, though I knew he had a brother and a sister in addition to his two sons. We knew each other just a short time, and I know so little about him. You were his younger brother, weren't you?"

"Yes."

"I'm surprised how soon you could be here.

Did you come through Los Angeles or San Francisco?"

"Actually I came last week and planned to meet Jonathan in Los Angeles. Our family was concerned that he was rushing into marriage so soon after Jennifer died."

"I can understand your concern, but I thought his first wife had been dead several years."

"She died a year ago."

"Well, I can see why you were concerned, and had I known that her death was but a year ago, I would have suggested to Jonathan that
we should wait."

"That wasn't our only concern." His tone and manner seemed to change.

"And what would that mean, Mr. Bird?" "We did a thorough background check on you, Miss Hansen, or should I say Mrs. Crazy Horse, and what we found was very unsettling. Yes, we know that you have an income that makes you quite independent, but frankly you're not the type of person that the family saw as Jonathan's wife."

Sarah was stunned. All she could think of to say was, "I see."

"It wasn't only the savage you were wed to that was the problem, it was the affair you carried on in Philadelphia with that lesbian artist that made you totally unsuitable."

"Well, I can see why Jonathan wanted to leave the East Coast, and as far as any affair I had with a woman, it's a figment of your warped imagination. Thank you for coming and helping avoid an uncomfortable encounter with you and your family. I bid you good day, sir." Sarah turned and walked out of the hotel.

CHAPTER NINETEEN

Tommy returned to El Paso, finished up his business affairs, and left El Paso six months later. With no destination in mind, he just roamed until he found his way to Mexico City. He felt compatible with the pace of life there while enjoying the city's culture and recreational pursuits. One evening he was having dinner at the hotel in Mexico City when the maitre'd approached him and said that the restaurant was full and he wondered if Tommy would mind if another gentleman could join him. The maitre'd said he could vouch for the gentleman because he came from a very well known family. Tommy was tired of dining alone and welcomed another to share his table. The man was Carlos Quintero who, after a few glasses of wine, told Tommy that he was attempting to build a railroad to El Paso but was constantly running into problems with local officials who felt their palms hadn't been sufficiently greased. He was getting so frustrated that he was thinking of taking two months off to go big game hunting.

They finished dinner and Carlos asked Tommy if he'd join him for some cognac in the hotel lounge; Tommy accepted. After the drinks were served, Carlos looked straight at Tommy and said, "Mr. Sanchez, you're not Mexican, are you?" Tommy was surprised, but saw no reason to be evasive. "As a matter of fact, I'm Sioux. Is that a concern?"

"Not in the least. In fact, I'm fascinated. Were you ever a warrior?"

"When I was a young brave, I went on many raids. I didn't see it as anything remarkable, just something we did to survive."

"I assume you've hunted buffalo and deer. How about mountain lion?"

"We hunted for food and didn't see the sense in hunting for the sport of it. Why do you ask?"

"My family has a small hunting lodge in the mountains northeast of here. It seems a mountain lion killed one of the locals, and I've been asked to go up there and terminate it. You seem like an adventurous individual. Would you like to help me track down the cat and kill it?"

"Those cats go up pretty high. I don't have the gear or equipment for such a trek," Tommy responded.

"I can get you outfitted and have several rifles that would do the job. What do you say?"

"Have you ever hunted mountain lion?" Tommy asked.

"Several times with my brother Juan." "Why not ask him?"

"He's in Europe with his new bride."

Tommy looked at his companion, trying to size him up, contemplating what it would be like to be on a hunt again. Then he reached out and shook the man's hand. Quintero made the arrangements for the trip, and they left the next day on two sturdy mounts that were owned by Quintero's family. They camped out the first two nights, and during that time the two men found out how compatible they were both in life and in business. Tommy learned that Carlos's mother and father lived in the southern part of Mexico and that his other sibling, Juan, worked the family's ranch. Quintero's money came from his family while Tommy's was earned, yet each was similar in how they approached situations.

They arrived at the hunting lodge on the third day. They rubbed the animals down, gave them some hay and water, and put them in the two horse stable behind the cabin.

The lodge was nicely furnished, not too expensive but utilitarian. The layout was similar in some ways to Geoffrey Combs's Mountain retreat. There was a large living area that contained a kitchen in one corner with two bedrooms off the living area. They built a fire and put some kindling in the stove and ate some stew they hadn't finished on the trip to the cabin. Carlos gave Tommy some blankets and showed him to his room. Tomorrow they'd find someone in the nearby village who knew about the killing and where it took place.

Tommy had never hunted mountain lion, and all he knew about the cat was that it was a predator that traveled alone and at large distances in search of prey or a mate. It was comfortable in a mountain habitat and liked to hole up in crevices and heavy brush.

They rose early and Carlos broke out two center-fire single-action Remington rifles with rear sights. Tommy inspected the rifle, and Carlos gave him some ammunition to try it out. With Carlos watching, he walked outside, spied a fallen log about one hundred feet away, and took aim. After several minor adjustments, he fired at an object two hundred yards away and told Carlos that the rifle was satisfactory.

"You appear to be a man who knows a lot about weapons," Carlos said. Tommy nodded.

That morning they rode into the small village near the base of the mountain and talked to a couple of the locals who had heard the villager scream while he was being attacked by the lion. They had scared the cat off and dragged the man back to the village, but he was too far gone to save. The cat apparently had attacked from above and broke the man's neck by grabbing onto his neck with his sharp teeth and strong jaw. It was attempting to eat the man when the other villagers came upon the scene. The cat had fled, but the villagers saw it two days later near the kill site.

Many of the villagers were now afraid and refused to wander too far away from the village. The problem was that the village relied on deer and elk that was abundant in the mountains and the villagers were anxious that the two newcomers kill the animal. Two of the men from the village agreed to lead Carlos and Tommy to the kill site. The four set out after lunch and found the site about two in the afternoon.

Tommy was a natural tracker and could follow the cat's footprints to and from the site. He also determined where the cat was before the attack. He climbed up on some rocks about twenty feet above the site and found some hair on the dirt. He assumed this was where the cat sat eyeing his prey. After accompanying the two villagers back to the village, Tommy and Carlos made their way back to their cabin and prepared for the next day's work.

When they awoke, there was snow on the ground. They agreed that it might be easier to track the cat in the snow. They packed for a three day trek, thinking that the cat might be elusive and it would take more than a day to track it down. They went back to the kill site and started in the direction the cat took after the kill. The terrain was difficult, and sometimes they had to backtrack and make a wider turn to travel in the direction they thought the cat might be. They were primarily looking for crevices and heavy brush that the lion might be hiding in.

By the end of the first day they reached an elevation of five thousand feet and set up camp; they hadn't seen any sign of the cat. They talked it over after they'd eaten and decided to continue going up the mountain the next day.

A light film of snow had fallen during the night and the wind had picked up. Tommy and Carlos were thankful they'd dressed warmly. The horses were jittery as they put on their saddles, and Tommy handed the reins to Carlos to hold while he made an inspection of the area around their camp. He was gone about thirty minutes, and when he returned Carlos was anxious to learn what he saw. Even though there was some new snow, Tommy could see an impression of the lion's paws and tell that the cat had approached within fifty feet of their camp.

"This is not good, Carlos. That cat may be tracking us. From what I've been told of the mountain lion, they don't attack humans. This one is different. We better be on our guard." Carlos agreed and handed him back the reins to his horse.

After two hours, they lost the lion's tracks. They stopped around noon and heated some coffee and had some jerky before they continued on. "I suggest we spread out about twenty yards apart and see if we can spot his tracks. Be careful, this one is full of tricks," Tommy said.

They spread out and then alternated between coming together and spreading out at as they climbed higher. They carried their rifles in their right hands and the reins in their left as they gradually ascended. Tommy had a six-gun in a holster on his hip, and although he knew that one shot from the Colt probably wouldn't bring down the cat, still he felt comfortable having it within easy reach. Most of their supplies were carried by the two horses, but at Tommy's urging they carried small knapsacks around their waists with some food, matches, bandages, and extra ammunition.

Near four o'clock in the afternoon they came across a patch of brush to the right and a ledge of rocks to the left. Suddenly Tommy heard the cat scream, then a shot was fired and Carlos yelled. Tommy let go of the reins and ran as fast as he could in the snow toward Carlos. He saw the lion mauling Carlos and fired quickly to scare the cat, which turned and escaped up the hill to Tommy's left. He snapped the bolt back and fired again; this time he hit the cat, saw it tumble, then get up and dive into brush and out of sight. Tommy knew that both horses had scattered as soon as the shots were fired and they'd be in trouble if he couldn't catch the horses, but Carlos needed his immediate attention.

Carlos was bleeding from a gash in his neck; the lion had probably grabbed him there. All their supplies were on the horses except for what he and Carlos carried in their little knapsacks. Tommy opened his and took out some bandages and pressed them against the gash to stop the bleeding. He then examined Carlos further and noticed large gashes on the left side of his face. Tommy cleaned the gashes as best he could with bandages and wet snow. The cat had been in a tree and as Carlos crossed under the tree, the cat sprang and hit Carlos from behind. The impact had rendered Carlos unconscious. Tommy wasn't sure how his friend was, but he knew that what he did in the next few minutes would determine his fate.

They were in a precarious situation. He had an unconscious man with a gash in his neck. They were at seven thousand feet in elevation and it was starting to snow and getting colder. Both horses had scattered with most of their provisions and he had to figure out how to get Carlos down the mountain. It would be better if he had the horses, but he didn't know how to get them unless he left Carlos alone, and that was out of the question. He decided to set up camp where they were and moved Carlos and their limited provisions against the rocks to his left. He rounded up some kindling and pine needles, gathered an armful of thin branches, dug out an area, and then lit a fire. The best he could do was to keep Carlos warm until morning when he would attempt to bring him down the mountain. He could hear the cat scream occasionally. He was positive the lion was a predator and they were the prey.

He stayed awake all night feeding the fire and checking on Carlos. Loss of sleep was never a problem for him. He'd gone without sleep many times when he was on raids. He probably could go two days without sleep with minimal impact, but the question was would he get the cat before he was too exhausted?

The next morning, Carlos had regained consciousness and Tommy explained their problem and told him what they were going to do. He changed the bandages on Carlos's neck, built a litter out of pine branches that he could drag in the snow, and tied Carlos to the litter. He made a rope strap that would wrap around his waist and tied it to the front of the litter. Carlos would be pulled in the litter at a slight incline. He carried his rifle in his right hand and started back down the hill. He was lucky that Carlos was a thin man and somewhat smaller than Tommy, because the footing going downhill was treacherous. He had to stop every thirty minutes and readjust the strap, which was rubbing on his waist.

Two hours later they came across one of the horses. It had been killed by the lion and partially eaten, but the supplies were intact. Tommy took the food, a canteen, some medical supplies, bandages, and extra ammunition with him and left the remainder there. On one of the stops he fed Carlos some jerky and used some of the water for himself and Carlos. There was a needle and thread with the medical kit, so he took his time and washed Carlos's neck wound and stitched up the gash. He was amazed at how Carlos took the torturous trek downhill and withstood the needle in his neck. Carlos was a man and Tommy felt good that he was helping such a courageous one.

He stuffed the remaining bandages and food into his parka pockets and picked up the litter and his rifle. He started walking down a slight grade when he was hit from behind. He dropped the rifle, and he tumbled down the slight grade. The cat was on him instantly, and he fought it off as best he could, but the strap holding to the litter impacted any attempt to defend himself. Finally, he pulled his Colt and shot the cat in the shoulder, but the cat escaped back up the hill.

The impact was traumatic for Carlos. The litter had turned over, pinning him face down; the gash in his neck opened again, and he was bleeding freely. When Tommy got to his feet, he started to attend to the gash and Carlos lapsed into unconsciousness. Tommy took off the bandage around Carlos's neck and cleaned the wound and put on fresh bandages. He checked himself all over and found that he had suffered one bite mark on his left hand and a claw mark on his forehead. He bandaged the hand and put some lotion on the scratch marks. He was exhausted but got to his feet, retrieved his rifle, and checked on Carlos, who was still unconscious. He put the strap around his waist, but he was too tired to pull Carlos, so he decided to make camp, rest, and then figure out what to do next.

It took all the energy he could muster to find enough kindling to last the evening. He knew he hit the cat but couldn't be sure that it was a mortal wound. He assumed the worst and that the cat would be back to finish the job. The problem was that they were most vulnerable when they were on the move. Pulling Carlos on the litter didn't give him enough flexibility to prevent an attack. He had to make his stand here; he had to outthink the cat. Until now the cat was the predator and they were the prey, and Tommy had to reverse this, but how? He placed Carlos close to the fire and sat back and thought about what he could do. His thoughts were interrupted by the cat screaming; it was close.

He cut a small limb about six feet long and pushed it into the ground and tied another one of equal width and about three feet long across it. He put his jacket and hat on the sticks simulating the shape of a man. He took all the bloodied bandages off his hands and those from around Carlos's neck and put them over the wooden figure. Next he placed some food about five yards from the fire and then some more food ten yards out. He knew he was gambling with their lives, but he was sure they couldn't make it going down the hill with the cat chasing them.

He gathered a lot of leaves and small twigs under the light snow, and when he had enough, he lay down with his back against the rocks and pushed the leaves over his body, waiting with the rifle in his hands. He heard the lion scream again and knew it was near. The question was would the cat take the bait of the bloody rags and the food he set out for it.

He heard a small twig snap as the lion deliberately walked into the light of the fire. It sniffed and gulped down the food at the ten yard mark and started toward the food closer to the fire. Tommy shot the lion in the head and it fell over dead. He brushed off the twigs and leaves and went over to check the lion. There were no previous wounds; this one looked to be about one hundred pounds and was a female This didn't make sense, other than he had missed it with his rifle shot on the first encounter and the handgun on their second encounter, but then where did the blood in the snow come from?

Not knowing what was out there, he decided to stay awake and keep the fire going. Carlos was breathing comfortably and was going in and out of consciousness; Tommy probably had a concussion and knew he would need a doctor. He had nearly dozed off when he heard the screaming again. That's when he realized there were two of them. He reloaded his revolver and grabbed his rifle and started up the mountain toward the screaming. The sky was clear and the moon was out. Though he couldn't pick up a trail of blood, he was able to track the cat's prints in the snow; the animal appeared to be limping.

He heard it scream again as he closed the gap. Tommy was determined to kill the lion tonight; he was angry. He knew it was near, and he sensed the cat watching him. He heard movement as the cat leapt at him from above. He shot the mountain lion three times before the cat hit the ground. He walked over and saw five different wounds in the animal, which was about eight feet in length, weighed about 150 pounds, and was a male. He walked back to the unconscious Carlos, put some more kindling on the fire, and took a short nap.

The female mountain lion lay where he had shot it. He wanted to bring both lions down to the village but didn't have enough hands, and besides, Carlos needed immediate medical attention. Tommy changed the bandage on Carlos' neck and cleaned up the camp site, tied Carlos to the litter, grabbed his rifle, and started down the mountain again. Two hours down the trail he came across the other horse, whose rein had caught in some branches. The horse was covered with sweat from his attempts to break free. Tommy calmed the animal, gave it some water, and rubbed it down. Tommy tied the litter to the saddle, made another small litter for the remaining supplies, and tied it to the one carrying Carlos. He mounted and set out down the mountain again.

His concern for Carlos increased as he stopped for the night. The man had eaten very little for three days, and although Tommy constantly put water in his mouth and saw that he swallowed the water, his condition seemed to be deteriorating. The next day Tommy made up his mind that they wouldn't stop except to give the horse some water until they reached the village near Carlos's cabin. The horse would have to carry him and pull the litters; he was too tired to walk.

He reached the village at ten that night and banged on several doors before anyone would answer. There was no doctor in town, but there was an old man who tended to those who were ill. One of the villagers went for the man; Tommy told him what happened and what he did to stop the bleeding. Two local women changed Carlos's clothes and cleaned him up. The old man said Carlos had a fever and they'd have to bring that down first. The women put Carlos into a tub of cold water and sponged his body. Tommy was concerned, but the old man said this was the best way to bring the fever down. Two hours later the fever broke and Carlos was dressed in warmer, cleaner clothes, but was only intermittently conscious. The old man said that Carlos had to be taken to a hospital if he was to survive.

"That's over two days away and across a desert," Tommy said.

"I know, but I've done everything I can; it's up to someone who knows about these things. You had a hard five days, but you need to go further if you want to save your friend's life."

He set out for Mexico City, which was a three day ride. Two of the villagers lifted Carlos onto a litter, and after being given two horses and enough food and water, Tommy thanked the villagers and left. He stopped only long enough to give the horses water and some grain and to change mounts; he arrived in Mexico City at noon of the third day. He was directed to the city hospital and delivered Carlos to the doctor on duty. Tommy filled him in on what happened, what he did to care for Carlos, and what the old man in the village had done. It seemed that everyone at the hospital knew who Carlos Quintero was and they sent word to his parents.

Tommy checked into the Juarez Hotel downtown and gave strict instructions not to disturb him for two days. Other than room service he stayed in bed through the next two days.

CHAPTER TWENTY

When Tommy finally emerged from his room he ordered steak and eggs and then went to the barber shop for a shave and a haircut. When he was presentable he hired a carriage to take him to the hospital where he inquired about Carlos. The physician treating Carlos Quintero asked to talk to Tommy in private. Dr. Santana led Tommy to a small room on the second floor of the hospital near the room that Carlos was in. He asked Tommy to be seated. "I need some of the details on Mr. Quintero's ordeal. I understand you were with him during that time." Tommy nodded.

"I assume the gash on Mr. Quintero's neck was caused by a wild animal. Is that true?" the doctor asked.

"It was a male mountain lion weighting about 15O pounds and about eight feet in length. From what I've been told, mountain lions don't normally attack humans, but this one killed a villager and attacked us on two separate occasions. My guess is that there was something wrong with the animal to make it act that way."

"Is there any way you can recover the lion and bring it here for examination?"

"I'm afraid not. It's at least a five day ride each way."

Dr. Santana asked him several more question, which he answered. and then Tommy asked about Carlos. "He's conscious, but that neck wound appears to be infected and we're just staying ahead of it. We've bled him twice, but I'm concerned that if we bleed him anymore, he may not have the strength to recover. He's lost more weight. I know you want to see him and he wants to see you, but could you possibly wait another day? There're some more tests we want to do to see if we can eliminate the infection."

Over the next two days Tommy visited the old city, sampled some of the nightlife, and enjoyed food and drink. When he finally reentered the hospital, he asked the nurse at the reception desk about Carlos. The nurse said he was better and that his parents were with him, but he could go up to the second floor and see him.

There were three people with Carlos when he entered the room. Carlos was awake but looked drawn. He introduced his father, mother, and sister and told the three visitors that Tommy saved his life. Dr. Santana came in while they were all getting acquainted and asked them to leave while he checked Carlos. The three family members and Tommy walked down the hall to the waiting room. The sister sat down and the mother hugged Tommy and told him how grateful she was. The father shook his hand and told him how much he admired him.

Tommy was humble in accepting their praise. "I did what anyone would've done in the situation. Tell me about Carlos's condition. Will he recover?"

"The doctor is encouraged. They were able to stop the infection, and though Carlos is weak and lost a lot of weight, the doctor expects him to recover fully."

Don Fernando Quintero was an impressive man, slightly taller than Tommy, with gray wavy hair and a strong handshake. "I wasn't only talking about what you did for my son, but what you did for my oldest and dearest friend, Don Hernando Lopez. You are a hero in my eyes and to everyone in Don Lopez's district. Knowing what you did there, I can imagine what you did to protect my son and bring him down from that mountain. One of the villagers is on my payroll. I sent him back up the mountain to bring back both lions you killed. My family and I will always be in your debt. I know you are a wealthy man, but if I could make you richer, I would do it now. What are your plans for the future?"

Tommy was moved. "I don't know what I'll try next. I've always wanted to see California; perhaps I'll see if there's a future for me there."

"My friend Don Lopez speaks of you as though you were a son. He misses you very much and wishes you would come back. I know you can't. I know the pain would be too great to endure. What I don't understand is why you went with my son. You hardly knew him beforehand."

"Your son is a very engaging man and he caught me by surprise when he asked me to accompany him. Before I knew what I was saying, I accepted. As it turned out, it was a two man job and I'm glad that I was able to spend time with such a dynamic man. You should be proud of your son, Don Fernando."

"I wonder if you would do us the honor of staying with us at our residence just outside Mexico City for as long as you're in the area. I know you're staying at the Hotel Juarez. I could have my foreman assist you if you accept our invitation."

Tommy didn't hesitate. "I would be delighted. As soon as I visit with Carlos, I'll return to the hotel and check out. Would four o'clock be acceptable?" Don Fernando said it was.

The family allowed Tommy to have an uninterrupted visit with Carlos. The two men talked about the hunt. Carlos didn't believe there were two lions even though his father told him that two were brought down from the mountain.

"I can't believe you killed two lion."

"I believe the male was the killer and tracking us. The female was probably hungry and smelled the food I laid out for bait and just walked in," Tommy told him.

"I know you pulled me on a litter some of the time and I remember when the cat hit us and we went tumbling down the hill. I thought it was over then."

"I know. I got a shot off after we wrestled on the ground and hit him in the shoulder, but it didn't deter him much."

"I blacked out after he hit us from behind. I don't remember much, though I had a feeling that I was in a cold tub and some women were washing me. Was that possible?" Carlos asked.

Tommy smiled. "Two of them were washing every bit of your body. Too bad you missed that. One of them was quite attractive."

The two laughed, and Tommy could tell it was time to leave. Carlos was looking very tired. "I'm staying with your family for a few days. I plan to leave after I'm sure you're on your feet."

Don Fernando's foreman picked up Tommy at the Juarez Hotel and drove him to the Hacienda Del la Soto, a magnificent estate with a background of the mountains to the east and a lazy river to the south. There was a main house, several guest houses, stables, corrals, and numerous other buildings near a race track. Tommy was in the presence of the really rich. The foreman escorted him to one of the guest homes with running water and its own out house. He informed Tommy that dinner was at six and the dress was casual.

Tommy cleaned up and at the appointed hour walked up to the hacienda and was greeted by Don Fernando and given a tour of his home, which consisted of six bedrooms off a large living area, a kitchen, and storage area in the rear. A servant served wine and a tequila milk drink; Tommy chose the tequila. Dinner was set for four to include the father, mother, daughter, and Tommy. He learned a good bit about the family during dinner, and after dinner they adjourned to the large living room for a glass of sherry.

Don Fernando told him that he and his wife, Alicia, had been married thirty years. They had two boys and a daughter, aged twenty six, un- married, who was an accomplished equestrian and fencer. She asked Tommy if he had ever fenced. When he replied that he hadn't, she smiled and suggested that she could teach him the fundamentals during his visit.

The women retired and the two men continued their conversation. "I know you've been on a dangerous hunting trip, but I propose that we have a little fun and go deer hunting tomorrow. We have a nice preserve on the rancho about two miles from here. We can hunt, get better acquainted, and perhaps provide dinner for the family." Tommy accepted.

They retired for the evening and met at five the next morning for a hearty breakfast and then the two rode out to Don Fernando's preserve along with two retainers. He outfitted Tommy with clothing, boots, and a Winchester single action rifle. They were in luck and each shot a small deer in the morning and then had a nice lunch with a bottle of wine. The two men relaxed and let the retainers prepare the lunch and take the two deer back to the hacienda.

"You are a natural hunter, my friend. I suspect that you've had a lot of experience. My son tells me that you are a Native American from the Sioux tribe. Is that true?"

"My father was Sioux and my mother white, but I was raised to be a warrior."

"But you seem to have many more skills than that of a warrior. Why?"

"My father was a man of vision. He fought for our way of life, but he saw that his people could not sustain that lifestyle with the corning of the white settler. He made sure that I would be able to assimilate into the white world by pushing me into that world when I was in my teens. I was able to learn from my white employers and adapt."

"My son alluded to your business acumen; how did you become successful?"

Tommy had never discussed his business with anyone before, but for some reason he felt comfortable with the older man and was willing to oblige his inquiries. "I started with something that I knew and was good at and gradually expanded into areas that were compatible but didn't interfere with my core business. When I moved to other locales, I followed the same blue- print and was successful. I've not moved beyond my capability so far, though I've expanded the areas of my knowledge and tried to see what would come next. It's a slow process, but one that I'm comfortable with and one that seems to work so far."

"You are legend among those who know about your exploits. My impression is that you are a very lethal man, yet you brought all four of those killers back alive. There seems to be a contradiction there. Why didn't you kill them when you had the chance?"

"Maria Conchita had been Don Hernando's daughter for twenty years but my fiancee for only a month. He had priority to deal with the four. It was my job to protect her and I failed. I wanted to kill them, it's true, but the revenge I exacted from them on the way back was more than satisfying."

"I sense that you are a very comfortable man, yet I also sense a large burden that you're carrying. Do you know what it is?"

"I killed a man in Laramie, Wyoming; he was a temporary deputy, and the sheriff he worked for has hounded me from town to town. It seems each time I become comfortable something hap- pens that forces me to move on. I would like to stop and fix it, but so far I've been unable."

"Have you applied for a pardon?"

"I had an attorney in Tombstone processing one, but he wasn't getting anywhere."

"I don't want to seem a cynic, but from my experience you can buy anything at the right price. What's your peace of mind worth? What's your ability to be free worth? Whatever it is, I think you should pay it, and if you don't have enough money, come to me. You are someone I would risk everything for because you would never disappoint me. Now let's get back to the hacienda and see what our cook can do with two choice deer."

Three days later Carlos was brought home. He'd lost about twenty pounds, but his color was returning. It was his radiating charm that the family had missed the most, and it was no time before he was charming them at dinner with his visions of the future and amusing stories. Carlos and Tommy walked around the beautiful grounds, had picnic lunches in the family 's orange grove, and went fishing in the lazy river. But the time had come for Tommy to move on. You could be a guest only for so long. The family tried to offer him lucrative incentives to stay in the area; in fact, Carlos offered him a full partnership in the El Paso to Mexico City Railroad. Tommy declined as graciously as he could. He knew they were disappointed, but he had to live life on his own terms. They all agreed to stay in touch. The foreman drove Tommy to Mexico City.

He had several options to choose from to reach San Diego. He had heard about a small: fishing village called Acapulco on the Pacific Ocean from Carlos and his father. They recommended that he visit the village and then go by steamer up the coast to San Diego. The problem was that there were mountains between Mexico City and Acapulco. He could go by stage or rent a guide and make the trip on horseback in a day. He chose the latter. His guide was named Felipe and was a charming fellow.

The horse provided by the company escorting Tommy to Acapulco was adequate and probably suited for such a trek. He and Felipe saddled up and left at eight in the morning. They reached the pass about noon and stopped long enough for a drink and sandwich that the guide provided. The company issued Tommy a map to use as he traveled over the pass. As he was riding along following the guide he noticed that they were taking a route other than that outlined on his map and he reined in his horse.

The guide noticed that his charge wasn't following him, so he turned around and reined in his horse next to Tommy. "What's the matter? Aren't you coming?"

Tommy reached into his vest and withdrew a Colt handgun. "Are you carrying a weapon?" he asked.

The guide said he wasn't. Tommy made him open his jacket and lift up his shirt to confirm what he said. "Who's waiting for us up ahead on this other trail?"

"I don't know what you're talking about," the guide responded.

Tommy ordered the guide off his horse and to walk in front of him. "If someone shows up, I'm going to kill you."

"Now wait a minute, who do you think you are?" The guide was seemingly nervous at this turn of events.

"If you're not off your horse immediately, I'll shoot you where you sit."

The guide dismounted, handed his reins to Tommy, and walked in front of him. After they had walked about one hundred paces down the other trail, the guide stopped. Tommy pressed the muzzle of his handgun in the man's back and urged him forward but the guide refused. "How many are out there?" Tommy asked.

"There're two around the next bend."

"Are they armed?"

"Yes."

"Call them to come help you. Tell them that the traveler has you down. Make it sound realis- tic and you'll live."

The guide yelled to his two companions to come to his aid. Though not perfect, his plea for help brought the two on the run. Tommy forced the guide to the ground while he hid behind a boulder. As soon as the guide's cohorts were abreast of him, Tommy ordered them to stop and throw down their weapons or he'd kill them. They looked to their companion lying on the ground and then threw the weapons down. He picked up their weapons and put them in his saddlebag and then asked about their horses. They told him they were tied to a mesquite bush down the trail.

He walked the three to the other horses, then mounted and tied the reins of one horse to the saddle of another and rode away with all four horses. "The three of you are on your own. If I see you following me, I'll kill all of you."

He rode back up the trail to where the two trails intersected and then went down the other trail. When he reached Acapulco, he sought out the local magistrate and asked him if there had been any recent robberies and/or murders on the trail between Acapulco and Mexico City. The magistrate said there had been at least a robbery each month in the past year. Tommy told him what happened and delivered the three horses to him and suggested that the three would be robbers would be coming down the trail eventually. The magistrate assured Tommy they'd be arrested when they did.

The Acapulco coastal area with its long, sandy beach and view of a beautiful blue ocean were something he'd never seen before. He marveled at the waves as they crashed onto the beach and then receded just as dramatically. This was well worth the trip over the hills in spite of the attempted robbery and perhaps something worse. He stayed at a shack on the beach and was awakened each morning by the crashing of the serf on the shore. He slept late and then walked on the beach before having breakfast at a small cantina that served eggs, sausage, and beans. He'd never been fishing in a boat and certainly not in the ocean, so he hired a boat for a day and went out about one mile and fished for tuna. He was tempted to stay a few more days. He'd heard about places like this but never saw them, at least not until now.

CHAPTER TWENTY-ONE

Sarah could sit in her Toom and feel sorry that her fiancé drowned and that his family considered her persona non grata or she could start the rest of her life. She chose the latter. Santa Barbara had some allure for her with its view of the ocean and cosmopolitan lifestyle, but she wanted to be sure that's where she wanted to settle before she made a commitment. She hired a carriage along with a driver for a week to serve also as a guide. His name was Jose Oliveros, and his family had been in California for over one hundred years. He was fluent in both Spanish and English and had worked for the carriage shop for six years. Sarah wanted to return to Santa Ynez. She especially wanted to visit with the priest at the mission. She wasn't Catholic, but she had felt a comfort level with the priest that she had found in no other.

Santa Ynez was a day away by carriage with a stop at the Kinevan Tavern atop San Marcus Pass. The weather was fair and the trip was without incident. The last time she traveled this way, they were robbed by two highway men. They checked into the Central Hotel and had adjoining rooms on the second floor. There didn't seem to be any concern about Naomi being an Indian; at least no one mentioned it to Sarah as she registered. The rooms were fairly austere with one bed, closet, marble-topped chest of drawers, pitcher and bowl, and a commode. The one redeeming feature was that the hotel provided breakfast, lunch, and dinner for their guests. Jose stayed with relatives in the volley.

Technology hadn't reached the Santa Ynez Valley, so the next morning Sarah sent Jose with a message to the priest at the mission and told him to wait for a response. She had asked for a meeting the next afternoon. Jose returned that evening with the response; the meeting would be at two the next afternoon. While waiting for Jose to return, she and Naomi walked around the town visiting the few retail shops along Sagunto Street, which included a general store, millinery shop, Chinese laundry, drug store, and grocery store and then returned to the hotel for lunch where she read again the newspaper account of the sinking of the Emerald Gay. She had to accept the fact that Jonathan had drowned and the life they had planned together was not to be.

Her meeting with Father Lynch focused on methods she could use to get over her grief and get on with the rest of her life. They walked while Naomi waited on a bench in the mission garden. The view from the mission was spectacular. To the east was the grist mill built by a man named Chapman, a mason from New England, and to the south was the Santa Ynez River that the priest said was fill of trout this time of the year. To the north were a few shops, primarily to support the mission. Many of the repairs that had been ongoing during her last visit had been completed, but there were still some remnants of the work still not finished.

She felt some of her inner strength return by just talking to the priest. He assured her that she would recover as long as she had faith in her own good judgment. What she liked about the priest was that he could counsel her without invoking God with every other word. Sarah wasn't opposed to Catholicism or any organized religion but relied more on the golden rule as a guide. She left feeling refreshed and invigorated with a renewed sense of empowerment. Father Lynch invited her for tea; she and Naomi accepted and then they returned to the hotel.

Sarah had met Felix Mattei on her last visit to Santa Ynez, and there he was standing in the lobby with his wife, Lucy, as she and Naomi returned from their visit to the mission. She had heard that they were contemplating building a hotel in Los Olivos and was curious why they were selecting that location since Santa Ynez was the hub of activity for the valley. They ex- changed pleasantries and small talk and Felix suggested that Sarah and her companion join him and his wife at dinner in the hotel dining room at seven; she accepted for herself and Naomi.

Felix was quite knowledgeable about what was going on in the Santa Ynez Valley. He first saw the valley while moving cattle from his ranch in Cayucos to Los Angeles; it was instant love. He suggested areas that Sarah might want to investigate before she made up her mind where to relocate. He and Lucy extended their condolences for her loss and hoped that wherever she decided to relocate, she would keep in touch with them.

Their talk turned to the hotel that Felix was planning for Los Olivos and why he chose that location as opposed to Santa Ynez. He told her that they hadn't finalized their plans. Two is- sues were still unresolved: one was the land he had under option and the other was adequate financing to cover the cost of construction and his expenses through the first year. Sarah asked how much he needed, and he indicated the total amount needed was fifteen thousand dollars to get started and five thousand to carry the operation through the first year.

Sarah asked Felix about land and he suggested a land broker in Ballard that he trusted. They finished dinner and wished each other good luck, and then they all retired to their rooms. The next day Jose drove Sarah and Naomi to Ballard to meet with Anthony Johnson, a land broker specializing in the valley.

Over the next two days they drove around the volley looking at land ranging in size from two hundred to two thousand acres. Each had its own positive features and each had some negative issues. After two days Sarah was exhausted and wanted to take the next day off by just being driven around the valley.

They were driving toward Solvang and came across the makeshift village of Chumash. Sarah asked Jose to stop and wait while she and Naomi walked into the village, which wasn't much of a village. There were three or four teepees and a couple of wooden shacks. None of the men were present, but children and women were sitting at a stream washing clothes. The women and children appeared to be suffering from malnutrition. She and Naomi attempted to dialog with the women, but their language was completely different from the Sioux that each spoke.

Sarah remembered how it was when she was initially captured by the Sioux and how she had to compete with the dogs for scraps of food. These people were free and yet were living at the same level she had when she was a prisoner.

They got back in the carriage and went to the general store in Santa Ynez and bought several months' supply of food and grain and delivered it to the village. At first the women and children retreated from the bundles of food that Jose set out in front of their tents. It took considerable encouragement by Sarah and Jose to get them to open the bundles, and when they did, the women looked around to see if anyone was looking before moving the bundles into one of the tents. An older woman in the group came out of one of the tents and smiled at Sarah; she took this as a thank you.

They'd visited the valley for a week and Sarah still couldn't make up her mind about the valley, so the three drove back over the pass and returned to the Arlington. It'd been several years since she last saw the McIntyres, so she decided to return to Los Angeles and visit with the couple and their daughter. The incident on the train had strained their relationship, but the couple had been so helpful to her when she was destitute that she wanted to see if their relation- ship could be mended.

CHAPTER TWENTY-TWO

The steamship was four hours late when it finally reach the port of San Diego. As he left the steamship and arrived at the port office, many of the passengers were milling around looking for those who were supposed to meet them. Children were crying and husband and wives were exchanging heated words as Tommy carried his bag up the hill to the Cortez Hotel and checked in. He was tired, ignored his hunger pangs, and fell asleep immediately after he was shown to his room. When he awoke it was noon. He cleaned up, shaved, and went down to the dining room and ordered a steak. Several other men, who he assumed were salesmen, were having coffee and discussing various business enterprises they were coiling on with limited or no success.

Tommy's plan to meet with bankers when arriving at a new location had proved successful in the past, and he intended to continue with that plan until he found another that was more successful. He inquired of the gentlemen in the dining room which banks seemed to be most aggressive. The consensus was that Wells Fargo and San Diego Bank and Trust appeared to be more receptive to business expansion. He rented a horse and carriage and drove into town to meet with both banks.

His first meeting with the manager of the Wells Fargo Bank was less than satisfactory. The manager treated him as though he was a peon and was reluctant to give him any insight into business in the city or the surrounding area. Tommy didn't get mad; in fact, he smiled at the lack of good sense on the part of the banker and went to the newer San Diego Bank. It was like night and day; the manager of the Wells Fargo Bank talked down to Tommy, while the president of the San Diego Bank, Harrison Guthrie, spent over an hour summarizing the economic outlook for the city and the potential that existed. It was then that Tommy shared with the banker his assets and suggested that he would transfer one hundred thousand dollars of his holdings from his El Paso Bank to the San Diego Bank; he asked Guthrie to handle it for him. Harrison couldn't conceal his good luck that had dropped in that morning.

"Can you suggest a good attorney?" Tommy asked.

"There are many good attorneys in the city, but if I had a particular problem and the money to hire anyone I wanted, I'd pick Michael Lund. He has a knack for getting the job done. He's located in the Farragut Building across the street. I know him personally and would be more than glad to walk over there with you now and personally introduce you." Tommy accepted.

It was about three in the afternoon. Michael Lund was planning to leave for the day when Harrison Guthrie led Tommy into his waiting room and asked the receptionist if he could see the attorney. She asked them to wait while she went in and asked Mr. Lund. Both Lund and the receptionist came out of the attorney's office together. Lund walked over and greeted Guthrie, who introduced Tommy and then excused himself and walked back across the street to his bank.

Lund's office was simple yet elegant. It was spacious with a few attractive printings, a large desk with a swivel chair, and two overstuffed chairs in front of his desk. Lund asked Tommy to be seated and how he could be of service. Tommy wanted to be sure that whatever he Lend would be kept in strict confidence. Lund assured him that would be the case. Tommy told Lund the entire story of the shooting in Laramie, his flight, subsequent flights, his attempts to seek a pardon, and his discussion with Don Fernando.

Over the next hour Lund asked many pointed questions and received candid answers from Tommy. The one that Tommy had the most difficulty with was how he arrived at his name. When he was finished asking questions, Lund asked Tommy for a few moments while he thought the whole thing over. Tommy sat patiently for over five minutes before Lund looked up at him and said he thought he could accomplish the task.

"It's going to cost you a significant amount for my services. I expect I'll have to make a trip to Wyoming, perhaps more than one, to resolve the issue. I also expect that I'll have to pay for other services while in Wyoming, and that may be expensive. I expect my fee will run between five and ten thousand dollars and I want a two thousand dollar retainer up front. I suspect that you'll have to pay that amount to others to obtain the pardon. I can't guarantee that we'll accomplish your objective, but I'll do everything I can to accomplish the task. Are you able to commit that amount of money to this venture?"

"Mr. Guthrie is transferring a amount of money from one of my accounts to his bank. I assume that will be accomplished within the week. You're welcome to talk to Mr. Guthrie about this matter. I have no problem with the amount you quoted for services as long as it's accomplished."

"I believe the first thing we should do is establish your name. It shouldn't take more than a week, but I'd feel more comfortable with that established."

"What do you need from me?" Tommy asked.

"I'd like some basic information and then I can petition the court to legalize your name."

After Tommy furnished the information Lund needed, the two men shook hands, and Lund told Tommy he'd have a written agreement drawn up tomorrow. As Tommy was leaving the office, Lund's receptionist gave Tommy a message. It was from Harrison Guthrie inviting him to dinner at his home and indicating that he had some potential business ventures he wanted to discuss with him.

He walked back across the street and accepted the invitation. Rather than give directions, Guthrie said he'd send a carriage to the Cortez Hotel for Tommy.

Harrison Guthrie lived about ten minutes from the Cortez Hotel in the hills overlooking the bay. The home was modest yet had a magnificent view of the ocean from every room in the front of the house. Guthrie's wife was a petite, handsome woman with short, dark hair and was of Spanish descent; her name was Esperanza. It was still daylight and they moved to the screened-in front porch and were served canapés and a glass of Madeira wine by their maid, after which they passed the time with light conversation.

When they were called to dinner, Tommy escorted Esperanza to the dinner table and con- versed in Spanish with her. Esperanza Guthrie was pleased that Tommy could converse in Spanish because her husband couldn't. The dinner was a mixture of local fish and vegetables. After dinner, Esperanza Guthrie excused herself, and Guthrie offered Tommy a cigar and some cognac. He declined both.

"From our conversation at the bank, I gather you're quite versed in horses, freight, and cattle. I'd like to introduce you to a new concept, if you don't mind?"

"Please continue," Tommy said.

"In San Diego, we have two different horse-drawn street car companies. Neither is making any money, and it doesn't look as though the future will be any brighter. The only value that I see in either company is the license for their route, which is assignable. With the advent of the electric engine, it seems to me that the era of the horse-drawn streetcar using iron rails will soon pass into history. They've had electric cable cars in San Francisco since 18 73, and it's only a matter of time before that'll replace horse-drawn streetcars here and throughout the country.

"Someone with foresight could purchase the existing horse-drawn companies here and with the licenses be first in line to install cable cars over the existing routes. It'll require some capital outlay for a power house and trenching to house a cable to run between the existing rails. I believe the existing streetcars could be used initially and then gradually phased out.

"But that's only the second stage of this venture. The third is the electric streetcar. The electric engine has already been invented and I believe that within five to seven years the cable car will be replaced by an electric streetcar. There's someone in the state of Virginia who's already in the development stage. The transition to cable will cost some money, but I believe you'll recoup your investment within two years and be ready for the next stage, which will be expensive.

"I prepared a pro forma for you; it looks like it'll take about fifty thousand dollars to include switching over to cable, digging the trench be- tween the rails, and putting in a steam-powered station to power the cable cars. It'll cost about one million dollars to go completely with electric streetcars, but the upside is out of sight. I've spent a lot of time reading about the technology and I'm convinced that this will be a sound enterprise, but it'll take someone with ambition and foresight to pull it off. I also know some people that would like to be investors in such an enterprise when the time is right."

Over a couple of cups of coffee Tommy read the pro forma and summary that Guthrie had provided. "You've really thought this through and presented me with an opportunity of a lifetime. I don't know much about cable cars or streetcars, but I like your thought process. I'd like to review the numbers for a day or so and get a feel for the business by riding the trolleys. If I agree with your plan, the first step as I see it is to visit San Francisco and see how the cable cars are operated and powered and whether it's feasible to transition to electric trolleys. How tight are those contracts with the city?"

"I can be some help there. My brother sits on the city council and tells me they're a very progressive group. It'll be to your advantage to consult with him once you've made your decision and once you own both companies. I'd like to be a part of this enterprise, not as an investor because I don't want to run into a conflict of interest with the bank, but as a representative of the bank looking out for a very special depositor. Perhaps we at the bank could negotiate with the two horse-drawn companies."

"I'll get back to you in a few days. In the interim, Mr. Lund needs to know that I have at least twenty thousand dollars on deposit with your bank, so let's expedite the transfer of funds from El Paso. If I decide to go forward, I'll transfer more funds and seek to have most of my funds transferred here."

The next day Tommy made a point of riding on each of the two horse-drawn company's carriages. One route went from the wharf to the center of town and the other ran for two miles along the coast. Each had limited passenger travel and the horses looked like they were suffering from malnutrition. Tommy talked to the drivers and found out they were being paid very little and were expected to maintain their carriages and feed their horses. Each carriage was allocated two horses. There wasn't much grain or hay for the horses. Tommy was appalled at the condition of the animals and asked the drivers why. "That's the way it is," one of them said.

Tommy spent some time driving around town with his own carriage looking at street patterns and the location of residential districts relative to the horse-drawn routes. The route from the wharf to the center of town seemed the more lucrative of the two. He felt that the reason why the other route wasn't drawing enough customers was that it didn't service the needs of the population.

He then talked to one of the city planners to get a feel for how building expansion, both retail and commercial, was moving and where it was moving. With this information he had a better feel for the business and what routes should be planned. He shared this information with Harrison Guthrie and that he was taking the steamer to San Francisco the next day to see first hand what the cable car business entailed. He checked out of the hotel for a few days but let the desk know that he planned to be back near the end of the week. The trip by steamer took thirty six hours. He met up with a couple of business men who were on their way to San Francisco and engaged them in conversation. Tommy was evasive when asked what line of business he was in but did let them know he was an investor looking for an opportunity. The food onboard was passable and they dined on a medley of fish and assorted vegetables. After dinner, Tommy and a few other men adjourned to the bar and had a nightcap. At nine o'clock he excused himself and retired to his room.

The next morning they served an assortment of eggs and ham. The ship docked at the Embarcadero around noon, and Tommy hired a carriage and driver to take him to the Bay City Hotel at the top Nob Hill, where he asked the driver to wait.

As soon as he registered and had the porter deliver his bags to his room, he got back in the carriage and drove downtown to the intersection of Clay and Kearney streets. He asked the driver to wait while he boarded and rode the cable car up the hill and back down. He talked to two of the conductors on the cable car route and learned that there was a vault between the rails housing a cable that was continuously moving.

The car was attached to the cable by a metal clamp that could be disconnected and reconnected through use of a foot pedal controlled by the conductor. This allowed the cable car to stop to pick up passengers. Of particular interest to Tommy was the power needed to pull the cable car up a hill and the ability to brake coming down the hill.

Tommy visited the power generation building and talked to the engineer in charge of the unit. Steam was used to power a generator, which then moved the cable on a continuous basis. It took a great deal of wood or coal to build up enough steam to keep the cable moving. He then wondered how they could use one generator for multiple routes. He saw that as the problem. One track of cable was fine, but the huge potential was with multiple routes. Could one generator service more than one set of cables?

Electric lights had been introduced to San Francisco as well as San Diego. Electric power to generate lights went out to multiple areas. Tommy wondered if this technology could be applied to multiple routes for the cable car. He visited the building where power was generated for all the electric lights. The building enclosed a 12S horsepower generator being powered by an adequate steam engine. He wasn't an engineer, but intuitively he felt that multiple routes could be powered by one large generator. When he returned to San Diego, he'd ask Guthrie to put him in contact with a good engineering firm and ask them about this problem.

The trip back to San Diego took thirty-seven hours. Several of the gentlemen who traveled north with him were on the return trip to San Diego. Tommy had a glass of wine in the bar area of the steamer and then retired to his cabin. When he arrived at the San Diego wharf, he found the same driver who drove him to the steamer earlier in the week waiting for him. Tommy hired the man for the next two days. As soon as he checked in at the Cortez Hotel, he asked the driver to return about nine the next morning.

He'd telegraphed Guthrie before he left San Francisco and set up a meeting at ten three days hence. Guthrie was anxious to learn what Tommy had found out and whether he'd made a decision on the venture. Before the meeting, Tommy took another carriage ride along the two current routes of the horse-drawn companies and arrived at Guthrie's office at ten in the morning. It was obvious from Guthrie's greeting that he was anxious to know what Tommy had found out. He offered him coffee or tea; Tommy settled for a cold glass of water. Both men sat at Guthrie's conference table, and Tommy set his notebook on the table.

Tommy smiled at Harrison Guthrie before he started to speak. "The cable car has been successful in San Francisco for two reasons. The first is that it satisfied a need and the second is because of the city's topography. The many hills leading up to the residential area create a need for some form of public transportation for people to access the city and return to their residences. I don't doubt that the time of the horse-drawn carriage is coming to an end. It isn't profitable and it doesn't satisfy the need for public transportation. I know that they'll be replaced shortly, but I question whether an interim solution of the cable car for San Diego is the way to go.

"The time of the electric light has come and from what I read, they can provide power to five thousand electric lights with three 125 horsepower generators serviced by steam. Electric generators are going to be continually improved, so why not go to phase three and skip the interim solution? The cable car has been in use for thirteen years. I just feel that it was good for San Francisco, but the amount of trenching required and the potential problem of a separate powerhouse for each traffic route make it unacceptable to me.

"The question then becomes what to do about the current companies? In my view they are practically worthless and not worth buying except for the charter or license they might have. I think you need to do some homework and find out from your brother and other members of the city council what the two companies have that's valuable to us or can impact what we plan to do."

"I'll get on it right away. Your funds transferred yesterday and I notified Lund that they were in your account. I think he expects to see you right after our meeting. I have a draft of two thousand dollars for you. Do you want to deliver it to him?"

Tommy nodded yes. Lund was in his office when he presented himself to the receptionist. Lund heard Tommy and walked out and greeted him. "I have our agreement ready for you to sign. If it's acceptable, I'll leave for Laramie tomorrow morning."

Tommy sat down and read the agreement. When he was finished, he signed it and handed a two thousand dollar draft to Lund.

"I've already made contact with an attorney in Wyoming who specializes in matters such as this. Would it be possible to have an additional three thousand dollars telegraphed to me at the Laramie National Bank in the event that I can finalize the agreement while I'm there?" Lund asked.

"The money will be available for you as soon as I leave your office. You can pick it up from Harrison and deposit it in the Laramie National Bank yourself," Tommy responded.

"I've had your named legalized. You are officially Thomas Sanchez."

"Thank you," Tommy said and shook Lund's hand.

CHAPTER TWENTY-THREE

Over the next year Sarah and Naomi worked with the McIntyres to provide food for the poor, counseling for the abused, and homes for the homeless. Sarah especially had a feeling of accomplishment when she was able to help the itinerant Indians. Through her help, they were able to house over one hundred of the homeless. She felt rewarded, but realized this was not her life's work. She and Naomi made plans to return to Santa Barbara and continue the pursuit of her artistry. The McIntyres were disappointed but knew that this was their calling and not Sarah's.

In spite of her comments that she wouldn't travel by stagecoach again, the alternative of steamboat travel brought back the horror of the day she lost Jonathan, so it was by stage- coach they traveled form Los Angeles to Santa Barbara. Instead of returning to the Arlington Hotel, Sarah had rented a furnished home in the Riviera district for the next year. The lease came with a live-in maid. The two story, five bedroom home was owned by a local family who were on a world tour for the next year. They had met Sarah previously when she was in Santa Barbara and had been corresponding regularly. When Sarah wrote that she was returning to the city and was looking for a place to live for a year, they immediately offered their home and she accepted. One of the rooms upstairs next to her bed- room had an unfettered view of the ocean. She decided to make this her study and workshop. Over the next month she gathered supplies and then began to paint. Her first effort was a painting of the ocean from her location.

Since Santa Barbara was a sea coast city with a beautiful beach, it drew a cross section of tourists from the surrounding towns, and the beach area was where the tourists liked to congregate. The city had provided a landscape area for picnicking and a path for pedestrians between the ocean and the road paralleling the water. Many of the local artists took this opportunity to display their art on the landscaped area, which was proximate to the pedestrian footpath. Sarah was one of the artists who liked to display their work in the landscaped area on Saturdays and Sundays. She and Naomi would bring a picnic basket and spend the day.

She received considerable attention and though her work was slow to sell, she made enough sales to pay for the effort. Sarah realized she liked the lifestyle of the artist. She also liked the magnificent weather of Santa Barbara, its pleasant sea breeze, and the ability to interface with people who stopped to look at her paintings.

One afternoon she was startled by a man and woman who were standing in front of her, admiring her work. "You've become a rather skilled artist, Sarah." She looked up and smiled at Felix and Lucy Mattei. "Well, what brings you to Santa Barbara on this beautiful afternoon?"

"We're here for a few days and decided to walk along the beach and then have some lunch. When we saw the congregation of artists, we decided to look for some paintings to put in our new hotel. Yours are the best we've seen so far."

"Instead of going to a restaurant, why not share our picnic lunch here on the lawn? Naomi always prepares more than enough, and besides, I'd like to catch up on what's going on in Santa Ynez and especially your hotel venture," she countered.

Naomi spread out two blankets and placed the picnic basket and jug of lemonade, and the four sat on the blanket enjoying fried chicken and potato salad. Mattei went on to tell Sarah that he and Lucy had met with a couple of bankers on Friday. They were seeking additional funds to complete the hotel.

"I don't want you to think I'm prying, but how much more do you need?"

"We put fifteen thousand dollars of our own money into the project and were asking for an additional five thousand to complete the structure and still have some operating funds," Mattei responded while chewing on a chicken leg.

"Do you think five thousand is enough? I mean, it'd be a shame to open and still be short of funds," Sarah responded.

"No offense, but we've been in the hotel business before and I can guarantee you that we'll be successful. Before we started construction, I found out that they were extending the track from Los Alamos to Los Olivos. It will be terminal size and stop directly across from the hotel. Though it'll be narrow gauge, it'll bring in a lot of tourists and be the main vehicle for moving goods from San Francisco south. Is there a particular reason why you're interested?"

"I might be interested as an investor, particularly if I could have a room in the hotel that would function as a gallery for my work. The idea of the train terminal across from the hotel is appealing for someone like me, who'd like to travel to San Francisco periodically to promote her work. Do you know how soon the line would be extended to Los Angeles?"

"My guess is that the extension is at least ten years away and perhaps more. I could provide you a room just off the lobby that would be visible from the registration desk, if you wanted to invest. How soon do you want repayment?"

"Why not pay in installments, say on a monthly basis with reasonable interest."

"You seem to be a woman who's well versed in investments. How do you come by this knowledge?"

"I have several commercial buildings that pay rent on a monthly basis. My brother spent some time training me to manage my investments. In addition, I have a trust that draws royalties from oil discovered on my parents' property. I can afford the investment, and I like the idea of a hotel showing my work and especially one with Teady access to a transportation system."

They finished lunch, and while Lucy was helping Naomi clean up, Sarah and Felix Mattei struck a bargain and agreed to meet tomorrow at an attorney's office to sign the agreement. Sarah knew she had made a wise investment. "Felix, our agreement need not be made public. As far as anyone else is concerned, you are the owner and I am your tenant. I'll remain in the background."

"I think I'm going to like doing business with you." He shook hands with Sarah then Lucy and she embraced.

CHAPTER TWENTY-FOUR

He didn't know if Mr. Sanchez was guilty, an innocent, or a victim of circumstance. He did know that he had the funds to pay for the pardon and enough time had elapsed that it would be difficult to bring charges against Sanchez, let alone find him guilty. From what Sanchez said, Harker, the former sheriff, would try to have him extradited, but again from Michael Lund's perspective that was highly unlikely. The trip to Laramie wasn't fun; it was long and tedious, but the pay was good. When Guthrie divulged that Sanchez had one hundred thousand dollars on account in his bank and substantially more in several banks, Lund knew that this was a client to go the extra mile for.

He arrived late and checked into the Railroad Hotel and the next morning met with his counterpart in Laramie, an attorney by the name of Matthew Dowl who was helping him on the pardon. The two men greeted each other and adjourned to Dowl's conference room.

"Judd Harker is raising UI kind of hell, but no one's paying too much attention to him especially since Sanchez's old mentor Mike Jacobs is pushing the governor to ignore Harker," Dowl said. "I've talked to the governor's administrative assistant and he says if we can produce a ten thousand dollar contribution to the governor's election campaign, he'll sign the pardon. Of course someone else will have to take credit for the contribution, but we can work through that. So what are the chances of giving to the governor's reelection campaign?"

"I can have the money wired immediately conditioned that he won't change his mind once the money is in his hands. It isn't that I don't trust your governor, I just want to protect my client."

"I've thought about that. Since Mike Jacobs was Sanchez's mentor, why don't we have him act as the intermediary? He holds the pardon signed by the governor and when he receives the cash, he hands you the pardon and the governor the cash. Is that okay?"

Two days later Lund left Laramie with the pardon. He didn't meet the governor nor he did he meet Judd Harker. He heard the stories of the attempt to arrest Sanchez at Mike Jacobs's ranch and another attempt in Tombstone thwarted by Wyatt Earp and his brother Virgil. So he was expecting a confrontation that didn't materialize.

Lund wired Tommy with the good news and congratulated him on being a free man. Tommy felt a huge burden lifting from his shoulders. He was now free to travel throughout the country, though he didn't plan to go back to Laramie. He wanted to see the Waidners and visit Santa Fe and Tombstone and see how his old businesses were faring. But first he wanted to get started in the electric trolley business.
The question was what to do with the existing horse-drawn carriages and their owners.

The next day he met with Harrison Guthrie and discussed the options available to him. They agreed that the first step was to see if either or both of the companies were for sale; Guthrie said he'd make the inquiry.

Tommy started making plans for the electric trolleys, although he knew he'd need some more technical knowledge before he could proceed. He made some inquiries and learned that there was a professor at the local college who specialized in electrical current and electric engines. Guthrie arranged for a meeting between Tommy and the professor at his home. Professor Hilliard was working on a large electric generator at his lab in a small building in the back of his house in the Balboa District of San Diego.

Tommy asked whether a source of power could be built to drive multiple commercial carriages. The professor said as long as the carriage had access to an electrical source that could run continuously, multiple carriages could be propelled by the same source.

"How is that possible?" Tommy asked.

"If you had some sort of electrical line that he carriage could touch continually, it would be possible."

"How about a rail on the ground that the carriage continually touches?"

"I don't think so. It seems to me that the amount of electricity in the rail could possible electrocute anyone who stepped on it. The answer has to be that the electric source has to be overhead and the carriage touches the source, perhaps by a rod of some sort that can carry electricity to a power supply in the carriage," Professor Hilliard responded.

"So, do we need some power source inside the carriage?"

"Right. You must have something to make it move along the rails. Why don't you take a look at the one that's being proposed in Richmond, Virginia? I believe his system calls for a rod attached to the roof and to an overhead electrical wire. I have some literature on his plans. You're welcome to read what I have."

Tommy met with Harrison Guthrie the next day and asked how he had fared with the two horsedrawn companies. "The company with the route from the center of town down Main Street wants to sell, but the one from the wharf to the center of town said he doesn't know. I think he suspects something is up and is waiting to see what our offer is," Harrison summarized.

"Did you make them an offer?" "No. I said I had an interested buyer and would they be interested in selling."

"What does your brother say about their licenses to operate the horse-drawn carriages?"

"They have a license to operate for three years on their respective routes."

"So we could get our license to operate over the same route and ignore them. We'd have to have our own rails, but once we're up and operating, they have to quit, because no one will ride in their carriages. We could save the cost of buying them out, but I think we can accomplish what we want without the hassle. I want Lund to apply to the city for an exclusive license to build a large power plant, erect overhead power lines throughout the city, and lay track in the center of the city streets. If your brother can deliver, then the two horse-drawn carriage companies will see the handwriting on the well and be easier to deal with. I want you to come up with a reasonable valuation of their business as it stands and after we get our license, we'll make them a reasonable offer."

"I'd be glad to do that, but what about money? I know you can handle the seed money needed, but the overall cost of one million dol- lars to put this all together may require outside help."

"I've been thinking about that, but let's get the license first and then shop for financing. I want to talk to a friend of mine to see what his interest might be. Do you need me to talk to Lund or can you handle that?"

"I'll see him today and get on with it. Do you see a role for the bank in your operation?"

"If this goes as planned, your bank will be the prime vehicle for funds coming in and out of the business."

After Michael Lund returned with the pardon, Tommy wrote to Don Fernando and told him the albatross was indeed off his neck. He went on to explain his new venture, what it entailed, and wondered if he or Carlos was interested in being investors in the project. Don Fernando responded that they were interested and Carlos would travel to San Diego in six weeks to discuss the project with Tommy. He passed on some sad news. Maria Conchita's father, Don Hernando Lopez, had passed away last month. Don Fernando felt his friend had died of a broken heart.

Tommy was sad about Don Hernando but ecstatic that Carlos was corning to visit. He arranged to have several rooms at the hotel set aside for his young friend when he arrived. He still had a lot of work to do in order to put together a workable plan. So he decided to travel to Virginia and meet with the developer of the electric trolleys and see what he could learn from the man. He asked Lund and Guthrie to continue their efforts and took the train to Richmond, Virginia, to visit with Frank Sprague, the developer of the electric trolley.

A graduate of Annapolis, Frank Sprague was an electrical engineer who left the Navy in 1883 to join the Edison Company, but by 1884 he wanted to branch out on his own and founded the Sprague Electric Railway and Motor Company. He developed a method of transferring power through an overhead electric line to a streetcar via a pole called the trolley. He was delighted that Tommy Sanchez was pursuing the same venture in San Diego and was most helpful in making Tommy understand how the entire development package went together and what was needed to maintain the operation.

Tommy returned after two weeks in Richmond thoroughly convinced that Sprague's trolley would be successful in San Diego. In addition to the technical aspect of the project, Sprague had impressed upon Tommy the social aspect of what was to come. The electric trolley would open up areas outside the city limits and would facilitate development in the suburbs.

When he returned from Richmond, Tommy met with Guthrie and Lund to discuss the status of obtaining the license to operate in the city. Lund said that the application had been submitted and was being processed through the planning department end soon would go before the city council. Both Lund and Guthrie were assured by Guthrie's brother that the votes were there to approve the license application. Tommy thanked them but didn't share with them the thoughts generated by Sprague's social benefit comment.

Carlos came to town two weeks later, and Tommy took a week off to go deep sea fishing with him. They hired a boat, stocked it with a week's provisions and a small keg of beer, and did nothing but party. Tommy filled him in on the entire plan including purchasing land at the city outskirts to eventually build homes for those coming to California. At the end of the week Carlos said he and his father would invest what was needed. Tommy shared with him his intent to trade stock in the new venture to the owners of the existing horse drawn companies.

"You don't need to give them anything," Carlos said.

"I know, but this way there's less hassle, and besides, there should be so much profit that we won't even miss the amount of stock we trade for their rights." Carlos accepted Tommy analysis.

They met with Guthrie and Lund at the Delmonico Steak House and finalized the new company, which was going to be called Maria Trolley Company. Lund had set up the company and the amount of stock it was going to issue. He thought that it might be wise to let some of the civic leaders have an opportunity to purchase stock. Sprague had recommended an electrical engineer, who Tommy interviewed and then offered him a position with the company. Don Fernando, Carlos, and Tommy would be the major stockholders with Lund and Guthrie being minority stockholders. Lund would be the company's attorney and Guthrie its treasurer. He'd received permission from the bank board of directors to participate in the venture. Maria Trolley Company took an option on a piece of land on the city outskirts of the city and planned to build the powerhouse on this site. They had the money and the knowledge and were Just waiting for their license before they'd break ground on their new venture.

It was a happy time, end all consumed a lot of wine; that is, all except Tommy. He never found a need to over indulge; he always wanted to keep his wits about him. It was about eleven when they got up from the table and the four walked to the front door. Lund and Guthrie were sharing a carriage and left Tommy and Carlos at the door as they walked to it. Just then two shots rang out, and Carlos and Tommy dropped to the sidewalk and sought cover, but there wasn't any available other than the carriage that Lund and Guthrie were sharing. But Lund's driver had pulled away at that exact time and so they dove toward their own carriage, but their driver wasn't present. As Tommy looked up, another shot was fired and hit the side of the carriage.

Carlos polled Tommy back. "I think it's just one person and he's across the street." Carlos was pointing to where he thought the shots were coming from.

"You may have paid for a pardon, Sanchez, but I'm going to make you pay for killing my son."

For the first time Tommy learned that Bull Larkin was Harker's son. Now he knew why Harker had pursued this vendetta for so long and why the only way out of here tonight was to kill Harker. He guessed it would always come to this, but he thought he'd have a chance. Harker was moving across the street as he was talking.

Tommy told Carlos to stay where he was and that Tommy was going to make a run for it. Harker would probably follow him and that would give Carlos the opportunity to get help. Without giving Carlos a choice, he started running down the sidewalk away from the carriage but keeping near the wall to give him some form of shelter. He heard two more shots and knew that Harker was firing at him. He turned left and had gone about ten paces before he realized that the alley was a dead end. He searched frantically for some weapon and at the same time some place to hide in the alley but with no success.

That's when he saw Harker come around the corner and walk slowly into the alley. He continued to walk forward at that pace, and when he saw Tommy, he couldn't help but laugh. "Well, Mr. Slick, it looks like court is finally in session for you. You're charged with murdering a law enforcement officer, my son, and the jury says you're guilty and you're to die by a firing squad. Well, I'm a one-man firing squad. Thought you were pretty clever getting that Jew lawyer to buy you a pardon. Now don't deny it. I have friends and they told me. Well, there's no pardon for you here. I don't even want to hear you beg. It wouldn't do you any good."

Harker raised his gun and took careful aim at Tommy's head. Tommy didn't move, didn't say anything, just looked at Harker and smiled.

The shot took off half of his head and when he fell forward, his head landed at Tommy's feet.

Carlos had gotten his gun out of the carriage and followed Harker into the alley just in time.

"I'd say we're even, don't you?" Tommy hugged Carlos.

Lund, Guthrie, and the police arrived simultaneously. As soon as the shooting started, Lund and Guthrie had gone to the police station and told them what happened. Sergeant Randolph arrived and took charge. He asked many questions, and when he was finished he told Lund that he thought it was a case of self defense but he wanted them all to come to the police station to make and sign a statement, which they did. An hour later, Randolph told them they could go home. There would be an inquiry in the next couple of days and they might have to answer more questions, but it seemed like self-defense and they should be in the clear.

The mood between the four was a sober one; even Tommy and Carlos didn't have much to say as they retired to their respective rooms. The next morning the two had breakfast together but talked only about trivial matters. The trauma of the night before was still with them. Even Tommy, who was a skilled fighter and had killed before, wasn't sure what the impact of the shooting would be.

The following day the San Diego Union featured the shooting with pictures and a front page narrative. It seemed that the only thing anyone talked about for the next two days was the story carried by the newspaper. But that was nothing compared to the feature story on the fourth day, which chronicled Tommy's life including the shooting of Bull Larkin in Laramie many years earlier and his subsequent pardon. The Union wasn't finished because their feature the next week was an expose on the application for the electric trolley car being sought by Tommy Sanchez and his associates.

Guthrie and Lund were very supportive, but Guthrie's brother said the chances of approval of their application wasn't very good at this time and suggested they withdraw the application and resubmit it later. The four met several times during the week and realized that if their application was withdrawn, others who saw the potential in their application would submit their own, and their application would never be accepted.

Their only choice was to press on. Tommy asked Guthrie to talk to his brother.

"I want you to ask him what the main obstacle is and what we can do to compensate for it."

Two days later the response was relayed to Guthrie, who passed it on reluctantly to the other three. As long as Tommy Sanchez was involved in the project, the application was dead on arrival. The council recognized that Sanchez didn't pull the trigger, but the whole issue of Laramie and the pardon were council didn't feel comfortable in giving him the license. They had no animosity toward Carlos Quinte To; he did what anyone else would have done under the circumstances.

"This is too good an opportunity to pass up. You three have got to continue the project. If you don't, someone else will pick it up and you'll be sorry that you didn't take this opportunity. I'm persona non grata and there's nothing we can do about that. It's what it is. Carlos, you and your father could pursue this with Lund and Guthrie." Tommy was very candid with his three friends.

"What about you? You're the one who's done all the legwork and you're the one who initiated the plan. I'm not comfortable without you in this enterprise." Carlos's comments were seconded by Lund and Guthrie.

"There's more to this enterprise than the trolleys. I believe the money is in land speculation. The most important thing I learned from Frank Sprague is that the trolley will be the vehicle for expansion. People need not live close to town if there's a trolley system available to bring them to the services in the center of the town. I think you three, along with Carlos's father, should pursue the application and I'll set up another company to speculate on land at the outskirts of the city. I would encourage 011 of you to invest in my company.

"I think the best I can do for 011 of you now is to leave the area. As long as I stay, the implication is that I'm involved. Besides, as long as I'm not here, they won't have anything to write about. I'll wind up my affairs in two days and then leave. I encourage you to continue with the electric trolley, but if you don't, the opportunity will be there for someone else. The greater opportunity is in land speculation. It will be there even if you pass on the trolley."

Lund was a pragmatist. "This will all pass after a year, and what you put together will continue to be valuable. I suggest the following: Carlos and his father fund the trolley enterprise through a corporation that I'll set up. You set up a separate corporation for land acquisition. Guthrie and I will be the managers of the trolley business and will let you know in advance where we plan our next track. This way we keep the city happy, and you can invest and eventually own stock in the trolley enterprise and profit by purchasing land in advance of our expansion. Perhaps there's a way that Guthrie and I can own twenty percent of your land acquisition company sometime in the future."

CHAPTER TWENTY-FIVE

The year was 1877. Felix Mattei had completed construction of his Central Hotel in Los Olivos the year before. This was the same year that the narrow gauge railroad was extended from Los Alamos to Los Olivos with a terminal directly across the street from his hotel. Passengers could unload, walk across the street, and stay at the hotel or hire a carriage to transport them to Santa Ynez or even board the stagecoach for points south. The hotel was a combination two stories and one story. The rooms on the second floor were pristine and included a bed, night- stand, and a basin and pitcher sitting on a chest of drawers. Restroom facilities were at the end of the hall on the second floor.

The first floor housed the restaurant, lobby, a small bar, and a room for Sarah just to the left of the entrance area. She was delighted to have a place to show her work. It also gave Naomi some- thing to do. She'd be in the gallery most of the time and could sell what paintings were avail- able. In the event the customer wanted to talk to Sarah, Naomi would send someone to their home and have her brought to the hotel. They were living in a rented home in Santa Ynez, but Sarah was looking for something permanent.

The first year had been good to Felix Mattei, and he hadn't missed a payment to Sarah. She'd been living full time in the valley for over a year and decided that she would buy this year. Her finances were in good shape; her two commercial buildings and four homes in Pennsylvania were fully occupied. The oil revenue was continuous and was expected to stay that way for the remainder of her life. What disturbed her was her relationship with her brother James. She wrote a letter to him every month, but his responses were sporadic. This was disturbing enough, but the biggest surprise was his marriage to Jennifer Crayloi. Sarah didn't attend the wedding because she wasn't informed. She found out about it from her banker in Harris- burg who didn't know it was a secret.

She wrote James and asked him why he didn't invite her; he finally responded with a weak excuse. He said the wedding plans were put together rather quickly and he and Jennifer felt there wasn't enough time for her to come back east. Sarah was crushed and didn't know what to make of it. Deep down, she felt that James had a character issue and probably would be a pawn of his new in-laws.

The big ranchos in the Santa Ynez Valley had been in the process of being subdivided over the past ten years. With the drought of the 1860s, there wasn't enough water to grow the grass needed by large herds, and consequently the ranchos couldn't maintain huge parcels with drastically less income. Sarah found a fifteen hundred acre parcel south of Santa Ynez that was about four miles from Mission Santa Inez.

The parcel included an area for raising cattle and horses, some rolling hills, and the Santa Ynez River, which bisected the parcel. What Sarah most liked about the parcel was its proximity to the mission, Santa Ynez, and Los Olivos. She was within thirty minutes of all three places. The parcel had been split off from a larger parcel, which was still retained by the seller, Don Ozteg. He and she shared a common entry and exit.

Her social life was non-existent except for a few parties at Don Ortega's rancho. It wasn't that she was lacking an escort for the variety of functions at the ranchos; there just wasn't any- one who caught her fancy. Most of the eligible men fell into two categories. They were either in their late fifties or early sixties or they were in their twenties. She wondered if her life was to be frill of work and financial success but void of a love life. She traveled to Santa Barbara and San Francisco promoting her work and other than an occasional dinner with an owner of a gallery, she was lacking male companionship.

As soon as the land acquisition agreement had been finalized, Sarah and Naomi started to plan their home. They met with an architect from Santa Barbara who gave them a preliminary sketch a month after their initial meeting. Sarah made some changes and, after a few more meetings, approved a set of plans and hired a contractor to build the home. It took six months to build the home and another three months to furnish it. During the interim, Sarah became fascinated with the small vineyards on some of the large ranchos and went to the mission to talk to Father Lynch and learn as much as she could about mission grapes. She purchased some cuttings and started a vineyard on one hundred acres in the southern portion of her property and over the next seven years read as much as she could about the growing and management of a vineyard.

Mission grapes had been introduced into the valley by the Spanish and cultivated by the missions because the wine was used in their religious ceremonies. The stalks were thick and sturdy and the light colored red grapes produced a rather sweet wine or brandy. Some of the other ranchos produced more wine, but Sarah was satisfied with her yield and continued to seek refinement in her produce. She introduced several European varietals and crossed those cutting with her mission grapes.

It was during this period that she experienced some difficulty with the adjacent owner, who'd sold her the parcel. He was constantly moving cattle over their common road and blocking her access and exit. She rode over in a carriage one day and complained to Don Ortega. He invited her to a light lunch that included some of his wine and thanked her for coming over and making him aware of the situation. He assured her that the matter would be taken care of.

But two weeks later, she encountered the same problem end spoke to the rancho foreman, Harold Meade, after the cattle had been moved. "Well, little honey, we'll do the best we can, but we still have to move the cattle and this is the most convenient way." He leered at her as he spoke.

Sarah didn't like being referred to as "little honey," but let it pass. "I spoke to Don Ortega two weeks ago, and he assured me that this incident wouldn't occur again."

"Well, little lady, he didn't say anything to me, and as I said, this is the most convenient way to move the cattle. Maybe if I knew when you wanted to use the road, I could accommodate you."

"I have as much right to use this access as you do, and I don't think I have to make an appointment to travel on my road. I'll speak to the owner again."

"Well, you do that, little lady. He'll let me know if I have to change my routine."

Sarah made one more trip to Don Ortega's rancho and complained again. He was sympathetic and assured her that he would handle the situation. She drove to general store in Santa Ynez the following week as Meade and several of his hands were in town having a few at Murphy's Tavern directly across from the general store. He and his hands came out of Murphy's at the same time that Sarah and Naomi were leaving the general store and Meade called out to her. She stopped in front of the store waiting to see what he had to say.

"Well, bitch, you complained to my boss about me; I'll1let you in on a little secret. He ain't going to fire me. So what do you think about that?" He continued to talk as he walked across the street to the general store.

Sarah fired back. "It wasn't my intent to get you fired but to have access to my road when I desire. That's what our contract says and that's what I expect and I don't appreciate being called bitch, so I bid you good day, sir."

Meade was now on the same side of the street and stood in front of her. She knew a confrontation was brewing. She also knew that Naomi carried her knife and any move on the part of Meade would be met with a quick thrust of that knife.

"You think you're so high and mighty, but maybe I'll come visit you some night and find out if that little patch between your legs is blond as well." He towered above her.

Sarah reached into her bag and drew a small handgun and pointed it at Meade. "If you don't get out of my way, I'll shoot you where you wish I hadn't shot you, and as far as visiting me at night, I'm a dead shot, and when I shoot it isn't to wound anyone."

Meade immediately moved out of the way and let her pass. As soon as she laid her bag on the carriage seat she turned to see if Meade followed. He did not.

Many people had gathered outside the general store and had heard the confrontation. A couple came up to Sarah and complimented her on her stand.

To be on the safe side Sarah purchased a large dog that had been trained for security and made a spot for the dog inside her home near the entrance to their rear door.

CHAPTER TWENTY-SIX

When it was evident that Guthrie and Lund would receive a license from the city of San Diego to operate the electric trolleys, Carlos and Tommy started to buy up large parcels of land on what Lund and Guthrie told them would be the future route of the electric trolley. They invested nearly one hundred thousand dollars each and felt comfortable that this was a good investment; time would tell.

Tommy needed a change of venue. The newspaper articles had been vicious, and wherever he went in town the issue was raised as to whether he was the one cited by the newspaper. He spent a few days in Los Angeles but didn't like the town so he continued northward until he arrived in Santa Barbara. Here was a city that caught his fancy. It was young and fresh but had a cosmopolitan air about it. Tommy soon fit into its daily routine. He wasn't ready to think of a business, but he met with several bankers and then chose a bank on south State Street that seemed to have the style of operation he was comfortable with.

He transferred fifty thousand dollars into his account at the new bank and immediately acquired a new friend in the bank president. It was he who introduced him in the town and sponsored Tommy at many of the impromptu meetings of town officials and local dignitaries. Tommy with his good looks and fine manners and especially his finances was in demand at various social events. The major events centered on several equestrian groups and Tommy, being an accomplished rider, was welcomed to ride in their events.

The memory of Maria Conchita was still with him, and although he escorted different women to social events in the city of Santa Barbara, he hadn't found someone that gave him the thrill that Maria Conchita had. Francine Guttierez was a member of one of the elite families in the area and went out of her way to make Tommy's acquaintance. She asked John Staton, the president of Tommy's bank, for an introduction. Being that she was on the elite list in town, Staton acknowledged her request and invited her and Tommy to his home for dinner. She was a gracious dinner companion, and Tommy was delighted with the quick witted, intelligent woman and thanked his host for the introduction.

He escorted her to half a dozen social events before they became intimate. The love making was enjoyable, but Tommy had no intention of anything beyond that. Francine was an eager companion but was expecting a more permanent relationship, and when that didn't materialize, she became impatient and possessive. This change had the opposite effect on Tommy. One evening they were attending a party in town and Francine objected to the amount of attention Tommy was giving to another young woman at the party. Francine stormed out of the party and demanded that Tommy's driver take her home   immediately, leaving   Tommy   without transportation.

He knew that their relationship was over, but terminating it wasn't going to be that easy. Francine told her family that Tommy had taken advantage of her and forced himself on her. Her family was well aware of Francine's wild temper- ament and numerous affairs and was hesitant to get involved. But they were constantly nagged by Francine to do something.

The responsibility of defending her honor fell to the oldest of her brothers, Lucien Gutierrez. Reluctantly Lucien challenged Tommy to a duel, which was outlawed in California. However, the local authorities turned a blind eye when a member of one the elite families was involved. The challenge came in the form of a note delivered to John Staton on Tommy's behalf. Since Lucien issued the challenge, Tommy was allowed to select the type of weapon.

Tommy asked Staton if there was some other way to satisfy the family short of a duel. Staton made the inquiry but was turned down; it seemed that Francine wanted blood Tommy chose six-guns. The duel was to be held behind one of the warehouses on the north shore of Santa Barbara at seven a.m. John Staton said he'd be glad to function as Tommy's second and handle the interface with Lucien's second if Tommy wanted. Tommy accepted.

At the appointed time Lucien, his second, and his entourage, which included Francine, arrived and took a position on the south side while Tommy and John Staton took a position on the north side. The two combatants were to stand twenty paces apart and at the count of three draw their firearms and fire until one or both men fell to the ground.

One of Lucien's entourages agreed to do the count. At three Lucien clumsily drew his weapon and fired twice at Tommy without hitting him. Tommy stood his ground and didn't draw his weapon. Lucien was stunned and didn't know what to do. He didn't want to be there and didn't want to kill a man who wouldn't defend himself. He just stood there with his weapon pointed at Tommy.

In an instant Tommy drew and shot the gun out of Lucien's hand and continued to fire, hitting the fallen weapon and driving it toward Lucien's entourage and specifically at Francine. When he emptied the weapon, he drew the other gun he carried and continued to fire and drive the weapon until it was at Francine's feet. She ran from the scene; the other members of the entourage didn't move. In fact, one could almost say they couldn't breathe. They never saw such an exhibition and probably were afraid for Lucien as Tommy strode toward him with his gun in his hand.

"Lucien, I apologize for my behavior. It won't happen again. May I consider your honor restored?" Tommy stuck out his hand. Lucien grabbed it as though he were hanging onto the lower rung of a ladder, thanked him, and slowly walked away with the rest of his entourage.

John Staton threw Tommy's cape around his shoulders and led him back to their carriage. "I think that puts this to bed. I'm sure we'll not hear anymore from Francine or her family."

Two days later Slaton brought word from Lucien that Tommy would not be bothered by
Francine in the future. "My guess is that Lucien told her you are a gentleman and couldn't have acted ungentlemanly toward her."

Tommy wasn't sure what his reception would be from the group that he socialized with. The fact is that he was treated with a great deal more respect by the men and a lot more under- standing by the women.

It was a week later when Slaton approached him with a problem. He needed to make a large gold shipment to San Francisco for a mining company in the area. The problem was that the train hadn't been extended north past Santa Barbara. Slaton needed someone with experience to ride shotgun on the stage from Santa Barbara to Los Olivos, at which point the shipment would be put on the train to San Francisco.

"You're quite proficient with a weapon, and I'd feel more comfortable with this shipment if you were on the stage. Now I know that you're a businessman and may not want to get involved in something like this, but if you did, my client and the bank would be very appreciative. They would make it worthwhile."

Tommy thought it over for a day before he agreed. "After the duel with Lucien, I need a change of scenery, and it might be fun transporting the cargo to Los Olivos."

The stage left in front of the State Street bank with only a driver, Tommy, and of course the strongbox, which was on the floor between the two men. The first part of the trip over the San Marcos Pass with a stop at Kinevan Tavern went without incident. The two men had lunch, changed horses, and mounted for the second half of the ride. They drove about a mile east. Then the road turned abruptly north and soon veered to the right as they came up on a flat portion of the trail.

As soon as they made this turn, shots rang out and the driver was hit and slumped over onto Tommy's lap. Tommy grabbed the reins and encouraged the horses forward. He saw two men trying to wave him down as he urged the horses onward. The two men mounted and gave chase. Soon they overtook the stage coming up on the left side of Tommy, who drew and fired at both men, hitting one and discouraging the other.

Tommy decided to take his chances with the one would be robber and polled on the reins until the four horses stopped. Tommy jumped down and drew his weapon, but the other rider was riding away as fast as he could. He checked on the driver who'd been wounded in the right shoulder. Tommy was able to stop the flow of blood, but the man was unconscious. He lifted the driver down and placed him on a seat in the carriage, climbed back up, and drove at a slower but steady pace to the Santa Ynez Hotel.

As soon as they arrived at the hotel in Santa Ynez, the manager sent for the sheriff and the doctor; both arrived at the same time. Several of the locals assisted the doctor in carrying the driver to his office. Tommy told the sheriff what happened and where he was shot at by the robbers. Within fifteen minutes the sheriff and a few of the male citizens mounted up and took off after the robbers. The sheriff asked Tommy if he wanted to join them. He declined, stating that he still had a strongbox to deliver to the terminal at Los Olivos. It took him an additional hour to reach the terminal and arrange for its storage in the terminal safe. Slaton had arranged for security of the strongbox once Tommy and the driver delivered it to the terminal.

It was too late to return to Santa Barbara, so he drove the team of horses over to the hotel, turned them over to an attendant at the hotel, and registered at Felix Mattei's hotel. Sarah was closing up her little gallery and stepped into the lobby as Tommy Sanchez registered for a room. She stopped and looked at the man registering and was sure she'd seen him before, but where? At that moment Tommy turned and stared directly at Sarah and smiled. "Miss Hansen, it's good to see you again."

It took a few seconds for the greeting to take hold. It was then that she recognized the man who'd foiled the robbery at the hotel in Santa Fe. Her heart skipped a beat; he seemed as mysterious as he was then. "Are you staying at the hotel, Mr. Sanchez?"

"Just for the night. I don't want to seem presumptuous, but we never finished our conversation in Santa Fe. I wonder if you'd be interested in being my dinner companion this evening at the hotel?"

The menu was sparse but the food excellent. The hotel had only been opened a year, but Lucy Mattei had earned a reputation in that short period of time as being an excellent cook. Sarah and Tommy talked for nearly three hours over dinner and only when they were interrupted by Sheriff Mason, did they stop.

Tommy saw the sheriff before Sarah and started to rise as the man approached their table. He nodded to Sarah, whom he knew, and shook

Tommy's hand. "I'd hope that you'd stay Our city council would like to have lunch with you around noon tomorrow and personally thank you for what you did."

Before Tommy could say anything, Sarah interrupted the sheriff. "What's this all about, Sheriff?"

"I'm not surprised that you don't know, but this man is a bona fide hero. To help a friend, he rode shotgun on the stage carrying a shipment to a San Francisco bank. On the way here, there was an attempted robbery and the driver was shot. Mr. Sanchez grabbed the reins and continued to Santa

Ynez, but the robbers rode after him. He shot one and discouraged the other and got the driver to Doc Roberts in Santa Ynez and then delivered the strongbox to the terminal across the street. Everybody is talking about it, and some of the citizens want to say thank him."

The sheriff turned to Tommy and asked him for an answer. But before Tommy responded, Sarah blurted out, "He'll come." Tommy looked at her and smiled.

The hotel was full and the hour late, so Tommy offered to escort Sarah home. She wasn't afraid to travel alone at night, but with that confrontation with Meade still in her mind, she welcomed the companionship. Sarah offered him their guest house so he didn't have to travel back late at night. He accepted.

It took about an hour to reach Sarah's home. Naomi was awake and nervously opened the door. Sarah introduced Tommy and told Naomi he would sleep in the guest house. Sarah gathered some blankets, sheets, and a towel and escorted Tommy to the small guest house located thirty yards behind the main house. She insisted on making the bed, and when she started to leave, Tommy put his arm around her waist and kissed her on the mouth.

She returned the kiss and then pulled away.

"I'm sorry, but this is coming too fast for me. You're a very attractive man, and I've had a little too much wine to know my true feelings." She left him at the door smiling at her.

Naomi was agitated when she reentered the main house. "He's not Mexican; he's Sioux."

Sarah was stunned by Naomi's suggestion, but decided to retire before she jumped to any conclusion.

Tommy was up at six the next morning and waited until there was movement inside the main house before he knocked. Naomi greeted him; Sarah was still in bed. "You're no Mexican, you're Sioux," she said.

"I am. I'm the son of Sitting Bull and Elizabeth Kelly, a white captive."

Sarah was standing in the doorway behind him as he acknowledged to Naomi who he was. "That's why you always looked familiar. I saw you one time, but it was well before Little Big Horn; I think it was at my wedding to Crazy Horse. When did you change your name to Sanchez?"

"I acted as a guide to several wagon trains in my late teens, learned to speak Spanish fluently, and lived with a family named Sanchez for a period of time, so it seemed kind of natural that while I was living with them I take their name.

Later I just continued to be identified at Tommy Sanchez. I've recently had that name legalized, so I'm officially Tommy Sanchez."

"That day in the hotel lobby in Santa Fe has been on my mind for UI these years. Were you carrying a gun when you forced the robbers to
leave the money?" He smiled.

"Yes."

"Are you really that fast?"

"I used to be, but maybe not now."

"Are you married?" She just couldn't control herself from asking the question, but as soon as she did, she blushed.

"No. I've never been married. Sarah, I'm a little uncomfortable being the center of attention. I don't know any of the people in Santa Ynez. Would you be my companion at the luncheon? I think if they see me with a beautiful woman, they probably won't be as concerned with me."

She didn't really wanted to go, but more than anything she wanted to be with this man, so she accepted. Before they left, she wanted to show him around her fifteen hundred acre mini ranch. They saddled two horses and rode out shortly after breakfast and covered the perimeter of her place and her small vineyard. She was proud of the ranch and from what she could tell from his manner, he was appreciative of her efforts in bringing the place along.

The luncheon was held at the Central Hotel in Los Olivos and was attended by about twenty of the elite in the valley, including Father Lynch. The sheriff introduced Tommy to the dignitaries, and to Tommy's surprise, John Slaton had come for the luncheon. As soon as lunch was served the sheriff gave a recap of Tommy's heroics, and the mayor of Santa Ynez issued a hand written proclamation making Tommy an honorary citizen of the valley and asked him to consider moving here.

After lunch most of the attendees were able to personally thank Tommy and reiterate what the mayor said about him relocating to the valley. Tommy was unaware that John Slaton had told Sarah about the duel that Tommy was involved in earlier in the month. She drew the conclusion that Tommy Sanchez probably would be in the middle of any confrontation whether he wanted to be or not. Slaton didn't disclose to her what the cause of the confrontation was, but she assumed a woman was involved.

The sun was shining and the weather temperate with not a cloud in the sky. Tommy asked if she'd like to go for a ride in her carriage. They drove toward Ballard and stopped alongside a small stream that flowed between Los Olivos and Santa Ynez. Sarah laid out a blanket and Tommy opened a bottle of wine he bought at the restaurant.

"I know you may say it's none of my business, but John Slaton told me about the duel. What brought two men to that point?"

"I was intimate with a woman and she wanted a permanent relationship, I did not, so she forced the issue, and her brother had to challenge me. I did my best not to kill him and yet make him believe that I was not the aggressor in my relationship with his sister. I think he believed me. Sarah, I'm attracted to you and I sense you are to me. I'm a grown man, yet I'm a half-breed and have to carry that with me until I die. I don't try to provoke anyone, but I won't turn the other cheek either. I've found that if you turn the other cheek, someone will want to slap the other as well. I'd like to spend more time with you. I've had you on my mind from the first time I saw you as a new bride and later in Santa Fe. I've been a very successful businessman and seem to be able to make good investments. I'm free at the time and could move here to see if our relation- ship could grow. That's if you are interested."

"That day in Santa Fe will be with me forever. I too have a slightly checkered past. I've been referred to as a squaw, and people have made snide remarks about my being married to a savage.
If you could ignore my past, I'd like to see if our relationship could blossom."

Tommy took her in his arms and smothered her with kisses, which she returned as passionately. She willingly gave herself to him and he responded with a passion that he didn't know he possessed.
Later as she lay in his arms, she said, "I don't know about you, but that was pretty fantastic."

"I couldn't have said it any better. I've had an image of you, but you've surpassed even that. You are a fantastic woman, and I hope I get to know you better."

"Well, I don't know if anyone could know me better than you." She playfully gave him a jab in the ribs.

After a whirlwind romance of two weeks, they agreed to be married in a month. Naomi would be her maid of honor and Tommy wanted Carlos as his best man. They shared with each other their other loves and Tommy felt comfortable in putting Maria Conchita to rest. She would always be his first love, but Sarah would be his last.

Sarah learned more about Tommy from Carlos at their wedding. He told her about his ordeal and how Tommy had carried him down the mountain. Although he didn't know 011 the specific details, he shared what he knew about Maria Conchita, her death, Tommy's near-death experience, and his subsequent capture of all four men who had killed Maria Conchita. This made Sarah even more certain that she had indeed found a soul mate.

They honeymooned in San Francisco, and Sarah was delighted that she could take the lead and show Tommy something he hadn't experienced before. He was like putty in her hands; he couldn't do enough for her, and he was surprised that he was able to subordinate his interest for her. She took him to art galleries, and while they were in San Francisco one of the galleries had a private showing of four of her works. Tommy was deeply impressed with his wife's talent and gave her a diamond pendant. They slept late, enjoyed elegant dinners, and tasted the best wine that money could buy.

After two weeks they boarded a steamer to San Diego. Tommy wanted to check on his property. Carlos had indicated that the electric trolley was successful and they'd probably want to sell some of their holdings.

Sarah and Tommy shared with each other what their holdings and assets were and agreed for the time being to keep everything separate until they returned from their honeymoon and hired a competent attorney to set up a structure for them. Sarah met Michael Lund and Harrison Guthrie and was surprised that the idea for their electric trolley company was Tommy's and that he had relinquished his interest. He and Carlos bought large parcels of land at the end of the existing trolley lines and where the extension of the trolley was planned.

Carlos had agreed to sell a five hundred acre parcel before he left for Mexico City. It was up to Tommy to finalize the deal, which is what he did. They sold the land for a substantial profit and deposited the money in their joint account in Guthrie's bank.

Lund and Guthrie were fascinated with Sarah, who presented each a signed painting. Tommy smiled; he knew that both were won over with not only Sarah's talent but her beauty as well. Tommy had Lund tell Sarah about the shooting. He wanted her to be aware of everything that he was involved with so there would be no surprises. She asked him questions about Judd Harker and Bull Larkin, and Tommy answered as truthfully as he could. For this she was grateful.

They took the steamer back to San Luis Obispo and the train back to Los Olivos; Naomi was waiting for them with their carriage. She brought them up to date on the gallery and the rancho. She was reluctant, but under Sarah's prodding she told about the cattle that were on the access road and that some had come down to the house. Meade wasn't apologetic and didn't seem to care about her complaints.

When the three arrived at the access road, cattle were being moved down the road. They waited about thirty minutes for the cattle to clear, and then Meade rode up and smiled at them. "Sorry about that. We thought you'd be on a much longer honeymoon." With that comment, he and two of his riders galloped off.

Tommy and Sarah didn't say anything until they arrived at their home, but Naomi kept looking at Tommy on the way back as though asking him to do something. "Does this happen often?" he asked Sarah.

"Quite often. In fact, as often as they want. I've talked to the owner twice, but it hasn't helped, and Meade is as arrogant as he can be. I don't know what we can do."

They retired early. About ten that evening, Sarah sensed Tommy getting up and asked him what the matter was. "Don't worry; I'll only be gone only a short time."

She knew in an instant what was on his mind. "Tommy. Don't. I can't afford to lose you. Please don't go."

"Don't worry, Sarah, this won't take long."

Don Ortega was a light sleeper and when he heard a noise, he wasn't concerned because the dogs hadn't barked. He started to go back to sleep, but something cold was pressing against his cheek.

"Good evening, Don Ortega. I haven't seen you since our wedding. How are you?"

Don Ortega started to protest, but Tommy pressed the blade of the knife against his cheek and drew blood. "I want to talk to you about our road problem. It seems that Sarah has asked you to live up to your agreement on several occasions and you've ignored her. That's not very neighborly. Do you think?" Don Ortega nodded that it wasn't.

"Now here's what we're going to do. You're going to find another way to move your cattle that won't interfere with our parcel anymore. Are we in agreement?" Don Ortega nodded that they were.

"Now I don't want you to think that once I leave, you can do whatever you want. I was able to come on your ranch, bypass your dogs, and enter your house without anyone knowing. I can do it anytime I want. Do we understand each other?"

"I understand." Don Ortega choked out the answer, but Tommy wasn't convinced of his sincerity.

"I had intended to cut off your right ear to show you my intent; however, you've said oil the right things, but somehow I don't believe you."

Don Ortega started to protest, but Tommy put a cloth over his mouth and cut off half the lobe of his ear. When the pain subsided, Tommy took his hand from Don Ortega's mouth. "Now I didn't cut off your ear, just cut the lobe a little. It'll heal, but I want to impress upon you that I'm not someone who makes idle threats. Now to show your good faith, I suggest you fire Meade this morning, and I wouldn't consider retaliating against me or my wife.

Do we have an agreement?"

Don Ortega was sobbing, but Tommy extracted an answer from him that they had an agreement. Ortega didn't hear Tommy leave his house nor did he hear any of the dog's bark. He placed a cold compress against his ear until the bleeding stopped and then went outside and called his dogs by name. All three responded and ran up to their master. If nothing else shook Ortega, that did.

Sarah couldn't sleep until Tommy slipped into the house around one a.m. She threw her arms around him and begged him not to take any more chances, and that's when she told him that she thought she was pregnant. "It must have been that hot carriage ride." She laughed when she made that statement.

She asked what he had done, but all he said was that he and Don Ortega had consummated an understanding and now it was up to Don Ortega to live up to the agreement. He said he loved her and was concerned about having a child at her age.

"I know it's a risk, but my first two children were easy births, and besides, I wanted to have a child with you. I want someone to perpetuate what we've accomplished, so please be careful. I know you can handle yourself, but bear with me that I'm a little possessive at this stage."

He kissed her, picked her up, and led her back to their bed. Naomi had heard the entire conversation and could only imagine what Tommy had done to Don Ortega. She was happy for her mistress and would be there when her time came. She'd grown fond of Tommy after being skeptical at first and thought her mistress had found a good mate.

CHAPTER TWENTY-SEVEN

Her letters to her son Lars were sent through James T. Jefferson, the Pinkerton detective. He was always quick to respond to her letters, but was unable to give her anything concrete about what Lars was doing or where he was. Occasion- ally he would tell her that he heard Lars was running with a group of Sioux who escaped the reservation. He was not offering much hope.

Just prior to their wedding, Sarah told Tommy about Lars and extracted a commitment that if Lars could be found and if he could be enticed to come live with them, Tommy would try to do everything to help him assimilate into white society. With that commitment, Sarah encouraged Mr. Jefferson to hire other agents to seek out Lars and report back to her.

Sarah was three months pregnant and hadn't slowed down. She still went to the gallery twice a week and did the shopping for the family even though Tommy suggested that he and Naomi were quite capable of selecting their food. This morning she informed Tommy that they were short on provisions and that she and Naomi were going to Santa Ynez to the general store. Tommy said that was okay as long as he went along and drove. She could lie back in the carriage and take it easy.

They usually used the four passenger carriage when they were shopping, and today was no different. Normally Tommy didn't carry a weapon, but today he took his six-gun and holster and laid it on the floor next to his feet.

He had all he could do to keep the number of purchases to a minimum, but Sarah was in the buying mood, and when she saw anything at the store that was for a baby, she bought it. Tommy's job was to carry the packages outside and place them in a boot at the back of their carriage. He'd just put the final packages in the boot while Sarah was settling up the bill with the proprietor when he saw Meade come out of the saloon with two other cowhands, cross the street, and walk toward him.

"You may have my boss buffaloed, but not me," he shouted.

Tommy ignored the three, but Meade kept up the dialog. "If you had a gun I'd show you what we think of half-breeds in this valley."

Tommy assumed that Meade was just letting off steam and was no threat, but when the other cowhand shouted, "You cost us our jobs and we're going to kick your ass," he knew that there was going to be a confrontation.

They were shouting obscenities at Tommy, working up enough courage to take action, and a crowd was gathering, which helped fuel the three. Tommy knew it was only a matter of time before one of them got enough courage and started something. The carriage was between him and the three who were still in the middle of the street. He reached into the boot and grabbed his holster and six-gun, strapped it on, tied it down around his right leg, and walked out into the street, stopping about twenty feet from the three.

At that moment Sarah and Naomi walked out of the general store and stopped in their tracks as they saw the scene unfold. She called out, "Please don't, Tommy!"

Tommy waved Sarah off and stood in front of the three for a few seconds and then, as fast as he ever was, drew his weapon and shot the hats off all three of the men and then reholstered his weapon. Sarah couldn't believe what she saw. No wonder that man in the lobby in Santa Fe fled and left the money rather than face Tommy.

Meade was on the left of the three and he stumbled backward while his two companions stumbled to the side. A look of fear was evident on their faces, but Meade was trying to hold it together.
"I'm not afraid of some fancy shooting half-breed; we can take him. Come on."

One of his companions wasn't so sure. "No way, man, I never saw anyone draw that fast and shoot so straight. He could have killed us easy; he's giving us an opportunity to walk away and I'm taking it." With that he walked away, and the other man followed him to stand in front of the saloon.

Meade was the only one left facing Tommy, and he was trying to figure how to get out of the situation alive. "If you didn't have a gun, half breed, I'd kick your ass right in front of your wife and then I'd fuck her."

Tommy walked up to Meade and with his open right hand slapped him across the face. Meade was more surprised than anything, and then a smile formed on his lips and he swung a hard right at Tommy's head. But Tommy had already planned a counter attack and was ready. He shifted his weight to his left foot and struck out with his right heel and hit Meade just behind his right knee, causing it to buckle and he started to fall on his right side. Tommy shifted his weight and hit Meade in the head with a left hook, breaking his nose and splitting his lip, and then crossed over with a right, snapping his head back. Meade fell in the dirt.

It was a devastating beating and drew some" ohs" from the crowd who was watching the confrontation. Those in the bar who'd been watching knew that Tommy Sanchez was no one to challenge. Tommy turned to Meade's companions.

"Get him out of here. I'm going to take my wife home and then I'm coming back and look for the three of you. It won't be wise if I find you."

Tommy walked back to the carriage, took off his gun, put it in the boot, and helped Sarah and Naomi into the carriage. It was as though it was just another day at the office for him. He was cold and calculating and had delivered a message that wouldn't be lost on the town or the sur- rounding communities.

Sarah kissed him on the cheek and held his hand as he drove them home. Naomi had an inner smile. She was employed by a wonderful woman and a powerful man who wasn't afraid to speak up and if necessary follow up with action. She finally felt safe.

In the next two months Don Ortega let it be known that his rancho was for sale. He wanted to move nearer to his children. He especially didn't want to explain to his friends how the lobe on his ear was damaged. Tommy made him a fair offer, and the sale was consummated soon thereafter. Tommy and Sarah were now the owners of the T & H Ranch. Tommy didn't want to concentrate on only one profit center for the ranch. Cattle were necessary, but the volatility of the market made him hedge and they decided to diversify into grapes and apples. He knew their main income was from other investments and didn't want to tax the ranch to support their lifestyle.

It took about a year for the confrontation on Sagunto Street to die a natural death. Meade, his two acquaintances, and Don Ortega were gone, and the memory of that day vanished like the wind. Tommy and Sarah were a part of the community and welcomed into the homes of the rich and elite. The community was growing, and soon very few carried a sidearm.

Sarah didn't give birth to just one child; she had twins, a boy and a girl. Both children were fair skinned but with black hair. They named the girl Helga Elizabeth Sanchez and the boy, Thomas Lars Sanchez. Sarah had a difficult time during the birth, but without Naomi it would have been a disaster. Tommy went for the doctor in Santa Ynez while Naomi cared for Sarah. The round trip took two hours, and during those two hours Sarah thought she would die, but she'd been through lows times in her life and was determined not to let childbirth be the last things she ever did.

Tommy was a father for the first time and vowed to spend as much time as he could with his children. He was a devoted father and not only spent time with his son, but his daughter as well. If he went fishing he took them both. He showed no partiality.

Playing with his two children brought back memories of his childhood with his mother and father. He couldn't remember a time when Sitting Bull spent time alone with him. He was always busy. Tommy didn't begrudge him that and he was proud of his father's accomplishments, but he missed the warmth as a child that he felt for Helga and little Tommy. He started to make inquiries about his father and found that the old man was still alive and living at the Standing Rock Agency on the border of North Dakota and South Dakota. Tommy wanted to see him and show off his wife and children, but the trip would be too difficult for the children, who were but one year old.

Sarah understood what he wanted and agreed that it would be best for him to go alone. He could take pictures of the family and show them to Sitting Bolt. "We'll be okay. I want you to have the opportunity to see your father one more time."

It took him nearly five days to reach the Standing Rock Agency. The lack of available transportation to the agency caused most of the delays, but he persisted and was welcomed by his father and his brother Crow Foot. Sitting Bull didn't recognize him at first. Tommy was dressed as a white man with short, cropped hair while Sitting Bull and Crow Foot wore traditional dress. Tommy showed them pictures of Sarah, Helga, and young Tommy. Sitting Bull recognized Sarah; he'd attended her wedding. He also made mention of Tommy's mother and said Sarah reminded him of his wife, Elizabeth. The old man was delighted that Tommy came to visit him and was proud that his son had assimilated into the white culture.

When Tommy arrived in June 1890 at the Standing Rock Agency, tensions were high. Fort Yates next to the agency was on full alert. A movement had started the year before and had permeated UI the tribes to the West Coast. The movement was called the Ghost Dance, and the Indian agencies feared Sitting Bull would use this new movement to stir up the tribes and mount another assault in the area.

What started as a peaceful movement by Jack Wilson, a Paiute holy man with a message of love for his people and a desire to work with the white people, was completely misunderstood. Jack

Wilson said he had received his message in a vision and used a circle dance or community dance to preach his message, and soon this dance was termed the Ghost Dance and became a rallying mechanism for an uprising.

Tommy asked Sitting Bell if he was going to start an uprising. The old man said his time had passed and the leader of his group in the agency was Kicking Bear. Subsequently Kicking Bear was asked to leave the agency by the com- missioner of Indian Affairs, leaving Sitting Bull as the focal point for their concern whether he wanted to be or not.

Tommy remained with the old man and his brother for another week and then it was time to go. He wanted his father and brother to come back with him to California, but his brother and father declined. "My place is with my people. They need my guidance." Sitting Bull said. He thanked Sitting Bell for pointing him on the right road; he would always be grateful. He was sad to learn six months later that the old man had been arrested for fear he would start a revolt and the next day was shot and killed by several of the Indian security personnel. That same month, a massacre occurred at Wounded Knee and over 150 Sioux were killed by soldiers after a weapon was accidentally fired. Tommy anguished over the plight of his fellow Indians and would dedicate the remainder of his life to help in any way he could.

CHAPTER TWENTY-EIGHT

It was 189 1, and the twins were three years old. Tommy was teaching them to ride. Sarah was teaching them to swim. They owned fifteen thousand acres with a small stream running through the property. The children loved to swim in the stream, but Naomi, who was like their second mother, was petrified they'd drown. It seems that she didn't like to swim since her experience on the

Emerald Gay. Whenever Tommy playfully threatened to throw her in the stream, she ran away and stayed as far as she could from him.

It was about this time that Sarah received a letter from Mr. Jefferson, the Pinkerton detective in Omaha. He told her that Lars was running with a band of no goods and though they hadn't been caught yet, the sheriff was waiting for an excuse to form a posse and get rid of the gang. Sarah had extracted a promise from Tommy when they married that if Lars wanted to, he could live with them until he was on his own. The problem was that Lars hadn't given any indication that he wanted to reunite with his mother, let alone her new husband. She wanted to go to Lars and beg him to come home with her because she was worried that he would do something foolish and wouldn't be able to recover. She wanted to go to him one more time, but she couldn't leave the twins. They needed their mother.

Tommy solved the problem by volunteering to go to Lars and attempt to bring him back. Sarah was happy and apprehensive at the same time. She worried that Lars would ignore Tommy's attempt, and Tommy was no one to fool with. He was a peaceful man, but like Crazy Horse, he wouldn't tolerate disrespect.

The trip to San Francisco and then on to Omaha was boring, and Tommy didn't know what kind of reception Lars would give him. He had known Crazy Horse and admired him as a warrior and as a man. He had fought to survive and protect his people. He wasn't the least bit jealous of Crazy Horse even though Sarah had confided in him that she had really loved her first husband. From what Sarah revealed, Lars had been difficult from the time Crazy Horse died and didn't want to acknowledge her as his mother. Tommy would do what he could, but it was up to Lars to make the effort.

He met with Jefferson in his Omaha office and discussed the situation. Lars was running with a group of Indians that had left the reservation and were using the smell town of Ralston, about thirty miles southwest of Omaha, as a kind of staging place. There was a saloon in town that seemed to attract a rough crowd. The sheriff visited only when there was trouble, which was about every other week. "There's nothing in the town but a general store, saloon and livery stable, so if we go, we'll probably have to camp out and wait until Lars and his band come into town." Jefferson said.

Tommy had brought a Remington and his six-gun and holster. He didn't have any intention of using force, but he didn't want to face a group of belligerent young Indians with a chip on their shoulders without a weapon. He purchased a week's provisions for two and rented a carriage. They left at five a.m. the next morning, arrived in Ralston about three in the afternoon, and checked out the saloon. It was empty save for the bartender who said Lars and his group hadn't been there for a week. Tommy wondered where they were getting the money for food and whatever.

He and Jefferson found a spot on a small hill with a vantage point to see who came into Ralston and where they went. During the next two days only a couple of cowboys came into town and left after having a quick beer.

On the third day, about four in the afternoon, six young Indians rode into town and tied their horses to the hitching post outside the saloon.

Jefferson pointed out Lars. "How do you want to play this?" Jefferson asked Tommy.

"I checked the saloon out, and the back door seems to be open all the time. I'll go in the front and try to talk to Lars. I'd like you to go in the back and keep my back just in case. Just because it's Sarah's son, don't take any chances. When in doubt, shoot. Are you okay with this?" Jefferson smiled grimly and pick up his shotgun.

Tommy had told Sarah when he left that he would do everything in his power to try to reason with Lars but that he wouldn't get killed by taking any unnecessary chances, and if Sarah wasn't comfortable with that, he didn't want to go. "I don't want to come back to you and tell you that your son created a situation and forced me to defend myself." "You're my husband and I love you with all my heart. I know I'm putting you in a dangerous position, but I'll rely on your good judgment. Whatever happens, happens."

He laid the Remington against the well just outside the front door of the saloon and carefully pushed through the café door and entered. He saw six men and the bartender in the saloon. Four of the Indians were at a table and appeared to be playing cards; two others were at the bar having a beer. Everyone looked up as Tommy entered the saloon. He was dressed in western wear, but his clothes were new and clean and he stood out among the six Indians who were mostly in rags and dirty clothes. It was obvious that UI were armed.

Tommy stood so that he had all six in front of him. "Sarah Hansen asked me to find her son, Lars. Is he here?" Tommy was looking directly at Lars when he asked the question.

No one answered, and the four at the table continued playing cards. So Tommy asked the question again, but this time in the Sioux language. Those at the table stopped and looked at him. Lars said, "There's no Lars here, only Tasunka Wilco."

Tommy responded that Tasunka Wilco was Crazy Horse's name and in order to use the name, the father had to vacate it and that since Crazy Horse died with his name, no one could use it.

"Who the hell are you?" Lars asked.

"I'm the son of Sitting Bull, and I'd like to talk to you alone."

One of the Indians at the bar went for his gun, and Tommy shot him in the shoulder and then slowly put his gun back in his holster. He saw Jefferson come in the back with his shotgun ready, but Tommy signaled him that it wasn't necessary the others looked at Tommy as though they couldn't believe anyone could be that fast.

The other Indian at the bar was angry and went for his gun, but Tommy shot him in his wrist before he could reach his gun. He then turned his gun toward the other four and ordered them to put their guns on the floor.

Tommy continued in Sioux, assuming they all understood him. "I want to talk to Lars. You three take the other two outside and see to their wounds. Bartender, I'll pay for a round of drinks so you won't be out any money, but I want you outside as well. Mr. Jefferson is going to keep an eye on UI of you with his shotgun until I finish talking to Lars."

When they were alone, Tommy sat down at the table facing Lars, who immediately asked, "What the hell do you want?"

"I'm your mother's husband and my name is Tommy Sanchez and I am the son of Sitting Bull and Elizabeth Kelly, a white captive. So as you can guess, I'm also a hair-breed. Your mother and I own a large ranch in California and we want you to come live with us until you're able to strike out on your own. I will teach you every- thing I know, but I'll expect you to work on our ranch and be respectful to your mother.

"I see no reason why you can't succeed in the so-called white world; I did, so can you. You and I come from good stock. Your father was a great man and your mother is a very talented artist. All she wants is for you to be happy. From what I can tell, you're one step away from starvation and another away from jail and probably a hangman's noose. You have nothing to look forward to the way you're going and everything to look forward to in California. You just need the courage to admit that what you're doing is foolish and you want a chance at a better life."

"You make everything sound so simple. I want respect. My men give me respect. I'm their leader," Lars responded.

"That rabble will leave you when someone else comes along that offers them a better deal. They're just like you. They don't know what to do, so they do nothing, and when they need money or food, they steal. People will only put up with so much theft before they band together and shoot all of you. That really is something to look forward to."

"How do I know I can trust you?" Lars seemed to be softening.

"What I'm promising is that you'll be fed, clothed, housed, treated fairly, and given an opportunity to grow and find your way in life. When did you sit down and say to yourself, what do I want to do with my life? I'll bet you never did. Your whole life is one of bitterness because your father is dead and you want to blame some- one. There's no one to blame. That's just life. You put it behind you and move on. I want to help, but I've learned that the only one who can help you is yourself. My only promise to your mother is that I would try to bring you home, but I'm not going to force you with a gun. I usually don't wear a gun. I grew up just like you. I made it, why can't you?"

Tommy thought he saw a tear form in Lars's eye, but the boy looked away and just sat there. "Would I have to go to school?"

"Only if that's what you wanted."

"What kind of ranch do you have?"

"Your mother and I have a large ranch with horses, cattle, and grapes, and we grow some hay for our stock. Your mother is a renowned artist who mostly paints Indian scenes, probably what she encountered when she was a captive and later when she was married to your father."

"I won't allow anyone to speak badly of my father."

"I've never heard your mother speak badly of your father. I believe she loved him, and from what she told me, he loved her. Your sister Naiwa is married and lives on the Red Cloud Agency with her husband and two children. You also have a brother and a sister who are twins and three years old. You'll have a great time with them. You have a family that wants you. The question is do you want them?"

"Where did you learn to shoot like that? You're the fastest man I ever saw."

Tommy smiled. "I was a guide for a wagon train, and one of the leaders of the wagon train taught me, and I practiced a lot."
"Could you show me how to draw and shoot
like that?"

"I'd be glad to, but as I said, we don't wear guns anymore. Cities are becoming more civilized, and the citizens back up the sheriff who they elect.
It's rarely that you'll need a gun un- less you want to go hunting, and we can do that on the ranch.
There's plenty of game." Tommy reached out his hand. Lars smiled and took it.

When they went outside, Lars said goodbye to his friends and said he was going with Tommy. The two men Tommy shot had only received superficial wounds, and after they were bandaged they didn't seem to have very much discomfort. The five Indians were curious as to how Tommy had learned to shoot so fast and yet be so accurate. They asked if he'd give them a demonstration.

Tommy felt that he had pushed them all a little hard and was willing to show off his skills for them. He asked the bartender to line up six bottles in the street about twenty paces away. When the bottles were set up and the bartender out of the way, Tommy drew and hit off six bottles and reholstered his weapon almost faster than the eye could see. Everyone, including Jefferson, was in awe of Tommy's skill; no one said anything, but Lars had a big smile on his face.

They cleaned up their campsite, and Jefferson, Tommy, and Lars went to Omaha that day. Lars had never been on a train and spent the entire trip peppering Tommy with all kinds of questions ranging from what made the train move to what were the names of the twins and would he have to go by the name Lars. Tommy laughed and said the name Lars certainly didn't fit him. He'd talk to his mother and see what she had to say.

CHAPTER TWENTY-NINE

Sarah couldn't believe her good fortune. She had a wonderful family, and her son, Lars, had agreed to come home. The young man and Tommy had developed a bond during their trip home, and Lars undoubtedly had a great deal of respect for Tommy's skills with a gun. He must have asked Tommy ten times if he'd show him how to shoot. There was tension between Sarah and her son, but not the twins, who learned they had a big brother. Tommy played peacemaker and found things for Lars to do that he liked as well as taking him fishing and hunting.

Sarah tried to spend some time with Lars, but he was at an age where he didn't want to be told what to do, especially by a woman, so she didn't press him. She was hoping that he would come around by himself and they'd be able to talk. He was, however, impressed with her art and especially the landscapes of the Indian villages, so she tried to use that as the catalyst to a better understanding between mother and son.

Lars was curious to know how Tommy became so successful, so Tommy told him how he started out with something he knew, did it well, and then tried to find some other business that complemented the first business.

Lars didn't like his name and asked Tommy to talk to Sarah about changing it. Tommy asked him what name he liked; Lars said he had always liked the name Juan. When Tommy told her this, Sarah said she wanted to honor her father. "Sarah, what do you want more, to honor your father or repair your relationship with your son?" he asked.

In the end she relented and started calling her son Juan. He felt he had won a victory and therefore could acquiesce to something she wanted, and that was to get him an education. She'd taught him to read and write when he was young, and although he had resisted, he was competent enough to be able to read most things. Tommy was a role model and Sarah deferred to his recommendations concerning Juan.

When they were fishing or out hunting, Tommy would tell Juan about Sarah's like after his father died and how she was treated as an outcast because she was married to his father and how her own brother didn't invite her to his wedding because their family thought she was nothing but a squaw. Juan started to have a better understanding and finally sat down with Sarah to talk. She told Juan that he wouldn't be forced to do anything, but he had to understand that he was their son and they wanted him to succeed and that the best way was to get an education. She slowly introduced the possibility of having a tutor come to the ranch to teach Juan. He was reluctant at first, but with Tommy's encouragement, he agreed to give it a try.

The relationship between Tommy and Juan was good, between Juan and Sarah tolerable, but Juan was afraid of Naomi. She reminded him of one of his father's sisters who was always on his case. He told Tommy that Naomi carried a knife. "And I'll bet she'll use it if anyone messes with Mom." Tommy laughed.

In spite of his reluctance, Juan took to studies and, after two years with very little encouragement, said he would like to study the law.

Sarah and Tommy couldn't believe it, but they weren't going to get in his way. Tommy introduced Juan to their attorney who agreed to take him on and train him in the law, but he was going to have to do what the attorney said or he'd be out, family friend or not. Juan agreed, and his first task was to cut his hair short and wear a suit with a tie. He took up the study of law with Joel Whitworth Jones of Santa Ynez. Sarah cried when Joel told them he would take Juan under his wing.

Tommy had discounted the livery and freight businesses to Henry Garcia in Santa Fe and Joaquin in Tombstone. The effort he had in El Paso had long since been closed out, and with the sale of his and Carlos's original land purchase in San Diego, Tommy had nearly one million dol- lars in cash assets, which he spread out between ten large banks. He and Carlos exercised their option and owned twenty percent of the San Diego trolley business, and there was a steady stream of income to oil parties involved in the enterprise. They, along with Lund and Guthrie, had purchased more land along the route where Guthrie and Lund planned to extend the trolley. His future income seemed solid. Sarah's commercial buildings and her four houses had been sold and she was liquid. With the income from her trust and sales of her paintings she had substantial assets. Their ranch and home were free and clear; they were a very wealthy couple with a grown son and two small children.

Sarah had received a few letters from James over the years, but none that said anything, none that congratulated her on getting married, and none that said what a joy it was to have a new niece and nephew in the family. However, his latest letter caused her great concern. He spoke of his financial situation and that he frankly was out of money and needed help and could she provide that help since he had come to her aid when she was in dire financial straits?

Sarah felt a need to help James and discussed it with Tommy. "I'll support whatever you decide, and yes, we're well off and can afford to help. My questions relate to what he needs, how long he'll need help, and what happened to his assets."

"What you say makes sense, but how do we get that type of information other than going back east and asking?"

"That's the only way I can think of to find out what we need to know. The twins are old enough to travel. We can leave Juan here to oversee the ranch and take the children and Naomi to visit with your relatives." He smirked.

The trip was long and tedious and the children were children, but Tommy and Sarah read to them daily and made a game out of most of the trip, and when they became too much for them, Naomi took over. Rather than go to Harrisburg, they decided to stay in Philadelphia and have James come to them at their hotel. Before contacting James, Tommy wanted to take a few days and see what he could find out about James and his predicament, so he hired a private investigation firm with offices in Philadelphia and Harrisburg to see what they could uncover. Additionally, before they left the valley, Tommy had his bank in Santa Barbara make inquiries to James's bank in Harrisburg to see what the size of James's debt was and who his creditors were. He asked them to telegraph the results to him in Philadelphia. He also contacted a respected attorney and told him what he was trying to find out and asked whether he could check on the Craylors to see what their assets were.

When they were ready, they sent a telegram to James and asked him to come to their hotel in Philadelphia. James came by train the next day.

The depression of 1893 was brought about by speculation, but this time it wasn't land speculation, it was the over building of railroads, with the Philadelphia and Reading Railroad being the biggest that collapsed from excessive debt in February 18 93. This was followed by the collapse of the Union Pacific, Northern Pacific, and Atchison, Topeka railroads. It extended to banks and many businesses. Unemployment was high and the severity of the depression spread to the West, but not to the extent as in the eastern industrial cities. Tommy was aware of the situation when he took the family east to meet with James.

James looked drawn and had lost nearly twenty pounds. Sarah was expecting to see a vibrant man in his early forties, but he looked like a whipped dog. He seemed nervous and on edge, especially around Tommy. He didn't know much about his brother-in-law and was surprised to see that he was a well-dressed man of Mexican descent. He finally realized that Sanchez and that man in the hotel in Santa Fe, many years ago, were one and the same. He talked to Sarah and the children and when the time came, he asked if they could help him.

Prior to their meeting, Sarah and Tommy had decided that Sarah would make the final decision on the amount of financial assistance they would give but that Tommy would handle the discussion and negotiations." Where's your wife, James?" Tommy asked.

James responded that she wasn't attending the meeting.

"There won't be any discussion of help unless your wife is present. You are still married, aren't you?"

"Yes, but what does that have to with any of this?"

Tommy continued while Sarah excused herself on the pretext of getting the children some lunch. "It has everything to do with it. I've done some inquiries and have found out a great deal about your financial situation, your creditors, and the reason why you're in this position now. In fact, after we talk about your situation and if we decide to help you, I'll talk to your in- laws and make sure they know the terms of our agreement."

James became red in the face. "Who the hell do you think you are? I helped my sister out when she was destitute and I didn't have to do that. All I'm asking is that she reciprocates." The problem was that James didn't know who Tommy Sanchez was, didn't know his back- ground, or what his relation with his sister was. He wondered if Sanchez controlled his sister's assets.

Tommy leaned back in his chair and waited until James calmed down before he continued. "I hired a private investigating firm and have their report here. I've made inquiries to your creditors and know what they'll take and I've had an attorney review your trust to see how you became entangled with the Craylor family to the point of being at the brink of bankruptcy. Here's the re- port if you'd like to read it."

James's anger didn't surface again; he seemed almost resigned. He took his time and read the report." I can get my wife here, but I don't know about her father and brother."

"Oh, they'll come. I've talked to all your creditors and have made an agreement with them to wait until they hear from me. Since you pledged ml your assets to your creditors, I could buy their liens at a discount and take over your assets and then foreclose if I so desired. You haven't paid any of your creditors for over four months, and they're anxious and could foreclose on you at any time. To stall them, I've permitted them to telegraph my banks and understand my financial capability. I haven't guaranteed that I will pay them, but I've indicated it's a possibility. I don't say you're stupid, James, I just think you let your heart get in the way of your better judgment. Before your wife comes here, I want her to read the report; I want her to understand what we all know about her and her role in your financial problems."

"You're a cold son-of-a-bitch," James blurted out

Tommy ignored the insult. "My wife and I'll be here another three days and then we'll go back home. It's your choice."

The investigators were expensive, but what they produced was shocking. James had borrowed heavily on his commercial and residential buildings and pledged his trust money from the oil revenue because Harold Craylor, his wife's brother, had embezzled funds from a bank where he was a vice president. The wife had pressured James to repay the funds so her brother wouldn't go to jail and her family wouldn't be shamed. James coiild've handled the shortfall if it hadn't been for the depression and his heavy investment in railroad stocks. The wife said her father couldn't help her brother because he'd lost his money in the same railroad stocks. The investigator found out that the father and the brother had used the embezzled funds in land speculation around Washington, D.C.

The report went on to state that the land the Craylors purchased was very valuable and they have a sale pending on the property. The investigator suggested that the family had a reputation of being slippery. Maybe the wife didn't know about it and maybe she did. But the Ciaylors were leaving James to shoulder the entire burden. Tommy showed the report to Sarah who felt that her brother had been betrayed. "What a family he's married into. Do you think he knows?"

"Probably not, but he will if he shows up here with his wife. I had the attorney look into the D.C. land purchases and see who the owners of record are. It might be interesting."

The meeting with James and his wife didn't take place until three days later. Sarah and Tommy wondered what was taking so long. She had her answer when the two showed up at their hotel room. The wife was arrogant and demanded to know why she had been dragged from her home to meet with people she didn't care to see. That about summed up her personality and the meeting didn't get any better. Tommy had gotten the answer to his question on the land in D.C. The owners were Harold
Craylor, his father, and Jennifer Hansen.

James and his wife were in for several surprises. The first was when Tommy told them that he did not purchase their debt from their creditors; someone else had and now was in a position to foreclose on ml their assets including the trust.

"Can't you do something?" James asked.

"The person who purchased all your debt has an issue with you. I understand the issue, and I don't want to get involved." James slumped deeper into his chair while his wife seemed very calm.

For the first time Sarah spoke to her brother and his wife. "I've been very disappointed in you, James. You were good to me when I was poor even though it seems you could've helped me sooner, but you did help, and that's what counts. But you've excluded me from your life for what- ever reason and that broke my heart, but I'm a strong person and with my wonderful husband and family, I'll survive. The question, James is will you? A marriage is a partnership, but from what Tommy and I have found out, yours is one sided."

It was at this time that Jennifer lashed out at Sarah. "I don't have to sit and listen to someone who married a savage and probably did it twice," she snarled as she glared at Tommy.

Sarah ignored the outburst and continued. "Before we left Santa Ynez, Tommy and I agreed that any help given to you was to be determined exclusively by me, and in spite of your shunning of me and my family, I purchased all your debt yesterday, including the pledge of all your oil revenue." James stared at his wife. Neither said anything.

"I'll give you back your life, but it's going to be conditional. Tommy will cover the conditions."
Tommy was looking directly at Jennifer
Cray- lor. "Before we continue, I'm going to ask our attorney and your father and brother to join us. They've been discussing certain facts that we've uncovered."

"This is ludicrous. Who the hell do you think you are? I'm leaving." Jennifer got up to leave, but James put out his hand and grabbed her arm. "Sit down, Jennifer. I want to hear what they have to say." She walked back and sat down.

The senior Craylor was a tall, distinguished man slightly on the thin side. He had an affable smile and shook Tommy's hand. Harold Craylor, his son, was about six feet two inches tall and weighed in excess of two hundred pounds; he was a large man.

The attorney by the name of Charles Good- win sat on a chair facing the two Craylor men, who sat on a couch. Everyone was seated, but Sarah begged their leave to attend to the children in one of the other rooms.

Tommy addressed the group. "I'm Thomas Sanchez, the husband of Sarah Sanchez, who is James Hansen's sister. We were asked by James Hansen for financial assistance because his assets were heavily encumbered and the creditors were putting pressure on him to pay or they were going to foreclose. Sarah finali7.ed the purchase of the creditors' liens yesterday, and she alone is now the creditor of James and Jennifer Hansen. The purpose of this meeting is to determine how James got into this predicament. My attorney, Charles Goodwin, will discuss this aspect."

Charles Goodwin stood up and in a very clear voice summarized what he knew. That Harold Craylor had embezzled funds from the Philadelphia Trust and Loan Bank and Jennifer Craylor had asked her husband to repay the bank so her brother wouldn't be prosecuted. Jennifer told her husband that Harold lost the embezzled funds by investing in railroad stock and that the rail- road went through bankruptcy.

"But that was not the case. Harold and his father and James's wife invested the embezzled funds into land surrounding the capitol in the District of Columbia."

Goodwin was interrupted by the father, who jumped out of his chair. "That's a bald-faced lie! We didn't do any such thing. Sir, I ask you to re- tract that misrepresentation immediately or you may be the subject of a very expensive lawsuit."

Goodwin took out a file from his briefcase. "I have in my hand the contract of purchase for the land to Mr. Craylor, Harold Craylor, and Jennifer Hansen. These are your signatures that were notarized. What I've said is not a lie but the truth. I also have the documents on the pending sale you're planning with Lancelot Corporation. I have placed a lien on this property in the name of Sarah Sanchez to stop this sale."

James turned on his wife. "How could you do this to me?"

"I haven't done anything. Your sister has bailed you out, so stop complaining and figure a way out of this." Jennifer was as arrogant as she could be.

Harold Craylor spoke up. "You can't prevail on a lien on the land. The bank was repaid, and they're not going to do anything, and if they won't do anything, you don't have a case." He smiled as he spoke.

"On the contrary, I'm a stockholder in the Philadelphia Trust and Loan. I've asked the bank president why he didn't press charges even though the loan was repaid. He said that Frederick Craylor told him his son lost oil the money in a now defunct railroad company. When I told him that father, son, and daughter used the embezzled funds to purchase land outside the nation's capital and showed him the documents, he said they were going to press charges against all three Craylors."

While he had a captive audience, Goodwin continued. "Now we have a solution that you may or may not like, but it is a solution. The three Craylors will transfer their rights in the land around the capital to Mr. and Mrs. Thomas Sanchez. Mrs. Sanchez in turn will release her liens on Mr. James Hansen's property. If this is accomplished, Philadelphia Trust and Loan won't press charges on the three Craylors."

Harold Craylor was immediately on his feet, shouting, "You can't get away with this!" He lunged at Tommy. But Tommy had been prepared for such an outburst and hooked his arm around Harold's waist, pivoted his hip into Harold's left side, and threw him over his shoulder. Harold crashed to the floor. He sat up, leaning against the wall adjacent to the hallway leading to the other rooms in the suite and drew a pistol from his waist band.

"I'm going to kill you." He raised the weapon and aimed at Tommy, but froze when someone behind him said, "Drop your weapon. I may not be as skilled as my husband, but I'll kill you if you even breathe too hard. Now drop the weapon."

Harold Craylor could feel the cold muzzle of Sarah's weapon against his neck and meekly dropped the weapon. Tommy picked it up and ordered Craylor to take a seat and shut up. The older Craylor started to protest, but Jennifer said,

"Shut up, you old fool, and let's hear what they have to say."

Sarah came into the room and put her arms around Tommy and kissed him. "You are the greatest man I've ever known and I'm proud to be the wife of the son of Sitting Bull, Tasunka
Lyotake."

One could see pride for his sister in James's eyes. This was what a marriage was supposed to be like.

After the tension eased, Tommy continued. "Let me cover the conditions again. The Craylors will sign over their interest in the D.C. property to Sarah and Tommy Sanchez, and Sarah Sanchez will tear up all the indebtedness that she purchased from the creditors of James and Jennifer Hansen. Mr. Goodwin will secure a release from the bank, which will sign a memo that they won't pursue the Craylors for embezzlement, and finally, Jennifer Craylor Hansen will not contest a divorce from James Hansen if he so desires. Mr. Goodwin will secure all the releases once everyone has signed the applicable documents."

When they left, Naomi hugged and kissed Tommy and told him she loved him. The two children were asleep during the entire confrontation.

That evening James visited them and asked if he could take the entire family to dinner; they ate in the hotel dining room. He spent some time with the children and told Sarah they reminded him of themselves when they were small. He said he had left Jennifer with her father. He and Jennifer had decided they needed sometime apart before they made any decision about their future. He nearly cried when he recounted how she begged him to help her brother and then they used the money to further their own inter- est. He had been shocked. He finally admitted that he had been dazzled by the Craylor name and subordinated his own interests to them. "What a fool I was, and what a lousy brother to eliminate you from my life. Is Tommy really the son of Sitting Bull?" he asked Sarah.

"He is. His mother was a captive like me and hailed from New Jersey."

"Sarah, do you realize you've been married to one of the greatest warriors in our lifetime as well as to the son of one of the greatest Indian chiefs in history? What a life you've led, and your talent knows no bounds."

"I certainly do. I loved both men, but Tommy is the greatest. Did you see him toss that big ape?"

"I did, but when you came up with the gun, I couldn't believe it. I don't think Harold will tell that story to any of his friends. Jennifer thought it was a lark, but I set her straight and told her how you backed that gunman down on the train to Los Angeles. I think she respects you. I always wanted to know whether Tommy had a gun with him that day in the hotel in Santa Fe."

"He did." She responded.

They departed the next morning, and Sarah and her family went by train to their beloved ranch in Santa Ynez. They'd come frill circle, and their entire family was now on the right track. They looked forward to raising the children and watching Juan seek his way in life.

They had just switched trains in San Francisco and were sitting down when Sarah remembered an incident in her life. "Tommy, were you ever in Independence, Missouri?"

"I was there in 1864. I was hired to act as a guide to a wagon train going to the Oregon Territory."

"Did you rescue a couple of kids in a stable one evening while you were there?"

He turned to her and smiled. "Was that you and James?"

ABOUT THE AUTHOR

James (Jim) Kelly is a retired U.S. Air Force Officer with combat flying experience. This is his fourth novel but his first attempt at publishing. The background for all four novels is the same Santa Ynez Valley.

Jim and his wife, Patricia Sullivan, own and operate High Meadows Ranch, an equestrian facility in the beautiful Santa Ynez Valley in Central California. The couple is actively involved in a program to "Support the Troops" at forward operating bases in Iraq and Afghanistan. Jim can be contacted via e-mail at jkelly2020@veri- zon.net.

A MAN OF BREEDING

Tommy Sanchez, the son of Sitting Bull, the victor at the Battle of the Little Big Horn and his captive wife, found out early in life what prejudice was for a half-breed. Initially, he was able to overcome the stigma, but one fateful day his entire world turned upside down and he was pursued from town to town by a vengeful sheriff who forced him to continually moved once he was established in a community.

Sarah Hansen was captured by indians when she was a teenager and forced into a marriage with Crazy Horse, the war chief of the Sioux. Upon his death, she had to fend for herself and two children in a white world that treated her with contempt, viewing her as a white squaw and the widow of a savage.

Unaware of each other, Sanchez and Hansen began a quest for self respect, overcoming many obstacles and finally meeting in the beautiful Santa Ynez Valley in California.

James S. (Jim) Kelly is a retired United Stated Air Force Colonel with over 100 combat missions in Vaietnam. Prior to his retirement, Jim was the Director of a Communications Program in Iran, working directly under the Shah. Jim and his wife, Patricia, own and operate

High Meadows Horse Ranch outside Solvang, California. Most of his novels, including 4 Westerns and 3 Mysteries, use Solvang and the Santa Ynez Valley as a backdrop. Over the past 15 years, Jim and his wife have been active in a charity, supporting our troops in forward operating locations overseas in hostile territory.

To contact Jim, send an email to: asyougo90@gmail.com